Campbell Armstrong was born in Glasgow and educated at Sussex University. He and his family now live in Ireland. His bestselling novels, *Jig, Mazurka, Mambo, Agents of Darkness, Concert of Ghosts, Jigsaw, Heat* and *Silencer*, have placed him in the front rank of international thriller writers.

SILENCER:

'A masterly work of suspense . . . like an icecube down the back of the neck.' *The Times*

'Among the most intriguing of blockbuster writers . . . near to unputdownable.' *GQ*

BLACKOUT

Campbell Armstrong

Doubleday

LONDON • NEW YORK • TORONTO • SYDNEY • AUCKLAND

JxlC

07680335

TRANSWORLD PUBLISHERS LTD
61–63 Uxbridge Road, London W5 5SA

TRANSWORLD PUBLISHERS (AUSTRALIA) PTY LTD
15–25 Helles Avenue, Moorebank, NSW 2170

TRANSWORLD PUBLISHERS (NZ) LTD
3 William Pickering Drive, Albany, Auckland

Published 1998 by Doubleday
a division of Transworld Publishers Ltd

A catalogue record for this book is available
from the British Library.

ISBN 0385 408315

Typeset in 11/13pt Sabon by Falcon Oast Graphic Act
Printed in Great Britain
by Mackays of Chatham plc, Chatham, Kent

For Roy Stevenson,
fisherman, bookman, friend,
and for Stephen Black for his help

This stuff will probably kill you
Let's do another line

– Tom Waits, *Heartattack & Vine*

1

THE JACKRABBIT, FROZEN IN TERROR BY THE HEADLIGHTS OF the car, appeared abruptly out of nowhere. Samsa – even if he knew it was completely the wrong response in heavy rain, that a jackrabbit's life wasn't worth a nickel in the larger scheme of things – slammed his foot hard on the brake.

Pure blind instinct.

The car went immediately into a searing skid on the slick blacktop and plunged off the road down an incline, overturning. Samsa found himself suddenly in a jarring upside-down world, an inversion of black sky and black rain glittering in the headlights, the passenger door bursting open and the girl screaming as she fell out, as if she'd been sucked into another dimension.

The girl. Oh, dear Christ.

He twisted the wheel, imagining there might be some corrective maneuver he could perform, but the car kept sliding on its roof across greasy terrain. Only the buckled seat belt, digging into his chest, kept him in place. The hazard lights came on, blinking and clicking crazily, and

9

the Billie Holiday tune playing on the tape deck slurred to a halt. He heard the malevolent roar of the useless engine, and the wheels spinning overhead as the car scudded along. A half-empty vodka bottle shattered the windshield, and Samsa had the frightening impression he was seeing the night through an opaque clutter of plastic packing pods, or in a spidery dream that obscured a terrifying mystery.

There was a stabbing pain in the region of his shoulder and the seat belt felt like a band of iron. But these sensations came to him dimly because of a whine deep inside his skull, and his heart was very loud, and he could still hear the echo of the girl's scream and feel wet air flood through the open passenger door. The car churned up soil and kept plowing forward and Samsa thought for the first time of a possible explosion, a punctured gas-tank, an electrical spark from somewhere, and boom.

Because of a goddam jackrabbit traumatized by headlights, because of some misbegotten respect he'd entertained for the sanctity of life, here he was in this upturned car, fighting panic and powerlessness and wondering how far the car might travel before it finally ground to a halt, or whether it would combust first. Stricken by an assortment of acute fears, he groped for the seat belt with the idea he could free himself and open his door and roll out of the vehicle, but he was fumbling, and his hands couldn't work the buckle, and the car was shuddering in a way that suggested it was about to fall apart in a disconnected series of bits and pieces, broken wing mirrors, hubcaps, misshapen engine parts. He imagined a field strewn with such things, like the horrific wreckage left by an airplane that had fallen out of the sky. Bodies burned beyond recognition. The sifting of charred bones.

He thought, *I'm dying, this is it. Big time.* Blood zoomed to his head, an almighty roaring.

And then it was over, the car struck something hard and spun round once and stopped. The engine died. Samsa clawed free of the seat belt and slid out into the rain.

Smoke hissed through the shattered radiator grill. The headlights, which somehow hadn't died, picked out the shape of the tree the car had hit. A leafy branch, bark violently stripped and raw, lay across the chassis. On his back in the wet grass, Samsa moved away from the vehicle. He was aware of how the wheels still turned in diminishing whispers, and of the sound of rain falling through leaves, and the odd silence that lay in a spectral place just beneath these noises.

He got to his feet. His legs trembled. The girl. Where was the girl?

His mouth ached. He must have broken a tooth along the way, although he couldn't remember how. He had to find the girl. Spitting out the gritty debris of the tooth, he walked the field in the direction of the blacktop, listening for some sound of her. But there was nothing except the goddam rain and mud sucking at his shoes.

When he came to the foot of the incline where he'd skidded off the road he stopped. For a time he didn't move, paralyzed by aftershock. His system shut down. A collapse was taking place inside. He shivered, closed his eyes, and the scary incident replayed itself in his head. He had to shake off this numbness and find the girl, nothing else mattered. He moved, lost his footing, went down in the grass. Pain penetrated his shoulder – a torn muscle, a dislocation maybe. He could tolerate that. He'd known worse. He got up again and called the girl's name a couple of times.

No answer.

She's unconscious somewhere nearby. Blacked out, lying in the warm rain. Yes.

He felt the need to check the time, anchor himself in the

familiar, the quantifiable. He glanced at his wristwatch, but the face was cracked and the hands bent and the luminous dots meant nothing. A wind came up and gathered the rain together and blew it directly into his eyes. Where was she – this girl he barely knew? He remembered her waiflike face and the detachment in her eyes and her long legs under the short blue velvet skirt, the white shoes with the thick clunky heels. He remembered how she'd drunk vodka like there was a new Prohibition Law about to be enacted. Sometimes she'd tried to make a fluting sound by pressing her lips against the neck of the bottle and blowing. He'd seen the shape of her mouth by the lights of the instrument panel and been distracted by it. Or enchanted. It didn't matter which anymore. Because of that fucking demonic jackrabbit.

'Say, where you taking me?' she'd asked.

And he'd talked vaguely about some place he knew, although in reality he wasn't thinking of a particular destination. His head was filled with motels. A key to an unfamiliar bedroom, a double bed and white sheets, a corny painting hanging on the wall.

His lightweight summer suit was soaked and clung to him like a second skin. He was oblivious to his discomfort. He was starting to experience another kind of panic now, different from the one he'd felt hanging upside down inside the car. This had its origins in a place less primal, that civilized intersection where you were supposed to know right from wrong. But he'd overridden all the internal controls that regulated everyday behavior. And now he wished he could turn the clock back to the point where he'd first decided to switch off these instruments and just go go go with his gut feelings and his needs.

Jesus, his needs—

He stumbled into her. She lay half submerged in a

hollow of water maybe five or six inches deep. He bent down, gripped her by the shoulders and raised her up a little way. Rain fell into her short soft hair and ran down her face, and mascara tracks that resembled some kind of weird shorthand message slid across her cheeks. His throat was dry as cinder.

There was a lawful procedure to follow, regulations to obey. He knew all that. You reported the accident and a cop duly arrived on the scene, and you uttered the details of the incident in the flashing glare of a patrol car's roof lights.

But he couldn't do that.

Not immediately.

His shoulder throbbed. With the tip of his tongue he explored the stub of the broken tooth and tried to gather his thoughts, but they were in disarray.

2

'TAKE A PEW, LEE,' JIMMY PLUMM SAID.

Lee Boyle, who hated being ordered around, sat down. The room was lit only by a single green-shaded lamp on the desk, which had the effect of making Plumm appear like something you'd encounter on a bad trip. He had enormous glowing green eyebrows and shoulder-length hair the same color. He wore a faded monogrammed smoking jacket that had the look of a garment passed down from one generation to the next, as if to impart the impression of a decayed English aristocrat who'd sold off the family estates and hocked the crested silver years ago.

Boyle knew better. He knew for a fact Plumm had been born and raised in Long Island. The closest he'd come to England was probably a travelogue about the Lake District on TV, or maybe some groveling documentary on the House of Windsor.

Plumm said, 'I do very much like that little gold doodah round your neck, Lee. Set you back a good sum, I imagine.'

'I got it pre-owned,' Boyle said.

'Pre-owned, eh? Good shoes, too,' Plumm remarked. 'Top of the line, if I'm not mistaken. Also used?'

'Who wears used shoes?' Boyle said. He didn't like the notion of Plumm running an inventory. He considered it an invasion of his private space. Plus, the obvious subtext here was criticism of his spending money he didn't have. And he didn't need to hear that either.

'Well, then,' Plumm said. 'Where exactly do we stand?'

'Basically, I need more time,' Lee Boyle said.

Plumm raised one of the big eyebrows. 'Let me guess. You're going through a bad spell.'

'Business sucks.'

'If I believed every sob story I heard I'd hang one of those sweet little Gone Fishing signs on my door.'

'I wasn't giving you a sob story, Jimmy. I'm only saying there's this cash flow problem, which is inconvenient and embarrassing.' Boyle leaned forward in his chair. He knew Plumm found him attractive – gays were always drawn to his yellow-haired blue-eyed looks and his physique, the good Aryan template that probably fueled decadent fantasies of a sado-masochistic Nazi nature. But when it came to business, Plumm's bottom line was cash. You owe. Pay up. Plumm's equations were very simple and sometimes vicious.

Plumm rose. He was massive, six-five at least, and broad-chested. He stepped round the front of his desk and looked at Boyle for a time. Rain swept against the window beyond the curtains. The summer night was profoundly foul.

'You do have somebody you could ask, of course,' Plumm said.

Boyle shook his head. 'Get real.'

'I am *being* real. Very much so. Dear old Daddy.'

'Dear old Daddy doesn't talk to me,' Boyle said.

'I hate to hear of estrangements in families. A

rapprochement would be in order, given the circumstances.'

'Daddy doesn't believe in forgiveness, Jimmy. You only get one chance with him, and if you fuck up you're through. And I fucked up years ago as far as he's concerned. End of story.'

Plumm didn't move for a while. He appeared to be considering the situation, sifting courses of action. Then he reached out and gripped Boyle's upper lip between his thumb and index finger and pulled on it hard. Boyle felt himself being drawn forward, his face level with Plumm's crotch. This was humiliating and disturbingly intimate. Nobody – *nobody* – treated him like this.

'My advice is simple, friend. Go to good old Dad,' and Plumm twisted the upper lip with nasty vigor, holding it a moment. Just as Boyle had had enough of this fiasco and was raising a hand with the intention of hammering Plumm's fingers away, the big man released him.

'What the *fuck*,' Boyle said.

'You don't like physical?' Plumm asked.

'I prefer to choose who touches me. And I don't remember giving you a free pass, Plumm. Don't *ever* pull that kind of stunt again. I mean that.' Boyle, who stored grudges the way some people accumulated price-saver coupons, sat back in his chair and thought murderous thoughts. He thought about the gun in his apartment, a Llama Compact .45 he kept stashed in the cabinet under the bathroom sink, concealed behind Almond's tampons and toiletries, and he imagined pressing the barrel into this phony's huge forehead just to watch the bozo sweat.

'I was only trying to emphasize my point. Go see Daddy,' Plumm said.

'I already told you, Jimmy. No can do.' Boyle's lip hurt. 'Daddy's not Santa nowadays.'

'Then Daddy and I have something in common,' Plumm

said. He sat behind his desk, opened a folder and lowered his head. Without looking up he added, 'The sands of time are just running and running, love.'

Love. 'How fast are they running?'

'Oh, let's say three days, shall we? I'm in a charitable mood.'

'Three days? Three whole days? Gee.'

'Don't tell me you have a problem with that.' Plumm flapped a hand.

Boyle realized he'd been dismissed just like a Domino's delivery boy. He walked to the door and looked back. Plumm was making a scratchy sound on paper with a pretentious gold-nibbed fountain pen, like he was answering an invite to tea from an imaginary fucking duchess or something.

Asshole.

Seething, Boyle let himself out and stood at the top of the stairs. Through the glass panel of the door below he could see rain brightened by street lights. He went down quickly, two steps at a time. On the sidewalk he hauled his jacket up over his head and hurried through the downpour. Halfway along the block he ducked inside a bar called Chang's, a big white-walled room decorated with pink plaster-of-Paris flamingoes, scores of them.

Busy place. Escapees from the weather crowded the joint, cluttering all the available floor space and tables. Raincoats had been hung over some of the flamingoes. The air stank of damp clothing. Boyle scoped out the faces, recognized a couple of dopers looking strung-out, and a few small-time hoods planning low-grade scams that were doomed from conception. A bunch of losers.

He eyed the women as he usually did. He didn't see Almond anywhere. He pushed his way across the floor, tense, hands knotted. Plumm might be a faggot and a fraud, but that didn't alter the fact he was a tumor

17

inside Lee Boyle's head and had to be excised somehow.

He made it to the other side of the room, where he took a pack of Camel Lights from the pocket of his jeans and lit one with a Zippo on which his name was embossed. Almond had given him the lighter on his last birthday. She'd wrapped it in tissue and put it inside a little cardboard box with a ribbon stuck to it. 'The big three-oh,' she'd said at the time. 'You're getting up there, babe.'

Where the hell was she? He touched his lip where Plumm had yanked it and he thought, *Three days and counting*. He gazed into the Zippo flame.

A girl in tight leather pants stepped out of the toilets. 'Hey, good-looking.'

She had a gaunt face, a little heavy on the make-up. He knew her as Krystal with a K. Her real name was probably something like Darlene. She had an accent that might have been prairie.

'What's happening?' Boyle asked.

'I'm thinking you need, uh, like a snorkel to work in this weather. Maybe a tank of oxygen strapped to your back.'

'Innovative stuff.'

'I'm running,' she said. 'See you around.'

'Say, Krystal. You seen Almond anywhere?'

'I saw her yesterday, I think. Maybe the day before. I never keep track of time, Lee. You know me. I'm scattered.'

Boyle watched the girl vanish in the crowd. He considered hanging around for a while, wait for Almond to show. Then he thought he'd go home instead. He made his way to the front door, working his elbows into a few spines and ignoring complaints – 'Hey, buddy, watch where you're going' – with a scowl. His car was parked in an alley about a hundred yards away. He ran splashing through puddles. At the end of the alley a solitary light hung above the back door of a seafood restaurant, illuminating the black dumpsters where he'd left his old Porsche. He took the key from the pocket of his jeans. He didn't see the man emerge from the cover of the doorway.

'Lee.'

Still cowled in his jacket, Boyle turned. The man stood under a black umbrella. He had a huge punched-out face and one bad eye that looked like somebody had used white-out on it. Tom Raseci, known as Bigshoes, was about the same height as his employer Plumm, except he'd gone to fat. He was carrying about 300 pounds of blubber.

'What is this, Tom? I just talked with your lord and master. Didn't he tell you?'

'Fine car,' Raseci said. 'Classic.'

'You want to make small talk in this weather? I'm going home.'

'Not in that car you ain't.'

Boyle looked at Raseci. 'Why? You intend to confiscate my vehicle as collateral, Tom?'

Tom Raseci shook his head. 'What I'm trying to say is, your car's got a problem.' He approached the vehicle, nodded at the front right tire. 'You ask me, I'd say somebody came along and slashed it.'

Boyle went down on one knee and fingered the soft rubber, feeling the ragged slit and getting angry. 'Nice fucking work, Tom.'

'You think I did that?'

'Yeah, I think you figured a little vandalism might hassle me. Keep the heat on.'

'More like some passing moron resented your Porsche, I'd say. You get guys like that. They work out their envy with a knife.' Raseci came closer. 'Myself, I'd never stoop that low. I appreciate classic cars. Hell, I wish I could *afford* one. But it's the upkeep. The specialty mechanics.

19

The spare parts. Must break your heart at times.'

Boyle stood upright. He looked into the other man's face. The weird thing about Raseci's bad eye was the way you were drawn to it, fascinated by the milky quality. You could imagine stirring your finger in it.

'Tell your boss, Plumm, to go fuck himself,' he said.

'Smart messengers don't deliver bad messages, sonny.'

Boyle gazed again at the trashed tire. The anger foaming through him had its sources scattered all over the place, the constant debilitating lack of cash, a sky that had been pissing rain for days and days, and the absence of Almond. And now this act of mutilation on his Porsche, which was one of his few assets at present.

'Got a spare?' Raseci asked.

'It's flat.'

'You'll need a ride home. My car's round the corner.'

'I'll walk.' Boyle turned and moved to the end of the alley.

He heard Raseci call out. 'Hey, rich boy. Maybe you could phone Papa and have his limo pick you up. *Har-har-har*.'

3

DARCY STARED AT HER SCRABBLE TILES. Q E K E L M I.

Milk, she thought. Or *meek*. Otherwise, what these letters looked like was the name of some Libyan despot.

On the other side of the coffee table Nick was wearing his smug expression. *I've got a great word.* She could see it in his eyes. Maybe he had a seven-letter beauty he could get out. He arranged his tiles just-so. The game had begun to drag on her, but she knew she'd keep playing because it occupied him; it kept his mind off his groin, which was where his thoughts tended to drift. She got up, slotted a CD into the deck. She was into her classical mode. Brahms.

'I don't know what you get out of that stuff,' Nick said after a while.

'Just listen,' she said.

'I've been listening and I still don't get it.'

'Try using both ears.'

Nick, handsome in a dark, gipsy kind of way – as if he knew ancient secrets, which wasn't even close to the truth – gazed at her across the table. 'It's not like you can

21

dance to it, Darcy. You can't even tap your feet.'

'I'm trying to upgrade you,' she said.

'And I'm trying to downgrade *you*,' Nick said. He stretched out his arm and laid his hand on the back of her fingers. He had soft hands. They felt like cotton handkerchiefs that had been dried outdoors on a spring day. He was eighteen and on his way to college in the Fall, and when he graduated he'd work in the family company, which produced something Darcy thought totally boring – paper products: napkins, towels, what have you.

She tried to imagine being married to him. Mrs Darcy Doily.

Nick's whole life was set out in front of him, predetermined and immutable. He'd never dream of straying off the path and going in an unexpected direction. All the Mancuso brothers worked in the family business. Nick, the youngest, would start out as a regional salesman, driving long distances to show samples of patterned paper plates to department-store buyers in towns bypassed by freeways long ago.

She felt him stroke the palm of her hand. What he wanted, she knew, was to make love to her. Desperately. There had been a series of urgent clumsy encounters in the back of his car, sweaty moments when she'd *almost* been swayed – more from curiosity than any lust, or affection even. In the context of her world, she and Nick were 'going steady'. They hung out together at school. They held hands at ball games and in burger joints. 'Going steady', that quaint phrase, seemed to her a suffocating kind of business. People made assumptions about you. *She's screwing Nick. She's gotta be.* Darcy Doily, prisoner of conjecture.

She liked Nick well enough. He had good qualities. Reliability. Generosity. But.

She stood up. She looked at the clock on the mantelpiece. Ten thirty-eight. Alongside the clock a sequence of family photographs had been arranged. She glanced at one of her mother, then turned away. Nick was watching her. He had the air of a faithful dog about him. Something that was always under the kitchen table or lying around by the sofa, waiting, hoping to be tossed a scrap. Or better still, stroked nicely.

Dream on.

Nick rose and stood directly behind her now, his arms crossed over her breasts. His breath was warm on the back of her neck. He eased his fingers between the buttons of her shirt, reaching for a breast. He was hard as a rock. She could feel it against her. He had only to come within an inch of her and his motor cranked up.

There was an intimacy here she knew she was supposed to enjoy. Sometimes she did, sometimes she didn't. Her feelings came and went for no particular reason. Fickle little breezes: yes, no, I don't want to, I'm not ready, I don't think I love you, I don't know what love is, Nicky, I'm too young.

She drew away from him. 'We were in the middle of playing Scrabble, I remember.'

Nick looked let down, slightly martyred. He shrugged and went back to the table to examine his tiles. At least he didn't pull the predictable crap – I can't go on this way, Darcy. It hurts a guy, you know? You get a pain in the groin. A knot.

She gazed at her letters. 'I'm not one of those . . .'

'One of those what?'

'Cockteasers.'

'I never said you were.'

'I think you sometimes *think* I am.'

Nick shook his head. 'I love you,' he said.

Love was supposed to light up in your heart like a big neon arrow. But the electricity just wasn't getting to her.

23

There was no real juice unless you counted the occasional little spark. And that wasn't enough for her.

'I figure you'll come round,' he said.

'Pretty sure of yourself, aren't you?'

'I'm a patient guy, Darcy.'

She pushed her fingers through her dark-brown hair. Patience, sure. He had it in spades. Another of Nick's qualities. Look on the bright side. He could be ugly, geeky, like one of those Internet chat-room addicts, a snail with myopia and acne. Instead he was easy on the eye, gregarious, polite to his elders. He didn't smoke cigarettes, didn't touch drugs. He played tennis and basketball. He was every father's ideal. Her own father, for one, approved of Nick Mancuso. 'Nice kid,' he'd said. The unspoken declaration was that she could do a whole lot worse.

She thought: *Just do it and get it over with, why don't you, Darcy? What are you saving it for?*

He played his tiles on the board slowly.

CUNT.

'That's the only word you can come up with?'

'Yeah,' he said.

'A suspicious person might say you're trying to tell me something, Nick.'

'I'll show you my other letters if you don't believe me.'

She pushed her tiles away. She was suddenly tired. It was ten forty-six on the clock. Where was her father at this time of night? Busy guy. Out there doing all the stuff he did. She moved, sat in Nick's lap, curled up against him, enjoying a sense of comfort. He seemed quite content just to hold her. He smelled of deodorant and aftershave and the underlying musk of the permanently horny adolescent. *He's a kid, really. A big kid.*

The telephone rang. She climbed out of Nick's lap and answered it.

'Darcy? You okay?' Her father, voice fuzzy, speaking on his cellular phone.

'Fine. Nick's here.'

The frazzle of static, and her father's voice fading in and out. She heard the word 'accident'.

'I can hardly hear you,' she said. 'What accident?'

There was a moment of clarity. 'I'm not hurt. I don't want you to worry.'

'What happened?'

But the connection was lost entirely and the sound Darcy heard in her ears reminded her of a locomotive vanishing down a long black tunnel.

4

THE COP WHO ARRIVED ON THE SCENE WAS A STATE TROOPER wearing a name-tag that identified him as Trope, Frederick. Samsa, who'd never seen or heard of Trope before, showed the trooper the place where he'd gone off the road. Trope, a gangly man in a glossy rainslicker, wrote a few words in his notebook.

Samsa mentioned the jackrabbit, knowing it sounded foolish. But sometimes when you admitted your own idiotic behavior you gave yourself a certain authenticity: people were inclined to believe you when you put yourself in a bad light. He was apprehensive anyhow, even though he'd rehearsed himself. What to say. How to act. He'd been over all that, checking the angles. But there were tightropes in his head and not one was entirely secure.

'You braked for this rabbit?' Trope asked.

'Stupid, huh?'

'Reflex action,' Trope said. 'Happens.'

'Still pretty stupid,' Samsa said. 'A rabbit. Jesus Christ.'

'You need medical attention?'

26

Samsa said, 'I broke a tooth and my shoulder's probably bruised. Nothing serious.'

'You might want a couple of X-rays to be on the safe side.' Trope turned his flashlight on Samsa's face at a considerate angle. 'Let's take a look at this car.'

They went down into the wet field and walked to where the overturned Chrysler lay against the tree. Samsa had turned off the headlights earlier.

Trope peered inside the wreck, working his flashlight into black crannies. *Looking for booze*, Samsa thought. Samsa hadn't drunk more than a mouthful of the vodka and he'd disposed of the broken bottle. He'd fly through any sobriety test, if it ever came to that.

'You're a lucky guy,' Trope said, and strolled round the car. 'So you overturned and slammed down the slope and traveled – what – about five hundred yards. I seen people croak in cars that looked a damn sight better than this. She's pretty smashed up.'

Samsa said, 'I guess my number wasn't written on this one.'

'With your kind of luck you ought to play the State lottery this week. Course, maybe you used up all your good luck right here.'

Samsa saw his dark muddy hands by Trope's flashlight, and streaks of dirt on his suit. He gazed at the big tree, the naked bruise where the branch had snapped off. He heard the sound of the girl's scream inside his skull and for a moment imagined he saw her trapped in the car.

He'd dreamed all that in a nightmare and now he'd come out the other side and everything was going to be okay. Everything was under control. Right.

Trope asked, 'You got any idea what time you skidded off the road?'

'Ten, maybe,' Samsa said. 'Earlier. Later. I'm not sure.'

'You called in at ten fifty-three.'

'I wasn't exactly thinking about time,' Samsa said.

'That's understandable,' Trope remarked. 'It's not important to be one hundred per cent precise. This is just for the incident report.'

'I used my cellular phone to call. But my watch is busted.'

'So you go off the road around ten and you report the accident at ten fifty. You black out for a while?'

Samsa said, 'I guess so. I don't remember much after slamming into the tree.'

Trope, who had an Adam's apple the size of a mandarin, again wrote something in his notebook, which he held protectively under his slicker. 'Where were you headed?'

Samsa hadn't expected this question. A cop being nosy, he figured. Gathering and storing snippets of intelligence for future reference. You never knew what might come in handy. Trope the trooper, doing his job.

'I was just driving around. Thinking. You ever do that?'

'I do my thinking in bed mostly,' Trope said.

Samsa had a sudden fierce urge to say to Trope, it was like this, Fred. Something happened. But Trope didn't have a confessor's face, and Samsa saw no chance of understanding there. Nor absolution.

'I need to see some ID,' the trooper said.

Samsa took out a wallet from the inside jacket pocket where he also kept his phone. He showed his driver's license. Trope looked at it, gave no sign of recognition. *He's a new kid on the block*, Samsa thought.

'I think the best thing is for me to drive you home nice and safe, Mr Samsa.'

'I'd appreciate that,' Samsa said.

'Sure you don't want to stop at the County Hospital first?'

'I don't think it's going to be necessary. But thanks anyway.'

28

They walked back across the field, and Trope placed a hand under Samsa's elbow, as if he expected him to collapse suddenly on the way up the incline. *I might just do that*, Samsa thought. The night was filled with invisible weights and burdens and they pressed down on him.

They climbed to where Trope's car was parked on the edge of the blacktop. Trope held the front passenger door open and Samsa got inside. He inclined his head against the back of the seat and tried to think his way into another state of mind. A well-regulated place where gravity wasn't defied and cars didn't slam down inclines and doors didn't burst open.

What you need is instant amnesia.

He turned to the trooper. 'You must have been cruising pretty close,' he said. 'I was expecting city cops.'

'I just happened to pick up on the call. I was in the vicinity. I've only been on the job two days, so I wasn't sure if I should leave this for the boys downtown.'

Two days and you're keen, Trope. Samsa shut his eyes briefly when the car moved forward. He didn't want to look out across the big field.

He looked anyway.

The land, some twenty acres clogged with weed and dandelion and untrimmed shrubs, and bisected by the blacktop, belonged to a family called Purchase who'd lived in the state since the turn of the century. It was used by people walking dogs, trysting lovers, kids firing air rifles, nocturnal junkies. He'd heard that the city council had tried to procure the property from the family with the intention of turning it into a park. But the Purchases wanted more money than the city could afford. It was a wilderness.

Beyond the trees that marked the boundary of the land he could see the lights of the Chackstone Acres subdivision, which was screened by a cedar fence. The houses

29

were too far away for anyone to have heard anything. Too far away for anyone to have *seen* anything either, unless some amateur astronomer happened to be adjusting his telescope. On an overcast rainy night like this?

The only telescope was the one in his imagination.

Trope said, 'You want to give me directions, sir?'

'Sure.' Samsa leaned forward. 'Turn round first chance you get. Go back toward downtown. I'll direct you from there.'

There was a wasplike hum in Samsa's head. *I wasn't thinking straight.*

I wasn't thinking at all.

He clenched his hands in his lap and listened to the rain drumming on the car, imagining it falling through the branches of the tree and over his ruined car and all the way across the tangled field to the subdivision, and beyond that into the deepest stretches of the night. His thoughts were all wild stampeding horses.

5

LEE BOYLE WALKED ABOUT A MILE, HIS MOOD FESTERING. HE passed steel-shuttered store fronts and a building site surrounded by a high fence. Urban renewal. There was no doubt some of Daddy's money was involved in this prettification. Hugh, bless his glacial heart, had built a pyramid of investment corporations and subsidiaries, through which he owned shopping malls in Alabama, a dumb country-western theme park in Tennessee, a marina in Southern Cal, and fuck only knows what else. Hugh's money was insomniac. It buzzed day and night, swelling as it moved.

All I need is a lousy twelve grand, Boyle thought. Which is beer money for old Hugh. Twelve grand! He'd used the cash borrowed from Plumm to settle some long outstanding debts, the bulk of it to dealers, but also his landlord, collection agencies and sundry other demanding bastards.

On a plot of flattened land a crowd of bums huddled around a blazing oil can that sizzled in the rain. People with sodden newspapers folded on their heads. One old guy with a sad broken umbrella. Boyle glanced at the flames. *If you're not careful, this is the kind of place you might end up.* It was the kind of thing Hugh would have said in the days when he acknowledged his son's existence.

He found a payphone, stuck a quarter in the slot and called Rudy Vass.

Rudy Vass said, 'I was just about to truck on over to your place.'

Boyle explained he was stranded.

'I'll come get you,' Vass said. 'Tell me where you are.'

Boyle mentioned the location, then hung up. He waited in the grubby glass phone booth. *While I sheltered in this archway from a day of driving showers.* He couldn't remember who'd written that. Sometimes things escaped him. He smoked cigarettes and wondered about Almond. Occasionally she disappeared for a day. Now and then she had an all-nighter. But she was supposed to have met him in Chang's. Where the fuck was she?

He didn't like to think of her wandering beyond his lines of demarcation. He had boundaries, strictly imposed. One time she'd said, 'You want to keep me in a goddam straitjacket, doncha?' He'd laughed and slapped her straight in the mouth, because what it all came down to in the end was control. She couldn't just go dancing off into the darkness unless it was on his say-so. You had to lay down the law every now and then.

His Nikes squelched. His green silk bomber jacket, acquired from a mail-order company by means of a bogus credit card, was ruined. Water from his gold necklace dripped down his chest. He suddenly thought about The Kid, popped another coin inside the slot and punched the numbers. All he got was an answering machine with The Kid's faggoty drawl. 'I can't come to the phone right now. Don't hang up without speaking. Your call is important to me, so please leave a message and I'll get back to you. Pax.'

Pax. The Kid was damn hard to reach. He'd need to go over there, wait outside The Kid's apartment. But he didn't have time for hanging around, he needed to score, he needed hard cash. And quick. Like now.

Rudy Vass's battered pick-up appeared. Boyle climbed inside the cab, which smelled of damp dogs. Wet dog hairs stuck to his black jeans. 'You want to invest in one of those deodorant tree-shaped things you hang on the mirror, Rudy.'

'The smell get you down? Funny, I don't notice it.'

Vass, a lean man with a goatee that gave him the look of a redundant hippie, changed gear and the old pick-up groaned. Empty beer cans rattled around in the back, where Vass kept a puzzling array of stuff: rope, a winch, hubcaps, discolored tools, dog bowls.

'Your place?' Vass asked. 'I got the goods.' He tapped the breast pocket of his leather jacket.

Boyle thought, *Tempting, very tempting*. He looked at the empty streets, scanning for Almond. Here and there the feeble lights of a bar or coffee shop burned.

'There's a guy I want to see first, Rudy.'

'Who?'

'Crassman.'

'Crassman? That guy with the funny leg?'

Vass snorted into a suspect old handkerchief he'd pulled from his pocket. He had a bronchial problem exacerbated by the fact he didn't look after himself. Boyle had once tried to impress upon him the merits of vitamin supplements. 'Fuck vitamins,' Rudy had said. 'Vitamins are so goddam bourgeois. Only the demented want to live for ever.'

'That raunchy trailer park,' Vass said. 'I hate going over there.'

33

'Take a few minutes, that's all. You got a gun on you?'

'Yeah I got a gun but—'

'It's only for show, Rudy.'

'Guns are never only for show,' Vass said. 'Forget Crassman, Lee. Let's go to your place and do this shit that's burning a hole in my pocket.'

Boyle said, 'It'll keep.'

Vass revved up the truck and drove through a variety of suburbs to the trailer park where Crassman lived in a camper shell supported by cinderblocks. He'd attached a half-assed wooden extension to it, which he used as a kind of living room. You didn't need planning permits for anything at Shadow Oaks. The place was a poorly lit slum filled with a jumble of trailers, campers, pick-ups, jeeps. There were always snot-faced screaming babies here, oversized women in baggy cheap floral dresses, and a range of animal life, some domestic, some not.

'This is the pits,' Vass said. 'Makes my place look like a goddam show home.'

'Everything's relative,' Boyle said. Vass lived in a converted gas station. He'd turned the interior into a workshop, and when he needed cash he carpentered furniture in blond Scandinavian style and sold it.

'Over here,' Boyle said.

Vass parked outside Crassman's place. A mutt chained to a metal pole barked a couple of times and then was silent. Shadow Oaks gave Boyle the impression he'd entered the sludge at the bottom of American life. You looked at the windows of campers and trailers and you couldn't help feeling that the people inside were busy rehearsing heavy family traumas – incest, repressed rape memories – in case they got the call from Oprah.

He stepped down into mud. Vass followed him reluctantly along the path to Crassman's front door. A light was visible in the wooden extension.

34

'You bring the gun?'

Vass patted his jacket. 'I'm a walking felony, man.'

Boyle slapped his palm on the door.

Crassman was a long time answering. The door opened a slit. The man's face was tiny and oval, his nose sharp. He reminded Boyle of a cross between a human and a ferret, the offspring of a bestial coupling.

'Why, hey, Lee,' Crassman said.

'Bad night,' Boyle said, and shoved the door and stepped past Crassman. Shrugging, Vass followed.

'Let's go inside this living room of yours,' Boyle said. He kept moving. The camper shell was cramped, the ceiling so low you had to stoop. The extension wasn't much higher. It had a sofa and an old velvet armchair. A lava lamp bubbled on a wooden packing crate.

'Look at this, Rudy,' Boyle said. 'When did you last see a lamp like this baby?'

'I read someplace they made a comeback,' Vass said. 'You don't keep in touch with trends, Lee. Retro, they call it.'

'You saying Crassman's at the cutting edge of style?'

'I don't know shit about style,' Crassman said. 'I got it at a garage sale.' He rubbed his hands together nervously. He had a gloss of sweat on his upper lip. 'Figured it was kinda nice. Cost me two bucks.'

Boyle picked up the lamp and watched the colors expand. 'You think it's nice, Rudy?'

'I covet it,' Vass said.

Boyle set down the lamp and surveyed the room. The paneled walls were buckled and the air smelled of kerosene. Copies of *Ring* and *Hustler* were scattered here and there. Crassman's fly was halfway open.

'I hope we didn't interrupt you in any self-administered five-fingered massage,' Boyle said.

Crassman tugged up his zipper. 'Nothing like that, Lee.'

'Tell me, sport,' Boyle said. 'How's your wallet?'

35

'Things ain't so good,' Crassman answered.

'How bad are they?'

'This leg's been acting up.'

'Oh, yeah, right. The hunting accident.' Boyle looked directly into Crassman's eyes. 'You ran into a stag with an Uzi, I remember.'

'Ha ha. You know damn well I shot myself in the knee,' Crassman said. 'Rainy weather affects it, Lee. So I can't go out and find work.'

'You never worked in your life. You're a welfare artist.'

'Now, Lee, that ain't exactly true—'

'You know every welfare scam going.'

'They tightened up on all that,' Crassman said.

'My heart is bleeding,' Boyle said. 'How about you, Rudy?'

'I'd be crying in my beer if I had one, Lee.'

Boyle stared at Crassman. 'It's payback time, sweetheart.'

'I'm not in a position—'

'Don't fuck with me,' Boyle said. He wondered if Plumm felt this way, if he had this same kind of exuberance going through him when he threatened one of his tardy debtors. This little rush of power you felt when you knew you had somebody by the balls. 'You owe me one thousand dollars, which I was foolish enough to loan you three weeks ago because you said you had this deal with a quick turn around that was going to net you *beaucoup* bucks. And my thou was going to grow like some magic mushroom into fifteen hundred overnight. Funny thing is, you don't answer my calls, you don't show up at my place with cash, you don't phone.'

'It didn't pan out, Lee. Some things went wrong.'

'Figures. So how much can you pay back?'

Crassman looked trapped and miserable. 'God's honest truth, I'm down to my last twenty.'

'Twenty? *Twenty?*'

Crassman tugged a crumpled bill from his back pocket. 'Here. Take this on account, Lee. Go on. Take it.'

Boyle knocked the bill from Crassman's outstretched hand. 'Pass me your gun, Rudy.'

'Lee, come on,' Vass said. 'Let's blow this place.'

'Give me the goddam gun, Rudy.'

'Gun?' Crassman asked. 'You don't need no gun, Lee. I swear I'll get the bread for you.'

Lee Boyle took the gun from Vass's hand and pointed it at Crassman's head. Crassman's expression was a mixture of despair and incredulity. Boyle poked the end of the barrel into Crassman's chin. *There was a pecking order of things*, Lee Boyle thought. Plumm picks on me. I pick on Crassman. Who does Crassman pick on? His mutt in the yard? A few harsh strokes of the whip?

'Twenty's a fucking insult, Crassman,' he said.

Rudy Vass made a clucking sound of disapproval. 'Be careful with that gun, Lee.'

'Give me one good reason I shouldn't just blow this roach into the promised land, Rudy,' Boyle said. He pushed the gun into Crassman's larynx.

'Because homicide's a very bad rap,' Vass said. 'Just take the guy's twenty, Lee.'

Boyle smiled at Crassman. 'So, Crassman. Do I take the twenty or pull the trigger? You see my dilemma.'

'I can raise another hundred tomorrow,' Crassman said. 'Somebody owes me, Lee. He's good for it.'

'I hate this shit. Somebody owes you. You owe me. I owe somebody else. I swear to God, I really hate these chains of debt. I gave you a grand in good faith. You exploited my generosity.'

Lee Boyle increased the pressure on Crassman's throat. 'Down on your knees, champ.'

'Good Christ, Lee,' Crassman said.

37

'Down.'

Crassman went into a supplicant's position. *This was it*, Boyle thought, *the undiluted essence of glee*.

'Please, Lee. Look, I can probably raise two, two hundred tomorrow.'

'Spare me the mumbo-jumbo,' Boyle said.

'Maybe even three. I don't know yet, I gotta do some chasing around.'

Lee Boyle struck Crassman's skull with the gun in a swift downward motion. Crassman pitched forward, covering his head with his hands and whimpering. Boyle stepped back. It wasn't enough. He felt unfulfilled. He grabbed Crassman's collar and hauled him halfway up, and this time hammered him with the butt of the gun across his nose. It made a hard cracking sound, steel on bone. Blood flowed from Crassman's nostrils. Boyle drove his knee into the guy's chest and Crassman slumped to the floor.

'This is only minor violence, Crassman,' Boyle said.

'Lee, forget it,' Vass said. He'd picked up the twenty and was holding it out to Boyle.

Boyle ignored the offering. He grabbed Crassman's hair and yanked it, forcing the man's face up into the purplish light from the lava lamp. He picked up the lamp and brought it down on Crassman's head and the glass cracked and warm colored liquid spurted out. The light went out and now the room was lit only by a bare bulb overhead. Crassman lay face-down in a small pool of his own blood and liquid from the lamp.

Rudy Vass said, 'This is a bad scene, Lee. Come on.'

Boyle squatted alongside Crassman, and with the tip of his finger opened the guy's left eye. 'I'm taking the pitiful twenty, Crassman. But if you don't call me tomorrow with some good news about a sizeable installment, you don't get off so lightly in the future. *Comprender?*'

Crassman's eyelid fluttered.

Lee Boyle gave Vass his gun back and went outside to the pick-up. Vass came behind him, blowing into his handkerchief. They got inside the truck.

'That was cruel, Lee,' Vass said.

'Yeah, well, I'm desperate,' Boyle said.

'You were crazy to invest in any scheme of his.'

'A moment of unjustified optimism, Rudy.'

'You know what I think? You don't like your life. That's what I think.'

'So it's not exactly a pleasure dome.'

Vass drove for a mile in silence. Then he said, 'I remember a time when you wouldn't even have considered doing that violent shit.'

'In my glorious yesterdays,' Boyle said. 'When I was a college boy and the world was all sunshine and I could get high on Keats and Shelley. When I didn't need substances. Yeah yeah yeah. *I am not the buoyant thing I was of yore*, quote unquote.'

'Fuck it. Let's just get wasted, Lee.'

Boyle thought about Crassman's blood, streaks of which dampened the twenty-dollar bill he held in his fist. Blood money.

'Yeah. Let's do exactly that.'

6

_____

SAMSA ENTERED THE HOUSE QUIETLY. HE WENT AT ONCE UP to his bathroom, where he removed a bottle of painkillers from the medicine cabinet and shook a couple out into his hand. He dropped them on the tiled floor, stooped to gather them up, swallowed them with water. Then he swirled Listerine round in his mouth, and when he spat it out he saw dark metallic pieces of an old filling.

He tried to avoid his reflection in the cabinet mirror. Blood had darkened and dried on his lips, and there were bruises and streaks of dirt on his face. He was white and unrecognizable, his eyes lackluster, as if somebody had turned out the lights behind them. His thick graying hair was wet and plastered flat across his skull, and his cheeks, normally full, appeared deflated.

This doesn't look like me. This isn't Greg Samsa.

He took off his shoes, undressed, stuffed his clothes in a closet alongside other garments he'd gathered to take to the dry-cleaners, then stepped inside the shower, where he worked a lather of warm soapy water into his face. He scrubbed his hands and fingernails briskly again and again

40

with a small hard-bristled brush, and ran shampoo through his hair. Wash, dry, put on a robe – it was a series of steps and tiny performances. Pantomime. Doing normal things. Looking the part. He was operating in a haze and it terrified him, and he couldn't allow himself to feel that way.

He heard Darcy's voice beyond the bathroom door. 'Dad?'

He said, 'A minute, honey.' He knotted the belt of the robe before he opened the door.

'You look bad. Are you hurt?'

'You should see the car,' he said.

'*Seriously*. Are you hurt?'

He placed a hand on her shoulder. 'I could use a drink.'

'What happened exactly?'

'Skidded,' he said. 'Off the road and into a field.'

'Where?'

'You know the old Purchase property?'

'What were you doing over there?'

'Just driving,' he said.

'I bet you were driving too fast. You always do.'

He thought how little he could see of Harriet in her. She had his coloring, his very dark-brown eyes, the same slightly stubborn set of mouth – but softer, infinitely more attractive. It was as if Harriet's involvement had stopped at the birthing process. She'd left no mark on this girl. Here's our daughter, Greg. She's all yours. I'm empty now. And she'd stayed that way.

They walked downstairs to the living room. He went to the liquor cabinet and poured himself a large cognac, noticing the Scrabble game on the coffee table. 'Nick gone home?' He needed to make small talk. Where you didn't have to think. As if you were concussed.

'A few minutes ago.'

He swallowed some of the brandy. He sat down, and

41

the room rushed at him all at once as if it had turned over just like the Chrysler. He was dizzy and faint and felt like an astronaut inside a space capsule. There were inversions, strange flips, optical illusions. A voltage spike on the graph of perception. Photographs turning over, Harriet's lovely face upside down on the mantelpiece, the hands of the clock hurrying backwards.

His fingers shook. The brandy in the glass rippled. He closed his eyes. What he saw behind his eyelids was the shallow pool of water and the broken branch and something black flapping in the air like a predatory bird, eyes lethal.

'Are you really okay?' Darcy asked.

'A little shook up. It'll pass.'

'I'll call Pascal if you like.'

'I don't need a physician, honey.'

'How do you know you don't? There might be internal bleeding or something.'

'I'd know,' he said.

'Okay, okay. I'm only trying to help.'

How can you help, dear Darcy?

He opened his eyes. The room had readjusted itself, but seemed to exist precariously in an unfamiliar dimension. Darcy began to stack the Scrabble tiles inside the box. He watched her. Fifteen, full-breasted, suffused with the confidence of youth and yet riddled at the same time by insecurities, the whole all-out nuclear rage of her hormones. Fifteen, a young woman, time flying away, and Nick Mancuso sniffing round her. He felt love and sadness simultaneously.

He finished his cognac. He needed another to blunt his mind.

'Your hand's shaking,' she said. 'Maybe you should take a tranquilizer.'

'What I need is another brandy,' and he rose to pour himself one.

42

It happened then, a zap out of nowhere, a crushing sensation around his heart, breathlessness. He reached out, supported himself against the liquor cabinet, thinking coronary, meltdown in the aorta. *Does she have parents somewhere wondering about her? In some faraway house in another part of the city, another part of the nation, were two people waiting for the phone to ring and a daughter to say, Hi, I'm fine, I'm doing okay?*

He raised the bottle. He could hardly hold it.

'Here,' Darcy said. 'I'll do that. You'll spill it all over yourself.'

He watched her pour into his glass. He said, 'That's a miserly amount.'

She added another tiny drop. 'It's all you're getting.'

'Come on,' he said. 'This is cruel and unusual punishment for a guy that just survived a car wreck.' He attempted to infuse a certain flippancy into his tone, but it was like trying to maintain a shuttlecock of lead in the air.

'Drink it slowly. I'm going to find you a pill. There's some upstairs.'

'Darcy, I don't want a pill,' he said.

But she was already gone from the room and he could hear her hurrying up the stairs. He imagined her rummaging in the medicine cabinet among the tablets Harriet used to take. He wondered why he'd never gotten round to throwing the entire pharmacy out. For the same reason he'd kept all her clothing, all her jewelry, he supposed. Whatever that reason was called. Something the heart stoked up. The demands of love, the deranged idea that you kept the essence of the person by hanging on to their possessions – as if one bright afternoon she might just materialize under a halo in the doorway and say, Sorry I left you alone this long, my love. He didn't need this and he didn't need to look up at Harriet's photograph either,

43

goddamit – that oval face and those solemn eyes with melancholy secrets hidden in them, things she'd never explained, couldn't have explained, monsters trapped in the dead-end labyrinth of her mind.

You drifted from me, he thought. *And I fill the cold emptiness any way I can.*

Darcy came back in the room. 'Here.' She was holding out a pill to him. 'I'm not sure it's the smart thing to take it with brandy,' she said.

He looked at the sky-blue tab. It was called Limbitrol, he remembered. It was only one of a bunch with names that rolled easily off the tongue. Elavil and Surmontil. They sounded like futuristic candies. Here, kids, chew these down. Try some Prozac while you're at it. They'd done nothing for Harriet except drive her deeper into that impenetrable pocket where she'd lived her life. He placed the pill in his mouth and swallowed it with brandy. Quickly. He didn't want the taste of it.

The telephone was ringing. The sound, shrill and un-expected and yet so goddam commonplace, went through Samsa's head like a vibrating ice pick. Darcy answered, then handed the phone to him. He heard Eve Lassiter's voice.

'The grapevine's buzzing. You hurt?'

'No. I'm fine.'

'This is what comes of driving on slippery roads in the rain,' Eve Lassiter said. 'You were brooding again, right? You were in a funky mindset and not paying attention. You took your eye off the ball, didn't you?'

'I confess.'

'What you need is a refresher course in careful driving.'

'Is this going to be a nag, Eve?'

'A half-nag, I'd say. Not the whole thing. If you were feeling low, why didn't you call me? Tell me it just never crossed your mind.'

44

'It never crossed my mind,' he said.

'A hundred times I've told you, Greg. You feel low, you phone me. You never listen.'

Samsa could hear noises in the background. A jukebox, the click of pool balls. Eve was having a late drink in a bar she liked, because she said she enjoyed the attentions of the young studs that hung out there.

'Go back to your beer and your boys,' he said.

'I'll come over if you need company.'

'I'm going to sleep.'

She was quiet for a moment. 'Okay. Sweet dreams.'

He put the handset down.

'She's got the hots for you,' Darcy said. 'She sees you and her mouth just kind of hangs open.'

'The hots? *Eve?* I don't think so.' He pulled his daughter toward him and held her, smelling a trace of herbal shampoo in her hair.

'You're going to meet somebody one of these days,' Darcy said.

'It's only been a year,' he said. 'One year ago to-morrow.'

'I'm having a problem breathing, Dad,' Darcy said.

He released her. 'I think I'll go upstairs,' he said. He kissed her cheek.

She asked, 'You sure you're okay?'

'Yeah. Don't worry about me.'

He went up to his bedroom, climbing slowly. His shoulder ached and he rubbed it. 'Sweet dreams,' Eve had said. Tell me how.

Restless, he rose and walked the room for a time. *His shoes. He had to do something about his shoes.*

He heard Darcy in the kitchen, the clack of a plate in the sink, water running. Then she was climbing the stairs to her own room. Her door closed. She sang a couple of phrases of some popular song. She had a good clear voice, but now the sound struck him as discordant, like an untuned harp randomly plucked.

He waited, then went inside the bathroom, where he picked up his shoes, carried them down to the kitchen and wrapped them inside a plastic bag he found in a drawer. He stepped out of the house. He dropped the bag in the trash can, rearranging garbage, concealing the bag under a pile of withered carrots and browned lettuce leaves and ancient celery. He stuck the lid on the can, went back inside the house and climbed once again to his bedroom. *I'm thinking like a goddam criminal.*

He walked to the window and parted the curtains and looked down into the street. Empty. A couple of lamps shining between the trees along the sidewalk, a nocturnal suburb. He watched the still scene for a while, expecting – expecting what?

He didn't know.

Something bad. Something that formed in the shadows.

He let the curtain fall from his hand and sat on the edge of the bed. Then he pressed his knuckles to his lips, as if to hold back a cry rising inside. He lay on his side and tried to eclipse everything from his mind. A process of emptying himself, draining the battery of his memory until it was dead.

7

RUDY VASS SAT ON BOYLE'S SOFA AND SAID, 'NOW THIS IS what I call great shit.'

Boyle was peering through the slats of the blind down at the street below, feeling the edge of paranoia he associated with speed that had been stepped on. He strummed the slats with his fingertips and chewed on the inside of his mouth, where he had a tiny ulcer. He'd been forgetting his vitamin regime.

His apartment was situated over a pawnshop protected by steel shutters and a state-of-the-art alarm system. Directly below he could see three brass balls glistening in the rain. 'It's cut with something. I don't know what,' he said.

'No way,' Vass said. 'It comes from my regular guy.'

Vass's regular guy was a postgrad chemistry student named Stretch, who paid his tuition by making up batches of drugs – speed, downers, hallucinogens – now and again.

'I'm too jittered,' Boyle said. His pulses were at the races. His head was out of touch with the rest of him.

'My guy doesn't mess around with his basic recipe,' Vass said.

'Then how come I'm feeling like this?' Boyle asked.

'Maybe it's your mood.'

'My mood's okay.'

'Not from where I'm sitting, Lee. That number you did on Crassman. That was *unreal*, man. There's a mean streak in you wasn't ever there before.'

Boyle popped a can of Coors and gulped it back. He studied his answering machine, stared at the zero in the little message window. Almond was out there somewhere. The rule he'd laid down was for her to call him every three hours, no matter what. He hadn't heard from her since – since when? Yesterday afternoon? The idea she might have acted independently was an insult to him.

Rudy Vass sipped from a bottle of Southern Comfort. 'You want to sit, calm down a little.'

'I don't know why I shoot myself up with this shit when it gets me so goddam *amped*,' Boyle said. He let his arms hang at his sides, loosened them up, did a couple of neck rolls.

'Drink some of this, take the edge off,' Vass said.

Boyle took the bottle and sipped. It tasted sour. He set it back down on the coffee table, which was littered with paraphernalia. Rigs, a little plastic baggie of speed, a few sparkly crystals that had spilled. There was a packet of Rizla and a small vial of Lebanese grass and a half-dozen tabs of pink downers made up by Stretch to a formula he'd concocted himself. The shooting-works to take you into orbit, the calming agents meant to restore equilibrium. Sometimes they didn't work and you just zoomed into a place in the ether, where you were frazzled and unglued.

Vass was rattling on about his opinion of Boyle's life. 'You want to bring your problems into focus and get a handle on them, Lee. Once upon a time, as I remember, you were going places. You had smarts galore. You might have become a fisher of men.'

'You're going to tell me where all that good stuff vanished. Right?'

Vass tugged his beard. 'You developed a fondness for this drug. You started to get like you just don't give a fuck about any goddam thing: where you're headed, what you're doing. You could still build a whole new life for yourself, Lee. I'm looking to give you advice. We go back a long way, you and me. Eleven years.' Vass ticked each item off on his fingers. 'One, give up the drugs, clean up your act. Two, this stuff with the chick. Set her loose, Lee—'

'Set her loose? She brings in around two thou on a good week, Rudy.'

Vass had veined eyelids and his cheeks were sunken. His pallor was like classroom chalk dust. 'It's a moral consideration. I remember we outlawed slavery way back. Lincoln et cetera.'

'Slavery my ass. She does her thing for me willingly. I tell her, do this, do that, she does it. I don't call that enslavement.'

The telephone rang. Boyle picked it up at once. He expected it to be Almond, all sweet and contrite. Instead he heard a man's angry voice.

'I been waiting at this hotel an hour for your girl, Boyle. Where is she?'

Boyle couldn't think a moment. 'She didn't show?'

'If she showed, would I be calling?'

'I don't understand,' Boyle said. Losing his grip here. Had he made an appointment for Almond through one of the phone services? He couldn't remember. His mind was in hyperdrive. He didn't even know this guy's name, and the voice was strange to him. He had the glimmer of a suspicion that maybe this call was some form of sting operation engineered by the vice cops. They were always trying to set up capers that were forever being tossed out

49

of court on the grounds of illegal entrapment.

The guy said, 'I'm out of here in ten minutes if she don't show. And I'll tell you this, Boyle, it's the last time I contact you. This is a waste of my time.' The guy hung up.

'Your little chickadee didn't keep a date?' Vass asked.

'Apparently not.' Boyle walked round the room, trying to remember. But it was gone. Slipped down some crevice. *Jesus. Where do lost memories go anyhow?* He checked the view again, a forlorn street of shuttered storefronts and apartments poised above them, and everything seemed to pulsate feebly like a light flickering on and off in a dying man's eyes. He didn't belong here.

'How much does she keep out of what she earns?' Vass asked.

'Enough.'

'You throw in what, nine or ten grams of *el cheapo* coke a week? You buy her some clothes now and then, you feed her when she feels like being fed, maybe some pocket money. Most of the time she's too zoned to give a rat's ass.' Vass sucked on the Southern Comfort and dragged his shirt cuff across his lips.

'She does all right,' Boyle said.

Vass said, 'It blows me away, Lee. The blue-eyed boy turns pimp.'

'That's a loaded word, Rudy.'

'It's your fucking *job* description. How would you describe what you do?'

'I'm in the lubricants business.'

Vass laughed. 'You're still a pimp. You lost your way. You detoured down some weird highway, and now you don't know what the hell you're doing with your life. I mean, you're even entertaining some weird-ass notion about going into the blackmail business with that guy you call The Kid, whatsisname. That is totally off the wall, Lee. And then there's this money you owe to Plumm, who's a ghoul. I swear I saw him in *Friday the Thirteenth Part Three*, man. When I think of the way you used to be . . .'

Boyle tuned Vass out. This was the point when Vass usually started to ramble about the old days. How he and Boyle met at the U of Penn, where Boyle was skimming through Eng Lit like a genius and Vass was losing his struggle with the mysteries of physics. How Boyle, despite his high grade-point average and his penchant for asking intelligently contemptuous questions at lectures, was obliged to drop out in his freshman year because Daddy Boyle didn't like the inauspicious reports of his son's activities, which included such misdemeanors as stealing the dean's car and screwing the dean's daughter in the back seat of it, no less. A dishonorable discharge from academia for young Lee, and no more of Daddy's money for future scholastic purposes. Vass himself had quit school after a weekend retreat, when he'd tuned into a message from a Nepalese guru. Set yourself free, young man, walk away from the chains of organized education.

So I took up my hammer and saw, Lee. And I kept on drugging. Ah, sweet Christ, I wish I'd been at Woodstock. Born too late. Vass kept coming back to this speech every time he was speeding.

Boyle, cresting the crystal arc at a slippery point, was thinking about that phone call again. If it was a set-up, it meant his name was in somebody's black book. He thought about a sleazy vice cop called Stephen Rebb who'd hassled him a few times in the past. Maybe Rebb, an altogether objectionable character, had set something up. Lee Boyle didn't like this possibility. He tried to maintain a very low profile. He wasn't one of those movie-type caricatures in a long fur coat and blinding jewelry and a broad-brimmed hat and bimbos hanging on both arms.

51

He picked up his telephone and unscrewed the mouth-piece.

'What are you doing?' Vass asked.

'I'm wondering about bugs, Rudy.'

'As in *listening* devices?'

Boyle nodded. He looked at the wiring. What could you tell from that? A listening device could be anywhere: under a table, inside a lampshade, in his bedroom. He had an urge to start dismantling things, stripping them down to basics. He'd get his screwdriver and go into the ventilation duct. Take apart the answering machine. On one level he understood this was speed causing havoc. On another it was all very real.

'Lee, nobody's got your place bugged.' Vass took the phone out of his hand. 'There's nothing wrong with this goddam phone. You're small change in the big network of sexual commerce, man. The idea of anyone taking the time and trouble to bug your apartment, hey, that's down-right laughable.'

Boyle walked to the sofa and sat and drummed his fingertips on his knees. He tapped one foot rapidly on the floor. He couldn't quit doing it. Moving, shaking, tapping. He flashed on The Kid, pictured his sweetly cut sandy hair, those floppy fag sweaters he always wore with the sleeves rolled up to the elbows, his ever-so-nice manners. *I'll get you something solid, Lee, it just takes a little time.* He thought about phoning him, but even though Vass had said the telephone was okay, Boyle didn't trust the goddam thing.

'Pop one of those pink babies,' Vass said.

'This shit's cut with something,' Boyle said. 'I'm telling you, Rudy.'

'Just take one of the pinks.'

'How do I know what's in the pill?'

'Don't go all funny on me now.'

Boyle stuffed his hands in his pockets and rattled coins vigorously. 'I ought to go out looking for her. Hanging out here's a waste of time.'

Vass said, 'Let's just stay right where we are, Lee. She'll show. You know she'll show.'

'What if she doesn't?'

'Then you're out of a bad business. Or else you'll have to get yourself another girl.'

Boyle listened to the rhythms of his blood and the wild timpani of his heart, and he wondered if this speed was taking him to outer space. It was a long trip back from there, crashing down through one depressing level after another. Grinding your teeth, chewing the inside of your mouth, pacing up and down.

'Tell me this,' Vass said in a quiet voice intended to soothe. 'You ever get it on with this girl?'

Boyle's scalp was tingling. It's all too much now: huge rushes of unfocused energy, thoughts that don't gell, collisions between what's real and what's not. Bugged rooms, people watching from the shadows of doorways, Revenue guys going through his canceled checks on microfiche at the bank, special warrants signed by judges – you could imagine the whole works.

'Well? Did you?' Vass asked.

Boyle scratched his head. 'No. I never did. But I was sorely tempted.'

'You had the will-power to resist.'

'You don't mix business with pleasure.' He remembered seeing her step out of his shower, and her supple little nut-brown body glistening with water, her hard flat stomach damp. She'd looked at him standing in the doorway. 'You like what you see? Come on, Lee. Do me.' And so he had, right there on the bathroom floor among damp towels, a sweet grappling, not once, twice, but three times. His own desire was a fever. And if she was faking passion, she was one hell of an actress. 'I don't do this for the tricks, Lee. This is special.'

Why had he lied to Vass about it? Some vestigial shame? *I don't feel shame*, he thought. Shame's what happens when you hand a megaphone to your conscience. And conscience was a loud-mouthed luxury.

Vass was quiet a moment. 'What age is she?'

'She could pass for twenty,' Boyle said.

'Yeah, but how old is she?'

Boyle stood up. 'You stay here if you want. I'm going out.'

'Wait—'

'Don't stop me, Rudy.' He was all haste now, looking for a jacket, shoes, rummaging around. It was important to hit the streets. When I find her, she's in serious trouble.

Vass said, 'You didn't answer my question.'

'Okay. Thirteen. One three.'

'*Thirteen?* Unlucky number, man. Real evil vibes.'

8

THE MAZE OF BASEMENT ROOMS BENEATH CITY HALL ALWAYS smelled of mildew. Damp infiltrated everything. Papers curled round the edges and folders felt gummy to the touch. Eve Lassiter had once found a fuzzy white mold growing on the wall behind one of the old-fashioned steam radiators. It became known in the department as The Blob. For a while it was an object of curiosity and a certain indignation. Sergeant Duff had taken a Polaroid of it with the intention of showing it to the mayor as proof of the inhospitable conditions in which the city's downtown cops were obliged to work. But the fungus had been forgotten in the flux of business.

Samsa found himself remembering the growth, thinking it might be expanding there still. He had an urge to get up from his desk and check it out, but instead he shifted papers from his in-tray to his out and back again. The muscles at the nape of his neck ached. That morning, shaving, he'd seen blue and yellow contusions on his shoulder, a whole map of discoloration as sharp as a new tattoo. The thought had occurred to him: *I carry a bad sign on my body.*

He rose, walked to the water-cooler, filled a dixie cup, swallowed a couple of aspirins. He was conscious of activities going on all around him – John Cullinan, an odd soul with a haunted look, muttering to himself at his desk, 'People don't have a fucking clue what it's like down here, what the hell ever happened to the new building the so-called city fathers promised.' Duff politely talking down the phone to some lunatic, 'You say you actually saw your husband being beamed up inside this craft, Mrs Gogarty, and the craft had a swastika sign on it. So what is it, like a Nazi from outer space?' Fogue lighting up one of his foul cheroots in flagrant disregard of the department's no-smoking policy.

Babble echoed down the interconnecting rooms.

Samsa went back to his desk, which was partitioned off from the hoi polloi. *Three hundred and sixty-five days ago. A year almost to this very moment.* He sat, gazed at some paperwork, feeling detached from his purpose in this place. Overhead, the fluorescent strip hummed. No natural light penetrated these rooms.

Eve Lassiter put her head round the door. 'Surprised to see you this morning, Lieutenant. Shouldn't you be taking it easy?'

'Why? I'm functioning.'

'I hear the car was a write-off. You look like a write-off yourself.'

She was tall and slim-hipped, thirty-three years old. She wore her red hair straight to her shoulders. She had green carefree eyes – some Irish filtered through her ancestry. You could imagine her playing a harp with those long fingers. Around the department she'd acquired a minor reputation for picking up younger men in a certain bar she frequented. Samsa considered this rumor for the most part macho talk down among the lockers. So she had a casual

56

dalliance now and then, that didn't make her a nympho-maniac. She was young, she had appetites.

Needs. He knew about needs. Where they led you.

'I slept badly,' he said.

'You sound a little off-key,' she said.

'I keep thinking . . .' He paused. There was a doorway here he couldn't open in a hundred years. He wanted to, he wanted to go inside that room and say, 'This is what happened, Eve. Try to understand. I took a very wrong turning.' It was the same feeling he'd had with Trope.

'Thinking what?'

'That car. I see that car slamming off the road.'

'Post-trauma,' she said. 'You'll have flashbacks.' She approached the desk. 'I have a suggestion. Why don't we have dinner at my place one night?'

'We'll do that,' he said.

'I'm not being pushy or anything. But when do you have in mind?'

He shrugged. 'Some night next week.'

'I've heard of pulling teeth. What night?'

'Whenever—'

'Enthusiasm would be a step forward, Greg.'

He raised a hand to his head. Pick a day. Any day from the deck.

'Wednesday,' he said.

'Okay. Seven suit you?'

He nodded. She said, 'I do good Creole. Tex-Mex, if you like that. I can cook. Really.'

'I believe you, Eve. I look forward to it.'

She leaned across his desk. She looked very young suddenly. He imagined her as a teenager, gawky and unco-ordinated. She spoke in a quiet voice. 'Know some-thing, Greg? There's this sad streak in you that really bothers me.'

'Sad streak?'

'I'm not saying it very well, I guess. A kind of lost quality. You're like an explorer who's mislaid his compass.'

'You want to mother me, Eve?'

'Shit, no. I'm not the mothering type. And I don't ever fall for any of that little boy lost jazz. I only want to feed you. I think you need it.'

'You can feed me Wednesday then.'

'Deal.' She turned to the door, then stopped. 'The Leeson case, by the way. I'm meeting with a guy whose phone number we found scribbled on a scrap of paper in Leeson's bedside drawer. I'm heading out to see him now. He didn't sound exactly over the moon to hear from me. Why don't you come keep me company? You look like you need just about any old excuse to get out of here.'

Samsa thought about Anthony Leeson, a retired pharmacist who'd been stabbed to death a couple of nights ago by an assailant in a frenzy. Zane, the coroner, had counted twenty-four stab wounds. The murder had all the hallmarks of a homosexual-related slaying. Leeson's neighbors were quick, indecently eager even, to point out that he'd often been seen bringing young boys back to his apartment.

'It's your case, Eve,' he said.

'I could use some help with it.'

He was reluctant. He wanted to stay behind his desk and shuffle papers and keep his head down until kingdom come. He'd given the Leeson case to Eve because he'd been entangled in other matters, and, anyway, he knew she was capable. There had been thirty-two homicides in the city during the last four months. It didn't compare with certain other cities, but it stretched the resources of the department.

Samsa spent too much time juggling manpower and schedules and asking the chief, Al Brodsky, for more qualified people. 'I've talked to the mayor,' was Al's stock response. The mayor's response was also stock: 'I'll look into it and get back to you, Al. It's a matter of money we just don't have at this point in time. We went way over budget building the new precinct house on the East Side, and refurbishing the South Side was more than we bargained for. You know how it goes, Al. The city's impoverished.'

Yackety-yack.

The mayor's idea had been for the bulk of the downtown cops to be moved to the new East Side precinct, but the building, incompetently constructed, had problems with the refrigeration system, the elevators were unreliable, the sewage pipes constantly backed up, and – a true brilliancy in planning – an inadequate number of phone jacks. Samsa remembered a time when the department had thirty precinct houses throughout the city, but policy – which he thought misguided – had dictated closing these houses and cramming as many cops into as few boxes as possible. Bigger boxes, sure, but better service?

A fortune spent nationwide on extra cops, on new jails. But very little of it seemed to be coming this way, to the hub downtown, this fetid basement that housed a total of 233 cops in the course of different shifts. This hell.

Eve said, 'I could use your input. You're sharp when it comes to assessing what people say. I'm still a little naïve.'

'Naïve? *You?* I don't really think so, Detective.' Samsa got up anyway, took his jacket from the back of his chair and slowly followed her. Naïve wasn't a word that came to mind in connection with Eve. She was sharp and persistent, qualities that had led to her promotion to detective only last year. Okay. She wants your company. She thinks you need to get out. And you don't have the energy to resist.

Fogue, a plump bald figure blowing perfect thick smoke rings, looked up from behind his chaotic desk and said, 'Hey, Lew Tenant.' Fogue always made Samsa's rank sound like a man's name. 'Heard you lost your bearings last night.'

'I had an accident, Billy,' Samsa said.

'You ever hear the theory there's no such thing as an accident? I read this guy, forget his name, says accidents are things you actually want to happen. No kidding.' Fogue laid a hand on his heart.

'Bullshit,' Cullinan said. 'All I hear in this place is bullshit. All I smell in my nostrils is this damp.'

'Hey, it ain't my theory, Cull. Can I help it if I'm well read?'

To the tune of 'Smoke Gets In Your Eyes', Cullinan sang to himself, 'Damp gets in my bones.'

Fogue said to Samsa, 'Seems you go out actually *looking* for accidents. Least, according to this guy I read.'

'The man cracks open a book and listen to what comes out,' Samsa said. 'One thing he hasn't read is the No Smoking sign.'

'Unconstitutional discrimination,' Fogue said. 'I belong to this group. Rights of Smokers in America. ROSA. We're fighting back against all those puritan clean lungs suckers.'

Samsa moved toward the stairs that led out of the basement. Eve walked just ahead of him. She had a loose-limbed motion, hips swinging just a little, her ass firm under her tailored black slacks. He thought, *I've never looked at her before from this perspective.* A little surprised, he lowered his eyes.

Fogue called out. 'Anybody searching for you, Lew Tenant, what'll I tell them?'

'Say I'm up to my neck,' Samsa said.

'In what?'

Samsa didn't respond. He listened to the sound of his footsteps click on the old marble floor of the entrance to City Hall, with its high neo-Gothic ceiling in need of a paint job. Upstairs were courtrooms and the DA's office and the mayor's staff. The place was riddled with dry rot and the marble was engrained with dirt, and in winter the outmoded boiler failed to send heat through the veins of the building.

Outside on the street he felt clamminess in the sunshine. It was one of those mornings when the atmosphere would agitate asthmatics and swamp-coolers stifle rooms. *Say I'm up to my neck*, he thought. That would be the truth.

Eve tugged his arm. 'You coming or not?'

He must have been standing motionless without realizing it. He had to prevent traffic jams in his head. Curtail them somehow. The plan, if he really had one, was simple: concentrate on what he was doing at any given time, rein in wayward thoughts and dispel tiny seizures of drift. It was more than just going through the motions. It had to be an act of belief. He had to get inside the memory banks and delete whatever he didn't need.

Accidents are things you want to happen.

He didn't believe that for a moment, because it implied some kind of ludicrous collusion between himself and a hapless jackrabbit on a highway.

He found himself moving slowly through the molasses of air. His mind was filled all at once with alternatives too late to deploy. *She was a hitch-hiker I picked up.* But she didn't look like a hitch-hiker. She looked exactly what she was. There would be suspicion, innuendo.

Okay. She was a hooker. And that's against the law.

Yeah, but why this particular hooker out of so many, Lieutenant? Why did she catch your eye?

She was somebody I was bringing in for questioning.

In connection with what, Lieutenant? What particular

61

case? Did you suspect her of something? Let's hear your story for the record.

'Greg,' Eve said. 'Are you orbiting the planet or is there some way I can connect with you? You're miles away.' She unlocked her car. 'You *sure* you didn't bang your head last night?'

'I'm sure,' he said.

She sat behind the wheel. Samsa lowered himself into the passenger seat. He felt the car slide forward out of the parking lot. He thought, *Maybe all our lives are lived through acts of dishonesty. The only way we cope is by lying to ourselves.*

He turned to look at Eve. 'I'm a good cop,' he said.

She glanced at him. 'Is that a question?'

'I've always been a good cop. It's all I know how to do.'

She said, 'What is *bothering* you?'

'Maybe it's a mid-life crisis.'

'Maybe it's loneliness,' she said.

He looked through the window. The city rose in a haze of towers, stacks of concrete and glass. In the downtown acre of greenery called Patriot Park, there was a birdshit-smeared monument to the man, Barnabas Sullivan, from Limerick, who'd first built a settlement here in the wilderness in 1835. All that energy and optimism only to have your effigy covered in droppings. Welcome to neglect.

It was still a fucking wilderness out there. It was just the savages that were different now.

Eve said, 'I didn't have any right to say that, Greg. About loneliness.'

'It's probably true,' he said.

'It's none of my business. I've never lost a spouse. I can't even imagine what that grief must feel like.'

Grief, he thought. Grief was like plugging into a connection that ripped the heart out of you. It was a demon you hadn't summoned, but it came without invitation, a gargoyle that gatecrashed your life.

Don't dwell on this. You don't need it.

He continued to gaze from the window. They were driving through an area on the edge of downtown that was seedy, old warehouses and dilapidated factories. It was a grim neighborhood. Early twentieth-century signs were still barely visible in dirty brick: 'Carstairs Mattress Manufacturing Company'. 'McPherson's Grain & Feed'. The area was known as Flesh Row. Sometimes Skin Street. At night this was the neighborhood where bodies were traded, boys and girls pacing round under weak street lights and cars cruising back and forth. This was the place where you came if you were lonely and your appetites had gone beyond any consideration of consequences.

'I'd like to see all this razed,' he said. He heard a little note of anger in his voice. 'I'd like to see them come in with a crew of wreckers.'

'No way. It's historic. If anything, they might pump some money into cleaning it up and preserving it. It has character. With a little work, maybe a few cafés and bookshops, it might even have charm.'

'Charm? I doubt it. It's always going to be sleazy.'

'Let's agree to differ,' Eve said.

She patted his knee a second. 'And, yes, you've always been a good cop. In my book, the best.'

'Thanks,' he said.

'Dignified and emphatic,' she added.

'Enough already.'

'And honorable.' She smiled. 'I hope I grow up to be just like you.'

'Yeah? Just be careful what you hope for, Eve.'

9

IN GINNY FLAGG'S BEDROOM, DARCY SAID, 'I THOUGHT YOU were supposed to be sick.'

'I am sick,' Ginny said.

'You don't look it.'

'I feel fluey.'

'Sure you do. You haven't prepared for Hump's test, have you?'

Ginny Flagg, a tiny girl with a red-dyed streak in her cropped black hair, took off her glasses and wiped them on the edge of the bedsheet. 'All that geography stuff is too, I don't know, blah. Like I need to know the capital of the Ukraine? I don't know where the Ukraine is even.'

'It's a former Soviet state,' Darcy said before she could stop herself.

She had a memory that was sometimes a curse. Everything got stored automatically inside her head. She could remember the names of minor actors in forgotten B-movies. She could tell you the line-up of rock bands and who split to form another group. She remembered all the things they crammed into her at school, even when they weren't interesting or useful. Lately she'd begun to let her mind stray in class, as if to spite this gift of recall. Besides, school had started to drag on her – the gossip, the day-after-dayness of it all. She'd found herself daydreaming and drifting, impatient to put the whole place behind her and move on to something else, even if she didn't know what.

Something exciting. It had to be that, at the very least.

Ginny's bedroom had black walls and glossy yellow furniture. The blinds were drawn, giving the place the feel of a cave.

'You on your lunch break?' Ginny asked. She ripped a pink Kleenex out of a pop-up box on her bedside table and held it to her nose.

'Yeah. I thought I'd just drop in and catch you slacking.'

'I am not slacking.' Ginny smiled and put her glasses back. She had a face like a myopic pixie. 'I was watching a video actually. Wanna see?'

'I don't have time.'

Darcy glanced at her watch. She supposed she could skip PE and get back for Hump's test. Ginny zapped the remote. A videotape clicked into play. Darcy looked at the TV in the corner.

'He's dreamy,' Ginny said. 'He's still the dreamiest babe imaginable.'

James Dean in *Rebel Without A Cause*. Darcy remembered that Ginny belonged to a group in school called The James Dean Appreciation Society, a cult of about ten girls who were enraptured by images of a dead man. They met regularly to watch the few movies Dean had made, and on the anniversary of the actor's death they wore black clothes and mooned around sadly and held a day-long wake. She could see Dean's appeal up to a point, but not the way Ginny did.

'Tell me he doesn't turn you on,' Ginny said.

Darcy shrugged.

'Come on. Look at those eyes. Look at that mouth.'

Darcy said, 'He's okay.'

'*Okay*? He's got something Brad Pitt doesn't have. He's got something Val Kilmer would *murder* to have,' Ginny said. 'You just want to get him in bed and make love for hours and then, when he's hungry afterwards, you'd scramble him some eggs and bring them on a tray. Like a love slave with an offering.'

Darcy stared at the screen. She thought Dean too moody, as if he was in a place he could never be reached. Maybe that was his attraction on celluloid. He was aloof, mysterious, and his death in real life had added to this allure. Now he was truly inaccessible.

'I'd be his love slave,' Ginny said. 'He'd only have to snap his fingers and boy I'd be there. Who am I kidding? He wouldn't even *need* to snap his fingers. He'd only have to give me one of those real cool looks of his and I'd wither, I swear to God.' Lips slightly parted, Ginny gazed at the picture, then pressed the remote and froze the image. 'Look at the way he wears his jeans. The way he stands, kinda hunched like that. If that's not a turn-on, I don't know what is. Okay, so it's Fiftyish, it's ancient, but that doesn't take anything away from the guy.' Ginny sighed and laid a hand on her heart. 'He's immortal. He's like some god. He knows something you don't. He's got secrets. You just wish he'd share one of them with you. He's so goddam romantic it's practically *unbearable*. It ought to be outlawed, for Christ's sake.'

Darcy propped her elbows on her knees and leaned forward. The static image of Dean flickered a little, traversed by lines of video interference.

'You also get the feeling he knew how to treat a girl,' Ginny said. 'He had to be a great lover.'

Darcy remembered reading somewhere that Dean was either homosexual or bi, but this wouldn't have made any difference to Ginny or her fellow members of the Appreciation Society. He was beyond criticism, beyond judgement. Beyond death even. The eternal lover. The endless dream. She could see the romantic strain in this notion. The guy you could never get. The one wasted before his time. The tragic figure.

'Is Nick a great lover?' Ginny asked suddenly.

This question bothered Darcy. It wasn't Ginny's curiosity, but more the casual assumption behind it. Nick and Darcy, Darcy and Nick. They were a couple, they had to be making out on a regular basis.

'Why don't you ask him yourself, Ginny?'

'Yeah. Right. I'll just walk up to him and say, ' "Hey, Nick, how are you in the sack?" '

'Maybe he'd answer you.'

Ginny plucked a Kleenex from the box. 'He's studly,' she said. 'I know a few girls that think so.'

'But I'm the lucky one he picked,' Darcy said.

'I hear a funny little note in your voice, Darce.'

'Like what?'

'Like you're not absolutely sure what you feel about this thing between you and Nick.'

'I guess maybe I don't,' Darcy said.

'Hey, if you ever dump him, let me be the first to know.'

Darcy smiled and looked back at the screen a moment. 'I have to run,' she said.

'Run,' Ginny said, and touched the remote. James Dean's image was reactivated. 'Who needs you for company anyhow? I have my boy, Jimmy.'

Darcy let herself out of the house. The noonday heat was a heavy shroud that hung over everything. She moved along the sidewalk, dragging herself through the humidity in the direction of school.

Get educated, her father had always told her. Like he really believed it was a key to some bright shining future. Ever since her mother's death, though, he'd lost a lot of his interest in her report cards. He'd lost interest in a whole bunch of things. Over the past two months he'd taken to driving alone at nights, never saying where he'd been when he returned, or whether his voyages into the dark were work-related or some solitary nocturnal way of killing time.

He'd become a mystery.

And last night he'd crashed, and this morning he'd been weird, scowling into dead space over his coffee, then for no apparent reason playing silly knock-knock jokes with her. Oscillating between moods, between sounds and puzzling silences. These were signs of some kind. Was he falling apart a year after his wife's death as the recognition finally socked him that he'd never see her again for as long as he lived?

But then she hadn't been present in any real sense for years before her death. She'd lived in a zone of withdrawal. Physicians had run brain scans that revealed no abnormality. Then they'd put her on drugs. But nobody had a connection to her head or what she was thinking. Her father had spent a great deal of time trying to coax her back into the world. He'd sit for hours on the edge of the bed and stroke her hand and whisper to her. Harriet had gazed vacantly into the distance most of the time. Sometimes at night she walked through the house like she was in a dream.

One time Darcy had found her in the kitchen and she'd asked, 'Is there any way out of this place?'

You found a way in the end, Darcy thought. She drew a hand across her sticky forehead. She thought about Eve Lassiter, whom she'd met a dozen times and liked. Why didn't her father just get it on with her? Why didn't he grasp the fact, so obvious to Darcy, that Eve had a *thing* for him?

She reached the entrance to the school, then stopped. She realized she didn't give a damn about Hump's test. She turned round and walked away.

10

LEE BOYLE DRANK THREE CUPS OF COFFEE IN QUICK SUC-
cession inside a café downtown. It was located in a new
pedestrian precinct cobbled in red stone, fancy black
wrought-iron street lamps here and there, flower boxes,
boutiques galore.

He was sweating under the whirring ceiling fan and
conscious of potted ferns made to sway by the breeze of
the blades. A minute ago he'd thought somebody was
watching him from behind, but when he swiveled his head
all he saw was one of the ferns shimmering. He wondered
about plant sensibilities – a random notion that just
chugged into his head.

He sucked urgently on sugar cubes and smoked cigarettes and made an inventory of his long trawl through the
city. Here, there, looking for Almond. Clubs, late-night
dives. Nobody had seen her.

He remembered going back to his apartment at some
point and opening the *Yellow Pages* and calling round
motels and hotels, asking if they had a guest called
Almond – which was pointless, because she wouldn't be

registered under that name. She wouldn't be registered at all. Night clerks tended to hang up on him when he started to describe her – beautiful little girl, about five-two, maybe eighty-five pounds, dark hair, kind of Latino looks, you'd remember if you ever saw her. But nobody wanted to get into long telephone conversations with a guy that sounded desperate and incoherent. *Well, fuck you, I happen to be looking for a missing person.* Click. Dead connections.

Somewhere in the course of all these phone calls he'd also tried to contact The Kid, but he didn't get anything except the answering machine again. He left a message instead of just hanging up. 'Hey, this is Lee. You got anything I can use? I need something, man. Anything. Get back to me.'

He'd snorted more of Stretch's powder, instead of mainlining, and it had burned his nasal passages like he'd inhaled Comet, but *Jesus!* the boost was there. Then he'd gone out and walked around some more in the dawn light, driven by manic energy, but the dives were all closed and the kind of people who might have seen Almond had gone underground. They were people of the night, couldn't hack sunlight, vampires. He'd left messages everywhere he could. Tell her to get in touch. Like immediately.

What he needed was sleep. But his mechanism wasn't even *close* to shutting down. He knew this condition. Restless, marginally demented. He tapped his fingers on the table.

The waitress, a fat girl with healthy rose-colored cheeks, came with the coffee pot. 'Another refill?'

'Sure. Why not.'

She leaned over and poured into his cup. He had a desire to engage her in conversation, but she'd already drifted away among the greenery. He drained the coffee

71

and left, walked back in the general direction of his apartment.

Almond. *Beautiful little girl, about five-two, dark eyes.* He had only to snap his fingers – like so – and she'd do whatever he wanted. Because she adored him. Because he was good to her, in his fashion. But strict, because she needed that.

He turned a corner and entered a street of derelict office buildings. His mouth was dry. He knew if he looked at his tongue it would be the color of coffee. He came to a cross street and popped inside a bar, thinking of ice-cold lager going smoothly down his throat. It was one of those Irish pubs of the 1930s immigrant school, dark and unfriendly – no plastic shamrocks here, no furry little leprechauns for tourists who'd lost their way.

He asked for a Heineken. He drank half of it, *aaah*, then scanned the clientele, a few pre-noon dark-faced boozers, who sat hunched over their drinks like men communing with private gods. He finished his drink, ordered another, chugged it. He liked the glorious icy feel.

He noticed a payphone by the door and he thought, *Why not? Why the hell not? Because he despises you. He sees you as a wastrel. Somebody down the tubes. A young man who didn't know what to do with the silver spoon.* In his present frame of mind, one of whirlpools and agitations, Boyle wasn't convinced that these were sufficient reasons, so he fished coins out of his pockets and went to the phone. He remembered the number, dialed it. He felt a great surge of confidence suddenly, above the hubbub of everyday life.

'Yes?' Always the same brittle response.

'It's Lee here.'

A silence you could cut with a chainsaw. Lee Boyle imagined his father behind the big walnut desk inside the fancy house on Cable Hill. The high-ceilinged rooms, cornices restored by craftsmen imported from Milan, antiques up the ying-yang.

'Lee,' Hugh Boyle said. The tone was deep-freeze.

'I just thought I'd give you a call,' Boyle said. 'It's been a long time. Last time we spoke was at Monique's wedding.'

'How dare you bring up Monique's wedding?'

Trying to ease his way back into his father's favor, Boyle realized he'd need one of those ice-cutting ships that negotiated the Antarctic. 'We talked about stuff.'

'What "stuff" exactly did we talk about, Lee?'

'I remember you—'

'Stop. Let me tell you what *I* remember. You got outrageously drunk and fell face-first into your poor sister's wedding cake. You brought with you – entirely uninvited, I might add – a couple of underdressed young women of dubious vocation, and that wretched crony of yours, Vann, Vass, whatever he's called. Your little crew then proceeded to disgrace itself. Do I have to go into detail? There was blatant evidence of drug-taking in a bathroom. A valuable hand mirror was shattered. Sexually explicit graffiti was lipsticked on walls. Sums of money and credit cards mysteriously disappeared from the pockets of coats in the cloakroom. I am not speaking of an isolated prank, Lee. I'm looking back over an entire history of misdemeanors, some of them utterly appalling.'

'You ought to let all that water flow under the bridge,' Boyle said. 'It's past. It's gone. I've changed my ways. I've just spent weeks in a rehab clinic. I'm clean. I've been doing social work.'

'I think I've heard this one before. It's the angular approach to asking for money.'

'Did I mention money? Did I *mention* money? You're the one that brought it up. Not me.'

'You're an embarrassment, Lee.'

73

The jay makes answer as the magpie chatters.
W. Wordsworth. It was weird what kept coming back to
him across the years.

'Goodbye, Lee. Don't call again. Do you understand
me?'

'I need a little help here, I'm tapped out, I'm having
difficulties, it would only be a loan, you'd get it back at
twenty, twenty-five per cent interest, I *mean that*.'

He was talking into a disconnected line. He slammed
the handset back in place, raging. He cut me off. His only
son. An embarrassment. Well, screw you too, Hugh.
You'll get yours.

He must have been speaking very loud because the
drinkers were watching him. He returned to the bar. He
was burning up.

The barman said, 'You okay, fella?'

'Nothing a chilled brew won't cure,' Boyle said.

The barman, who had fat tattooed arms, slid a green
bottle across the countertop. Boyle felt the urge to talk to
this guy, explain his outburst on the phone. 'I don't get
along with my father,' he said. 'Oil and fucking water.'

'Mine's dead,' the barman remarked.

Boyle leaned across the bar. 'You know what name he
gave me when I was born? Huh? Lee Harvey Boyle. Lee
Harvey. You carry that round and see where it gets you.
You know why he did it?'

The barman shook his head slowly. 'Tell me.'

'Because Lee Harvey Oswald shot John F. Kennedy,
which made Oswald a big-time hero in my father's book.
He hated Kennedy. Loathed him.'

'The name's a weight all right,' the barman said.

'Fucking right it's a weight.' Boyle felt spit gather like
cotton at the corners of his lips. 'My fucking sister, little
Miss Precious, she gets Monique, ooh la la, and what do
I get? Huh?'

'It's a hard road any way you travel it,' the barman said.

Boyle poured his lager into his glass. He wanted to forget Monique, and all of his family, but sometimes Monique's face came drifting up to him, out of the shallows of memory, pale and pretty and utterly despicable. Her and her fucking wedding to that geek stockbroker type called Austin Arganbright. What kind of name was that? It sounded like a goddam mouthwash.

He said to the barman, 'All I want is *Love in a hut, with water and a crust*. Keats. You know what I'm saying?'

'Keats,' the barman said, like a man chewing on an unexpected bit of tofu.

Boyle took a great swallow of his lager, then asked, 'Where's the toilet?'

The barman pointed to the other side of the muggy brown room. Boyle crossed the floor, entered the john. It was scented with pine, but that didn't disguise the fact that somebody had recently taken a highly fermented dump in one of the cubicles. He unzipped, leaned against the urinal, cursed his father.

Lee Harvey Boyle. The gunman in the book depository in Dallas.

He looked at the stream of his urine. *That goddam Almond*, he thought. *Had she just upped and left town? That was like giving him the finger. He'd get to the bottom of it. He'd track her down. She wasn't getting out from under him. And if she thought that—*

'Hey. You. Bright boy.'

Boyle, lost in his roiling thoughts, hadn't heard anyone enter the john. He turned his face round. There were two guys. One was tall and ponytailed and wore a leather jacket, the other was short and thick-necked with an off-center mohawk that gave his skull the look of a lopsided skunk. Bad hairdos, both of them. The one with the slanted mohawk was carrying a lead pipe, maybe a foot long.

Uh-oh. Boyle zipped up quickly.

The guy in the leather jacket had a severe case of acne. 'You know Vern Crassman, I understand.' He had a country twang to his voice, maybe hick Kentucky. It was a voice Boyle associated with mangy dogs, tar-paper shacks, haggard old women shucking corn.

He turned from the urinal. He was thinking rapidly. 'Crassman,' he said. 'Vern Crassman. Umm. Do I know Vern Crassman?' He glanced at the lead pipe. Mohawk was holding it against his side and emitting unambiguous rays of impending brutality. From the corner of his eye Boyle realized the john had no window. Ergo, no escape route. So it was down to him and these two bad-looking hillbillies Crassman had despatched. The prospect of pain sizzled in the air.

The one in the leather jacket said, 'You hurt Vern, buddy.'

'There might have been a minor fracas, I guess,' Boyle said. 'Some kind of misunderstanding.' He wondered how long this pair had been following him.

'A fracas,' the guy with the lead pipe said.

'Yeah, a fracas,' Boyle said. He looked at the squat man, who was overweight and probably ponderous in his movements. He was the kind of guy who always got the heavy shit to lift when you needed something moved. Here, grab this grand piano, Mohawk Man. All dumb strength, a real grunt.

Boyle walked to the washbasin and turned on a faucet. Thinking, thinking. He wasn't going to be able to schmooze his way out of this situation because neither of these guys looked like a good listener. They'd been sent by Crassman and they were here to redress the balance of things, plain and simple. Violence begets violence.

The one with the ponytail suddenly grabbed the lapel of Boyle's jacket.

Boyle said, 'Take care. This is an Armani, friend.'

'It don't look it.'

'Like you'd know?' Boyle asked.

'Armani. This is a fucking rag, what it is.' The guy tugged hard, bringing Boyle's face close to his own, affording Lee Boyle a close-up of acne pits, pustules, blackheads. It was like the surface of some hostile planet.

Boyle pulled his face back. He heard stitches pop in his lapels and he was aware of the squat fellow with the lead pipe coming up from behind.

This is total squalor, Boyle thought. *Violence in this shithole.* He knew there was a better life. If this was the best the human condition had to offer, somebody had a whole lot to answer for.

He said, 'I do judo. Be warned.' It was worth a try.

The mohawk snorted. He probably thought judo, like Armani, was another fashion designer, a Jap one.

The lead pipe was raised in the air and coming hard and fast toward Boyle's skull. He reacted without any thought, because the time for thinking was past, everything was measured in microseconds, and the idea of a lead object embedded in your head concentrated your goddam mind like nothing else. He made a great effort to free himself from the grip of the guy in leather, twisted his face to one side, and the pipe whoomed past his head and crashed against the sink, cracking the ceramic. Boyle saw his lapel come away and saw the guy in leather holding a strip of what had once been a fine jacket. So the jacket was a write-off, but on the plus side he was free, he could move now, he could act. He felt energy come up from his feet and rush through his body. He was spiked.

The mohawk made a snarling noise and drew the

pipe back up a second time. 'Judo my pecker,' he said, and the pipe began its spooky descent.

Boyle's perceptions were suddenly unlimited, as if he'd just become plugged into an all-encompassing awareness he never knew existed. He was conscious of a flood of brilliant light. Watching from a place above, he saw himself bring his knee up into the pipe-wielding guy's groin and, in almost the same instant, headbutt the one in leather and watch him stagger back against one of the urinals, while the mohawk – squawking – was doubled over like a constipated man with his asshole stitched shut. The pipe had rolled out of his hand and Boyle bent down to pick it up and whacked it against the mohawk's head. Next he turned to the guy in leather, who was crouched in a urinal, holding his face in his hands as water flushed automatically down the tiles and diluted his blood, turning it pink like the juice from certain grapefruits.

What the hell. Sweating, heart roaring, Boyle smashed the guy's kneecaps with the lead pipe.

The guy went all the way down. His mouth was open but nothing was coming out. He was in that place where pain made you mute. Boyle turned and gazed at mohawk, who was flat on his back and gazing up at the ceiling with a deeply dazed expression. He wasn't seeing anything except maybe his own private planetarium.

It was a moment of huge satisfaction. *Incalculable* satisfaction. Boyle pondered some extra violence, but decided the best idea was to blow this place entirely. He tossed the lead pipe inside one of the cubicles, walked out the john and through the bar to the street. He went several blocks in his ruined Armani, but, hey, what was a jacket? You kicked ass, Lee. You took the pair of them and you *destroyed* them. What you ought to do next is go over to the trailer park and have a word with Vern Crassman. Surprise the hell out of him. See Crassman cower.

It was only when he'd made it back to his apartment that he felt the symptoms of collapse. He looked at the drugs on the coffee table and contemplated the notion of dabbling in just a tad more, enough to get him through the rest of the day so he could continue to look for the bitch.

Runaway.

His hands were wet and they'd begun to tremble beyond all social acceptability, and when he shut his eyes he could see that lead pipe smash the mohawk's head and he could smell the rancid stench of the toilet. *You got lucky*, he thought. *It could have gone the other way: your skull caved in, your all-American looks demolished.*

He went inside the bathroom, dipped his face under the cold-water faucet. The inside of his mouth tasted foul. He walked back into the living room and surveyed the crystals of speed.

You don't need it, Lee. Yes you do. That little nagging voice in his ear.

He wandered to the answering machine. The message window read '2'. He pressed playback. Almond. Let it be. But the first voice was Jimmy Plumm's. 'I hope I'm not pressuring you unduly, love. But time is passing. Time is indeed passing.'

The second message was uttered in a hushed voice he recognized immediately.

'Lee, you old speed-freak, I hear you're looking for your little Almond,' it said. 'Maybe I can be of some tiny assistance?'

11

EVE SAID, 'I'M DETECTIVE LASSITER. THIS IS LIEUTENANT Samsa.'

The young man, Joshua Gold, stood in the doorway of his apartment and looked defensive. 'I was under the impression you were coming alone, Detective.'

'The lieutenant doesn't bite, Mr Gold.'

Gold held the door open and, frowning, indicated that Eve and Samsa come inside.

Samsa surveyed the living room quickly. An aquarium stocked with salt-water fish occupied one corner. Flutters of yellow and green, translucent flashes. The filter pump throbbed. The walls of the room were covered with photographs of young men, some of them naked, others in briefs. They weren't beefcake shots. They were *artsy*, young guys with broodingly sensitive expressions. On the bottom of each framed photograph was the signature J. Gold in copperplate.

Gold, who wore a purple cotton shirt and white cut-offs, said, 'Sit, if you like.'

Eve sat on a beige leather sofa. Samsa remained standing, watching Gold. He was a pretty kid, Samsa supposed, slim, with very fine hair that he kept sweeping back from his forehead. His legs were suntanned, his feet bare. He wore a slender silver bracelet around one ankle and a small pearl earring. He sat down on the arm of the sofa with his knees clamped together and his long fingers intertwined. Then he got up and walked to the aquarium, where he lounged with a fretful expression.

He stared at Samsa. 'Anyone ever told you you have a lived-in kind of face? Faces are like houses, I always think. Some occupied a long time, others just sort of blank and *totally* without soul. You have soul, Lieutenant.'

'Is that a good or bad thing?' Samsa asked.

'Oh, I think it's good. It's very good.'

Samsa gazed at the young man a moment and then, for a reason he didn't understand, had to look elsewhere. Perhaps it was the way he felt Gold was studying him. Whatever, he was uncomfortable. He looked down at the smooth pine floor, so highly varnished it created reflections. He saw himself there, his image distorted in glossy wood. *I have soul.* Or maybe I traded it away, made a deal with my own personal devil.

Eve opened her notebook and tapped it with a ballpoint pen. 'Let's talk about Anthony Leeson,' she said.

'I told you when you phoned, Detective. I gave him my number. That's all.'

'In what circumstances, Joshua? You ran into him in a bar, something like that?'

Gold was hesitant. He strolled the room, tapping his hands against his thighs.

Eve said, 'I don't have to remind you that this is a homicide inquiry, do I, Joshua? You don't keep information back when it comes to murder. It's not very bright.'

Gold stood still, took a couple of deep breaths. 'Okay. I sometimes go to a certain ... *risqué* area close to downtown, which I guess I don't have to spell out for you, do I?'

Samsa listened to the filter. He gazed at the fish. Bubbles rose spiraling in the water.

Gold was saying, 'I was very strapped for cash, you understand. I do mean *strapped*. So I did what I sometimes do when the old bank balance goes into the red and that nasty manager writes me shit letters. I know I shouldn't go down there, but I do it anyway.'

'Let's just say you were looking for companionship,' Eve suggested.

'And then what?' Samsa asked, turning to look at Gold.

Gold said to Eve, 'I think your lieutenant is judging me, Detective. I feel a condemnation coming on.'

'I am not judging you, Joshua,' Samsa said.

'He isn't usually the judgemental type, I promise you,' Eve said.

'Well he's certainly shooting me some pretty dark *looks*,' Gold said.

Eve leaned forward on the sofa. 'Just tell us what happened, Joshua.'

'Do I really have to?'

'You have to,' Samsa said. 'Get it through your head.'

'See,' Gold said. '*More* dark looks.'

'Forget my looks,' Samsa said. 'Just answer the questions.'

'I'm not terribly proud of some of the things I do,' Gold said.

'Your pride isn't our concern,' Eve said.

Gold pressed his hands to the sides of his face. 'About a week ago I went down to that particular stretch of town we're talking about and I hung out for a while, which I don't like, because you do get some terribly sick boys and girls round there. There's one girl with full-blown Aids, my God. She's literally *dying* on the sidewalk—'

'The point,' Eve said.

'Okay. This green car comes along. It pulls up beside me, I get inside. The man behind the wheel takes me out to his apartment in the suburbs.'

'And this man was Anthony Leeson?'

'Right,' Gold said quietly.

'And you spent how long with him?'

'Most of the night. He was quite a gentleman. I suspect he wanted company as much as, you know . . . And I left, oh, just as it was getting light. He asked for my phone number and I wrote it down for him.'

Samsa stared into the tank of water, and suddenly remembered how her mascara had run. *What the hell did I think I was doing? Where was my fucking head at the time? What lunacy afflicted me?* A terrible fear descended on him. There was pressure behind his eyes. He forced himself to concentrate on the conversation between Eve and Joshua Gold, but he'd missed some part of it already. You have to pay attention. You have to believe the world goes on and you're an active participant.

'So when you went back downtown again on the night Leeson was killed, you saw him, but he didn't pick you up this time,' Eve was saying.

'Right. He drove past, signaled to a boy a little way down the block, and this kid got in the car. And off they went.'

'This kid – you ever see him before?'

Gold shook his head. 'Never. And the next day they found Anthony slaughtered. I read about the knife wounds and I freaked, I just *freaked*. And I thought, *Nobody's safe down there*. Not if there's somebody going round with a knife.'

Samsa said to Eve, 'Let's take him downtown.'

'*Downtown?*' Gold was horrified. 'Am I a suspect?'

'We need a description of the kid you saw, Joshua,'

Samsa said. 'You get to sit in a room with a very patient man who'll show you a book of facial characteristics and you'll tell him what you remember. And he'll come up with a composite.'

'You haven't answered my question,' Gold said. 'Am I a *suspect*?'

Eve said, 'Nobody's saying you're a suspect, Joshua. Anyhow, yours wasn't the only phone number in Leeson's possession. We have to check them all.'

'But nobody's ruling me out either, are they?'

Eve said, 'We're only asking for your co-operation at this stage.'

'At *this* stage? What does that mean? Is there a *next* stage where you try and pin this murder on *me*?'

Eve spoke with great patience. 'Joshua, I have no reason to consider you a suspect. You say you saw somebody get into Leeson's car, fine. I have to take that as a truth unless I find out otherwise. I *could* say it worries me a little that you didn't report the fact you saw Leeson on the night of his death – but I'm giving you the benefit of the doubt where that's concerned. Obviously you don't want it known what you do on your nocturnal jaunts.'

'Damn right I don't,' Gold said.

'And I understand that,' Eve said. 'So let's co-operate on this description.'

'It was so dark,' Gold said. 'I don't know if I can do it.'

'You'd be surprised what you can remember,' Eve said, and closed her notebook. She got up from the sofa.

'When do you want me to do this thing?' Gold asked.

Eve put a hand on the young man's tanned arm. 'How about coming in now?'

'Now? I always visit my mother at lunchtime. She's in St Jude's, poor dear. If you ever need to put your mother in a nursing home, I certainly *don't* recommend St Jude's. The nurses are absolute Fascists.'

'After lunch then,' Eve said. 'Say three? I'll set it up. It won't take more than thirty minutes or so.'

'You're sure this isn't some kind of devious ploy to get me downtown and interrogate the hell out of me?'

'We don't need ploys to do that,' Samsa said. 'Believe me.'

'Okay. Three o'clock.'

Gold showed them to the door. As Samsa stepped past him, the young man said, 'Have we ever met before?'

'I don't think so,' Samsa said. 'Maybe I remind you of somebody else with a lived-in face.'

Gold tapped a fingernail a little nervously against his teeth. 'Could be,' he said. He stood behind the screen door after Samsa and Eve had stepped out.

The interior of Eve's car was like a sauna. Samsa rolled down his window, slipped the knot of his necktie, undid the top button of his shirt. This air was unbreathable. He heard something click in his shoulder and experienced a short thrust of pain. *Have we ever met before?* He felt the pinching movement of dread in his heart. Dread was new to him. He didn't have a place where he could store it.

Eve said, 'I don't quite see Gold stabbing Anthony Leeson. He doesn't strike me as the homicidal-frenzy type somehow. But you just never know, do you?'

Samsa said nothing. He gazed up at the red-brick apartment building. He thought he saw Joshua Gold watching from behind a window on the third floor, but he couldn't be sure.

Eve laid her hands against the steering wheel. 'If I'm wrong, forgive me, but I'm getting the distinct impression this case doesn't entirely intrigue you.'

'Why do you say that?'

'Normally you're more animated. More alert. You didn't seem too interested in Gold. You had an elsewhere kind of look on your face.'

'I don't have high expectations of him, Eve. You heard him. It was dark, and he's not sure he can come up with a description. I don't rate him as a suspect either—'

'That's not the point I'm making, Greg. There's some other thing troubling you. And whatever it is, it's been bugging you all morning. So why don't you just take a chance and tell me—'

'Look, if I wanted advice I'd go to a fucking therapist.' It was out before he could stop it, the snappy remark, the uptight tone. He was sorry immediately.

Eve stared at him with a look of annoyance. 'Fine, *fine*. There's nothing on paper that says you have to tell me anything, Lieutenant. Let's just drop it, okay? I'm sorry I bothered.'

'Eve,' he said. 'We're good colleagues, we're friends—'

'I always thought so.' She turned the key in the ignition.

'Okay. I'm not myself. I've been thinking a lot about Harriet these last few days.'

Eve leaned back in her seat. 'God. It's been a *year*, hasn't it? I totally forgot, Greg. I'm so sorry.'

'There's no reason you should remember this particular anniversary,' Samsa said. 'I've been reliving some things, that's all . . . You know what the worst thing is? I'm never going to know why she did it in the end. For the rest of my life, it's going to be one big mystery. The physicians and the shrinks talked about clinical depression, but that doesn't begin to explain anything, Eve. That's just a goddam label they hang on something they don't understand.'

Eve touched his hand sympathetically. He looked into her candid green eyes. He could read the message there: share this with me, Greg. He felt fraudulent and cheap. He was stealing from her fund of compassion. Of course he thought about Harriet, because there was hardly a moment when she didn't come into his mind, and he was choked with memories of the better times before she plunged irretrievably into her own black world – but he was cheating Eve by omission.

'I'm glad you told me, Greg. I thought maybe it was something like that. I wasn't sure.'

He shrugged. He had a sense he was melting, changing forms, turning into something else. 'Let's get back,' he said.

She drove most of the way in silence. At one point she talked about what she might cook for dinner next Wednesday, and he understood she was trying to lift his spirits. She had a generous uncomplicated heart.

She parked in the lot behind City Hall. They walked together down to the basement. Eve vanished in the maze of rooms, saying she was going to look for Ross, the guy who put together the faces from his big book of features.

Samsa entered his office and switched on the tiny portable fan on his filing cabinet. He stood close to it, letting the blades blow directly into his face. The air churned but didn't cool.

Al Brodsky, Chief of Police, appeared in the doorway. 'I heard about the bust-up, Greg. You hurt?'

Samsa said, 'Nothing serious. I broke a tooth.'

Brodsky had a big round face and slitted eyes. He was an untidy man, his neckties always loosely knotted and hanging wrong, his suits crumpled, usually a shoelace undone. He was sharp where it mattered, though. He had a mind like a carving knife and a low-key ability to terrify interviewees, whether they were suspects in a crime or cops who'd transgressed. Fogue had nicknamed him Brodsky the Blade, and it had stuck. Samsa had a genuine fondness for the man. Their relationship went back years.

'How are you getting along otherwise, Greg?'

'I'm fine.'

'How's Darcy?'

'She's doing all right at school.' Brodsky's questions, he knew, were not entirely idle. The chief was checking on

87

him, because he wouldn't have forgotten the anniversary of Harriet's death. He'd have it memorized.

'She's a bright kid,' Brodsky said. 'She'll go places.'

'The right ones, I hope,' Samsa said.

Brodsky placed a hand on Samsa's shoulder, an affectionate little contact. 'You're a good father. Always have been.'

Samsa adjusted the fan, but it didn't help. Sweat ran from his scalp down his face.

Brodsky asked, 'How's your caseload?'

'Heavy enough.'

'Anything new on Leeson?'

'We might have a witness. Then again, we might not. There's also the Dell thing, which isn't going anywhere.'

'Homicides involving transients are goddam knots. Drifters kill other drifters, then they just keep drifting right along.' Brodsky leaned toward the fan, running a finger under his collar. 'The Gavency case looks pretty good. I've been reading the reports.'

'It's taking shape,' Samsa said.

'He killed his wife. I don't think there's any doubt. A sweet little confession might be welcome.'

'And we might just get one, Al,' Samsa said. This catalogue of murders dismayed him. He remembered a time when he'd done the work and it hadn't touched him quite this way. Sure, he'd always felt a certain shock when he thought about what humans inflicted on other humans – the extremes of brutality were appalling, deadening – but you dealt with that, you just closed down part of your heart and went about your business. Only it was getting more difficult. It was like a long slope and all you could see at the very bottom was darkness.

Brodsky was observing him. 'We don't have the one-on-ones we used to. We ought to have a couple of beers one of these days.'

'I'd enjoy that.'

Brodsky moved toward the door, then stopped. 'Say. What about tonight?'

'Tonight?'

'Unless you've got something else going on.'

'My calendar isn't cluttered, Al.'

'Your place around eight thirty? I'll bring some of that foreign beer you like. Grolsch?'

'Right.'

'Fine, I look forward to it, Greg. There's something I want to discuss with you anyway.'

Samsa watched Brodsky go out of the room. He stood a few moments longer in front of the fan and then, thinking of Darcy, feeling an urge to talk to her, picked up the telephone and dialed his home number. The phone rang unanswered.

He looked at the travel clock on his desk. Two thirty. It was too early for her to be home from school. He hung up, wondering what it was that Al Brodsky wanted to talk to him about.

12

LEE BOYLE LAY ON HIS SOFA AND HUNTED SLEEP, BUT HE WAS too whacked, too *spun*, and a line of Shelley's kept going round inside his head. *The awful shadow of some unseen Power, Floats though unseen among us.* Tell me something I don't know, Percy.

He heard the sound of his door buzzer. He was dry-mouthed, and when he rose his legs were stiff. The buzzer went on and on. Whoever the stubborn fucker was down in the street, he sure as hell wasn't going to give up and go away.

Boyle entered the kitchen. Tiled surfaces gleamed and there were no dirty dishes in sight. The pine-top table had been scrubbed. He'd done all this cleaning in an energy fit before trying – fruitlessly – to get some sleep. Buzzing round the kitchen with Spic 'n' Span and two whole rolls of paper towels. He swallowed a handful of vitamins, washed them down with a glass of water. Finally he flipped the intercom switch. 'Yeah?'

'Tom Raseci here. Open the door, Lee.'

'I'm just leaving. I have an appointment.' He looked at

the kitchen clock, a Bart Simpson timepiece Almond had hung. Three forty-three. He had to be somewhere at four-thirty.

'Buzz the fucking door, I said.'

'Is this some rough-house stuff, Tom?'

'The rough stuff don't start until your clock's run out, Lee.'

Boyle pressed the button that unlocked the street-level door. He heard Raseci climb the stairs. Bigshoes. What was he here for? Boyle opened the door and Tom Raseci entered the apartment.

'I never been here before,' he said. He sniffed around, touching this, that, like a goddam landlord checking out the condition of his property. Boyle kept the lid tight on his resentments.

Dressed in an expensive black linen suit, Raseci stared at a couple of titles on the bookshelves. 'What's all this shit you read. *The Mirror and The Lamp*. Is it some kind of thriller or what?'

'I've never met anybody who thought so,' Boyle said. 'It's a book about poetry.'

'Poetry, huh? I wandered lonely as a daffodil, har har.' Raseci tugged a volume off the shelf and flicked the pages. '*Culture and Anarchy* by Matthew Arnold. You got some high-tone tastes, Lee.'

'Souvenirs of a gentler time, that's all.' Boyle hadn't looked at his books in years.

'Hey hey. Now this is more like it. *Confessions of an English Opium Eater*. What is this? Like a how-to manual?'

'You want to come to the point, Tom?'

Raseci sat on the sofa and sifted through the drug paraphernalia on the coffee table. He pushed the hypodermic needle aside with a look of distaste, then rubbed some spilled crystal between thumb and forefinger. 'Speed?

Can't get off it, huh? I was hooked on dope one time. Then I discovered Narcotics Anonymous. Changed my life around.'

'My name is Tom R and I am a drug addict,' Boyle said.

'Don't knock it. It worked for me,' Raseci said. 'This shit must cost you.'

'I get high with a little help.'

Raseci held up the baggie in which the crystal sparkled.

'Be very careful with that,' Boyle said. He took the baggie from Raseci's hand and put it in the pocket of his crumpled shirt. He was feeling sluggish, bottomed-out. 'I was just leaving, Tom.'

'What it is, Jimmy Plumm hears the word going round that you've misplaced your little income machine. Which doesn't make him happy. He was figuring maybe this chick would be good for some of the money he's got coming from you. She's a working girl, after all. Not all of the cash, but a little. A thou, say. A gesture of goodwill that might just buy you another day. *Might*. Mr Plumm doesn't really *want* to see you damaged, Lee. I think he kinda likes your face. So it worries him when he learns your main asset appears to have taken a hike.'

'That's street gossip. You don't want to listen to that stuff. I have that girl where I want her.'

'So you say. But Mr Plumm keeps an ear real low to the ground. He's a guy that don't let anything escape him. And what he hears is that you've been running round like a headless chicken looking for your little meal ticket.'

'Untrue,' Boyle said. 'She was doing some high-paid out-call work, that's all.'

'Yeah? So explain how come you been asking for her all over the place.'

Boyle nodded at the table. 'Blame the drugs, Tom. Sometimes they make you forgetful. I sent her someplace, only I don't remember where exactly.' He laughed at his own carelessness. Silly me. He wondered if his lie had any plausibility. Raseci's discolored eye fixed him without expression.

'You're saying she'll be back soon.'

'Right, right.'

The big man rose from the sofa and wandered the room. He gave Boyle the impression that he was looking for something to break, preferably a visible part of Lee's anatomy. 'What I've done in the present uncertain circumstances, Lee, is I've sold your Porsche.'

'Sold it? *Sold* my car?'

'Following Mr Plumm's instructions, you understand. There's a guy paid two grand for it.'

'Sold my goddam Porsche for *two grand*? It's worth seven or eight.'

'There's widespread body rust. The engine needs work. Two grand was the top offer. That cash goes directly to Mr Plumm. Comes off your debt, see. Now you're down to ten. And if your little squaw shows up, let's just hope she has some bread for you. Which you'll hand right over to Mr Plumm. This way the debt is whittled down. And you get some breathing space.'

Boyle thought about his Porsche. He tried to reduce its loss to the simple proposition that it was only a car, just metal and wheels and an engine and shit. That didn't make it any easier, though. He'd had that Porsche five years. And now it was gone, and he was embroiled in the crazy world of Jimmy Plumm's bizarre accountancy system. 'So what are you saying, Tom? I have an extra day on account of the Porsche.'

'That depends on if your girl shows up.'

Boyle felt he'd entered an area of total perplexity. Plumm's world, he understood, was whimsical, his calendar capricious. What Plumm was doing was fucking with his head. You get an extra day, you don't get an extra day. Plumm, fraudulent Englishman, played master of the cosmos. He could give you time, or take it away from you.

'Yesterday I had three days. What have I got now? What's the bottom line here?'

'You're down to two and a bit. That hasn't changed. Unless the girl shows up with an installment. Or, alternatively, you come up with the whole ten grand, which is what is left after taking the Porsche into account.'

'Who bought the car anyway?' Boyle asked. It dawned on him immediately that the question was dumb. He knew the answer and it riled him. He stared hard at Raseci. 'I hope you get into a serious wreck when you're driving it. I hope you become one of those veggies on a life-support system.'

'Tut-tut.' Raseci produced a familiar set of keys from his pocket and dangled them. 'I'm keeping the Porsche keyring too. Comes with the deal.' He rattled the keys in a hugely aggravating manner. Chinkety-chink.

'I have to run, Tom. So if you don't mind?'

'So long as we're straight on a few things.'

'Yeah. We're straight.' Straight as you could be in Plumm's bent universe anyway. Two days and a bit and the sands running. Sweet Jesus. *My heart beats loud and fast.*

Raseci went to the door, opened it. He turned to look at Boyle. 'One last thing, Lee. Don't even *think* about splitting. Because it's a very small world and Mr Plumm has friends in a whole lot of places. See you.' Raseci went out, closing the door quietly.

Boyle stripped, showered, shampooed, gargled with a vile-tasting substance reputed to have a curative effect on mouth ulcers. He took a pair of clean blue jeans and a fresh shirt from his closet, where some of Almond's clothing hung. He fingered the dresses, the skirts. *It doesn't make sense,* he thought. *These things hanging here like this. Abandoned.* A strange kind of loss hit him, made him a touch sad. Where the hell was she?

He brushed his hair. He contemplated shaving, but decided against it. He didn't trust his unsteady hand with a razor. Looking in the mirror, he remembered that years back some drunken old biddy in a bar had told him he was a dead ringer for a long-ago movie star. Tab somebody. Or was it Troy? He couldn't recall. A lot of his memories must be wandering the back roads of his head like lost orphans crying for attention.

He cleaned the drug paraphernalia off the table, scooping it inside a leather shaving bag which he squeezed under the sofa. Then a quick snort of Stretch's crank – *whooo* – and he was out of here. Zip and into the street. No Porsche. No wheels. He felt stripped of citizenship. The disenfranchised American. Take a man's car away, you might as well take his goddam democratic birthright to vote while you were at it.

He looked for a cab, but they rarely cruised this neighborhood. He walked several blocks quickly, then he was into the heart of downtown, passing between office towers. Men and women hastened here and there with briefcases, lawyer types and cops entering the hive of City Hall. *The everlasting universe of things flows through the mind.* He wondered if Shelley had ever shot himself up with speed.

The air he moved through was lifeless. It was like walking inside the cellular structure of a warm wet sponge. He glanced back the way he'd come, scanning quickly for a sight of anyone following him, perhaps a reappearance of Crassman's ruffians, maybe somebody Plumm had tailing him. *It's a small world.* Crowded sidewalks, how could you tell? He skipped past a guy selling hot dogs under a colored umbrella. The stench of onions assaulted him. He

95

turned a corner where a blind man seated on a soapbox was playing saxophone.

He saw the silver and maroon canvas awning of the Rialto Hotel, formerly one of the city's classiest gathering places, but fallen now on tough times. The Rialto wasn't exactly a flophouse, but all its airs and graces were threadbare, and the doorman – who had a rummy's cracked red nose – was missing a brass button.

Lee Boyle went through the revolving doors into the empty lobby. He headed across the faded red carpet and into the coffee shop. It was a big room and there was only one customer and she was sitting in the far corner wearing shades and a black velvet jacket. Her hair matched the color of the jacket. Her make-up was white. She gave Boyle the impression of somebody returned from the grave on a temporary visitor's pass.

Boyle sat facing her. She wore an assortment of crosses round her neck, which were mainly Celtic and chunky.

'Warding off the evil spirits, I see,' he said.

'Plenty around.' She slipped her glasses down her nose and gazed at Boyle briefly before she replaced them. Her eyes were a very pale blue, which he'd always found unsettling, like looking into a couple of dyed ice cubes. 'You look as handsome and edible as ever, Boyle. Save for those dark puffy things under your eyes.'

'I work hard for these dark puffy things, Sartora.'

'I'm calling myself Cass these days, Boyle. As in Cassandra.'

Before Sartora, she'd been Divina. Before that – what? He couldn't keep track.

'You gotta keep altering yourself,' she said. 'I'm a work in progress.'

'Aren't we all?'

'I'm into things like shape-shifting,' she said.

This babe had a quality Boyle found oppressive, and he

didn't want to linger discussing her weirded-out belief system, so he didn't ask for details about shape-shifting. He tapped the face of his wristwatch and was conscious of the jerking movement of the second hand.

'I got your message,' he said.

'Oh, yeah, that. The message.'

Don't go vague on me, Cass, he thought. He leaned across the table. The ashtray was crammed with hand-rolled black-paper stubs.

'Are you carrying?' she asked.

'Sorry,' he said. 'I could probably find you something in an hour or so, Cass.'

'I'd appreciate it, Boyle. I really would.'

'No problem. Now this message.'

'Ice,' she said. 'I want high-class ice.'

'I hear you,' Boyle said. *Jesus Christ, tell me about Almond.*

'The best, Boyle. I'm running on fuck knows what adrenalin. And the gauge is way low. So I'm antsy. Also there's an affair of the heart that's a total fucking *disaster*. Which isn't contributing to my well-being.'

'I'll *deal* with it, Cass. Can we talk about this message?'

She examined her black-glossed fingernails, one of which was broken. 'She got in a car, Boyle. This was around nine-thirty last night. Quarter of ten.'

'You know the driver's name?'

'I look like a fucking phone book to you?'

'Okay. What did he look like then?'

Boyle had known Cassandra a long time. She'd stripteased, worked as a call-girl in a few ritzy resorts out west, then slithered somewhat from that summit. She was queen of vague. She perceived the world through a sensory net that was like a blackout blind. He'd hung out with her for a while a year or so back, a casual thing, and although the sex was good and hungry, she was too

97

spacey for his liking, and, besides, commitment – which she valued and needed – was a major chuckle from his point of view.

'I didn't actually see any of this *transpire*, you understand. My days of hanging out in certain places are past, Boyle. I know what's good for me.'

'Listen, Cass. I don't need a guided tour of your learning graph. I need to find the girl.'

'The person that saw her said she got inside a dark-blue car.'

'A dark-blue car. That's truly helpful, Cass. Who was this eyewitness?'

'You don't know this individual, and I'm not revealing my sources.'

'Fuck. Now you're a journalist with privileges.' Boyle had a sudden flash. *Goddam! She was the fucking eyewitness*. Nobody else. She was back hitting the sidewalks and she didn't want him to know, so she'd dreamed up this fictional observer. Well, well. There was pride at work here. In a calmer state of mind Boyle might have found this little act of deception touching.

She said, 'Now don't go all wigged on me, Boyle. I'm trying to help. You score me some dope in return for info. Scratch my back.'

'I'll score you the goddam dope, Cass. But I need more than a dark-blue car, you see. The world is filled with dark-blue cars.'

She said, 'My nameless friend remembers a detail of the license plate. It was nine two K something.'

'Nine two K something. That's all your nameless friend got?'

'That's all, Boyle.'

Boyle asked her for a pen, which she took out of her cavernous purse. He scribbled '92K' on a paper napkin. It was a beginning. How much of one, he wasn't sure.

'Meet me back here in an hour and I'll have what you need,' he said. He started to rise from the table. 'Incidentally, you didn't happen to see the guy's face, did you?'

She stared at him. 'Oh, fuck you, Boyle.'

'Old dogs and new tricks, honey. I don't think this shape-shifting shit is working for you.'

'Fuck you again.'

'I take that as, no, you didn't see his face.'

'Take it any way you like. Just bring me ice, Boyle.'

He was about to step away from the table when he was assailed suddenly by an unexpected sense of doom. It was as if a hood had been pulled over his head and he was being smothered. This goddam tricky powder that fueled you. He breathed deeply a couple of times and the bad sensation passed. *Scary Moments in Lee Boyle's Life*.

'My pen,' Cass said.

'Almost forgot.' He dropped the pen on the table.

'One hour,' she said. 'Don't pull a stunt on this, Boyle. I'm in serious need.'

He pointed a finger at her – *okay, babe, you got it, you got Lee Boyle's word, the ice-man will returneth* – and then he took a few steps across the room. She called out to him. 'Hey, Boyle. One last thing. The car was a Chrysler.'

13

DARCY WAS WAITING OUTSIDE CITY HALL WHEN SAMSA emerged at ten past six.

'Surprise,' she said.

'What are you doing down here?'

'I ditched my afternoon classes. Don't you ever get one of those days when you just don't feel like doing what you're supposed to be doing?'

'Sure. All the time.'

'But you're too conscientious to defy expectations,' she said. 'You don't break the rules.'

She linked her arm through his and they moved along the sidewalk. Downtown was beginning to empty, stores were closing, office workers were calling it a day. *You don't break the rules.* 'So what did you do instead?' he asked.

'I hung out. I just walked around downtown. Looked in some store windows. Nothing special.'

Samsa thought how ordinary this was, a man and his pretty daughter strolling along a city sidewalk in the early evening sun. The proud father smiling. A casual observer might think, *That's nice. I seek the ordinary*, Samsa thought. The commonplace. That elusive place where life is humdrum. And secure.

'So you're a little down?' he asked. 'Is that the message I'm getting?'

'I don't know what message I'm sending,' she said.

She looked gloomy. He wondered if her mood had anything to do with Nick, if something had gone wrong there, but he'd never intruded on that area of her life. Maybe he should have established better links of communication, because love alone wasn't ever enough. He often thought that Harriet's years of silence and withdrawal had established a pattern, and Darcy had grown up accustomed to the impotence of language.

'Sometimes I get this feeling of confinement,' she said.

'We all get that, Darcy.' It wasn't an adequate response. He knew that at once. Maybe what was really bothering her was this wretched anniversary. It was bound to be somewhere on her mind.

'Other people expect things from me,' she said.

'Like what?'

'Let's start with good grades.'

'And this is a burden I impose?'

'Yeah, a little. But mainly it's teachers,' she said. 'There's other stuff. Like Nick.'

He wondered if she was still a virgin. It was a question he'd relegated to the back of his mind, where he didn't have to deal with it. Some horny young guy fucks your daughter, how are you supposed to react to that anyway? Outrage was old-fashioned. The age of the shotgun was dead. And he couldn't summon up shock. He had no rights in the matter.

'Sometimes he stifles me,' she said.

They were in the parking lot now. Samsa had borrowed a car from the department pool. It was a late-model beige

Chevrolet in need of a wash. He unlocked it.

'New wheels,' Darcy said.

'Temporary. I'll work out a hire car with the insurance gangsters. I just haven't gotten round to it yet.'

Darcy sat in the passenger seat. 'Ooo-eee. Tobacco Row,' she said, and made a face. The ashtray, stuffed with butts, hung open.

'If Nick's stifling,' Samsa said, 'maybe you should think about cooling the whole thing.'

She slumped back in her seat, hands in the pockets of her jeans. He could tell from her expression that the subject of Nick was closed for the moment. He saw a distance in her eyes. She was so damn *changeable*. One moment up, the next down. One minute she was all hugs and kisses, the next she was about as approachable as frozen tundra.

'I have an idea,' he said. 'Let's go eat at that place you like.'

'Lucky's?'

'We'll pig out.'

She turned her face and there was a trace of a smile. 'I'm sorry if I'm moody. I don't mean to be. It's just stuff, that's all. I'll deal with it.'

'Sure you will.'

He drove through the stop-start traffic of downtown. Darcy fiddled with the radio, found a rock station. She was tapping her fingers on the dash, animated all at once, the funk sloughed off. Moods were like clothes she tried on, then discarded.

Beyond the city center Samsa headed north through suburban streets, passing gardens where people clipped hedges or dug out weeds, and kids played frisbee along sidewalks. Ordinary life as it was lived.

Lucky's, formerly a branch-line railroad station, had been converted a few years back when the railroad company was going out of business. It prospered as a restaurant whose clientele was mainly young and noisy. Samsa had never felt comfortable there. Always geriatric, over the hill.

He parked in the busy lot and went inside with Darcy, and they found their way to a table overlooking the rusted old rail tracks. The floor was strewn with sawdust for a rough-hewn rustic look, and the air, stirred by huge fans, was heavy with the smell of meat charbroiling. Most of the tables were occupied. Teenagers, twentysomethings.

A waitress brought menus, talked her way through the specials – 'Try the crab claws in lemon butter, they're scrumptious' – then left. Darcy studied her menu a moment before shutting it. 'How's the homicide business these days, Dad?'

'There's no danger of it slacking off. You can count on that.'

'Anything juicy?'

He thought juicy a peculiar choice of word. 'There's Anthony Leeson. If you're into blood and gore.'

'I read about that one. You got any clues?'

'We had a guy who said he might know something. It didn't pan out.' Joshua Gold hadn't been able to remember much when it came right down to it. Too dark. Not sure about the guy's height. Couldn't say he'd noticed any special characteristics. But Eve, tenacious as ever, wasn't going to let go of young Joshua just yet. She had other plans for him.

He said, 'You slog on these cases and sometimes you don't turn up a thing. So what happens? You become weary and frustrated, and you start wishing it was like a cop show: everything neat and tidy in the end.'

'Bad day, too, huh?' she asked.

What else could this day be? 'Yeah,' he said, and examined the menu.

When the waitress returned they ordered ribs with barbecue sauce, fries, Diet Cokes. Darcy looked out of the window at the tracks. She plucked a straw from the container and unwrapped it, rolling it back and forth across the table.

Samsa watched her for a while, then cleared his throat and asked, 'You miss her?'

Darcy didn't look up at him. 'She was never really there, Dad. I don't mean that to sound cruel or anything. She was like this presence that was always around, but that was all. Know what I mean?'

He reached for her hand and squeezed it. 'I know,' he said quietly.

'It's not like we were bosom buddies. I couldn't sit down and talk with her about things. I couldn't say, Hey, what do you think of this haircut? Or this shirt? Or these sneakers? What do you make of Nick? Could I?' Darcy picked up a napkin and held it against her face. 'I mean, really. *She was just never fucking there.*'

Samsa had a sensation of ice packed round his heart. This was too painful: her words, the look on her face. If he could defuse the anger and disappointment in the words and alter that expression, what fortune wouldn't he give? He loved this child to the limits of himself. 'She was sick, Darcy.'

'I *know* she was sick. Why didn't you send her away where trained people could look after her properly? And I don't mean that to sound cruel, either. Why did you have to take on the burden by yourself?'

'Because I kept thinking, one day she's going to snap out of it. Misguided optimism. Faith. My foolish heart. Call it what you like.'

'And all her stuff is still in the house. I mean, why are you keeping it? It's unhealthy. Spooky.'

'I'll get rid of it, if that's what you'd like,' he said. He thought of cardboard boxes, filling them with forsaken possessions, the attachments of a life cast away. He wondered if there was any activity more emotionally brutal than sifting the belongings of the dead.

'And you found her. You were the one that found her. Jesus Christ, I can't even *begin* to imagine how you felt.'

'I try not to dwell on it,' he said.

Darcy blew her nose. 'Let's drop this subject, Dad. Why don't we just stuff ourselves with ribs and make a really gross mess on the table?'

'And spill stuff on the floor,' he said.

'And make loud chomping noises like two animals in a zoo.'

The waitress came with stacks of ribs in a glutinous dark-red sauce. Samsa stared at the food. His appetite, small to begin with, had shriveled. He watched Darcy pick up a rib and chew on it, then she let the stripped bone sink inside her finger bowl, where it left a slick of red grease. *Pink water in the bathtub*, he thought. *Stained scissors lying on her stomach. Her hair, razored and chopped brutally short, sticking up from her scalp*. He felt haunted, ghosts stalked his life. What he needed was an exorcism. But incantations and the sprinkling of holy water weren't going to do the trick.

Darcy stared at him over the mound of ribs. 'I have a question for you. When you go out nights, where do you actually go?'

'Mostly it's work,' he answered. He chewed slowly on a fry.

'You don't have a woman you're seeing, do you?'

'No. Did you think I might?'

'You just get up and go, you don't say where you're headed. It can't be night shift all the time.'

'Homicides happen round the clock, which is inconvenient.'

105

'When it's not work, where do you go then?'

He picked up a rib, but he couldn't bring himself to taste it. 'I like the feeling of solitude I get in a car at night. There. Does that answer you?'

'I guess,' she said. 'I don't know why you sound so defensive, though.'

'I wasn't aware of it, Darcy. I get in the car and it's dark and I look for quiet roads. It's a peaceful sensation.' This intricate web of fabrication. Once you'd started to spin it you couldn't stop, because the strands would strangle you.

Was he supposed to tell her the truth? He could hear gates clang shut inside himself. He was barricaded behind his own evasions and lies. Gregory Samsa, a cop for twenty-one years, twenty-one fucking years of completely honest uninterrupted service to the inhabitants of this gritty threadbare city. Never on the pad, never on the take, never a goddam hint of graft or corruption; he slips up one time, he makes a serious error of judgement—

He crumpled his napkin with a violent gesture and pushed his plate aside briskly. *I was sick to my heart with solitude, Darcy. Can you understand that?* He wondered how he looked to his daughter, if she could read anything in his face. But she was staring into her food, wasn't even looking at him. He gazed round the room, experienced a great rushing blur of sensory impressions, then he remembered the feeling he'd experienced last night when he'd stared at the street from his bedroom window.

Something bad was coming down.

Something he'd be powerless to prevent.

He picked at a couple more fries, but that was all he could manage. Darcy, too, seemed uninterested in eating. *A flop*, he thought. Pigging out together. There had been a breakdown of sorts. It felt like a party where all the balloons had deflated and hung wrinkled.

'If you're finished, I'll get the check.' He looked at his

watch, remembered that Al Brodsky was dropping over. He raised an arm to attract the waitress. He paid the bill with a credit card. On the way out he noticed that Darcy had disappeared inside herself again. She looked distant and secretive.

We all have secrets, he thought. *It's how we handle them that matters. Or if we handle them at all.*

14

LEE BOYLE LOOKED OUT OF THE WINDOW OF VASS'S PICK-UP, which was rattling down a pocked road of old row houses. This was flinty blue-collar territory. Since the steelworks had shut down and the power plant replaced half its workforce with silicon chips, most people in this neighborhood were on welfare and hard times. Politicians didn't give a damn. That's what politicians were for anyhow. Vote for me, I won't do shit. But I'll do it better than the other candidate.

'So where does this guy live?' Boyle asked.

'It's not far.'

'And he can do the job?'

'In his sleep. It's nothing to him.'

'You known him long?'

'A few years,' Vass said. 'I met him through Stretch.'

'You can vouch for him.'

'Fuck's sake, relax.'

Boyle thought, *92K, 92K*. It was like a mantra going round in his head. He gazed at the dreary little houses. Old men, most of them black, sat on porches and read newspapers back to front, then started the whole process all over again. Boyle had a sense that there were drawers inside these houses stuffed with losing lottery tickets and unopened brown envelopes with windows.

'We there yet?'

'You're like a kid who sits in the back of his Daddy's car and can't keep still, Lee.'

Anxiety, Lee Boyle thought. *Time on whirring wings.* He remembered he was supposed to meet Cassandra at the Rialto, but he'd let that slide. He might not run into her again for weeks, months, by which time she'd have forgotten the deal anyway. You could count on that.

'This guy really calls himself Data?'

'Thirty-seven and a Trekkie to the max. You meet him, just don't mention Captain Kirk or that bald guy Picard, or *any* of those assholes, or it's going to be a long night listening to some very tedious details about the righteousness of the Federation.'

Vass slowed the truck, turned a corner, braked outside a row house painted battleship gray and peeling like bad skin. Boyle got out and followed Rudy Vass to the front door. Vass pressed the bell. The guy who answered had a shaved head. His eyes were stone-colored.

Vass said, 'Data, my man.'

Data had a smile like a crack in a rock. 'You're late, Vass.'

'Traffic's a nightmare,' Vass said. 'This is Lee. Lee, Data.'

Data's voice was deep, out of his chest. 'Before you come inside, you oughta know I have two strict rules in here: no smoking, and no drinking anywhere near the equipment.'

Data opened the door a little wider. Vass and Boyle went inside the house, which consisted of small interconnecting rooms, drab and dark and steamy. There was a smell of wood polish or air freshener, Boyle wasn't sure which.

A woman's voice, emerging from one of the tiny rooms, called out, 'Don't go making loud noises up there, Joe.'

'Right, Ma,' Data said.

Data reached the landing and opened the door to a room that burst on Boyle like a *Star Trek* museum. Posters depicted Spock and Kirk and others whose names were unknown to Boyle – he rarely watched TV, it was a foreign country to him – and a whole array of books, magazines, fanzines, miniature replicas of alien life forms, copies of Trekkie weapons. It was some kind of sorry shrine. Joe, aka Data, thirty-seven and still lives with his mother in a *Star Trek* alternative reality. All this kid stuff. Boyle had an urge to say, Look, I'm goddam serious. This isn't some space soap baloney.

'Rudy explain the fee?' Data asked.

'Twenty-five bucks,' Boyle said.

'That's the going rate,' Data said. He was wearing Osh Kosh overalls with big patchy pockets. His arms were hairy and muscular. Boyle drew crumpled notes from his jeans, counted out twenty-five dollars in fives. He wondered if he had anything left in his bank account. Fifty, sixty dollars tops. He knew he had about a hundred bucks in a coffee can stuffed at the back of a closet. His nest egg. Peanuts. All the money you spent down the drain of your veins or up your nose, and nothing to show for it but a serious taste. You've got a Mercedes, a speedboat, and probably a goddam Lear jet lost in your bloodstream.

Data pocketed the cash and walked to a table in the corner of the room, where a black laptop computer was located. It was attached to a box Boyle had no way of identifying. He was computer illiterate. He wasn't one for zipping along the information autobahn.

A tangle of wires dangled from the table and out of sight. Data sat down in front of the computer and pressed a button. Boyle heard a whir and then a series of beeping sounds, followed by what seemed like a strange hoarse wind blowing out of the laptop.

'Okay,' Data said. 'Rudy tells me you want some material outta the Department of Motor Vehicles?'

'I've got three digits of a license-plate number, a make and a color.'

'Shoot,' Data said, his hands poised over the keyboard.

'Ninety-two K. Chrysler,' Boyle said. 'Dark blue.'

'Ninety-two K.' Data's fingers tapped quickly. Boyle watched Data lean back in his chair while the machine whined.

'What's that box attachment?' Boyle asked.

'You never seen a *modem* before?' Data had a look of bewilderment, like he considered Boyle some primeval life form. 'This box connects to the phone lines. Which means the whole wide world.'

Boyle said he saw, but he didn't really, and, besides, he didn't give a damn. He was nervous. Because of the crank. Because of sleeplessness. *The modem's connected to the phone line, the phone line's connected to the phone poles, the phone pole's connected to the exchange.* He understood that in Data's world this was a holy moment, like making contact with God.

'Right, we're in,' Data said. Boyle saw what seemed to be names and numbers scrolling across the screen. Data leaned forward toward the monitor.

'Already?' Boyle asked.

'I got three Chryslers here, all Le Barons, all with the same partial, all in the color specified,' Data said. 'Get a pen and paper and write down this info.'

Vass took from his pocket a Bic, which he handed Boyle, who couldn't find anything to write on except for

111

a hard-top pack of Camel Lights. He scribbled the names and addresses quickly in tiny crabbed handwriting, a kind of shorthand he hoped he'd be able to decipher later. Data pressed a key and the screen blanked.

'I told you he was good,' Vass said.

Boyle stuck the pack in his pocket. 'He's good all right.'

Data rose. Business concluded. 'I'll show you guys out.'

They went down the stairs and toward the front door. 'You don't know me,' Data said to Boyle. 'We never met.' He eyeballed the street, presumably for a sign of alien life forms, then quickly shut the door.

Boyle and Vass walked back to the pick-up. When he was inside, Boyle sat with his head slumped back. 'She vanishes inside a Le Baron and nobody's seen her since,' he said. 'And that makes me feel a tad uneasy.'

'I still say she split,' Vass said. 'She wanted a clean break.'

'Hey, I know this girl. No way would she just up and vanish on me.'

The pick-up shuddered over a pothole in the road. Bumping up and down in his seat, Vass said, 'What now?'

Boyle took a cigarette from the pack of Camel Lights and lit it, gazing at the names and addresses through strands of smoke. 'Check out these names, what else? One of these cars is the only connection I have to Almond.' And he thought of the small girl with the lovely Latino features, damp towels on his bathroom floor and her glistening pubic hair and the sweet honeyed taste of her kiss, and he felt bereft, as if she might somehow have slipped through a crack in the earth's crust, forever lost to him.

15

DR LEWIS DICE WAS A PINK-SKINNED INDIVIDUAL WHO HAD A local reputation as something of an oddball on account of his hobby: taxidermy. Kids brought him dead animals – roadkill, creatures blasted by gunshot – and he restored the more salvageable specimens with a needle and surgical thread, then stuffed and mounted them in glass cases and contributed them to auctions for charitable causes. He had a squeak of a voice. At times he sounded like Mr Rogers through a flute. He wore flip-flops and Bermuda shorts and a Miami Dolphins T-shirt that revealed scrawny nut-brown arms.

People who visited his home invariably noticed such things as the severed heads of birds suspended in jars of preservative and the kitchen sink, usually filled with pale-green fluid, in which organic matter floated. His neighbors sometimes referred to him as Doc Dicenstein.

With a pack of big plastic Ziploc bags under his arm, Dice strode in his purposeful way out through the door in his cedar fence and headed for the great open field that bordered his property, where weeds and tangled thickets of long grass grew riotously. Every now and then he paused to contemplate an unusual arrangement of daisies or dandelions or wild flowers. He disturbed a red admiral on a grass stalk still moist from last night's rain. The butterfly took flight, fluttering past his face, color in motion.

He heard in the distance the *pock* of a rifle. He winced. A second *ping*, then a third. Why did parents give their children air rifles? And why did the children use these weapons for what they called sport? Killing wood pigeons, shooting cats, crippling wildlife. Where was the sport in that?

Shielding his eyes from the setting sun, Dice watched the butterfly go. Then he stared across the meadow, his attention drawn by the sound of machinery. A truck with the sign 'MARTIN'S 24-HOUR BREAKDOWN & RECOVERY SERVICE' was hauling a car from the base of an old tree. The car, strangely enough, was upside down. Men were busy attaching chains to the overturned automobile. A winch began to grind.

Some gosh-darn fool had smacked into the tree, Lewis Dice thought. A drunk in all probability. He looked in the other direction, noticing flattened grass and threadbare places and seeing, at the place where the incline rose to the road, a darkened area of churned ground. The hapless driver had come off the blacktop, *whoopsadiddley*, and slammed several hundred yards into the tree.

Upside down. My lord.

Lewis Dice approached the truck. 'Was anyone hurt?' he asked.

The two men from the recovery service were taciturn. They regarded Dice, with his high-pitched voice and baggy shorts and funny sandals, as if he were some crazy old coot who'd wandered away from an old folks' home without written authority.

'Don't rightly know,' one of them said. 'We just pick 'em up and drag 'em off, dude.'

'It's in bad shape,' Dice said. He looked at the car, the passenger door of which was unhinged and buckled. 'I've seen plenty of accident victims in my time. I spent a few years in ER. I'm a physician, you know. Was. Retired.'

'Zatso,' said the younger of the two men, a boy in his late teens. He had brown teeth. Dice, senses honed by a lifetime of abstention from drink and cigarettes, could smell tobacco on him.

'When did this happen?'

'Dunno. We just haul 'em away,' the kid said. He wore big leather mitts. 'Zatsall we do.'

Dice lingered a few moments and, since the likelihood of further conversation was clearly nil, walked off through the grass. He thought of all the casualty cases he'd attended: the gunfire victims, people with third-degree burns, folks hauled from car wrecks.

Pitiful situations.

Ah – what was this?

The dead swallow was delicately balanced on a pyre-like arrangement of grass. Dice went down on his knees and picked the creature up very carefully and placed it inside one of his plastic bags. The bird was riddled with pellets. Those boys with goddam airguns – why didn't somebody drum into their fat heads that people and creatures shared this planet, that respect was due every living thing?

He sealed the bag, rose and continued to walk. He scanned thickets, looking for casualties. Some days he found none, others he picked up two or three. A few he could repair and stuff, most he rejected as beyond restoration. Now and again, driven by the curiosity that had propelled him all his life, he performed very delicate post-mortems on his kitchen table.

He came upon an umbrella on the ground, one of those plastic transparent jobs people picked up cheaply when they were caught in an unexpected rainstorm. He gazed at it a moment, then walked on. Utterly disgraceful what he came across out here at times. Junkies' needles, shriveled condoms, used tampons, sometimes discarded underwear, shoes, a pair of jeans once. The place was a dumping ground.

He kept going. Grass grew in places as high as his thighs. The air was richly scented with wild flowers. A barbed growth snagged his shorts and retarded his progress a moment. He freed himself carefully and continued, and the stalks of long grass parted reluctantly as he moved. What one really needed here was a machete. Chop chop, slash slash, clear a path. Slice and hack, hack and slice. He hummed a remembered snippet from *The Pirates of Penzance*. Many years ago he'd played the role of the Pirate King in an amateur production staged by the staff of St Dominic's General Hospital, and he'd been good, very good.

He stopped suddenly in front of a thick stand of unruly bushes. A rat, sleek and gleaming, scampered out of the undergrowth and startled him. He watched it vanish, thinking there was something odd about the creature's appearance, something he couldn't put his finger on immediately.

He frowned, bent down, peered through the impenetrable tangle of leaves and limbs.

What was it about that rat?

Its whiskers, *of course, of course.* Wet, stained as if by red wine.

It had been disturbed in the act of feeding. *On a dead bird*, Dice thought. Some fledgling fallen from a nest,

116

perhaps. A defenseless little thing. An innocent. Such was the cruelty inherent in nature.

He reached forward and parted the strands of shrubbery with his hands.

16

———————

AL BRODSKY ARRIVED PROMPTLY AT EIGHT THIRTY, CARRYING two four-packs of Grolsch in paper sacks. Samsa opened two bottles, handed one to Brodsky. Inside the living room Al sat down close to the fireplace, where the last of the sun created a fuzzy yellow rectangle around his feet.

'Cheers, Greg.'

'Better days.' Samsa sipped the Czech lager. What was it Brodsky needed to discuss?

Brodsky stretched his legs out, relaxed. 'Darcy around?'

'Out on a date.'

'Who's the boy?'

'A kid called Nick Mancuso. He's at the same school. A senior.'

'Nick Mancuso . . . Isn't he the kid of that guy who's big in the paper products line? Bobby Mancuso?'

'That's him,' Samsa said.

'Is it serious?' Al asked.

'She says he stifles her.'

'She's young.' Brodsky slipped off his shoes. He had a

118

hole in the heel of a sock. He studied it a moment, then said, 'It gets easier, you know. In time.'

For a second Samsa thought Brodsky was referring in some oblique way to Darcy, but then realized Al had just skipped to the subject of Harriet. 'Tess has been gone five years now. I still catch myself talking to her. There's an absence. But the pain dims to a minor ache.'

Two widowers examining grief. Terrific. Was *this* what Al had come here to speak about? Samsa didn't want to talk about the dead. He wanted another kind of conversation: feathery, inconsequential. Department rumors. Dumb jokes. Anything.

He stood at the window and stared out into the street. The sky was suffused with yellows and pinks. A few stray clouds hung in the still air. *I want to be free of myself*, he thought.

Al said, 'After a while, you have this need to socialize, check what's happening, what you might be missing. Then, one day, a lady catches your eye.'

'And that's happened to you?' Samsa asked.

'More than once.' Brodsky smiled. The small slitted eyes disappeared in the folds of his face. He looked jovial. 'I can still get it up. It's a bit of a crank, I admit. But the machinery's basically sound.'

'I hadn't heard any rumors about you and women,' Samsa remarked. 'Either I'm sleepwalking through the department or the grapevine's shut down.'

'Maybe I'm just discreet in my old age.'

There's a future, Samsa thought. *That's what Al is trying to tell me.*

'Off the record, are you handling things okay?' Brodsky asked.

'Department things? Personal things? Which?'

'Either. Both.'

'I'm doing just fine, Al.'

Brodsky had a stare that at times could penetrate. He fixed you with those small eyes and they bored into your head like two power-driven diamond drill bits. 'You sure?'

'Sure.' Samsa had the sudden thought, *Al knows something*. But that was ridiculous. What was there to know? Everything had been dreamed, everything was effluence that had seeped from his head.

'I want to ask you something,' Brodsky said.

Samsa was holding his breath. This sudden tension was an arrow in his throat. He touched the edge of his broken tooth with the tip of his tongue.

'I'm thinking of the internal reorganization. I'd like your feedback on how it's going.'

Samsa relaxed now, drank some beer. Internal reorganization. That was easy. He could deal with that. He could talk about that all day long. All night.

'I can't think of any problems,' he said.

'You're getting total co-operation?'

'Total.'

Brodsky looked a little doubtful. 'Charlie Bird and Casey are coming through for you?'

'Religiously,' Samsa said.

'I just figured there might be some envy, that's all. When you got Charlie Bird working the East precinct, and Jack Casey the South, you worry about empire-building. They're good guys, don't get me wrong. But if there's the smallest sign of private fiefdoms I want to know about it. I don't want any hostility to get in the way of shared information, because it means the chance of something vital getting lost in the shuffle.'

'I get daily updates on the homicide investigations being conducted by Bird and Casey. They file copies of all their reports with me. I see something I don't like – work duplicated, fruitless inquiries, guys going off at stupid tangents – I talk with Charlie or Jack and we try to fix the situation. That was the mandate you gave me, Al.'

'Charlie Bird wasn't happy in the beginning,' Brodsky said. 'Three months ago, when I told him I was re-organizing homicide, bringing it under one roof so to speak, he pitched a fit. "So Downtown controls every-thing," he says. "Downtown wins the blue ribbon and Samsa gets to be like the guy on top of the pyramid. What does that make him? Some pharaoh or something? Samsa the First?"'

'Charlie's been with the department longer than me,' Samsa said. 'He had every right to feel aggrieved.'

'The only thing really aggrieved him was the fact he knew you were better equipped for the job than himself,' Brodsky said. 'He doesn't have your . . . call it diplomacy.'

'I never thought of myself as diplomatic,' Samsa said.

'With a slight edge,' Brodsky remarked.

An edge. Samsa wondered about this, whether he'd lost that edge, if it had become blunted by circumstance. He wasn't sure.

He was ready for another beer. He moved toward the kitchen. Al Brodsky, shoeless, followed him. Samsa opened the refrigerator, removed two Grolsch bottles.

'Understand, Greg. The first time you think there's any blockage in this pipeline, you come to me. No hesitation. No misplaced cop-loyalty crap.' Brodsky sat on a kitchen stool. He could look intensely serious, as he did at that moment.

'No, the co-operation's fine,' Samsa said. 'The only draw-back from my point of view is strictly personal. I don't spend enough time with Darcy. She's at a strange age.'

'Show me an age that isn't strange,' Brodsky said. He wiggled his toes inside his dark socks, staring down at them. The heel that showed through the hole was like a small albino eye. 'Are you saying in a coy roundabout way that you wished you'd never assumed this responsibility?'

'No, nothing like that, Al.' Samsa had the feeling he was being challenged, pinned. *I'm not the man for this job. It's some kind of sham. But life goes on, you told yourself that already. You're swimming, you have to keep your head above the turmoil of the waters. Everything is dandy. It was a world of appearances. I'll continue to be the good cop.*

He said, 'If it was the kind of thing that kept me tied to my desk, it might be different. But I still get out. I have cases I work.'

'I never saw your role as administrative,' Brodsky said. 'But any time you think it's too much, or you start to get that *stuck* feeling, say so. Jesus Christ, we've known each other too long to go beating about bushes, Greg. What is it? Seventeen years?'

'About,' Samsa said. *That stuck feeling*, he thought. The glue on the surface of fly-paper.

Brodsky knocked his beer can against Samsa's bottle and smiled. 'Seventeen years, Greg. Weddings and funerals and kids growing up. Laughter and grief. The whole damn thing. And here we are, a couple of hardened survivors.'

'Just about,' Samsa said. 'Let's go back inside the living room.'

Shadows had lengthened, the sun had almost entirely gone. Samsa switched on a lamp. The telephone rang and he picked it up. It was Eve Lassiter.

'I'm hitting the streets with young Joshua,' she said.

'I figured you would.'

'There's always a slight chance he'll see this kid he says Leeson picked up. If that happens I want to be there.'

'You're dressing for the part, I assume,' he said.

'Short skirt, long boots, very glossy. This little blouse you can just about see through. I don't want to be conspicuous. I'm wearing *mucho* make-up too. Master of illusion.'

Samsa imagined her in short skirt and boots, face made up, strutting her stuff like a hooker.

She said, 'Have you decided if you're joining me or not? All you'd have to do is park your car in the vicinity where we can keep in touch. And if anything happens, I know you're there.'

'Take Billy Fogue.'

'Fogue's loud and sexist. I'd prefer you, Lieutenant.'

'Get Duff then. He's on duty.'

'I'll get Duff if you're chickening out.'

'I'm not chickening out. I've got company.'

'Female by any chance?'

'The chief.'

'Oh, hobnobbing.'

Samsa caught his own reflection in the darkening window. 'I'll be home all night if you need me.'

'I wish you could see me in this outfit. You'd froth at the mouth.'

'Are you flirting with me, Eve?' Darcy had said Eve had the hots for him. He thought about that. Out of the mouths of kids.

'Could be. Or maybe I'm getting inside this role,' she answered. 'I might enjoy trawling the sidewalks. I might just quit the department and take up hooking.'

He pictured her strolling the night, looking provocative but hanging back from the action, turning cars away on some pretext when they approached her. 'Take good care,' he said.

'I always do.'

He hung up, feeling for some reason a little empty.

'Eve Lassiter?' Brodsky asked.

'Yeah. She's working the Leeson case.'

'From what angle?'

Samsa told him.

Brodsky said, 'That neighborhood's a blight. Vice

rounds these kids up, they're back on the street next day. What can you do? Eve's a resourceful girl. She just needs a little looking out for. You get along with her pretty well, I hear.'

'Is there gossip?'

'Not so much gossip, more a quiet underswell. You have to listen real hard to pick up on it. They say she's fond of you. Ditto for you.'

'I like her,' Samsa said.

'You got something stronger than beer? I'm starting to get into the mood.'

'Vodka, cognac.'

Brodsky wanted vodka. Samsa went to the liquor cabinet and poured a glass. Brodsky took the vodka and tasted it, then settled back in his chair with his hands clasped across his stomach. Facing him, Samsa thought, *This is a pleasant illusion. This is how it's meant to be: two old colleagues having a drink, comrades in arms, old times, weddings and funerals.* Somewhere there were photographs, Brodsky stiff and ludicrous in a tux, standing directly behind Samsa on the day of his marriage to Harriet. Happy days. Better times.

He turned to the window just as the street lamps came on and cast their customary dullish yellow glow. He drew the curtain, enjoying the idea of keeping the outside world at bay. Nothing existed beyond these walls.

Brodsky said, 'I'll help myself to some more of this vodka,' and he walked to the liquor cabinet.

Al was a lightweight when it came to drinking. He held it up to a certain point, but he reached that borderline fast, and then he became loquaciously sentimental – which meant he'd begin to trample through the undergrowth of the past, and next thing he'd want to drag out the old photograph albums. Remember that time, Greg? You and me and Harriet and Tess, that day on Lake

Maska when we hired a boat that almost sank? Remember?

I don't want to go there, Samsa thought. There were too few pictures of Harriet involved in any kind of activity, outdoor or in. She'd passed through the world like a pale shade, leaving barely a fingerprint.

'You ought to take it easy, Al,' he said. 'If you're driving.'

'I'm over the limit, I'll call a cab.'

Samsa was restless suddenly, thinking of Eve Lassiter, the dark places, the headlights of prowling cars. He understood he should have gone down there to provide back-up. Eve was his protégée. He'd taken her under his wing when she'd first joined the department. He'd recommended her for promotion.

But. *Have we ever met before?*

Brodsky appeared somber all at once. 'A year ago already. Hard to believe.'

Here we go. 'Al, I don't want to talk about it.'

'Sometimes you got to air the linen closet, Greg.'

'I just don't want to talk about it.'

Brodsky was going back for more vodka. On the way to the liquor cabinet he ran his knuckles across the keyboard of the piano. The sound rolled around the room. Samsa heard the strings vibrate under the lid, the afterwhisper of notes struck randomly. *This house*, he thought. *This whole goddam house whispers. It never stops. Day and fucking night I hear it.*

He opened the front door and stepped onto the porch where the air was muggy. Brodsky came after him, glass in hand.

'I'm out of line,' Brodsky said. 'I know it.'

'It's not that, Al. It's me, it's my fault. Sometimes I think I have a grip, and then it just goes, and fuck it, *fuck* it.' Samsa quit talking. He looked the length of the street,

125

seeing hordes of moths dart and flutter under the lamps. A million potential suicides. The air was strong with the scent of cut grass and chlorine from neighborhood pools.

Al clapped him on his bruised shoulder. 'I get maudlin. You don't need to tell me—'

Samsa heard the car before he saw it, a patrol car that loomed out of the dark, roaring down the center of the street, roof lights slicing the night. It drew up at the end of Samsa's driveway, and the first thing that came into his mind was the idea that something had happened to Darcy. An accident, Nick Mancuso's frail little VW convertible had crashed, and his head was crammed with pictures of blood and emergency rooms, doctors and orderlies, nurses hurrying with IV drips. Everything hasty. Everything out of control. Madness.

'Sweet *Christ*,' Brodsky said. 'Is there never any peace?'

A cop Samsa recognized as Randy Harrilyn got out of the cruiser and moved up the driveway to the porch.

Don't let it be Darcy. Don't let it be.

Harrilyn was a tall man with a tendency to stoop. He reached the porch steps and looked up, his face the color of a tangerine in the porch light. He stared at Samsa. In that moment, for no good reason he could think of, Samsa knew that Randy Harrilyn wasn't here on account of Darcy. He just knew, and his heart flopped over into a void, and he was hearing an old Billie Holiday tune slurring and dying inside a cassette deck.

17

IT WAS A LONG HAUL FROM ONE SIDE OF THE DARKENING CITY to the other, and Lee Boyle felt a persistent jumpy urgency and the occasional haphazard skip of his heart. It was weird how the mind had a wayward life all its own and thoughts roared around in a carousel of graphics and bizarre sound effects that eventually distilled themselves in the repetition of one word, one picture – Almond, Almond, Almond. *She left me at the silent time.* Yes indeed, Percy. She left me.

Only I don't believe that. I don't believe she'd *ever* do that. So where the hell is she?

Vass slowed the pick-up, checking street signs. 'This is Oakleigh,' he said. 'What number are you looking for, Lee?'

Boyle flicked on the interior light and studied his cigarette pack. 'Eight three six,' he said. 'Guy's name is Silas Goba. Or Gora. I can't make out my own goddam handwriting.'

Vass drove slowly along the street of frame houses. This was one of the city's older neighborhoods, *circa* 1950.

Dense trees camouflaged the homes, and great branches reached out luxuriantly, blocking street lights. A phantasmagorical effect, a jungle suburb. *Trippy*, Boyle thought. He half expected neon parrots to come screaming out of the leaves, like beasts from some acid flashback occurrence.

'Let's hope this is a better candidate than that last one,' Vass remarked. 'She must've been pushing a hundred, man. She'd never driven that Le Baron further than the local mall, for Christ's sake.'

Boyle pondered Mrs Clyde Fodor, whose Chrysler – license plate 92KB67 – had been parked in the driveway of her home out in Stanhope on the eastern edge of the city. Mrs Fodor, all glassy old skin and liver spots and knobby bone, had bought into Boyle's story that he and Vass were landscapers – well, artists, to be frank – scouting commissions. Boyle, who'd pitched his floral notions with extravagant enthusiasm, had an expression he could do in his sleep. It was one of wide-eyed purity, and it charmed birds from their nests and had old ladies wet-eyed and reaching for photographs of sons who'd vanished in the vastness of the continent, with new wives, new jobs, grandkids who existed only in color snapshots, phone calls at Thanksgiving. *You okay, Ma? I've been kind of busy.* Boyle touched their hearts in a mysterious way.

Picture this, Mrs Fodor, a whole bed of azaleas over here, maybe a fine array of marigolds there. The whole thing kind of bound together with a charismatic carpet of, shall we say, snowdrops? Babble babble, envisage the flowery magnificence.

It was bullshit, but he'd even begun to believe it, which was the real secret of any con. He'd put a slight fag spin on his words: *I can just imagine a tiny pond, too, lily pads, a frog or two croaking. How very bucolic, Mrs*

Fodor. While the old lady had considered Boyle's panoramic concept, Vass had sneaked off to check out the Chrysler, whose odometer had a grand total of 905 miles on it.

Mrs Fodor, a lonely soul, enjoyed company. She offered tea and a whole family history to go with it. She was a widow. Dear Clyde had died last year of complications arising from diabetes. Their only son lived in Europe. She didn't get out much. Didn't do a whole lot of driving. Eyesight failing. In an innocent way Boyle had asked if she'd ever loaned the car to anyone, a neighbor, say, or a friend, but the old lady told him she'd never done that. End of story. *Come back soon and talk to me about begonias,* Mrs Fodor had said when they were leaving. *I just love begonias.*

Right, Mrs Fodor. We'll be back.

One down, two to go.

Vass parked the pick-up. 'This is the place. You want to do the landscape shit again?'

Boyle opened his door, stepped down. The sticky night air had the stealthy feel of a mugger's breath. 'Let's play it by ear until we get a sense of this guy.'

He walked under a canopy of branches toward the pathway. Vass, hitching his jeans, followed. Number 836 Oakleigh, a somber brown house, was surrounded by garden gnomes. Jesus Christ, there must have been thirty-five of the squat fuckers on the lawn. Plaster-of-Paris elves skulked in the poor light, bearded leprechauns with pipes. Cute, if you liked little stone squadrons. Boyle found it unsettling, those expressionless eyes watching him as he moved in the direction of the porch. He half expected sudden animation, elves creaking to life, leprechauns deciding to form a debating society. Speed made you imagine all sorts of stuff out of the corners of your eyes.

A Chrysler was parked in the covered carport. Boyle

was about to step toward it when a porch light came on and a man appeared behind the screen door. Boyle couldn't quite make out his features.

'Help you fellas in some way?' the man asked.

Boyle, trying to think on his feet, detected unmistakable hostility flowing out toward him. He moved a couple of yards toward the porch. 'Mr Goba?'

The guy said nothing. He pushed the screen door open a few inches. A hinge squeaked. Boyle considered the idea of saying he was a lover of garden gnomes and had heard about this amazing collection, which he simply had to see for himself, but there were some kinds of bullshit that just coagulated in your throat. In any event, he didn't feel like going through another faggoty act, swishing and swooning over the clay figures like a queen of kitsch.

'I understand you have a Chrysler for sale,' Boyle said.

'I don't know where you heard that, fella,' the guy said, 'but you got the wrong information.'

'This is eight three six Oakleigh, and you're Silas Goba, right?'

'You got that right. But I don't have any car for sale.'

'You're sure?'

'You hard of hearing, fella?' The man stepped out under the porch light. He wore a white T-shirt. He was big, beef-bellied, no neck. His hair was marine-style crew-cut. He had the look of a man who ate light bulbs for breakfast and then, still hungry, chomped on razor blades. 'You know what I think? I think you and your buddy there come round thinking this place might be empty, might be an easy score.'

'No way,' Boyle said.

'I had this house burgled two times before, jack. And I swore to God I wasn't gonna be ripped off a third time, because I had it up to here with thieves. Take a hike, get the fuck off my property.'

130

Boyle didn't move. The air was alive with atoms of potential violence. He tried to imagine Goba picking up Almond. He pictured this: Almond steps inside Goba's Chrysler. Her neat little body settles in the passenger seat. A transaction is discussed, terms agreed. Does Goba fondle her knee? Slip a hand under her skirt? Delve inside her panties? Is he businesslike about it? Does he slobber? Is there the strained desperation of a rock-solid hard-on? Can't wait to get Almond to spread her legs, show him her cunt? Does she go down on him in the car, her beautiful little face in his fat lap, and his fly undone and his boxer shorts open?

Boyle had an awful moment, a sharp racket in his head, a small steel ball rattling through a variety of hooped circuits, as in one of those noisy Japanese pachinko arcade games. He drew a hand over his face. His fingertips were numb and his scalp tingled. *Rush this guy*, he thought. *Rush him and bring him down and stomp the truth out of him.*

'What you're telling me is the car's not for sale,' he said.

'You're real quick on the uptake,' Goba said. 'Lookit. Just get the fuck off my property. Don't make me come down these steps to you, fella. I got a short fuse.' He moved in an off-center way to the edge of the porch. He'd clearly been drinking. Boyle pegged him as the kind of solitary sociopath you sometimes saw sitting alone in bars, whispering menacingly to themselves.

Boyle glanced toward the Chrysler, which gleamed dully in the carport. If he opened the car and scoped it out would he find some evidence of Almond? A heart-draining trace of her perfume, say? A cigarette butt of the brand she smoked? An earring on the floor? Something tangible. He heard Rudy Vass sigh, a let's-blow-this-place sound. But Rudy, old friend that he might be, didn't have a vested interest in Almond, didn't worry about her the

131

way Boyle did, didn't have bad feelings of the kind Boyle was beginning to experience just about now.

She's hurt.

And then he thought, *This goon Goba fucked her and murdered her. This sick sack of shit maybe choked the life out of her and stashed her in the trunk of this fucking Chrysler in the carport. Her lithe body twisted, her face bloodless, her dress crumpled.*

Suddenly these possibilities took on the patina of absolute certainty, and Boyle, who didn't give a damn about Goba's threats, walked directly to the car.

'Hey,' Goba said, and came down from the porch to intercept. 'Don't you listen, fuckface? Ain't you heard a goddam thing I been saying?'

She's in the trunk, Boyle thought. *She's under a threadbare plaid travel rug. She's entombed alongside a spare tire and a jack and cans of oil and all the other greasy crap people store in their cars.* He'd never been so sure of anything. He saw the license plate number. 92KC700.

Goba shoved him in the chest with the flat of his fat hand and said, 'You're outta line here, fella.'

'Don't touch me again,' Boyle said.

'Don't touch you? Don't *touch* you? You're trespassing, shithead. I got rights.' Goba pushed a second time.

Boyle couldn't stop thinking about the trunk. It consumed him. It became a vast space inside his head. He stepped to the side, tried to pass Goba, who grabbed him by the arm and twisted it at a painful angle. Boyle, smelling a serious stench of whisky on the man's breath, made a huge effort and wrenched himself free.

'Where is she, Goba?'

'Where's who?'

'I want to see inside the trunk of that goddam car.'

Goba looked at Vass, who was standing back from the situation. 'Your pal outta his mind or what?'

Vass took out his handkerchief, coughed into it and said nothing.

Boyle reached for the trunk lid and Goba, coming up from behind, seized him, wrapped his thick arms around his ribs and squeezed. Lee Boyle felt air being forced out of his lungs and dizziness descend on him. He slammed his elbows with as much force as he could gather into Goba's ribs and the big guy slackened his hold and Boyle spun around to face him.

'You picked her up and you fucked her, and then something snapped in your sick fucking head and you stashed her in the goddam trunk—'

'Jesus, Lee,' Vass said.

Goba took a step back from Boyle and asked, 'What'n hell you talking about?'

'Absolutely no way she'd have vanished without saying anything to me,' Boyle said, vaguely aware of slippage inside, like he was sluicing down a water slide with no bottom in sight. 'She wouldn't have left her clothes behind. She liked the stuff I bought her. She liked those goddam clothes. You understand what I'm saying?'

Goba looked at Vass again. 'What is this guy *on*, for Christ's sake?'

Vass looked slightly tubercular in the poor light. 'He's worried sick,' he said.

'I don't know about worried, but sick, yeah, I grant you sick,' Goba said.

'I'm opening the trunk,' Boyle said.

'You think there's a *body* in there?'

'That's exactly what I think,' and Boyle turned back to the car. He couldn't get the trunk to budge and wondered if maybe it only opened if you pressed a button or pulled a lever inside the car. He beat the palm of his hand on the lid.

'Let me get this straight. You're saying I picked up some

chick and then . . .' Goba tossed back his head, and when he laughed his belly shook. 'Is this some kind of put-on, buddy?'

Boyle hated the sound of that laugh. He glared at Silas Goba. 'Open the trunk,' he said.

'Piss off.' Goba looked at Vass. 'Why don't you do your pal a favor and drive him down to the psycho ward at St Dominic's? Because if you don't I'm gonna rip his goddam face off.'

Boyle noticed a wrench lying on the floor of the carport, and he stooped, picked it up and held it out in front of Goba. The tool was rusty and brittle and might snap if he struck Goba with any force, but since it was the only possible weapon to hand what choice did he have? Unless he hefted one of the gnomes and used it to launch an assault on Silas Goba, a notion that struck him as only slightly plausible. MAN STRUCK BY GNOME-SHAPED MISSILE.

Goba smiled at the wrench and said, 'Hotshot, huh? Tough guy, huh? Come on. Come on. What you waiting for, asshole?' He made beckoning gestures, inviting Boyle forward even as he struggled to maintain his own balance.

Vass said, 'Lee. Let's get out of here.'

Goba said, 'Yeah, Lee, why don't you listen to your friend?'

'I want that fucking trunk opened,' Boyle said.

Goba took up the stance of a prizefighter and feinted to one side, tossing out a telegraphed punch that flicked past Lee Boyle's face. Boyle swung the wrench and missed, thinking how all of a sudden this little outburst of violence had the dreamy feel of a quiet foxtrot to it. Each movement might have been plotted by a choreographer on ludes. Goba, an adherent of the Marquess of Queensberry rules, sneaked in a stiff uppercut that went whooshing close to Boyle's chin, creating a warm updraft of air. Boyle raised the wrench, brought it down, caught the back of

Goba's wrist. Goba grunted, shadowboxed a few moments, shuffling his feet back and forth like a sand dancer in a ridiculous old vaudeville routine, but he was visibly losing energy.

Boyle considered the diversity of violence. Sometimes it was hard and sharp and brutal. Sometimes it just iced the breath in your throat. Other times it was almost hallucinogenic. This situation between himself and Goba belonged in the dreamlike category, slow slow slow, elementary box-steps at the Arthur Murray School of Terpsichorean Violence. This was burlesque.

'For Christ's sake,' Vass said, stepping between Boyle and Goba, who was breathing hard. Boyle shoved Rudy aside, thinking, *Goba is all huff and puff and threat. He doesn't have the stuff it really takes. He's a drunk windbag.*

Boyle swung the wrench again, this time in an angular fashion, and it struck deep into Goba's ribcage. The big man moaned and went down on one knee, clutching his side. Boyle had the urge to drive the wrench into the guy's head and feel the sweet smack of metal on bone, but he was going through a dip in energy, and all he really wanted was access to the goddam trunk. Goba was staring up at him, mouth open.

'The keys,' Boyle said.

'Fuck off.'

'The keys, man,' Vass said to Goba. 'Just give him the keys.'

'You can take a runnin' fuck, too,' Goba said. 'My goddam rib's probably broken. Sweet God.'

'You want your brain stoved in?' Boyle said.

Vass said, 'Best give him the keys. Don't push him.'

Goba said, 'If I was younger, by Christ—'

'Yeah yeah yeah,' Boyle said and held out his hand. This humidity was wilting him.

Goba said, 'One time I coulda had you for a snack between meals, shithead.'

'The fucking keys!'

'Crazy bastard,' Goba said, and dug in the back pocket of his blue jeans. He groaned and tossed a set of keys to Boyle. 'Go ahead. Open the trunk. You'll find this chick you're missing all wrapped up in a roll of linoleum under a pile of oil rags and old newspapers.'

Boyle walked to the Chrysler, unlocked the trunk, hesitated.

He felt the full cold terror of awful expectation.

He flipped the trunk open.

The interior light came on, illuminating thick volumes of drapery samples. He reached in, rummaged, threw the books out, yanked the carpet up, saw the jack neatly tucked away, the spare tire in the well, examined the space in the manner of a demented forensic scientist hunting minuscule clues – a pubic hair, a smudge of dirt, anything at all. He saw nothing, no sign of Almond, no tube of lipstick, earring, errant shoe, discarded panties, sweet fuck all. He slammed the lid shut and lowered his face until his forehead touched metal.

'You satisfied now?' Goba said. 'Huh? You happy now?'

Boyle experienced a strange zero condition. The night was collapsing about him, like he was coming undone in various stages, flesh peeling from bone, his gut falling and falling. Speed wearing off. He was crashing like a machine-gunned hot-air balloon.

He heard Vass at his side. 'Let's split this scene, Lee.'

Lee Boyle raised his face, looked at Rudy. 'Maybe he buried her some place. Maybe it was like that. Killed her, dug a hole.'

'Come on, Lee. This guy's done nothing. Look at him, for Christ's sake.'

'Fucking right I've done nothing,' Goba said. He was hunched among his gnomes and leprechauns, rubbing his rib area and looking fat and pathetic. Spit flecked the corners of his slack lips.

Vass said, 'Come on. We'll go back to the truck. Check out this last address.'

Boyle walked to where Goba crouched and stood over him. 'I'm not crossing you off my list, Goba. Understand that. You're still a candidate.'

'I see you back here, it's shotgun time,' Goba said. 'No questions asked. I blast at the first sign of the whites of your goddam eyes.'

'Yeah yeah.'

'I'm fucking serious, fella,' Goba said. 'A twelve-gauge right in the breadbasket.'

Boyle threw the car keys away among the plaster figures, went to the truck and climbed in on the passenger side.

From his shirt pocket he removed the baggie, laid a tiny mound of crank on the back of his thumb and tried to keep his hand still as he inclined his face toward it. He closed one nostril with the tip of a forefinger and snorted up the other, then repeated this with the second nostril. The crystal hit his throat like a rasp of buckshot and his eyes smarted and he tilted his face back and waited for the familiar acceleration, the quick-quick tango of his heart.

18

EVE LASSITER LEANED TOWARD THE GUY IN THE CAR. HE WAS middle-aged, paunchy, looked respectable. He could have been a store clerk. You could imagine him ringing up your haberdashery items on an old-fashioned cash register in a room smelling of sawdust and kerosene. She saw herself through his eyes, thigh-length boots and a criminally short skirt and her nipples visible through her blouse.

'All aboard for the razzmatazz express, sweetie,' he said.

'Sorry. I'm waiting for somebody,' she said.

'Your waiting days are over, sweet thing. Get in.'

'Not tonight, honey,' she said.

'You just out here flashing your ass for the good of your health?'

'I told you. I'm waiting for somebody.'

'This could be construed as false advertising, bitch.' The guy flipped her a finger and drove his car down the block. Eve turned, strolled along the sidewalk. That was the third approach she'd rebuffed so far.

The smell of reefer was strong in the close night air.

Twenty or so girls walked up and down under the street lights. Kids. Difficult to tell their age. They wore heavy make-up, smoked dope, some huddled around crack pipes, some sharing joints. A couple of these kids looked like basket cases, undernourished. A few older professionals hung together away from the dopers. Eve found the situation depressing. The drugs, the cracked sidewalks, lives casually wasted.

On the next block, where the male hustlers congregated, she saw Joshua Gold beneath a street lamp. There was segregation at work here. Females on one stretch, guys on the other. Gold wasn't looking at her.

She walked to the other corner. Ed Duff's car was parked some way down the block. He was a shadow behind the wheel.

She wished it was Greg in the car instead. He was pow-wowing with the chief, he'd said. Even if he hadn't been, would he have provided personal back-up anyway? You could hardly expect that of him. First, he was *Lieutenant* Samsa, and he couldn't be asked to perform such a dogsbody function, even though he'd generously gone out of his way for her in the past because he felt some touching custodial thing toward her, which caused some minor gossip in the department and a few snide remarks about favoritism. Second, he'd been acting weird all day, understandable in the context of his wife's death. But still, she'd never seen him quite so *uninterested* before. That glazed look. That sense of something smoldering inside him. The way he'd exploded briefly at her in the car.

Not quite right, Greg. Not in keeping with yourself.

She found herself wondering when he'd last been laid. You didn't have to read between the lines to get the picture that Harriet, who'd lived sealed off from the world, God knows where, hadn't been sexually active. *Maybe for years*, Eve thought.

I want to get him into bed. I want to make love to him.
She was tired of self-centered bar-stool cowboys with
great pecs. She was weary of narcissists who were basically fucking themselves.

A limousine with tinted windows drifted past.
Somebody slumming. Somebody looking for a little sleazy
action on the wrong side of the tracks.

She gazed toward Gold, who turned his face in her
direction and made an almost imperceptible shrugging
movement. She'd pressured him into coming down here to
look for the young man he'd failed to describe. The last
person known to have seen Anthony Leeson alive. His
possible killer.

She looked at her watch. Three hours had passed.
Maybe it was time to call it a night. But she didn't like to
think she might miss anything.

Gold was walking away now, drifting along the sidewalk. He turned a corner. She wondered if he'd just
decided to blow the whole thing off. She moved after him,
caught up with him in an alley.

'Taking a break, Joshua?'

He stuck his hands in his pockets and leaned against a
wall. 'This is like a *total* waste of time. This kid Leeson
picked up might just have been passing through. Anyhow,
I'm not really in the mood for being down here. It's a
major bummer.'

'I'm real sorry it's such a drag for you, Joshua. But I
want you to stay down here with me.'

'I assume I can't refuse?'

'I might take a very dim view of a refusal,' she said.

He pushed himself off the wall. 'Okay. I wouldn't want
to be an unco-operative citizen, would I? It might make
me look more a suspect than you already think I am.'

'Did I say you're a suspect?' she asked.

'Some things you don't have to say out loud, Detective.'

140

Gold frowned. 'A question for you: am I going to need a lawyer somewhere down the line?'

'You're asking me to predict the future,' she said. 'That's not my line of expertise.'

'Look at me, Detective. Take a good long look at me. Now tell me I resemble the kind of guy who'd slash *anybody* to death.'

'Killers come in all shapes and sizes, Josh.'

'God in *heaven*. I did not murder Anthony Leeson.'

'I don't recall ever saying you did.'

'You know, you have a knack of saying things that don't match the expression on your face. You must play a very mean hand of poker.'

'Sometimes I play mean regardless of the game.'

'I bet you do.'

They walked together to the corner of the alley, where Joshua Gold stopped and snapped his thumb against his index finger. He laughed suddenly in an excited way. 'I just remembered something.'

'What?'

'Your lieutenant. What's he called? Samson?'

'What about him?'

'It's probably nothing,' Gold said.

'Tell me anyway.'

'Oh, gladly, gladly,' Gold said, and laughed again.

19

SHE LAY ON THE GRASS, HER FACE AND LEGS COVERED WITH
flecks of dried mud and streaks of black dirt. Her position
was fetal, short skirt drawn up to her thighs, panties white
and lacy and discolored. Samsa hunched down beside her.
Make her go away. He'd stepped inside a hinterland he
didn't recognize, a place where laws didn't apply, logic
had no role.

The little man called Dr Lewis Dice, struggling against
hysteria, stood a few feet away alongside Al Brodsky.
He'd been out walking with his Ziploc bags, looking for
samples. *Ziploc bags*, Samsa thought. *Samples of what?*
He wondered how any of this fitted into the scheme of
things, or if there even was such a scheme. Or if the world
was just altogether random and a person's history nothing
more than a series of accidental occurrences.

A half-dozen uniformed cops prowled the area, direct-
ing flashlights into the tangled bushes where Dice said
he'd discovered the body. A couple of portable lamps had
been rigged up, but they failed to penetrate the sheer dark
secrecy of the thickets. Beyond the lamps, half hidden in

shadow, stood a small gathering of observers attracted to the field by the sound of sirens and the lights. They were silent and watchful. This was better than TV. It was live, unfolding in front of their eyes. Why didn't they just go the fuck home?

Samsa was having a problem swallowing. His hands sweated, his shirt stuck to his skin. He needed air, but there was none to breathe.

You need more than air. You need salvation.

Brodsky came forward, loomed over the corpse. 'Broken neck,' he said. 'And look. I'd say a rodent got at her fingertips.'

The girl's head hung at the kind of angle you never saw on the living. If you raised her face up in your hands, even with the greatest care, it would loll from side to side. Samsa was immersed in feelings he couldn't quantify, couldn't differentiate – a terrifying sadness, a murmur of panic, imminent danger. Faded mascara tracks, zigzagged by rainfall, lined her cheeks. Her little mouth was closed in a kind of pout, and her eyes, mercifully, were shut. He wanted to draw her skirt down, cover the underwear, but he couldn't bring himself to touch her. It was the very last thing he could do.

Brodsky kneeled beside Samsa and spoke quietly. 'There's bruising round the neck.'

Samsa hadn't noticed this. Particulars escaped him. Details he had no eye for. He remembered the contusion on his own shoulder and laid a hand against it, covering it, as if he were afraid that somebody might see it, despite the sports coat and shirt he wore.

He turned to look up at Dice. 'How did you come to find her?'

The discovery of the corpse had dismantled Dice. He was shocked, even though death was an old acquaintance. He related the sequence of events to Samsa, a tale that

143

included a dead swallow, taxidermy, air rifles, altogether incoherent and surreal. But the whole night was surreal: the portable lamps, the mention of Ziploc bags, the creaking noises of cops parting shrubbery and the ghouls watching from the shadows.

And the girl. Above all else.

Samsa glanced at the fingertips on her left hand. Bitten, gnawed. He got to his feet. His legs were stiff. 'You collect dead birds?'

'I do a little taxidermy, you see,' Dice said.

Samsa exchanged a glance with Al Brodsky. 'You stuff *birds*, Dr Dice?'

'Not just birds,' Dice said. 'Snakes. Cats.'

'And this is what, like a hobby?'

Dice said, 'More than a hobby.'

'Had you ever seen this girl before?' It was the kind of question he felt obliged to ask. A cop's question. Let's establish a few things for the record. Let's stake out certain parameters. This is the way the business of homicide is conducted. And I'm all business, Dice. I'm Lieutenant Samsa.

'No, never. How could anyone do . . .' Lewis Dice left his question unfinished.

Bad things happen, Samsa thought. *Would that answer you, Doctor?* No, because it didn't go far enough into the rotted infrastructure of the human heart. The things people do to one another. He remembered suddenly a homicide some fifteen years ago, when a man called J. J. Coleman had stabbed his wife, and then butchered her into pieces small enough to fit inside shoeboxes, which he had sent by special delivery to addresses picked at random from phone directories. Strangers opened the boxes, wondering maybe if they'd won some kind of free gift from a department store or a mail-order house.

Only to find otherwise.

Samsa looked at the girl again, wished he hadn't. He wished for a lot of things: to walk away from here, to travel back down through the crooked passageways of time all the way to last night where he might choose a different turning, to go home and lock the door and draw the curtains and lie down and sleep for ever and never dream.

He stared at Dice's pink face. Taxidermy. He thought of the dead girl filled with embalming fluids and laid out in a coffin. He imagined parents, sisters, brothers. Heartache and anguish, wreckage.

Dice was talking about a rat he'd seen come out of the bushes. Samsa tried to concentrate, but his mind was scattered and circuits were jammed.

'So you found the body and reported it at once?'

Dice said, 'I live just over there,' and he pointed toward the lights of Chackstone. 'I ran all the way back to my house to call.'

Samsa turned and looked beyond the lamps across the great field. He felt unsteady. *How long did you think she'd lie here undiscovered? For eternity? Her bones found a hundred years from now? But you knew she'd be found sooner or later. You were waiting, in a state of fearful suspension, for it to happen. You just didn't expect it this soon, did you?*

He saw the faint outline of the big tree in the distance, then he walked a few yards away from Dice. Brodsky followed him.

'You okay, Greg?' Brodsky asked.

'I'm hot.'

Brodsky sighed. 'So much for a quiet evening's drinking and shooting the bull.'

Samsa smiled in a strained way. He tried to imagine how his expression looked to Al Brodsky. He guessed weak, unconvincing.

'I wonder if she was killed here,' Brodsky said. 'Or if it happened someplace else and she was dumped in these bushes. I don't see any tire tracks.'

Tire tracks, Samsa thought. *Go back across the field, Al, and you'll find tracks that reach from the blacktop as far as that goddam tree.*

Brodsky was gazing down at the ground. 'But we'll find footprints all right,' he said. 'Place like this, we'll probably find more than we need. What I hear is kids come out here with rifles trampling all over the joint. And junkies. Also teenagers with kegs of beer. Party animals.'

He gazed across the property. Samsa thought he could hear things click into place in Brodsky's mind. Before the chief had the chance to state what he was thinking, Samsa said, 'Over there's where I came off the road last night. Straight into that tree.'

Brodsky said, 'I *knew* there was something about this place at the back of my mind.' He took a piece of chewing gum from his pocket and stuck it in his mouth.

'I wasn't in the right frame of mind to notice much of anything at the time,' Samsa said. Make light of this. File it under unhappy coincidence. 'There could have been a whole gang of killers dumping bodies all over the place and I wouldn't have noticed a damn thing.'

Brodsky laid a hand on Samsa's shoulder and squeezed it in a manner that was both friendly and concerned. 'I guess not,' he said. 'You're just lucky you didn't do yourself some serious damage.'

'Lucky is right,' Samsa said.

Brodsky glanced at Dice, several yards away. 'What do you make of our embalmer?'

'Eccentric at least,' Samsa said.

'But no more than that.'

Samsa shrugged. 'I don't know, Al.'

Brodsky looked in the direction of the dead girl. Lamps

146

illuminated her in a cruel way. 'Christ, she's so *young*. What do you think? Fourteen? Fifteen? And the way she's dressed – it doesn't leave a whole lot to the imagination, does it? You think she was hooking, picked up the wrong guy?'

'It's a possibility,' Samsa said. He ran a finger under his collar. He felt like some fluffy whipped-up concoction melting.

What have I done to my life?

It was easy to fabricate excuses: I was thinking of my daughter and how the truth would affect her. I was thinking of the department's reputation.

Bullshit.

You were only thinking of saving Gregory Samsa's ass, except you didn't think it through too well, did you?

Brodsky said, 'Let's play this. Some weirdo picks her up. He breaks her neck, wonders where he's going to stash the body, thinks this is the perfect place. So he drives here, parks his car somewhere up on the road, carries her across the field. Which pretty much rules out Dice, I guess. He doesn't look like he can carry anything heavier than a dead bird in a plastic bag.'

'On the other hand, she might have been dragged,' Samsa said. 'The mud on her clothes and legs could be consistent with dragging.' What was he saying? He realized, with something of a painful jolt, that he didn't *want* to rule out Dice so easily. In some subterranean aspect of himself, some corner he was ashamed to discover, he wanted Dice to be a suspect. But Brodsky was right. If the girl was carried across the field, or even dragged, Dice didn't seem a likely candidate. *What is happening to me, for Christ's sake?*

Brodsky said, 'Let's walk a few yards, Greg. I want a little privacy.'

Samsa strolled through the grass after the chief. He had the feeling of being poised on a needle. A little privacy. What did Brodsky have to say that required privacy? They moved about twenty yards beyond the lamps and Brodsky stopped, took the chewing gum from his mouth and slung it away.

'I know it's basically Charlie Bird's territory out here, Greg, but sometimes I have to think beyond zonal parameters. Social Services and Child Welfare and the good folks of our local press are always griping about how little we do about these kids. They claim we just look the other way when anyone mentions child prostitution. Turn a blind eye, sweep it under the rug, et cetera, which is only a perceived truth. We round them up every now and then, but what good does it do? They get rapped on the knuckles and they walk. A few go to juvey. The rest are just tossed out of court.'

Brodsky was silent. Samsa waited, conscious of his own shallow breathing.

'What I'm trying to say is I think it might be appropriate if you took this one yourself, Greg.'

Samsa closed his eyes for a moment. He wondered if he swayed just a little. 'Appropriate? How?'

'If this kid was hooking, and the head homicide honcho is assigned to the case, I can tell you, without fear of contradiction, that it's going to go down pretty damn well in certain quarters. It shows a caring face. We're not assigning your average homicide hack, we're putting the Man himself in charge. We're not sweeping this one under any rug. We're giving it top billing.'

Samsa thought about things being swept under rugs. Secrets. Lies. Terrors. He couldn't do it, didn't have whatever skills it took for this masquerade Brodsky was unwittingly suggesting. He'd say something wrong, make a slip, damn himself somehow.

'Well?' Brodsky asked. 'Give me some feedback here, Greg.'

Samsa stared across the property. He remembered how rain had roared. He remembered the way his body had been stooped as he moved through the long grass.

He remembered the weight of death most of all.

'Charlie Bird isn't going to like it,' he said.

Brodsky said, 'I don't give a shit what Charlie Bird likes. I'm thinking of the department as a whole.'

'This isn't a political campaign, Al.'

'Don't talk political campaign to me,' Brodsky said. 'This isn't about politics.'

'PR then,' Samsa said.

'Beyond PR, Greg.'

'The department with heart.'

'What is wrong with you?' Brodsky asked. 'You know I don't give a fuck about PR. I'm thinking about this kid. There are whackos out there. Guys that don't think twice about wasting a hooker. If I put you in charge of the case, it's like sending a double-edged message. One, we treat all homicides with equal seriousness, whether it's a kid prostitute like this or the president of some goddam corporation. And two, we highlight the tragically real perils of the street.'

Brodsky had it down pat. The quickness of his brain, his agility in seizing upon a situation and exploring its opportunities. You had to admire it. Samsa felt mosquitoes buzz around his face and he swatted them away, but they kept coming back.

'And we score some easy brownie points,' he said.

'Look,' Brodsky said, 'if you don't want to take the fucking case, don't take it.'

'I didn't say that, Al.' He imagined Bird working this homicide, picking over details, sifting the ashes, reconstructing the crime. Bird wasn't smart. He was better than smart when it came to this kind of thing. He was dogged. He couldn't be moved. He caught a whiff and tracked it like a demented hound and pursued it all the way to the gates of hell if need be.

'You never know,' Brodsky said. 'You could even be saving some other kid from ending up like the one here.'

Samsa heard movement and looked back at the crime scene. A photographer had arrived, and so had a couple of guys from the coroner's office. They were kneeling, examining the body. Usually they were chirpy, off-hand, just another stiff, so what. Tonight they were solemn. A flashlight popped and the corpse was captured on film for a new homicide folder. 'I'll just get this from another couple of angles and I'm outta here.' *Pop pop*.

The lights stung Samsa's eyes. The girl was surrounded by retinal disturbances, small prancing glares.

Move. Hadn't he told her that? *Get up and I'll help you out of here. But only if you move. Just give me some goddam co-operation*. And then he'd placed his palms on either side of her face, as if he might somehow realign the broken neck, but her head slid from his damp grasp. He'd never forget that. That was one for his nightmare files.

He was struck by an absurdity. The girl was dead. The jackrabbit was still alive. *The rabbit was running around out there someplace*. Life was a series of cruelties and imbalances. One hapless moment and you're ruined, and there's no way back, no road to the high ground of redemption.

A girl dies in the rain.

You want to scream.

He heard Al Brodsky just behind him and, without turning to look, uncertain of whether he could face Al at all without giving something away, he said, 'I'll do it.'

'Good man,' Brodsky said.

I'll do it, Samsa thought. *For all the wrong reasons, I'll do it.*

And he imagined a killer, somebody who'd prowled the rainy dark with his burden, a murderous stranger it was his job to track down and apprehend.

20

LEE BOYLE SAT IN THE PASSENGER SEAT OF RUDY VASS'S PICK-up, his body hunched a little way forward. He was studying the house across the street. Number 1900 Devine, nice two-story home in a good suburb. Trim lawn, flowers around the porch. A flagpole even. The American Way. But no sign of any Chrysler, 92K something something something.

Where was it? Tucked at the back of the house, hidden from the attention of vandals that might stray through a prosperous suburb at dark? Or was there a garage he hadn't noticed? A beige Chevy in the driveway was the only vehicle he could see.

'So what do we do?' Vass said. 'Wait here until this guy shows up with the car?'

Boyle didn't answer. He hadn't really heard Rudy's question. He was shivery, set apart from the humidity of the night inside his own little cell of frost. He chewed on the soft tissue around the ulcer in his mouth.

With great patience, Rudy Vass said, 'He could be a traveling salesman for all we know. Maybe he's gone on a trip or something. What I'm saying, we could be waiting here a long time.'

Lee Boyle lit a cigarette. He looked at the front windows of the house. The only light he saw was one that burned in the downstairs hall. He stared at the Chevy for a time, thinking of the ludicrous struggle with Silas Goba, the empty trunk, the books of drapery samples. The bad feeling he'd had about Almond hadn't gone away. If anything it was more concentrated now, a calcified deposit that had formed in his brain. He was uptight, gripped by wild notions, tidal anxieties.

Vass said, 'The longer we sit here the more chance of some neighbor calling the cops. Next thing you know, a cruiser pulls up and we're talking to some hard-ass cop who wants to know why we're hanging out on this well-heeled street.'

Boyle said nothing. Rudy was getting on his nerves somewhat. A small patronizing note had crept into his voice, and Boyle wasn't pleased with it.

'We should call it quits for the night, come back again in the morning. I'd be happy to drive you home.'

Boyle didn't want to go home yet. He told Vass so.

'Lee, you can strain friendships, you know. You can ask too much of a person at times.'

'Any time you want to let me out, just say the word.'

'I'm only pointing to a fact,' Vass said. 'I don't remember signing on as your chauffeur. You need some sleep anyhow. The way you acted with that guy Goba. I mean, *a body in a trunk?* Let's get a little reality into the situation.'

Boyle looked at Vass's face, the skin yellow under the street lights. He had the appearance of a man in the grip of a terrible disease. 'Suddenly you know something about reality, huh? What are you telling me? I'm suffering from sleep deprivation and imagining things?'

Vass tugged his little goatee. 'All I know is I'm sitting in this truck twiddling my thumbs on account of you having some great burning need to track down this bimbo.'

Boyle dropped his cigarette on the floor, crushed it. 'Say that again.'

'I take it back, okay? I take it back.'

Boyle said, 'You called her a bimbo—'

'I also retracted, Lee. Okay? I happen to be weary. The shit I do for you. Sometimes I wonder, am I weak? Is this a dependency thing I have? Or is it because I don't want to get on the wrong side of you because secretly you kind of scare me? Do I need your approval? What the fuck is it?'

'I don't want to sit here and dissect relationships,' Boyle said. 'If I wanted that I'd be sitting in an art house watching a French movie.'

Vass was quiet for a while. 'Let it go. Forget the girl, blow town for a while, take a trip, straighten out a few things in your life. That way the girl's out of your system, and you're out of Plumm's clutches.'

'I can't get out of Plumm's clutches,' Boyle said. 'He's like an octopus.'

'You just walk down to the bus station and buy a ticket to Nowheresburg.'

'Plumm's got people watching me.' Boyle took the baggie out of his shirt pocket and snorted, fighting back a need to sneeze. The speed zigzagged to his brain after a fiery detour around his heart. He imagined he could see it traveling in his bloodstream, shooting little trails of harsh white flak.

Vass looked doubtful. 'He can't have you under observation *all* the time, Lee. It's just not possible.'

'It's a feeling I get,' Boyle said.

'You know where that feeling comes from? Out that goddam bag you carry around.'

Boyle ignored this. He didn't need Rudy's disapproval. He didn't need criticism. He was listening to the hue and cry of his pulses. He was hearing Almond call out to him from a deep dark place. *Come get me, Lee. Come find me.*

Vass said, 'Know what I really think? You got a taste for this kid. You fucked her, and you liked it. Did you fuck her, Lee?'

'She's strictly business. That's all. I can't just abandon her.'

'Who abandoned who in this case? I mean, what are we *talking* about here? You're not thinking straight, Lee.'

'Don't tell me how I'm thinking, Rudy.' Boyle thought, *I've had about enough of this.* He grabbed Rudy by the collar of his denim jacket and dragged his face forward a few inches. 'Don't *ever* tell me how or what I'm thinking. You don't have some kind of probe that goes inside my skull.'

'Lee,' Vass said. 'Let go. Don't get into this.'

Boyle saw it in the depths of Rudy Vass's eyes, a judgemental quality. Vass was silently accusing him for the actions of his life. The girl, the dope, everything.

Vass sighed long and deep. 'Take your hand away.'

'You make me.'

'You're in this contrary mood I don't like.'

'I don't give a fuck what you like. The hand stays.'

'So what do we do? Sit here all night like this? This is childish. I don't want trouble with you, Lee. Of all people. I'm about the only friend you got, man. Keep that in mind.'

'I've got scores of friends,' Boyle said.

'Name one,' Vass said.

'You're trying to put me on the spot. I can see straight through you, Rudy. You want to be completely indispensable in my life; Lee Boyle's only buddy. I know him from way back, U of Penn. We hit it off from the start, we're

155

fucking inseparable, we're like *that*, twins. You're possessive, Vass.'

'Christ's sake,' Vass said. 'I can't hack this. You're gonezoid.'

Boyle tugged harder on the collar. Anger *pumped* in his blood. He resented Rudy's self-righteousness. Who did Vass think he was kidding, coming off like he was Mr Twelve-Step, certifiably straight? 'You're up there with your halo on and you're looking down at me and I don't approve of that, Rudy.'

'It's not like that, Lee.'

'It sounds exactly like that to me,' Boyle said. He clicked the glove compartment open, and a tiny light bulb came on and flickered meekly. The gun lay under some documents – vehicle registration papers. He pulled it out, a Colt Government model 38, and turned it over in his hand.

'Just put the gun back, Lee.'

Boyle pushed the barrel into Rudy Vass's cheek. 'You think I'd shoot my one and only friend?'

'This is a rotten feeling, Lee.' Little slicks of sweat ran over Rudy Vass's eyelids.

'I can hear your heartbeat,' Boyle said.

'Loud, aintit,' Vass said. 'So put the gun back and let's get on with our lives and we'll forget all about this little game you're playing. You proved you can scare me, okay?'

Boyle thought of life and death, fragile balances, the way things were poised so very delicately. He thought about pulling the trigger, blasting Rudy's face. Imagining it, the ferocious kick in his fist, Rudy's head all over the place like a pizza splashed against a wall. He lowered the weapon slowly, tossed it back inside the glove compartment, laughed for a time, then couldn't remember why he was laughing. The sound dried and faded in his throat, but he could still hear an echo of it.

'I don't fucking *believe* you pulled a gun on me,' Vass said. 'That's it. I'm out of here. This is the end of the line for me.'

He started the pick-up. Boyle had a moment of indecision. He knew Vass was correct on one level: waiting here could turn out to be pointless, and some snoop neighbor was likely to call the cops. At the same time he was reluctant to leave, because maybe the key to Almond was somewhere in that house across the way. Maybe the solution was concealed beyond that porch, that front door. He listened to the whine of the engine, closed his eyes, felt the lids flicker, little tics, small muscular spasms.

'I don't give a shit, man. But are you coming, or you hanging out here?' Vass asked.

Boyle opened his eyes, looked at 1900 Devine. The house appeared to shimmer in his vision. The light burning downstairs was fragmented, casting pale white splinters. He imagined a bulb exploding and felt shards of flying glass in his scalp like small barbed airborne insects.

'I'm going,' Vass said, and he slipped the truck into gear. It rolled past the house and Boyle turned once to look back. I ought to stay. I ought to wait. He was aware of the neighborhood changing, the freeway approaching, and then Vass was driving down the access road. Boyle saw the lights of downtown in the distance. He had the feeling he'd left something of himself behind on Devine. Something he ought to go back and recover.

He looked at Vass, whose face was stern.

'Pull over, Rudy.'

'Pull over? On the freeway?'

'I don't care where. Just drop me.'

Vass said fuck, he wasn't going to stop on the freeway. He came off at the next exit, and Boyle opened the passenger door and stepped down onto the street outside a twenty-four-hour video store. 'Go home, Rudy,' he said.

'Is that what you want? Me to leave you here without wheels?'

'That's what I want,' Boyle said.

'You're sure?'

Boyle looked along the sidewalk and then up at Vass in the cab. 'I'm sure.'

Vass seemed relieved. He needed a break from Boyle's company. 'Whatever you say, Lee. Whatever you say.'

Boyle slammed the door shut, *good fucking riddance*, slapped a hand against the panel and watched the pick-up disappear at the end of the street. He walked to the window of the video store and gazed through glass at the empty aisles, the glossy displays and posters advertising moronic movies.

The girl at the cash register was reading a magazine under fluorescent light and Boyle thought, *Almond, this is Almond*, and he pressed his face to the pane with his palms flattened against the glass and his expectations soaring into flight, but then the girl turned her face to one side and he saw he was mistaken, he'd forced a resemblance on a total stranger, only the black hair was similar, nothing else. He watched her for a time anyway, until she began to throb and brighten in his vision, as if she were on the point of combustion.

21

SAMSA CHECKED HIS WATCH: 1 A.M. HE FILLED A WAX CUP with water from the cooler and gulped it. The basement rooms were stuffy, unbearable. From his position at the cooler he could see through an open door into another room, and beyond that another room, and beyond that yet another. It was like an infinity of reflections in angled mirrors. He imagined himself trapped in endless boxes, dwindling in size the further he looked.

He crumpled the cup and dumped it just as Brodsky appeared. Billy Fogue, white shirtsleeves hanging loose, stood behind Al. His hairless head glistened. Here and there other cops wandered back and forth or worked the phones. The graveyard shift, energized by a fresh homicide.

Al Brodsky said, 'Fogue got a fingerprint match through the computer.'

Fogue said, 'The girl was one Cecily Suarez, reported missing by her parents in Denver. Seems she made running away from home something of a habit. She was thirteen years of age.'

159

Thirteen, Samsa thought.

Christ. One-three.

He felt the clamminess of the rooms invade his heart. Cecily Suarez. She'd told him her name was Almond. Two years younger than Darcy, for God's sake. He ran a hand across his face. He was thinking of Zane the coroner, the slab in the morgue where the girl had lain, Zane examining the dead flesh. The cause of death was easy for Zane, who'd seen every kind of fatality. The pattern of bruising appeared to be consistent with the use of a blunt instrument of some kind, and he'd studied what he referred to as 'areas of ecchymosis'.

A blunt instrument, Brodsky had said. *Like what? A rubber hose? A baseball bat? A karate chop?*

Zane, a skinflint with loose opinions and facile conclusions, had simply said, *People just don't realize how easy it is to break a neck.*

The girl had tracks on her arms. Zane had peered at them closely, but with a certain clinical indifference. *I wouldn't say she was a heavy user of a needle. I think we'll find out more about her drug habits when we've examined her nasal passages.* Samsa thought of instruments: steel scalpels, probes, the hard awful tools of Zane's trade.

She's been dead twenty-four hours, I'd say. Somewhere between ten and eleven last night.

Billy Fogue said, 'Let me add this news flash. Our girl was picked up a month ago on a streetwalking charge, fingerprinted and kept overnight in juvenile hall, then released on the order of some bleeding-heart social worker because she promised she'd take the next bus all the way home to Denver. She even bought a one-way ticket to Denver, which convinced the dickhead do-gooder that the contrite young Cecily had good intentions. Cunning little number. Did Cecily, aka

160

Almond, catch the bus? Oh, yeah, sure she did.'

Samsa thought, *I carried her through the rain, I hefted her wet body on my shoulder and carried her across that field, and even though she weighed practically nothing in life, in death she was heavy.* He shoved the memory away like indigestible food, but it kept coming back, a regurgitation of the slog, the mud, the grass, the jagged highs of panic. He'd thought of burying her, but he didn't have the implements and he didn't have the time, all he'd wanted was to hide her and get out of that field quickly, a vanishing act, oblivion. But there were no guarantees of oblivion.

No guarantees of anything. Not now.

Samsa stared into the middle distance, as if he were trying to distort the focus of his eyesight.

'Rebb is on his way,' Brodsky said. He held a hand in front of Samsa's face and clicked his thumb and middle finger together. 'Are you with us, Greg? You remember Stephen Rebb? Long-time vice cop?'

Samsa said, 'Sorry, I was thinking.'

Brodsky asked, 'Anything you want to share?'

Samsa shook his head. 'Not yet.'

'Give us a holler when you do, Lew Tenant,' Fogue remarked cheerfully, plucking a cheroot from his shirt pocket and then, glancing at Brodsky, thought better of lighting it while the chief was around.

Samsa remembered the thickets, the way he'd placed the girl among them, how he'd protected his hands from barbs by tugging the sleeves of his jacket down over his fingers. He remembered the wild rain slashing at his face. He remembered her on the coroner's slab, and how very young she'd seemed, with all the life gone out of her and the make-up washed from her face. Young and very small and soft. A life unlived, an empty bedroom in a house in Denver. Probably posters thumbtacked to a wall. Maybe a secret diary stashed under a loose floorboard. The relics of a person.

Like Harriet's clothing hanging in closets.

He turned his face as Stephen Rebb came into the room.

Rebb said, 'Whatcha got for me?'

Brodsky said, 'A dead girl.'

Rebb was a walking offense, a tall cadaverous man with sunken cheeks and dyed crow-black hair and a serious case of body odor. He'd worked so long in the world of vice it was as if he'd decided that the smells of dark streets and illegal massage parlors and humid whorehouses were preferable to basic hygiene. Dandruff littered the collar of his black jacket and there was always dirt under his fingernails, which he picked at from time to time with a nail file. He was in search of authenticity with a capital A, Samsa sometimes thought. The underworld man with an almost encyclopedic knowledge of the city's illicit flesh trade. You wouldn't want Rebb in your home. It was hard enough to accept him around the office.

Rebb asked, 'How old?'

'Thirteen,' Billy Fogue said.

'Streetwalker?'

'You wouldn't be here at one in the morning if she was a goddam jaywalker, Rebb,' Brodsky said, with a measure of impatience and distaste.

'So I'm not the best-loved character in the department. I accept that role willingly,' Rebb said. He smiled, showing his crooked upper teeth. He courted unpopularity, wanted to be seen as a night creature, a sleazy outsider who operated on the far margins of the law. 'The way I see it, I don't get paid for my charm. I get paid because I'm the only sucker you got who knows what shit really smells like down at street level.'

Samsa said, 'We all admire your talents, Steve.'

Rebb came close to Samsa, leaving a little cheesy cloud

of halitosis in the air. 'I like to be appreciated, Lieutenant. So who's the dead babe?'

The dead babe. Rebb had a way of putting things.

Samsa told him.

Rebb, tapping the side of his nose, made whirring sounds like those of a computer scanning a hard disc. 'She's coming into view . . . yeah . . . yeah . . .'

'Forget the sound effects and cut to the goddam chase,' Brodsky said.

Rebb said. 'She worked for a guy called . . . *got it*, real small-time hustler, name of Lee Boyle. Odd case. Wealthy background – father rich as fucking old John D. – disowned by family, drifted downhill. Drugs, the usual. Excuse me if I don't find it altogether an all-American tragedy, because this Boyle isn't a nice guy.'

'Somebody check Boyle's sheet,' Samsa said.

Fogue said, 'Only too happy to oblige,' and left the room.

Rebb asked, 'How did the kid get it anyway?'

Brodsky told him.

Rebb said, 'Busted neck, huh? I think it's a risk-type thing these lowlifers actually like. Life on the sordid edge. The next trick may be your last, honey. The next blow job might be HIV-pos, the next fuck might have a short-handled ax in the glovebox.'

Samsa said, 'You know Boyle?'

'I squeezed him once or twice for the hell of it. You got to apply some pressure on these guys now and then just to keep them in line. He's strictly from Peanuts Street. Smart, but missing the essential nuts and bolts that differentiate a regular guy from a slimeball. He used to run a girl called Nancy, who took a hike. But Lee didn't take kindly to this. So he tracks Nancy down and kicks the shit out of her, and she goes to County with serious fractures and a face that won't look the same again. But, hey, does she

163

press charges? Does she point the finger at Lee? Fuck she does. I fell down an elevator shaft or I was hit by a god-dam car, bullshit stories. See, there's some real off-the-wall loyalty out there at times.'

'Could Boyle have killed Cecily Suarez?' Samsa asked. The question seemed to him to hang in the air a long time. But this is the way it works. The creation of diversions. He was building thoroughfares in his head with no master blueprint, trying to believe they might lead somewhere in the end. Somewhere away from him. He felt shriveled, and wondered if this was what fear and shame did to you. And he remembered his disappointment at dismissing Lew Dice as a suspect. He'd taken Dice aside, questioned him briefly, as if to make sure he could be discounted. The motions of a pointless inquiry. *I know you're inno-cent, Dice. But this is what I have to do. I am the lieutenant. This is expected of me. You don't know you're talking to a shell. You're just an involuntary participant in a drama.*

Tell me what it's like to stuff dead animals, Doc. But you couldn't jump from the fact that a guy had a bizarre hobby to the idea he might have killed a kid hooker. Not even in the real world could you make that leap.

Rebb said, 'Could Boyle have killed her? Depends. If the crystal's good and it's coming nice and regular, he's okay. Take away his pacifiers, who knows? Or maybe he shot up one time too many.'

'But it's a possibility,' Samsa said.

'So's the idea of me getting it on with Sharon Stone.' Rebb picked grime out of his fingernails with his nail file and, leaning into the light of a desk lamp, examined it studiously. 'So's life on Pluto.'

Samsa looked at Brodsky, who was gazing at Rebb as if the vice cop were a mutant life form spawned in the sewers under the city. Rebb stuck the nail file into his pocket just as Billy Fogue returned to the room carrying a printout.

'He's been a bad boy,' Fogue said.

'Let me see that,' Samsa said.

Fogue passed him the sheet, which Samsa scanned quickly.

LEE H. BOYLE SOCIAL SECURITY NUMBER 074-05-2515.

One count of grand theft auto, September 1992. Six-month sentence, County jail. Served ninety-seven days.

One count of aggravated assault, January 1993. Thirty-day sentence, County jail. Served thirty days.

One count of possession of forged credit cards, March 1993. One year probation.

One count of possession of amphetamine (9.4gms), November 1993. Voluntary psychiatric counseling for three-month period.

One count of sex with a minor, April 1996. Dismissed. Lack of evidence.

One count of aggravated assault, January 1997. Dismissed. Lack of evidence.

Samsa handed the sheet to Brodsky, who looked at it and said, 'It's penny-ante stuff generally.'

'Aggravated assault twice,' Samsa said. 'Maybe this time he just goes overboard. He crosses the line. Hits a little too hard. I wouldn't mind paying him a visit. You know where to find him, Rebb?'

'Not offhand. He doesn't stay long in one place. I can make a few calls, ask around.'

'Do it,' Samsa said. He thought about Darcy. He walked into his partitioned space and dialed his home number.

She answered on the first ring.

'I'm going to be very late,' he said.

'Is this business or another nocturnal voyage?'

'Business,' he said. 'Are you okay?'

'Sleepy,' she said.

'How was the date?'

'I wouldn't write a book about it. He took me to see an Italian movie because he knew I wanted to see it. Halfway through he fell asleep. "I don't like films where you have to read subtitles," he tells me.'

'You're too bright for him,' Samsa said. 'Listen, sweetheart. I've got to go.'

'Any idea of your ETA?'

'Not a clue,' he said. 'Make sure everything's locked up. Leave the downstairs light on.'

'Done that already.'

'I'll be home as soon as I can.'

'Oh, one last thing. Eve called. No message.'

He blew a kiss down the line. He thought of her in the empty house as he replaced the handset. The empty whispering house.

He looked at Rebb through the open doorway. Rebb was talking into a phone, his voice hard and aggressive. 'Yeah, you say you don't know where Boyle lives, asshole, but maybe I don't believe you. Maybe my instincts are telling me something else. And maybe I just happen to remember those scuzzy videos you're selling out the back of your goddam shop . . . Yeah, the ones with women and fucking camels, dufus, the Egyptian filth that comes to you straight outta Cairo . . .'

Samsa stepped away from his desk and felt suddenly light-headed, thinking of going out into the darkness and looking for a stranger called Lee H. Boyle and wondering if a murder rap could be pinned on him. Where was all this leading him except deeper and deeper into a night-world that had no basis in any reality he'd ever known

166

before? Would his life always be like this now? He saw himself carrying the burden of an enormous lie, an evasion that hummed inside him constantly, like the vibrations of a machine. He suddenly remembered the fungus that had been growing behind the radiator and he wondered if it thrived still, if it was spreading, changing shape as it did so.

22

EVERYTHING IN LIFE GETS TAKEN AWAY SOONER OR LATER.

Your Porsche. Your inheritance from Daddy.

And your girl vanishes.

You don't know where. You don't know why. But a whispery little voice in your head keeps telling you it's bad.

Lee Boyle walked under street lights, aware of the webby effects they created. He passed a half-built apartment complex sealed by boards and wire fences. A large cat thumped past. He wanted to get his gun and blast the furry thing into bits and bloody pieces and see its entrails hang on the wire, brain blitzed and strewn around. But the death of a cat wouldn't cut what he was feeling any more than the act of pressing a Colt into Rudy's face had done – this surging anger followed by weird moments of detachment, then anger again. Then something he couldn't identify, loss maybe, a sense of amputation.

He realized he was in an unfamiliar neighborhood. Old brownstone houses with broken-down stoops and darkened windows and a corner grocery steel-shuttered for the night. He heard the sound of a couple squabbling from an upstairs apartment. All about him the night seemed suspended in a troublesome way, as if the darkness were held aloft on precarious stilts.

I need wheels, he thought. He was weary of walking. Wheels would boost him. He wasn't fussy; he'd take the first unlocked car he found. There was always somebody careless, even in a neighborhood like this. You could bet your ass on it. He moved along the sidewalk, checking the handles of parked cars.

Eventually he came across an old black Pontiac with leprous rust spots. The door hadn't been locked. He slid behind the wheel. The upholstery was stripped down to basic sponge. The interior smelled of sour milk. Toys littered the floor. A GI Joe figure, a broken-headed Barbie, an eyeless dinosaur with the stuffing coming out. The kids that rode in this car were brutal to their toys. Little delinquents.

A brother and sister, he figured. Always at each other's throats.

Like the way he'd been with Monique, back when.

Monique – what a fucking *pretentious* name – Monique, you giggling twat, Daddy's little girl, his favorite. Sit on my knee, Monique. Aren't you pretty? Aren't you cute? Can you sing something for us? *Ask me to sing*, Boyle would say. *I know all the words of 'Dixie' and I'm only five*. And then, always rebuffed by Daddy, he'd appeal with his curly blond-haired drop-dead charm to his mother, a cowed woman of some social ambition, whose marriage to that sphincter of a human being named Hugh had pounded her into timidity and alcoholism. Hugh called her the Gin Queen. Sometimes just Queenie. Here comes Queenie. Doesn't she look a little unsteady, children?

Queenie was wasting away in some goddam drunk

clinic the last Lee Boyle had heard. Banished just like himself. Discarded, tossed aside. Hugh had a whole lot to answer for. Hugh damaged people.

Boyle peeled back black masking tape under the dash, exposed the wires and connected them. He'd done it a hundred times before. Straight or fucked-up, he knew what he was doing. Spark and sizzle. The motor rumbled. He drove to the end of the street, the boneshaker spluttering. And then he was back in familiar territory, Central, driving past City Hall and Patriot Park.

He turned down side streets, alleys, parked outside a doorway splattered with spray-painted graffiti. A sign above the door read, 'The Half-Moon'. Boyle went inside, nodded at the big bouncer in the charcoal *Hey-I'm-connected* silk suit and climbed a flight of stairs into a room with black walls. A dilatory jazz trio was taking liberties with 'Every Time You Say Goodbye'.

He walked to the bar, asked for a vodka, slammed it back, repeated the action. This takes the edge off. But it didn't, not really. What it did was deceive you into *thinking* it calmed your system. He lit a cigarette, hand trembling slightly, and surveyed the few customers who sat here and there at tables. No Almond, of course. He hadn't expected to see her anyway. He was beginning to wonder if he'd ever see her again. The thought panicked him. He placed the cigarette pack on the bar and stared at his handwriting.

Mrs Fodor. No.

Silas Goba. Question mark.

Gregory J. Samsa. Who knows?

The file on Samsa. Very thin indeed. Practically empty. House in that neighborhood suggested he was probably employed in something quite profitable: financial consultancy, accountancy, maybe an executive sales position. Income what? $60–70,000 range? More? You could only hazard guesses. *You don't even know Samsa's age, what he looks like. You don't know the first goddam thing about him.*

Boyle pushed the Camel pack back and forth with the tip of his finger. He ordered a third vodka, sipped it, smoked another cigarette and stood against the bar with his eyes shut.

The girl behind the bar, skinny with big hair and a skirt so short it would have caused cricked necks and traffic chaos on Central, leaned toward him. 'You say something, Lee?'

He opened his eyes. 'No,' he said.

'Talking to yourself, huh?'

'I guess I must've been, Kiki,' he said.

'You want to watch that kind of thing,' and she winked. 'They take you away for that, I hear. Padded rooms and such.'

Padded rooms.

He remembered padded rooms.

He remembered straitjacket nightmares where he was clamped to iron beds, and thugs dressed like male nurses sat on his chest and shot him with Dilaudid to bring him out of orbit.

They called it 'voluntary' treatment.

Yeah, I asked for it. Take me in, please.

The resident shrink, Lannigan, had stuck him in a treatment group where you got to sit around and discuss your 'addiction' with a bunch of fucking wasted losers for two hours every day. He wasn't ever going back to that sweatpit to listen to drained old dopers talking about how they'd bottomed-out, grizzled old farts who droned on about broken marriages and lost kids and ruined careers, and cried into Kleenexes or unintentionally pissed on their paper slippers.

He realized his face was sweating even if he was still

cold. His gold chain stuck to his neck. He wiped his skin with a paper napkin.

He looked at the girl and asked, 'You seen Almond around?'

'You're slipping, sweetie. You came in here and asked me that same question, oh, about twenty-four hours ago.'

'Did I? Premature senility.' He had no recollection of ever having come in here asking for Almond. All he remembered was the relentlessly driven way he'd traveled through the crazed hours of darkness and into the first pale-blue horrors of dawn trying to find her. The bars and clubs he'd zoomed through blended into one another like the elements of a long-lost memory.

'She hasn't shown up, I take it.'

'She will,' he said. 'I'm not worried.'

'Why worry,' Kiki said. 'That's my philosophy of life.'

'Positive thinking,' he replied.

'The only kind.'

He leaned across the bar toward her. He was desperate enough to play a shot in the dark. 'You meet a lot of people, Kiki. Does the name Gregory Samsa mean anything to you?'

She appeared to think for a time before she shook her head and said, 'I don't hear any bells, Lee. Sorry.'

'That's okay. No big deal.'

Samsa, he thought. *Who are you?*

He crumpled the cigarette pack.

Get with the program, Lee.

Take steps. Find out.

He left the Half-Moon, walked to the big Pontiac, fired it up. He drove toward the freeway, took the exit marked Skyville. He found the street, parked halfway down the block, cut the engine. Then he waited, didn't move, checked the area. He contemplated dipping inside the baggie just for a boost, but talked himself out of it. He still had some energy burning.

But the next crash was just around the corner.

He got out of the car and walked quietly to the place he wanted. There was still only the beige Chevy parked in the driveway. No garage. *No fucking garage.* What was this? Your basic home with the no-garage option? Save a few bucks, build one yourself later?

He lingered, feeling just a little cold now. A warning sign. Ignore it, keep going. Poor circulation, something, who gives a shit?

He listened to the neighborhood. The hum of freezers and air-conditioners, all the little clicks that regulated the civilized world. He reached the place where the driveway ended at a fenced backyard. A lamp was lit in an upstairs window, throwing enough light down for him to see that the area behind the house was all lawn.

No Chrysler here.

Suddenly he heard a girl sing from a place above. He couldn't make out the words, but the sound was quicksilver and lovely, and he listened to it with unexpected delight, possessed by the notion that the voice originated from no external source but a place inside himself. And he was reminded of the way life had been once upon a time: carefree, vibrant with rich possibilities, notions of a future. *You're going places, Lee—*

But the mountains were always just too high and the distractions too great, and after a time you got used to the troughs, you became an inhabitant of the gloomy valleys whose slopes were made out of scree you couldn't ever climb because it collapsed and crumbled the more you scratched at it.

This sweet voice. It transfixed him. *What soft incense hangs upon the boughs.*

He collided with a trash can and the lid came off and

173

rattled on the ground and spun to a standstill, and the singing ceased abruptly.

Lee Boyle holds his breath. He steps back in shadow. The invisible man.

The curtain at the lit upstairs window is parted slightly.

A girl's face appears.

The girl with the nightingale's voice.

Her face, half lit by a lamp behind it, is young and beautiful. He can't tell the color of her hair, the color of her eyes, he just has this impression of purity and perfection.

He watched the curtain fall back in place and then he turned and hurried away in the shadows, moving quickly along the sidewalk, the voice still echoing inside him and the vision printed on his brain.

What a divine young thing.

Ripe.

Primo.

23

SAMSA DIDN'T LIKE THE LOFT, THE HUGE UNFURNISHED SPACE, ceilings twenty feet high, the brilliant white glossy walls that reflected light from a series of recessed bulbs of various colors – pinks, oranges, mauves. He had a sense of being dwarfed, as if he were shedding inches, diminishing until finally nothing would be left of him except for a pile of clothing and a pair of shoes.

Fogue and Rebb circled the woman, who sat in the only chair in the room. She was unflustered by the cops' presence. She rolled a cigarette carefully, filling black paper with tobacco. She stuck the cigarette between her lips and leaned toward Fogue, anticipating a light, which he supplied with a parsimonious flick of his lighter. According to what Rebb had said in the car on the way over, this woman had a track record: prostitution, operating a house of ill-repute, a couple of dope misdemeanors. Like Boyle, she was somebody who didn't stay in any one place too long, and Rebb had tracked her through a series of increasingly threatening phonecalls to his network of night animals – a porn-flick merchant, a crack dealer, a guy who specialized in sending pictures of naked infants over the Internet.

'Fatima—' Rebb said.

'You're behind the times. I'm not calling myself that these days,' she said.

'Oh, beg your pardon,' Rebb said.

'Cassandra to you, Rebb.'

'Cassandra, huh.'

'Names are limiting, I find. You get one at birth you didn't ask for. Who says you have to keep it for the rest of your life?'

Rebb said, 'There's no law.'

'*Au contraire*, there are too many laws,' she said. 'We are drowning in laws. There's a fucking tidal wave of laws. Traffic. Vice. Drugs. Let's have some anarchy about the place, for Christ's sake. Let's tear down the structures before they choke us to death.' She stared across the room at Samsa. She had eyes too pale to be described as blue. They had a bleached quality. They might have been fashionable contact lenses with a slick marketing name – Arctic Dawn, Cobalt Innuendo.

'Who's your friend, Rebb?'

'This is Lieutenant Samsa. Excuse my manners.'

'A big wheel,' she said.

'He's the Man,' Rebb said.

'Hey, the Man,' she said to Samsa. 'Do I consider this like an honor?'

Samsa stepped forward a few paces. She blew a stream of smoke in his direction, her head tilted back a little. He noticed discarded black pantyhose under her chair.

'Take it any way you like,' he said.

'That's generally how I take things,' she said.

Rebb said, 'You got to understand, Lieutenant. Fatima here – excuse me, Cassandra – she's got this self-image of a free spirit. Back in the old days she'd have called herself

176

a hippy. I got other names for her, though. Whore comes charging to mind.'

'Tut-tut,' she said, pointing her cigarette at Rebb. She looked back at Samsa. 'You ought to demand a refund from whatever charm school you sent Rebb to.'

'Also a jester,' Rebb said.

Samsa said, 'Rebb's style doesn't include charm.'

She smiled and got up from her chair. Trailing smoke, she walked to a big powerful stereo set against the wall in the corner. She pressed a button and the room filled up with the frantic angry sound of rap. The speakers thudded. The walls shook. Cassandra lowered her head, shut her eyes, clicked her fingers in time to the hefty bass beat, sashayed a few steps across the floor.

'*I hate that shit music,*' Fogue shouted.

She smiled *too bad* at Fogue, waltzed past him, approached Samsa with a flirtatious look. The music, a deafening series of staccato phrases, thumped in Samsa's head, which was already delicate. He watched the woman dance in a circle around him, the cigarette stuck in her mouth. Fogue walked to the stereo and killed it with a hasty gesture, and the room was suddenly silent.

Cassandra said, 'You're a fettered little fart, aren't you, baldy?'

Fogue said, 'I'm not listening to that kill-a-honky-cop crap.'

She took her cigarette from her mouth. 'Why? Does it scare you? What would you prefer? Garth Brooks? Maybe Henry Mancini? I got "Moon River" somewhere.'

Fogue scowled at her. 'My taste in music is irrelevant, lady.'

Samsa had a sense of things going out of focus, the real purpose of being here diffused in assorted squabbles and insults. If you could describe it as real. If anything could be described that way any more. He laid his hands against the back of the chair and said, 'We're looking for Lee Boyle.'

'You're not alone,' she said.

Rebb asked, 'Meaning?'

'Meaning I'd like to see him.'

'I'm hearing irritation,' Rebb said. 'He owes you? Left you holding the bag or something?'

'I didn't say that. I only said I'd like to see him. Sort of for old times' sake.'

'You know where he can be found?' Samsa asked.

'The Man speaks,' she says. 'I hear the voice of authority.'

Rebb said, 'Drop the attitude, Fatima.'

'Cassandra.'

'Whoever. The lieutenant asked a question. Give the man an answer.'

'What's your problem? Lost track of Lee? Why don't you look him up in the phone book?'

'Because he ain't in the phone book, honey,' Rebb said. 'Not under Boyle anyhow.'

Samsa intervened again. 'If you know where he can be found, it's in your best interest to tell us.'

'Why? What's he done now?'

'We want to talk with him,' Samsa said. 'That's all you need to know.'

'He's a persecuted soul,' she said.

'Also a shit,' Rebb said.

'So he's a persecuted shit. He's tormented.'

'Aw, fuck's sake,' Rebb said. 'Don't yank my chain, honey.'

'Tormented and misunderstood.'

'Look, he's a fucking junkie and low-rent pimp, who screwed up his chances in life. You know it, I know it, so skip the crap and just tell us where he lives.'

'What are you hounding him for?' she asked.

Samsa said, 'He's not being hounded. He might be able to help us in certain inquiries. That's all.'

'Ooh, what a phrase that is, covers a multitude of sins.'

'She's got a soft spot for Lee. Screw it. Let's just book her,' Rebb said.

'For what?' she asked.

Rebb said, 'Possession of narcotics. Posing for porno pics. We'll think of something.'

'Your aura's the color of dishwater, Rebb. You know that? You're like a coin: you got two sides. One side works for the heat, flip it and you get total sleaze. You'd have made a great pimp. Also you want to brush your teeth now and then.'

'You got me down pat,' Rebb said.

Samsa didn't like Rebb's confrontational approach. He never had. He said, 'You know where he lives or don't you? It's a simple question.'

She fingered the cross that hung from her neck. 'Am I throwing Lee to the lions if I tell you?'

'Yes or no, Cassandra.'

'There's a kindness in your voice that's noticeably absent from Rebb's,' she remarked.

'Which means what? You'll tell me?'

She walked back to the stereo and switched it on again, then returned to the spot where Samsa stood. She must have been very good-looking at one time, even beautiful. Her bone-structure was exquisite, but little lines spread from the corners of her mouth and her powder-white make-up didn't conceal the tiny incisions of age at the corners of her eyes.

'Is this loud enough for you?' she asked.

'Do you want it to be?'

She touched his arm. 'I don't want to hear what I'm going to say, Samsa. Sometimes I just don't like the

179

sound of my own voice. And sometimes I don't like the infernal noise of my own thoughts. Do you understand that?'

'Yeah,' he said. 'I think I do.'

24

THE TELEPHONE ON DARCY'S BEDSIDE TABLE RANG, AND SHE reached for it, expecting to hear her father's voice. Maybe he was calling to say he was on his way. He'd sounded rushed when they'd talked before. She wished he would come home. She was still thinking about the noise of the trash-can lid falling. Her first thought was that it had been the wind, but the night was perfectly still. Okay, a cat, a dog, maybe even one of those raccoons people said they saw scavenging every now and then. And then the word *prowler* had popped into her head. Somebody out there in the dark.

The voice on the phone wasn't her father's. It was deep and rich, a smooth baritone, an actor's voice. It reminded her of one she'd heard on a hot-chocolate commercial. 'Who am I speaking with?'

'First tell me who *you* are,' she said. She'd been trained by her father, who worried about the possibilities of threats from the criminal community, never to talk on the phone to people she didn't know, especially if they didn't state their name. The number wasn't unlisted, because he had the belief – civic-minded but wrong-headed, she thought – that anyone on the taxpayer's dollars should be accessible.

'You wouldn't know me,' he said.

'Then I'm hanging up.'

'No, don't do that. Don't hang up.'

'Give me one good reason.' Breaking her father's rule: always cut the connection. Don't get involved if you're not sure. But the voice had a pleasing quality, and wasn't menacing.

'Is this Gregory Samsa's home?'

She said, 'Yes. But he's sleeping.' She wasn't about to say he wasn't home. She didn't know this caller and she didn't want him to think she might be alone. You don't take that kind of risk.

'I don't suppose you can wake him up.'

'You suppose right.'

'Too bad,' he said.

'You want to leave a message or call back again?'

'Are you his daughter?'

Hang up, she thought. *Just don't get into this.* 'I don't like questions from strangers in the dead of the night.'

'I was only curious.'

She thought she could hear voices in the background. 'I'm hanging up,' she said.

'Before you sever the connection, do me a favor.'

'What?'

'Tell me your name.'

She stuck the handset down. She lay without moving for a time. Then, a little disturbed by the lateness of the call and the way the guy had asked for her name, she went downstairs. She stared through the kitchen window, which faced the side of the house where the trash was stored.

Darkness. Only darkness.

She flipped the switch for the outside light. In the driveway she saw the unfamiliar car her father had borrowed from the work pool, saw light fall against it and fade out in a feeble fashion among the shrubbery that surrounded the house next door, where the Petersons lived, prissy George the bank manager, wife Millie the social psychologist, their brat twins Leonard and Leonora – those names, *really* – nine years old and always spying on her. She hated the brightly colored plastic dental braces they wore. When they smiled they looked like a pair of stupid stunted clowns.

In the living room she helped herself to a drop of her father's cognac. She liked the way it burned. She gazed at the drawn curtains. She thought about the Italian film and Nick sleeping through it, even snoring at one point.

What she hadn't told her father about the date, what she *couldn't* tell him, was that Nick had detoured on the way home from the cinema and parked his car up near the Purchase property and suggested, with some urgency in his voice, that they *do it*. She'd walked with him into the meadow under a white quarter-moon blurry with moths and mosquitoes. She'd lain on the grass and he'd pushed her skirt up over her thighs and kissed her with such ferocity she felt nauseous, gagging on the deep reaches of his tongue and his fingers roughly inserted in her vagina. And she'd *wanted* to fuck him, but it had all gone wrong because she became *dizzy* with that awful throw-up feeling, and in the end she'd said, *I'm sorry, Nick, this isn't the time. I'm truly sorry.* She'd felt like a bitch-wife with a prophylactic headache. She hadn't meant to come off that way.

The phone was ringing again.

She picked it up.

'Just your name,' he said. 'That's all I ask.'

She slammed the handset back in place, finished her cognac and wished her father would come home.

25

WHEN BOYLE DIDN'T ANSWER HIS BUZZER, BILLY FOGUE picked the front-door lock with a pocket knife and said, 'Easy does it,' and the door opened, revealing a narrow staircase that led to the apartment. Fogue worked his trick a second time on the apartment door. Samsa didn't tell him to stop, that rules were being transgressed, the rights of the citizenry ignored.

Rules. Rules were what you made them. You break one, the rest collapse, the whole damn locomotive comes off the tracks at speed. He stood in the center of Boyle's living room and watched through the bedroom doorway as Rebb and Fogue prowled around, opening and closing drawers and closets.

Rebb found a couple of dresses and held one against his body. 'You think this is me, Billy?' he asked.

'Polka dots, nah,' Fogue said.

'Just put it back, Rebb,' Samsa said, a little sharply, and turned away from the skimpy polka-dot number and tried not to think of the girl dressing and undressing in this apartment, mirror-gazing, applying make-up, brushing her hair, all her little vanities past and dead.

Rebb hung the dress in the closet and shut the door and hummed a few bars of 'Polka Dots and Moonbeams', sounding vaguely like a guy playing a trombone. 'Hey, panties,' he said, dipping his fingers inside a drawer and pulling out scant filmy things in an assortment of colors.

Samsa said, 'This isn't a goddam department store, Rebb.'

Rebb stuffed the lingerie back where he'd found it and said, 'I've always been intrigued by the mysteries of female underwear. Bras especially. Hooks and clips and such.'

Billy Fogue said, 'This place is real clean. You notice that?'

'Speed-freaks have a lot of time and energy to kill,' Rebb remarked.

Samsa watched them go inside the kitchen. Fogue shuffled through the drawers of a cabinet and Reb peered inside the refrigerator, which contained only a few cans of Coors and a bunch of shriveled green grapes.

Rebb said, 'Another thing about speed-heads is they're not famous for having a whole load of food on hand. They got no appetite.'

A herb chart hung on the kitchen wall. Samsa gazed at it. Marjoram, Thyme, Basil. How to Use Them. It was a chart he'd seen in many kitchens. There was also a Bart Simpson clock: 2:20.

He worked his tongue against the edge of his broken tooth. The absence of Lee Boyle somehow reinforced an illusion of his presence. He was missing, and yet he wasn't. He was everywhere in this apartment, among the books on the shelves, the toiletries in the bathroom, the towels placed neatly on the rack.

Samsa wandered toward the books and found himself thinking about the distance between his smashed car and where the girl's body had been found, and he was assailed by the notion that somebody would eventually start to think how strange it was that the lieutenant had wrecked his car at roughly the same time the girl was killed, and only a few hundred yards from where her body was found. An unhappy proximity.

Coincidence. The world was filled with coincidence. Brodsky had accepted that without any problem, Brodsky hadn't been troubled by it at all.

Just tell them, he thought. *Kill this travesty. It cuts against the grain of your whole belief system. If you ever really had one.*

Who are you, Samsa?

He looked at the stereo and Boyle's eclectic collection of CDs. A little jazz, some classical music by composers unfamiliar to him – Schoenberg, Alban Berg – as well as Bach, Beethoven. Eighties pop, Dylan Thomas reading his own poetry. One odd item, a collection of Christmas favorites sung by the Mormon Tabernacle Choir. Was Lee Boyle, pimp, a closet sentimentalist?

He felt like a trespasser, a home-invader. He stared at the coffee table, seeing, under the soft glow of an angular lamp, circular streaks where the wood surface had been cleaned.

He listened to Rebb and Fogue clattering around inside the bathroom, the sound of a shower curtain being slipped along the rail, the chink of tiny plastic hoops. *What the hell do they expect to find in the shower?* he wondered. This was like a recreational outing for them, where they could poke among the stuff of another person's life. They enjoyed being snoops. He understood he should put a stop to it, tell them to cool it until Boyle showed up. They weren't here to ransack his property, they were here to ask him some questions, that was all. But they had a momentum going now and he felt removed from whatever they were doing.

He heard Fogue say, 'Now lookee here, Rebb. You suppose he has a permit for this?'

'Nice little gun,' Rebb said. 'A Lama forty-five. Compact Frame model. The idea of him having a permit is highly implausible, I got to say. A guy like Boyle, he wouldn't be big on paperwork. He's an outlaw. Or he likes to think he is anyway.'

Fogue appeared in the bathroom doorway with the gun, the handle wrapped in tissue. He had a cheroot hanging from his mouth and the smell was beginning to drift through the rooms. A heavy sickening odor.

'Item. One gun,' Fogue said. 'Too bad the little hooker wasn't blown away by this very weapon. Then we'd have something straightforward.'

'I suggest you put it back where you found it.'

'Anything you say, Lew Tenant. Back in the tampon box it goes.'

Samsa strolled the room. He walked to the window and peered into the drab street below. He saw the pawnbroker's sign and wondered what effect it might have on somebody to live above a business that dealt in desperation and poverty, wedding rings hocked, war medals traded away for a few bucks and never reclaimed. Maybe despair seeped through the building like a gas.

He still wore his own wedding ring. He looked at it now, a plain gold band. Why did he keep it anyhow? He had an urge to yank it off. He wasn't married. In a sense he hadn't been married for years and years.

He moved toward the answering machine, and pressed Playback.

The first message was a man's voice with a pseudo-English accent: *I hope I'm not pressuring you unduly, love. But time is passing. Time is indeed passing. Beep beep.*

The second was from a woman. *Lee, you old speed-*

freak, I hear you're looking for your little Almond. Maybe I can be of some tiny assistance? Meet me at the Rialto coffee shop around four thirty, okay? Beep beep. The machine stopped.

He recognized that voice.

Cassandra.

He stood with his hands pressed against the back of the sofa, his legs spread slightly, his head inclined downward. He realized he was holding his breath and his nerves were jangling. Tiny assistance? What assistance could Cassandra possibly give? Did she know something? Had she seen something? Like what? Had she been in the vicinity and seen Almond approach his car? Was that it? But Cassandra had given no indication that she recognized him. Not a flicker, a sign. It had been dark last night anyway, moonless and rainy. And Cassandra, even if she *had* been around the place, couldn't have seen much of anything.

He was jumping to wild conclusions, lost in a fog of possibilities and questions that were like darts. Stakes driven into his heart. His mind scampered this way and that, circled around on itself. Had Cassandra met with Boyle, imparted whatever information she had?

He couldn't let that be true. In this new world of his a fact was no longer a fact, it was something you could twist. He wiped the messages from the answering machine, even as his brain was racing to the notion that there was technology capable of restoring voices from erased tapes, there were instruments and audio experts who could find traces and amplify them to the point where meaningful sounds could be discovered, and if it came to that . . .

He heard Rebb say, 'Anything interesting there?'

Samsa wheeled round quickly, wondering how long Rebb had been standing in the doorway. He wasn't breathing properly. A constriction in his throat, like a cherry stone lodged there. His chest felt tight.

'A couple of messages, nothing that serves our purpose,' he said.

Rebb shrugged. 'I guess all we can do is wait for our wandering boy to show.' He approached the answering machine and stared at it. Just for a moment Samsa thought he was going to press the playback button, and he'd hear only a blank cassette, at which point he'd realize Samsa had been lying when he'd referred to a couple of messages that were of no interest.

But then Samsa would say, I must have wiped them inadvertently.

And Rebb might think, What? Very unprofessional, Lieutenant. Wiping a tape by accident. Clumsy of you.

There's no fucking end to this. It's a maze. At the heart of the maze is a monster with your face.

Samsa said the first thing that came to mind. 'You mentioned Boyle came from a rich family?'

'You ever heard of Hugh Boyle?'

'The tycoon?'

Thankfully Rebb had lost interest in the machine. 'Yeah. He's got this slew of companies all over the place.' He sat on an arm of the sofa, took out his nail file and dug away. 'Hugh's the father.'

Samsa said, 'And he disowned his son.'

'Would you want a kid like Lee Boyle?'

Samsa heard movement on the stairs. He made a shushing gesture, index finger to his lips. Rebb stared at the door. Billy Fogue, wandering in from the bathroom, was also silent.

Waiting, waiting.

A key was turned in the lock, the door opened.

Lee Boyle entered the room.

If he was shocked to find visitors, he didn't show it.

'Gentlemen callers. Including Detective Rebb, unless my eyes deceive,' he said. He walked into the kitchen and came back with a can of beer. 'Beer's there if you want to help yourselves, guys.'

Samsa got up from the sofa and said, 'I'm Lieutenant Samsa.'

Boyle looked at Samsa for a moment with an odd expression, and then smiled. 'Lieutenant. Nice to make your acquaintance.'

'Polite fucker,' Rebb said. 'It's all surface. You see those blue eyes and that face and you smell apple pie. Don't be fooled, Lieutenant. You're looking at low-level scuzz.'

Fogue blew smoke directly into Boyle's face. 'It's question time, buddy. You ready?'

'Is there a prize?' Boyle asked. He seemed undeterred by the smoke, didn't even bother to wave it away. He gazed through the disintegrating little cloud at Samsa and the smile didn't leave his face.

Cool, Samsa thought. *Or acting hard to seem so.*

Fogue said, 'The prize depends on your answers, Boyle.'

Boyle said to Fogue, 'Do I know you?'

'Detective Fogue. Sir to you.' He shoved his cheroot at Boyle like a tiny weapon.

Boyle relaxed against the wall, sipping beer. He looked at Rebb and Fogue, and then his gaze settled on Samsa. *'Struck to the heart by this sad pageantry, Half to myself I said, And what is this?'*

'He memorizes poetry like a fucking parrot,' Rebb said.

Samsa said, 'He's got the poetry down all right. Let's see what else he's got down, shall we? Let's see if he remembers where he was around ten o'clock last night. You recall that, Boyle?'

'Ten o'clock, let's see,' Boyle said. 'I was with a man called Jimmy Plumm.'

'Jimmy *Plumm*?' Fogue asked, and blew more smoke.

Samsa thought how crude Billy Fogue and Rebb could be, compared to Eve.

'Moneybags Plumm will vouch for you, will he?' Fogue asked. 'You into him for some cash? Plumm'll say just about anything to keep you out of trouble if you owe him. Duh. He doesn't make a profit if you go to jail.'

'Jail?' Boyle stared at Samsa for a moment over the rim of the Coors can. The look, which struck Samsa as secretive and knowing, was unsettling. *Had Cassandra talked to him? And what could she possibly have said?* The questions were trapped in the revolving door of his head. The questions were Semtex primed and wrapped in old newspapers.

'Excuse me. What's this talk of jail?' Boyle asked.

'Fogue gets carried away sometimes,' Samsa said. 'What time did you leave Plumm?'

'Around ten fifteen, ten twenty, then I went directly to a bar called Chang's.'

'Anybody see you there?' Samsa asked.

'I ran into a girl called Krystal,' Boyle said.

'Last name?'

Boyle shrugged. 'I wouldn't know her last name. She's a casual acquaintance.'

'Then what?'

'I left the bar. I met a man called Tom Raseci around eleven. We discussed the fact that somebody had slashed a tire on my car.'

'Bigshoes Raseci?' Fogue said. 'This just gets better all the time.'

'Without wheels, I had to contact a friend for a ride home. He picked me up at about eleven fifteen, eleven thirty. Vass, Rudolph Vass. You want his phone number?'

Samsa said, 'We'll get in touch with these people, Boyle.' He shoved his hands in his pockets. His palms were damp and stuck to some coins.

Boyle said, 'I guess you'll also get around to telling me what this is all about?'

Rebb put an arm on Boyle's shoulder. 'Here's the story, Lee. Your little girl was found dead. You know who I mean? Cecily Suarez. Almond by her other name.'

'*Dead?*'

'Murdered. Sorry to break it like this,' Rebb said in such a way that you knew he wasn't sorry at all. 'Somebody snapped her neck.'

'Is this a sick joke?' Boyle asked.

'I wish it was,' Samsa said. 'But it's not.'

'*Murdered?*' Lee Boyle looked as if he'd been struck on the face with a sledgehammer. He slumped, the beer can dangling loosely from his hand. He stared at Samsa, but he wasn't seeing anything, his eyes had a vacancy. A sign had been turned off inside him.

The smile was gone, the face empty. The beer can, angled slightly, oozed foam. *There was feeling here*, Samsa thought. *Something between Lee Boyle and the dead girl. A genuine affection maybe.* The expression on Boyle's face suggested he'd lost more than a hooker he had on a chain, a girl he worked. All right, he was lowlife, his world was one of dope and hookers, he had violence in his history, even so – even so Samsa felt an unexpected twinge of sympathy he couldn't afford. He had to be hard. He had to be made of metal that couldn't be broken. *Boyle's a suspect. Boyle has to be scrutinized.*

A long silence. Fogue and Rebb had subsided surprisingly into quiet. Boyle inclined his head now, eyes shut. 'Where did you find her?'

Rebb said, 'You know the old Purchase property?'

Boyle shook his head.

'That wilderness out near Chackstone,' Rebb said.

Boyle appeared to absorb this information absently. He

crumpled the beer can with a tensed hand. Foam exploded over his fingers.

'Who'd kill her, for Christ's sake?' he asked.

'That's what we're trying to find out,' Samsa said.

Rebb said, 'Which is why we're here, blue eyes.'

Boyle said, 'Why you're here . . . Now wait a minute. Hold on. You think I might have done it? No way. She was just somebody crashing in my apartment.'

'Somebody you took in under your mighty generous wing,' Rebb said. 'Some poor little thing in need of shelter.'

'Yeah, absolutely.'

Some poor little thing, Samsa thought. He was back in the Chrysler and the sky was turning over and his world was hemorrhaging.

'But she turned a few tricks on the side,' Rebb said.

'What she did in her spare time, I couldn't begin to guess,' Boyle said quietly.

Fogue pulled the dead cheroot from his lips. 'You were living off her earnings, Boyle.'

'She contributed to the rent. I never asked her how she earned her money.'

'Ho ho ho,' Rebb said. 'And I'm fucking Father Christmas. See my elves, Lee?'

'Fuck you, Rebb. She was a nice kid. I met her somewhere, she needed a place to live, and I suggested my apartment. Our paths didn't cross a lot. It was a temporary arrangement, that's all. What's so terrible about hospitality?'

'Hospitality's just fine. I just happen to think it's pretty scuzzy putting her to work on the streets,' Rebb said.

'Putting her to work? If that's an official accusation, Mr Rebb, and if you also seriously think I had something to do with the death of this girl, then I'd better call my lawyer. What do you think, Lieutenant?'

Samsa said, 'I think we'll check your story, Boyle. If it

193

hangs together, then you've got nothing to worry about, have you? If it's got holes, then you can bet your ass you'll be seeing more of us. As for you pimping, I don't give a damn. All I care about is who killed this girl. Nothing else.'

'I think you'll find my alibis are sound,' Boyle said.

'Ain't you the lucky one,' Fogue said.

Samsa felt weariness come down on him, a fatigue in his bones. His shoulder ached. He wanted very badly to lie down. 'We'll call it a night for now.'

Fogue looked disappointed. He dropped his cheroot butt casually on the rug. 'I'm only just getting warmed up, Lew Tenant.'

Samsa walked to the door. Boyle stepped in front of him, collided with him gently.

'Sorry,' Boyle said.

Rebb and Fogue went out. Samsa's way was blocked by Boyle.

Boyle said, 'I didn't catch your name, Lieutenant.'

Samsa stepped back from Boyle a couple of inches. The physical contact with the man discomfited him. 'Samsa.'

'As in S–A–M–S–A?'

'Right.'

'Unusual name,' Boyle said.

Samsa tried to imagine Boyle and Cassandra meeting someplace, whispering, sharing a confidence. *I saw Almond,* she might say. And Boyle would say, *Yeah? Where? Under what circumstances?* And then what?

What did she tell him? What *could* she tell him?

Maybe Boyle hadn't checked his messages, didn't know Cassandra had telephoned. But she'd call again if she didn't hear from him. Of course she would.

This is guilt run riot, Samsa thought. *This is a mind operating on desperation. You're walking through a forest and the trees are whispering your name and the clouds*

194

scudding overhead are spelling it out in great unfolding
banners.

'Do you have a card?' Boyle asked.

'A card?'

'Yeah, you know, if I find out anything about Cecily or her movements, then I'll know where to reach you.'

Samsa reached inside his pocket and gave Boyle one of his PD cards.

Boyle said, 'I can't believe somebody would kill her. She was only a kid.'

Samsa couldn't look at him. He stepped out of the apartment and moved to the edge of the stairs. Fogue and Rebb were already halfway down. He could see them in the pale stair-light, two faint shapes. He paused and imagined he heard a sound like a dam cracking in the distance, and water, as it gathered force, spewing through.

26

SAMSA WENT BACK DOWNTOWN AFTER HE'D LEFT LEE BOYLE'S apartment. He sat in his office, listening to Fogue speak on the telephone outside his door. 'Okay, Raseci, just see if you can remember the exact time you were with him. Shouldn't be too difficult if you apply yourself . . .' Stephen Rebb was working another phone, calling God knows what sources in the murky places where Cecily Suarez had worked.

Samsa put his hands on the desk, fingertips touching, almost a gesture of prayer. He'd been raised a Catholic, and in the early days of his marriage – those days before the darkening shadows began to form around Harriet – he'd attended Mass regularly with his wife. He'd never considered himself a deeply spiritual person. At best the church offered comfort and consistency, the center-stone of Sunday mornings. Then he'd lost interest during the years of Harriet's disintegration, and it was a long time since he'd prayed. But he had the urge now, because he had nowhere to turn, and if the slightest possibility of a God of any kind existed he'd run to it, he'd go down on his knees and ask for guidance and forgiveness.

He thought about Lee Boyle.

He'd come back to that subject later, when he was alone. He'd clear a space in his mind and analyze the situation. He'd try to remember if anyone had seen the girl get in his car: a witness he'd overlooked. But he'd been so fucking *careful*, so *discreet*. He'd driven past in the rain and signaled to her from a block down from the main action, and she'd come hurrying toward the car under her transparent umbrella with the rain slicking off it. The *umbrella*. For one dread moment he couldn't remember what he'd done with it. Then it came back. He'd tossed it away in the long grass as far from the wrecked car as he could.

Right now you're conducting a homicide investigation. That's your priority. Making the moves, sifting, gathering information. Seeing what can be fabricated out of the bits and pieces.

Except you can't forget Boyle.

He felt squeezed, pinched. The room closed in on him. He rubbed his eyes. He thought, *I've never been in a lonelier place*.

On a notepad in front of him were two numbers Billy Fogue had given him. He didn't feel like making either call. He had to raise his energy level, infuse himself with an enthusiasm he didn't have. You have to be keen. You have to maintain a façade of professional devotion. Be determined. A girl is dead out there.

He reached for the phone, picked it up, punched in the digits of the first number. Samsa found himself connected to a certain Sergeant Lucinda of the Denver PD. She had a sympathetic voice. He informed her about the death of Cecily Suarez, and the fact she'd been a runaway from Denver. Sergeant Lucinda said she'd check for an address, then have somebody call on the kid's parents. Samsa imagined a cop turning up on the doorstep of the Suarez household: It's about your daughter. I'm sorry. I have to tell you. I hate to bring this kind of news. There was never anything new to say, never a sentence with a glint of consolation. Words were dross at the bottom of a worked-out mine shaft.

He imagined a mother, imbued her with a sorrowful face, dark hair with a few steely strands. He pictured her walking up and down, chain-smoking and clock-watching, a low humming sound of terror forever in her skull. Imagining she hears Cecily's footsteps on the porch. Never again. The child isn't coming back. He had a curious feeling, something draining out of him. His eyes watered a moment.

Sergeant Lucinda said, 'You got anyone in custody for this, by the way? The parents might ask. They often do.'

'We're working on it,' he said, 'but we don't have anybody yet.' *In custody*, he thought. No, the killer was out there in the night. He was skulking down an alley or he was fast asleep in his bed or he was sitting in some late-night dive. Samsa pictured the murderer through a mist: a guy of about six-one, short black hair, add a scar, maybe a tattoo. The more details, the easier to make-believe. Easier to distance yourself.

'Runaways,' Sergeant Lucinda said. 'Break your heart every time.'

Samsa agreed, yes, they break your heart. Lucinda said she'd get back to him after the parents had been informed, and then there was the question of formal ID of the body by next of kin, so a family member would most likely have to fly out, and transportation arrangements would need to be made if the parents wanted the corpse brought back home for burial. All the usual business of death.

Samsa thanked her, then hung up. He listened to the

fan, watched how it oscillated, like a strange blind metal face scanning for something beyond its range.

He dialed the second number on his notepad. It rang for a long time, and he was about to hang up when the call was answered.

'Yes?'

'Lieutenant Samsa, Homicide,' he said. 'I want to speak to Jimmy Plumm.'

'This is he. You realize you woke me up? You know what time it is?'

Samsa didn't say he was sorry. 'I'm checking on a guy called Lee Boyle.'

'I'm more than a little pissed off by this intrusion,' Plumm said. 'By God, couldn't you have waited until a decent hour?'

Samsa recognized the voice. The first message on Boyle's answering machine. Something about time passing. He'd been too distracted to store the exact words in his memory. According to Fogue, Plumm was a moneylender whose rates of interest were usurious. He backed up his operation with muscle, hard stuff. You don't pay, say goodbye to a limb, an eye, whatever. His main enforcer was Tom Raseci, a name Samsa had heard around, always in association with violence.

'I guess I didn't realize it was this late,' Samsa said.

Plumm made a clucking sound. 'Homicide, did you say?'

'Right.'

'And you want to ask about who? Lee Boyle?'

Samsa rolled a yellow pencil under the palm of his hand. 'When did you last see him?'

'What kind of trouble is he in?' Plumm asked.

'This is routine.'

'Routine? At this hour? Come come.'

'Just answer my question, Mr Plumm.'

'I can't remember precisely.'

'Try,' Samsa said.

'Monday night, I believe.'

'At what time?'

'Mr Samsa, I'm a busy man. I run several businesses that make excessive demands on me—'

'I know about your business dealings. Let's skip the detours, okay? Monday night. When?'

'I'm sorry,' Plumm said. 'Maybe eight. Nine. I can't really be sure.'

'But definitely Monday?'

'Yes, Monday.'

'It could have been later than eight or nine?'

'Perhaps.'

'Or earlier?'

Plumm said, 'No, not earlier. It was after dinner, I remember that. I always eat between six and six thirty.'

Samsa said, 'Go back to sleep. Maybe you'll remember more when you're refreshed.'

He replaced the handset just as Rebb stepped into the room. 'You ever get the impression the world's filled with liars? There's hardly a fucking whore or pimp or porn-merchant I don't know in this whole city. I mean, sleaze is my specialty, Jesus – but nobody out there is talking. Nobody is *talking*.'

Samsa could see Rebb took this personally. He was insulted because his channels of information were dysfunctional. He'd spent years building delicate networks in the lower depths. He had his own payroll out there, people he greased. But sometimes grease didn't get you anything more than stained hands.

Rebb said, 'The best flash I got was she was seen checking into a room at the Starlit Lodge two days ago, which is ancient history. The guy she was with registered as Jack

Spratt. Ho ho. I suppose she called herself Mrs Lean. They checked out again an hour later, the clerk says.'

'Go home,' Samsa said. 'We'll pick it up again after we've had a few hours' sleep.'

'Go home?' Rebb asked. He was worked up. His unnatural black hair seemed almost navy in the fluorescent light. 'This is the time when my people are up and around. They don't keep normal hours, Lieutenant. Soon as it's dawn, *poof*, they're gone.'

Billy Fogue appeared in the doorway. 'I can't locate anybody who remembers seeing Boyle in Chang's. I talked to the manager, who wasn't overjoyed to be roused. And I haven't run down anything on this Krystal who Boyle claims he saw.' He looked at a notebook in his hand. 'Rudolph Vass says he picked Boyle up somewhere downtown at about eleven thirty, or maybe quarter to midnight. And Tom Raseci admits he talked to Boyle at some point in the course of the evening, but he isn't sure when.'

'Same with Plumm,' Samsa said. 'He saw Boyle, doesn't remember the time.'

'Plumm's thinking percentages,' Fogue said. 'Boyle's into him for some money, but is it worth perjury just to protect your investment? Right now I'd bet my ass he's on the phone to Raseci and they're trying to find out why we're asking questions about Lee Boyle.'

'So now we just keep backtracking,' Samsa said. 'Who saw her last. Where she was seen. We need a timetable of her movements.' He looked at Rebb, who had an unsettling light of determination in his eyes.

Rebb said, 'I'm hitting the streets. As of this moment.'

Samsa understood he couldn't stall Rebb. Nobody could have chained him in his present frame of mind. Besides, how would it look if Samsa ordered him to go home, start work afresh tomorrow? Illogical. A lack of

201

enthusiasm. Out of focus. *Play the game.* 'See if you can get anything on this Jack Spratt character, Rebb,' he said. 'A make on his car. A description of the guy. Anything.'

Rebb said, 'Spratt's two days old, and that's no fucking good.'

'He might have picked her up again on the night she died,' Samsa said.

'I'll lean on that night clerk at the Starlit. He's a Libyan and he doesn't have a green card.' Rebb turned away. 'See you.'

When Rebb had gone, Billy Fogue said, 'The whole alibi bit is looking damn iffy, I think.'

'For the moment,' Samsa said.

'What else do you want me to do before I collapse?' Fogue asked.

'Get some sleep. We'll let Rebb run with this for a few hours.'

'I can go home?'

Samsa nodded. 'That's where I'm headed.'

Fogue looked pleased. 'Later, Lew Tenant.'

Alone, Samsa stood in his partitioned space. He listened to phones ringing, cops answering. Accidents in the small hours, domestic squabbles, home invasions, violence. It never stopped. The world screamed and screamed. He walked out of his office and remembered as soon as he was on the street that he had no transportation. He'd left the Chevy at home, ridden in the squad car to the Purchase property, then he'd gone to see Boyle in Fogue's Buick.

Boyle. So there were holes in Boyle's story. So what? They were temporary. They'd be patched and grouted. He needed to think harder about Lee Boyle.

But not now. His head was overloaded. He didn't have clarity.

He looked the length of the street. A cab came into view

and he hailed it and slumped in the back seat. He was about to give the driver his home address, then changed his mind. It was very late, and no time to be paying social calls, but he didn't want to go home just yet. He told the driver where to take him, then he sat back, gazing absently at the night. He thought of Darcy. She'd be fine. She'd be fast asleep by this time. The house was secure.

He got out of the cab in a street of turn-of-the-century houses, many of them ornate, a few with elaborate gingerbread touches. Somebody with vision and an eye for profit had saved these places from the wrecker's ball and restored them, turning them into apartments. The street was leafy and suggestive of a prosperous time in the city's history, when the railroad had flourished and commercial barges hauled huge loads along the canal and factories smoked and thrived. Apart from a brief revival of fortune in the early 1950s the city had been on a general downward slope for a long time. It wasn't a terrific history. It was no American success story.

He paid the driver, walked up a driveway, stopped outside a door and pressed a buzzer. This was a bad idea altogether.

He heard Eve's voice through the intercom. 'Who is it?'
'Greg,' he said.

The door clicked open. He stepped inside a high-ceilinged hallway. Eve, tying the cord of her robe, appeared at the top of the stairs.

'Come on up,' she said.

He climbed, followed her quietly along the corridor at the top. Her apartment was spacious and filled with plants. A few throw rugs and very little furniture – a big sofa near the carved fireplace, a couple of chairs, and that was it. He sat on the sofa and wondered why he'd come here. She stood in front of the unlit fire. The only light in the room came from a lamp close to the window.

'This is a surprise,' she said. She had her red hair tied back. Her face glistened. *Some kind of moisturizer*, Samsa thought. She looked very young without make-up.

'I woke you,' he said.

'I'm a light sleeper.'

'You're alone?'

'I'm alone most of the time, contrary to what you might hear. You want a drink?'

'No, I'm fine.' He tapped his fingers on his knees. 'There was a homicide tonight.' He told her the details, how the body had been discovered, the coroner's interim comments. His narrative was brief and superficial. Whatever had brought him here, it wasn't to tell Eve Lassiter about the dead girl. He had a sense of banishing silences, talking because quiet was intolerable.

She listened. Sometimes she smoothed strands of hair from the sides of her face. She sat alongside him on the sofa, drew her feet up under her body. The robe she wore was cotton, blue-and-white check, and several sizes too big for her, and he wondered if it belonged to somebody else, if a man had left it behind. A lover.

'Thirteen,' she said. 'A child. It's so . . .'

'Yeah, I know, I know.' Samsa made a meaningless little gesture with his hand. 'I heard you called me at home.'

She said, 'I was going to tell you how my night turned out. I can report this much: I don't have what it takes to be a hooker. It's bleak down there.'

'Joshua Gold saw nothing?'

She looked just a little preoccupied. Then she smiled. 'You just came here to pass the time or check on your phone messages?'

'I don't know,' he said.

'You didn't want to go home,' she said.

'It's where I ought to be. It's late.'

204

'Or early.' She reached out, held his hand and ran her thumb back and forward across his knuckles. The intimacy was easy on him, the contact pleasurable. It rushed into the spaces inside him. He moved his head against her shoulder, smelled the scent of her soap, which was suggestive of crushed Fall fruit.

He could lose himself here, he thought. He could travel this road with Eve and he'd be safe from harm. He saw her undo the cord of her robe, and watched the robe part and the way the lamp shone against her inner thighs and highlighted the soft delicate hairs there. He didn't move, thinking how short the distance between them was. She pulled a pin or a clasp from her hair – he couldn't tell which – and it tumbled to her shoulders. He looked at her face, and how the open robe revealed her breasts, and he grasped the extent of his solitude, the way his life had been for too many years, and the silent disoriented woman who'd been his wife; all the years he'd waited for her to re-enter the world, and she never had. The wrists razored in the bathtub, pink water. That was what she'd left him in the end. She might have been saying, with the inexplicable malice of her derangement, Here, Greg, remember this when you think of me.

He kissed Eve, possessed by an excitement he'd half for-gotten, a shadowy fuse from his former life, and his blood changed course, his heartbeat became chaotic. She stood up, took his hand, led him inside her bedroom. A big dark-green room, a brass bed. She told him to lie down, and he did. He was willing, obedient.

She removed his shoes, his socks, unbuckled his belt and said, 'I've wanted you. I've wanted this to happen. You knew that.'

'Maybe,' he said.

'No maybe, Greg.' She undid the buttons of his shirt.

He couldn't wait. He couldn't hold back. There was

nothing elaborate in his desire and excitement, it was primal and urgent, he wanted to be inside her and discover in the act something of the life he'd lost, and dissolve the whole conundrum his existence had become. It was more than flesh, the conjunction of bodies. He had the sense she could rescue him somehow, that she was an angel who could reach down and bring him back from the place where he'd fallen. He looked up into her face and those disturbingly honest green eyes. She hid nothing. Concealed nothing. He watched her red hair swing against the sides of her jaw, and when she spoke her voice was a whisper. 'You need me.'

'Yes,' he said.

'You need me so badly.'

'Yes.'

He felt himself lifted upward, floating to meet her, sliding inside her. The impact was narcotic. He was suddenly in a dream where no external world existed. It was him and Eve and it was going to stay this way for as long as he could make it. This was real. Everything outside her bedroom was ashes.

She bent forward and her hair touched his forehead, then she swayed back from him and her breasts shook as she straddled him, and he was moved almost to tears by her marvelous tenderness. Her mouth was open, her face angled back now. She was all concentration and purpose, and as he looked at the smooth curvature of her long neck and the tightened veins and the shadows around her throat, he had no idea how long he could sustain this.

Not long, he thought, *not long at all*.

He was lost, frenzied and joyous, and already beginning to fall apart inside. He realized he'd barely understood the real nature of his yearning down the years. He'd been caged, grounded. Liberated now, the air all around him seemingly rocked with turbulence, he felt himself come, a fire searing through him. He was in pieces, and the pieces were burning.

Samsa aflame.

He heard himself call her name out loud.

She collapsed against him, her hair on his face, her mouth locked against his. He thought he could suffocate gladly in this way, expire here and now. Go out on a cloud of brilliant light. He'd recuperated after a long life-threatening illness. He was without burdens suddenly. A miracle. He wanted to tell her all this, but the feelings that ran through him couldn't be uttered.

She was quiet a long time before she said, 'I'm all you really need. And just think, I've been around all this time.'

'Waiting,' he said.

'Not always patiently.'

He stroked her hair, the side of her face, touched a breast. 'I wasn't exactly observant,' he said.

'Blind,' she said.

'Or distracted.'

She reached down between his legs and closed her palm around his cock and held it. 'Also some self-pity.'

'Probably that.'

'I *pushed* myself at you. God. I used to think up ways I could get you into my bed. If this hadn't happened now, it was going to happen next Wednesday anyway, because I'd made up my mind. As soon as dinner was over I had these sneaky plans . . .' She stroked him and he was hard again, and he felt unexpectedly young and vigorous, as if she'd stripped years from his life. He rolled her over onto her back and looked down at her. Gazing up at him she seemed vulnerable. If she was an angel, she was one without defenses.

'Again,' she said. 'I want you again.'

Again. Yes, again. It was a more delicious loss this time,

a shucking off of the self, slower now, carefully rendered. He kissed her throat, shoulders, tasted her skin, her hair, the uncharted territory of Eve. He was a man given the key to a room he'd only heard about before, but never entered. It was a room of flesh and bone and joy and honesty. It was where you went if you wanted unfettered exhilaration.

This time she came, and he understood he was receiving a gift of her most private secrets: the intimate sounds of pleasure she made, the way she buried her face in his shoulder, and how her body went rigid for one breathtakingly scary moment. His own climax, which rocked him to his spine, seemed like a note in a minor key by contrast. She said his name three, four, five times, and each time was a different riff on the same three syllables. She lay very still under him, staring into his face.

'Thank you,' she said. 'Thank you, thank you.'

'I should be saying that.'

She extended an arm in a lazy way across the sheets. 'Let's just say the gratitude's mutual, Lieutenant.'

A lovely sharing, he thought. An end to the winter inside himself. A thaw. He touched the side of her face, realized he didn't want to leave her. The notion of rising, getting dressed and going home appalled him. The reality check, the first light of dawn in the sky, the hideous bright face of the sun and all that it involved. He wondered how long it might be postponed. He wanted to draw the sheets over his head and sleep beside her and never stir again except to make love. He clasped her hand and held it tightly and raised it to his lips.

She propped herself up on an elbow and gazed at him. 'That's one hell of a bruise there.'

'I banged my shoulder.' The bruise on his flesh. 'I guess it happened when I wrecked the car. I didn't feel it at the time.'

She said, 'Say, you want to hear something hilarious? Gold says he saw you trawling.' She kissed his mouth.

'*Trawling?*' He was jolted suddenly, as if the atmosphere in the room had become charged with static electricity. Something very fine but ultimately fragile had been damaged in a matter of seconds.

'As in cruising.'

'Where?'

'Along Flesh Row. Where else?'

Samsa shook his head in an emphatic way. 'He's mistaken, Eve. He's got it wrong. He's way off.'

'That's what *I* told him. He's not exactly a wizard when it comes to ID-ing people, is he?'

'Okay, I might be lonely at times, and I don't deny I get depressed. But Flesh Row. No. No way. Christ, absolutely not.' He closed his eyes, remembering the nights he'd driven down there, the times he'd slowed the car and surreptitiously studied the eager girls beckoning from the sidewalks, imagining what it would be like, and how he'd always changed his mind at the last moment. He remembered the temptation, his nerves jazzed, the curious amalgam of desire and emptiness and self-disgust.

'You have to leave, don't you?' she asked.

'Darcy's alone.'

She placed a finger on his mouth. 'It's okay. I understand.'

He thought he hadn't been spotted. He'd considered himself anonymous, driving along, never stopping to buy. Except once. Just that once. One goddam time.

All your precautions, he thought. But somebody always noticed. Cassandra maybe. Now Gold. There were no hiding places except denial, and that was a besieged fortress. He rose from the bed, feeling desperate.

'I'm here for you,' Eve said. 'Remember that.' She

reached out and clutched his wrist. She released him, then watched as he gathered his clothes.

'You've got a broken tooth at the back of your mouth,' she said. 'I could feel it. Kind of jagged and rough.'

'Another souvenir of the crash,' he said.

'You want to get it seen to, Greg. Before decay sets in.'

27

THE TELEPHONE RANG AT 7 A.M. LEE BOYLE REACHED OUT TO pick it up. He'd lain on the sofa for hours without catching even a glimpse of sleep, because his head was a satellite that wouldn't quit transmitting images of Almond.

'Lee? I got your message.'

'You're a tough sonofabitch to find,' Boyle said. He was weary, dry-mouthed. The little ulcer in his gum was stinging suddenly. He had layer on layer of black feelings. Was this how sadness engraved itself? *Mournful surges that ring the dead seaman's knell?*

'I can't imagine why. You know my haunts, don't you? Maybe we just kept missing one another.'

'Maybe.' His interest in The Kid had been dwindling lately. *Almond dead. I can't grasp that one.*

'You want to come out to my place, Lee?'

'I'd prefer if you came down here,' Boyle said.

'No, I'll tell you why. I keep all my stuff here, and it's just more convenient, that's all.'

'I have to drag myself out there,' Boyle said. 'Is it worth my while?'

'I think so, Lee.'

'It better be. Give me an hour.'

Boyle hung up. He showered, gargled, brushed his teeth. His mouthwash agitated the ulcer. The tiny fucker throbbed intermittently, like a miniature lighthouse in his mouth.

He'd breakfast out of Stretch's baggie. He considered the needle, but that was a whole ritual, and he didn't feel up to it. He laid out some crystal on a mirror that he placed on the coffee table. This shit, one fine day in the future he'd give it up. But not now. He needed it. Even if he didn't trust Stretch's product, even if it amped him out of control, it was the only game in town right now.

He chopped the speed swiftly with a razor blade until it was a fine powder. He stared at the white mound a moment, wondering how many thousands of times he'd done this over the years, then shaped the stuff with the blade into two generous lines. With a cut plastic drinking straw between his fingers, he lowered his head. He saw sparkle, fragments that glinted. He saw his nostrils reflected in the mirror under the lines. *Gimme glass, I need glass.* These two lines were tracks that would carry him express-style for the next four or five hours.

After he snorted he felt the stuff coagulate in his sinuses. He remembered to take his multi-vitamins. He brushed his hair back, ran a quick mirror check. *You don't look the same, Lee. You look older this morning. Depressed. Something's gone out of you.*

He ransacked a closet in the bedroom, found a blue silk shirt and gray jeans hanging among Almond's clothing. He gazed at her dresses. He imagined her presence. Her white smile. The little generosities she bestowed. Any moment now she'd come through that goddam door and she'd have some convoluted tale about why she'd

212

disappeared. These are dreams, Lee. She's lost to you for all goddam time. She's gone where nobody comes back. So you put the thought away, stuff it someplace.

Don't think sorrow.

Zip. He was out of here. 7.30 a.m. and already on the streets, driving the stolen Pontiac through hard sunshine and heat you could taste. No air-conditioner in this heap.

Gregory J. Samsa.

A cop, for Christ's sake.

Now you know what he looks like anyway.

For the sake of argument, say Samsa was the one that picked up Almond. Not the ponderous Silas Goba, that slob drunk, but Samsa the respectable cop. You couldn't blame the guy for that. Almond made all heads swivel like they were on stalks. That strut she had down to perfection, the pert little breasts, the luscious mouth, the sexual confidence she oozed. He'd seen all that the first time he'd met her in a bar, when she'd been in the city only two days, escaping from some family hell out west, and was wandering like a soul in purgatory.

A week later she was working for him. Mainly hotels, outcall services, where the money was good, 150, 200 a throw. But sometimes the street, although he'd always thought that the saloon of last resort, a place she went when the phone wasn't ringing off the hook. He didn't like her out on the sidewalks.

It was from those black sidewalks that her killer had plucked her. Taken her to the Purchase field. Broken her neck.

Had the killer been Gregory J. Samsa? He fucked Almond and took her down to that unruly place, and then, consumed by an enormous guilt, murdered her.

Just try proving it, Lee.

He rolled down the windows. Muggy air that smelled of gasoline and slow death blew through the car. He wondered if cancer had a scent. If leukemia had its own aroma. He wondered also about rigor mortis and when it set in, and if Almond was stiff and lying in a chilled drawer at the morgue. He had an image of her flesh turning blue, which caused him to sense an impending angry derangement, gray vapors forming around the margins of his vision, and his brain like something in a boxcar hauled by a freight train through bleak railroad yards and alongside drab fields.

This day is unreal. This day is totally fucked before it's even begun. The jitters are arriving in hyped-up droves, like hordes of ravenous black flies.

He drove past shopping malls and through suburbs, his thoughts turning to the nightingale. The chime of her voice. That innocence. *Perilous seas in faery lands forlorn.*

She had to be Samsa's daughter. Who else could she be?

Gregory J's little girl.

He looked in his rearview mirror. He didn't believe what he saw.

He pulled the black Pontiac over and, with a feeling of concentrated tension, waited. He heard the flies drone malevolently in his head. He glanced in the wing mirror and watched Tom Raseci step out of the Porsche and walk toward the Pontiac. Raseci, wearing a lurid Hawaiian shirt, stuck his head in the window.

'Nice wheels, Lee,' Raseci said. 'Very nice. Where'd you get them? Gossamer?'

Gossamer Avenue, despite its poetic name, was the pits, a row of sleazy used-car lots that provided their own extortionate credit and specialized in selling junked-out gas-guzzlers to itinerant Mexican workers or deadbeats who couldn't raise a cent from any bank. The guys that ran the lots on Gossamer were always busy repossessing their junkers and making a quick turnover.

'I stole the car, Tom,' Boyle said. 'Happy now?'

Raseci kicked a tire idly. 'I hate to see the mighty fallen.'

'And I hate this shit of being followed around.'

'All that dope's made you schizoid, Lee. I happened to see you boogie past, was all. So I swung round for a better look. Lee Boyle in a beat black Pontiac. What is it? Seventy-four? Three?'

'Who cares?' Boyle said. He didn't believe Raseci had been driving along casually at all. At this time of the morning?

Raseci kicked the tire again with the toe of his size thirteens and the hubcap fell off. 'Not put together real well, is she, Lee?'

Boyle got out of his car. 'Okay, Tom. You've seen the car. You've noted my humiliation. Is there anything else?'

'That Porsche,' Raseci said. 'I had it tuned up. Running like a dream. Real sweet. A Swiss fucking clock.'

'Do we stand around in this God-awful humidity and talk cars, Tom?' He looked into Raseci's face. He couldn't see the eyes because Bigshoes was wearing black shades.

'Hell, no,' Raseci said. 'Let's talk about the morning news, Lee. Let's discuss this fresh-breaking story about how a certain young girl was found dead not three miles from where we're standing.'

Boyle gazed along the street. Boxy houses built too close together, spindly young trees, the roar of a diesel-driven lawnmower. 'What can I say, Tom?'

Raseci said, 'Mr Plumm is very distressed by the news. He had the cops talking to him about your whereabouts at a certain time. So did I, Lee. We're not happy with cops phoning. Especially Mr Plumm. Apart from the inconvenience, he sees an income problem for you now.'

'Her death's a tragedy.'

Raseci took off his black glasses and slipped them into

his pocket. His pecs shuddered under the fabric of his garish shirt. He touched his bad eye with a fingertip. His battered nose gave him the look of an ex-slugger, somebody who'd been knocked around a few rings in his time. 'Yeah, it's a real tragedy all right, Lee.'

Raseci suddenly grabbed him, got a tight lock on his neck, forced his face down against the hot hood of the Pontiac and pushed his knee directly into the crack of Boyle's ass.

'Christ, Tom. What the hell are you doing?'

'Consider this a freebie, a taste of things to come.'

'Tom, it's broad fucking daylight, there are people in these houses, you're probably scaring the shit out of them—'

'Fuck 'em, it's you I want to scare,' Raseci said. 'Only you. Dum-di-dum. How's that song go?'

The blow was deft and painful. Raseci drove his big leaden fist into Boyle's back just below the shoulder blades. Then Raseci raised him up from the hood, swung him round, and delivered a second punch with great impact into the solar plexus, that intricate network of nerves and ganglia. Boyle felt as if he'd been vacuumed by a very crude sucking device that also crushed and hammered as it cleaned. A Hoover with attitude. He slumped, slithered against the side of the car and groaned. The pain was excruciating. What made it worse was the fact that Raseci was singing 'Only You' as he worked.

Boyle's head rolled to the side. Dizzy. Seeing swirls.

Raseci picked him up and dusted blades of grass from his silk shirt in a manner that was almost tender. 'Nothing personal, you understand,' he said.

Boyle blinked, groping to make sense of his fractured perceptions.

'I don't *want* to bust your face, Lee. I don't *want* to break bones. But I'll do it with great pleasure in' – he looked at his watch – 'let's say about thirty-eight hours from now. Unless, of course, there's a hefty infusion of money before then.'

'Thirty-eight hours,' Boyle said, dazed.

'Time just evaporates,' Raseci said. He stepped back, gazing at Boyle. 'You feeling okay, Lee?'

'I'll survive,' Boyle whispered. He saw Raseci walk back to the Porsche, get inside and drive away, his big ugly face grinning, and he was filled with assorted notions of getting even.

He edged himself carefully into the Pontiac. He lowered his face against the warm plastic of the wheel and gripped the steering column for support. Even though speed anaesthetized up to a point, this pain was going to take some time to pass away. Time he didn't have. Time was a hummingbird, darting, elusive. Now you see it, now you don't. Thirty-eight hours. Was that all he had left? He needed to move. He felt sick. He opened the door and puked what looked like thin minestrone on the sidewalk, and let his head dangle for a while.

He couldn't linger. He had to get his hands on some hard currency. He was trembling as he wired the car, and there was a painful stiffening in his gut, but this was a trifle compared with the damage Raseci could *really* do.

Blow town. What Vass recommended. Walk down to the bus station and say, I want fifty bucks' worth of motion in any direction, Mr Greyhound, sir. No way, he wasn't going to let Raseci and Plumm hound him, he still had thirty-eight hours, enough time to work something out.

Like what?

Your prospects are zero.

He decided he could live with pain. If you focused it could be controlled. He thought about his gun. If it came right down to it, if he was really backed into a corner and there was *absolutely* no way out, okay, screw it, he'd shoot Raseci, and then he'd go after Jimmy Plumm. He'd do that. He wouldn't even think twice.

He drove, listening to imaginary gunshots and struggling to contain his physical distress, to where The Kid lived. He parked outside the apartment complex and didn't move for a moment. Then he got out of the car and walked toward the entrance. Jesus, there were stairs to climb. He'd forgotten that. Halfway up a flash of pain caused him to pause. His animosity toward the world in general was gigantic. Beyond management.

Die, Raseci. Die, Plumm.

And you, Hugh.

He imagined Hugh lined up with his head in a hood, body staked to a post in a lonely place. *A last cigarette before the ultimate beddy-bye, Hugh?* Except Hugh didn't smoke. It was unhealthy. Jesus, how he loathed Hugh. His hatred was like some heavy mahogany yoke around his shoulders.

He continued to climb, and reached the third floor. His heart was slogging. The Kid must have spotted him getting out of the car, because he was already opening the door and beckoning Boyle inside. Boyle nodded, but didn't feel like smiling. He needed to sit, made it to the sofa, and looked at The Kid, that soft wholesome face, hair light and floppy and no doubt shampooed in gentle herbal matter, the sleeves of his sweater rolled.

'How are you, Lee?'

'I've had better days,' Lee Boyle said, trying to recollect when he'd last been in this apartment. Months ago, when he'd run into The Kid in a bar downtown and they'd drunk a few beers together and smoked The Kid's hash, and then they'd come back here and Boyle had provided a little speed from his stash. The night was spent hatching vague plans and plots, ways of making a quick buck. The stoned babble of mendacious conspiracies. Blackmail, that was the word The Kid had used – *I have it scoped, Lee. Trust me. This is a solid proposition.*

'You look somewhat piqued, Lee.'

More tweaked than piqued, Boyle thought. 'Late nights.'

'Do you know your name means a calm sheltered place, Lee? Did you know that? A lee.'

'I enjoy a little irony this early in the day,' Boyle said. 'You got a cold beer handy?'

'Coming right up.' The Kid vanished into the kitchen, gliding off in his bare feet, then came back with two bottles of chilled Amstel.

Boyle guzzled half of his quickly. He looked at The Kid and said, 'Okay. This better be good.'

'I think we've got something, Lee. You want to come this way?' The young man beckoned to a door. Boyle got up from the sofa, stepped after The Kid into a small room where a blackout curtain was drawn over the window and a light bulb hung with red crêpe paper.

Boyle saw various bottles of chemicals, trays, prints hung on a plastic line with clothes-pegs.

'Now, let us see, let us see.' The Kid began to unhook prints from the line. He cleared a space on his work surface, shoving aside the chemicals, then spread out a bunch of prints. Boyle leaned over them, feeling an ache deep in his stomach. He wondered about internal damage. Maybe rupturing inside. A crab clawed at his intestines. He imagined pincers digging.

'The idea was I'd photograph only those guys that looked respectable, right?'

'Well-heeled,' Boyle said. 'Moneyed.'

'Nice cars. No scrapyard candidates. No riff-raff.'

'Exactly,' Boyle said. He peered closer at the prints, which were generally of a poor fuzzed quality. Mainly they showed shadowy figures of men sitting inside cars, occasionally somebody on a sidewalk.

'These don't look too sharp,' Boyle said.

'Consider the circumstances. I'm working in the dark. I can't use a flash, *obviously*. I have to conceal the camera. You try taking photographs in those conditions, Lee.'

'I'm not criticizing you,' Boyle said. 'I'm not expecting Karsh of Ottawa.'

'They can be enhanced, of course. That isn't a problem.'

'Okay. What am I supposed to be looking at?' Boyle asked.

The Kid, smirking a little, hovered over the spread of photographs like a magician about to play a card trick. He slid two prints toward Boyle. 'Check these out.'

Boyle picked up the prints and moved closer to the light and examined the dark images. It took him a moment before he focused, before he understood what he was seeing. Suddenly he was beyond pain. He was flying where the air was thin and he couldn't catch his breath. It was like hanging by a parachute caught on an updraft and all the green countryside spread out way below you.

Thank you, Jesus. This is what I need. This is *the break*.

The Kid asked, 'You'll see the image in one is sharper than the other. You want me to improve them even more?'

'No need. They're perfect. You any idea what you've *got* here?'

The Kid nodded and looked gleeful. 'Yeah. I know *exactly* what I've got. What happens next?'

'You sit back. I'll take it from here.'

'You walk out with the prints?'

'You got a problem with that?'

'I'd like, uh, some kind of guarantee.'

'Guarantee? What kind of partnership is this?' Boyle asked. 'You don't think I'm running a risk here? I'm putting my neck on the line, and if it goes wrong your name doesn't even come up. That's *your* guarantee. I'm the one burned.' He brought his face close to The Kid's, a belligerent little motion. 'Or maybe you want to do the whole thing yourself, huh? You want to look this guy in the eye? He'd fucking eat you and spit out the bones. You want to mess with that, sport? Huh?'

The young man shook his head timidly. 'I'd rather not, actually.'

'You better believe it, *actually*. So don't give me shit about guarantees. I'm about to commit a felony here. You want to stray that far on the other side of the law? You'd be in way over your head, man. You leave this to me, and I'll be in touch the very moment our ship comes in.' *Some people*, Boyle thought. *They think they have the balls for the real hard stuff. Ooh, taking pictures in the dark, how awfully dangerous.*

Boyle stepped back into the living room. He stared at the fish swimming round in the big tank. 'I'm thinking, if you ever fall on hard times and you're really hungry, Kid, you could stick one of them in a sandwich.'

'You are so *gross*.'

'People eat *sardines*, for Christ's sake.'

'They're pets, Lee. Pets.'

'I don't see any point in keeping pets that don't know you from one minute to the next,' Boyle said.

'I have a dim memory of having this exact conversation last time you were here.'

'I don't remember that.' Another little amoeba of memory destroyed. He realized he'd even forgotten The Kid's real name. He went to the door. 'I'll be in touch.'

'I'll be waiting, Lee. *Anxiously*.'

Boyle went down the stairs and outside. He sat inside the warm car for a time, trying to herd his thoughts. Corral them. Line them up. See what they amount to. Then he drove the dying black Pontiac – he'd have to dump this wreck soon – until he came to a payphone out-side a convenience market. He dropped a coin in the slot, dialed Vass's number and waited an age for an answer. He tapped his fingertips restlessly on an empty metal phone-book container. Come on, Vass. Pick up the fucking phone.

Vass sounded distant, pissed with him still. 'I'm making a table, Lee. I'm up to here in sawdust.' A dog barked in the background, one of Vass's menagerie of mongrels.

'Do me a small favor,' Boyle said.

'Lee, man, I'm busy. Also, I had the cops calling me at some unholy hour asking about you. What the fuck trouble are you in?'

'Don't worry about the cops. What I'm asking you will take about five minutes out of your day.'

Vass said, 'Being your friend isn't the easiest thing, Lee.'

'Especially my best friend,' Boyle said.

'Just spell out the favor, man. And I'll see.'

28

SAMSA DRANK HIS COFFEE QUICKLY. DARCY SAID, 'YOU really ought to eat something, you know.'

'I'm rushed.'

'You need cereal. Fresh fruit. You look wan. You don't get enough sleep.'

The portable TV was playing on the kitchen counter. Samsa saw a picture of the Purchase land and the blonde reporter from Channel 5, Linda Kisminski, talking into the camera. A caption along the bottom of the screen read, 5 LIVE AM in orange letters. He got up to switch off.

Darcy said, 'No, wait. I'm watching this. Is this what kept you out last night?'

Samsa said yes, it was, and fidgeted with his cup.

'How did she die?'

He told her. She made a face and continued to look at the picture. For as long as she could remember homicides had been part of her daily life. Her father never talked about the specifics, the blood details, but he carried the burden of them. You could tell when he was brooding: he'd disappear before your eyes, lost in God knows what investigation, what pieces of evidence, what ambivalent phrase from an interview with a suspect.

'How old was she?'

Samsa drained his coffee before he said, 'Thirteen. She was a runaway.' He looked at Darcy and there was uneasiness in his expression. 'You'd never do that, would you?'

'Run away from home? Come on. I can't imagine the circumstances.'

Linda Kisminski was saying '. . . from the details we've been able to gather, the dead girl worked as a prostitute in the city's sleazy and shameful sex trade, which continues unabated despite local complaints. Unless something is done about the situation, how many more girls like this one will be at risk? I talked earlier with Police Chief Al Brodsky, who says this tragic case has top priority, and the department is – I quote – "determined to find this girl's killer". Linda Kisminski, Five Live a.m.'

Darcy had seen the place, known locally as Flesh Row, sometimes Skin Street. She'd driven past there once or twice with Nick and looked at the girls on the sidewalks, and she'd wondered what they were thinking, what they felt when they were in some stranger's car or bed, if they distanced themselves and everything was mechanical.

'She was on drugs,' Samsa said. 'Have you ever . . . you know?'

She laughed, shook her head, no. It was a lie. She'd smoked dope a few times, and tried cocaine at a party a couple of months ago. She'd gone into the bathroom with Ginny Flagg and a college girl she knew only as Spyder – a Goth with torn black leggings and a pin in her earlobe and scarlet lipstick – and Spyder had produced a little brown bottle and a tiny spoon. For twenty minutes or so Darcy had felt a lift of exultation and energy, but then she'd wanted more. By that time Spyder had disappeared upstairs with a boy.

'Any leads?' she asked.

'Not yet.'

'Some sicko picked her up and killed her,' Darcy said.

He rose, touched her under the chin. 'I have to run.'

She sipped her orange juice. She watched her father take his sports coat from the back of the chair.

'You're not cutting classes again, are you?' he asked.

'I'm being dutiful and conscientious today.'

'Good.' He leaned to kiss her on the top of her head. She thought there was something a little tentative about him, a lack of the adrenalin he usually had when a new homicide occurred. Maybe you just got tired of death after so many years. She was about to mention the phone call she'd received last night, but the idea of a stranger calling out of the blue like that would bother him, and he was clearly flustered anyway. Why add to his concerns? The good daughter, considerate to Dad. *Sometimes.*

'I don't know when I'll be back,' he said.

'I'll be fine. Call me when you have a chance.'

He hesitated in the kitchen doorway. 'We should spend more time together, Darcy.'

'Yeah. On your retirement,' she said, and smiled.

She listened to him drive away, dumped her cereal bowl in the dishwasher and threw in a couple of cups and glasses. She brushed her hair in the bathroom. She thought about changing her hairstyle, which she wore short. Let it grow out, maybe shoulder-length. Sometimes you got bored with the same face in the mirror. She thought her eyes her best feature – deep brown, almost black, like her father's. 'Eyes like Hershey pools,' Nick had told her once. Mancuso, master of imagery.

She picked up her books from the table in the kitchen and left the house, locked the door, headed toward the corner of the block where the schoolbus arrived. Lately

Nick had been in the habit of giving her a ride, but she'd told him she'd rather bus it. It was a small act of rebellion and pretty pathetic really, but it was a start. If she was to dig out a claim to her independence and free herself from Nick without cruelty, it would need to be accomplished in small steps.

She heard the car cruising behind her before she saw it. She turned her face. The driver had one arm hanging from the window as he brought the car alongside her and said, 'Lovely morning, don't you think?'

She turned and continued to walk. The car – a pale-blue Mercury, finned, prehistoric – kept pace with her, which she found irritating. She stopped.

'Something I can do for you?' she asked.

'What's wrong with saying a simple hello,' he said.

'I'll tell you what's wrong: I don't know you, I've never seen you before, and you're disturbing me.'

'You going to school? Hop in. I'll drive you.'

Fat chance. She walked a few paces, stopped again and stared at him. 'What is it you want exactly?'

'Why do people always leap to the conclusion that other people always *want* something? It's an unhealthy way of looking at life. It's a sign of the paranoid times we live in. Everybody's scared. Nobody wants to connect. We live in our own sealed boxes.'

She shaded her eyes against the brightness of sun. She saw how sunlight was reflected from his shirt and his hair and the windshield.

'Hey, I'm harmless,' he said. 'Ask any of my friends.'

'I don't know any of your friends.'

'I'll introduce you to some,' he said.

'Yeah, right,' and she turned and kept moving. The car slid along beside her.

She said, 'You're being a nuisance.'

'You want to tell me your name?'

226

'Wait,' she said. 'You're the one that phoned! I recognize your voice.'

'I didn't phone you,' and he stopped the car and got out, leaving the engine running. 'Carry your books in time-honored fashion?'

'I can manage.' *Just walk*, she thought. *He's lying about not phoning*.

'Your heart is spoken for? Don't tell me.'

'*Jesus*. What business is it of yours?'

'You think I'm too old for you?'

'I think you're goddam presumptuous,' she said.

He was in step with her now. 'You're not exactly keeping company with the Ancient Mariner. So your heart isn't taken, huh?'

'What will it take for you to leave me alone,' she said.

'I'm just compelled by curiosity. You quit being curious, you might as well be dead.'

'This is where I catch my bus.'

'I'll drive you to school in my chariot.'

'Uh, don't think so.'

'Come on. Do I look menacing? Do I look like somebody who goes round offering rides to unfamiliar young women?'

She stared at him. 'Yeah, I think maybe you do.'

'Your father warned you against guys like me. Right? Candies-from-strangers syndrome.'

'I don't always listen to my father,' she said. Why had she said that? Why had she sounded so . . . *defensive*? She could hear the school bus rattling a block away. 'I make my own decisions.'

'I bet you do. So why won't you let me drive you?'

'No way.'

'I am crushed.'

'Good,' she said, and glanced at him.

He feigned an inconsolable look and laid a hand across

his heart. He had an expressive face and gestures. The eyes were bright and smart and – yeah, all right – attractive. He exuded an energetic confidence, as if life was something to be taken lightly, nothing was too serious, problems were just tiny obstacles you skipped around.

'Here's my bus,' she said.

'Go,' he said. 'Sit with the clones. Conform. Be like everyone else. Ride the bus. Sit in classrooms. Take notes. Regurgitate. Blah-blah.'

'You don't know the first thing about me.'

'I'd say you're intelligent. You're independent. You don't like school. You know there's more to life than books and teachers. You're a prisoner of the system. You're not free. You haven't tasted liberty.'

She smiled at him, didn't really want to. The way he pinned her down, defined her. Accurate enough.

She said, 'You're guessing now.'

'I'm a great guesser,' he said. 'I do a lot of things well, as a matter of fact.'

The big yellow bus drew up and the doors opened.

'Here,' he said, and shoved a piece of paper into her hand. Puzzled, she closed her fingers around it and boarded the bus, and saw him watch her from the sidewalk with a curious smile on his face as the doors hissed shut.

29

YOU DON'T GET ENOUGH SLEEP. SAMSA, TURNING DARCY'S
remark around in his head, thought, *I'm afraid of sleep,
of dreaming.* He entered City Hall, where Al Brodsky
greeted him and drew him aside from the flurry of clerks
and secretaries, lawyers and municipal officials arriving
for work. It was obvious to Samsa that Al had been waiting for him, and he had the nervy thought, *It's coming
down on me now.* But Al, hands stuffed in pockets and tie
undone, had other things on his mind.

'You want to hear a brand-new twist, Greg? We've got
a confession in the Cecily Suarez business.'

'A confession?'

'I don't know how much water it's going to hold. Come
downstairs and see for yourself.'

'Somebody just showed up and said what? He killed the
girl?'

'Popped in half an hour ago with a *mea culpa.*' Al
Brodsky steered Samsa toward the basement stairway.

'One of the usual nuts?'

'Not this time. This one's new.'

Samsa descended alongside the chief. Homicide cases brought loonies out of the woodwork, people anxious to confess for any number of reasons – attention mainly. Notice me, please. Here I am – deranged persons living bitter lives of excruciating anonymity on the fringes of society. Samsa had encountered a good share of these in his career. Usually you could dismiss them after a few questions. They spoke of demonic connections or mind-altering influences from outer space, or how they were the reincarnations of notorious serial killers, some of whom were still actually alive on various death rows.

Samsa and Brodsky entered one of the interview rooms. Billy Fogue was there, and Sergeant Ed Duff, who looked like a middle-aged Boy Scout, suntanned and healthy, the kind of dependable guy you just knew would have a way with sheepshank knots and how to pitch tents on mountainsides.

Billy Fogue said, 'Lew Tenant. Meet Ryan Pritt.'

Ryan Pritt sat at the table in the middle of the room, his hands clasped in front of him. He was a thin-faced man who wore a plaid shirt and neatly pressed khaki pants and shiny brown shoes. His hair was receding. He had a relaxed air about him, an absence of desperation, distress.

'How are you, Ryan?' Samsa asked.

'It's a load off my mind,' Pritt said.

'You really killed this girl?' *Tell me you did*, Samsa thought. *Prove it to me. Let your story be watertight, Ryan. What am I thinking? I want Pritt to be guilty.*

Pritt said, 'Yeah. I killed her.'

Fogue said, 'Ryan's a construction worker, Lew Tenant. Presently unemployed. Married. Two small kids.'

Pritt nodded. 'Evangeline and Angelique. One's three, the other's five.'

'Pretty names,' Samsa said. He looked at Pritt's hands. The fingers were callused.

Pritt said, 'I got pictures in my wallet, you want to see them?'

'Maybe later.' Samsa sat on the edge of the table. The guy had none of the usual behavioral give-aways of the nut: no rapid speech pattern, no weirded-out light in the eye. 'You want to run through your story for me?'

'I already told these officers,' Pritt said.

'Now you get to tell me, Ryan. Start with when you met her.'

'I picked her up Monday night.'

'Where?'

'That area they all go. You know it?'

'What time?'

'About nine, maybe nine thirty.' Pritt adjusted a cuff of his shirt. 'I drove out of town. Took her out to that field near Chackstone Acres.'

'What did you do next?'

'I don't have to give you all the details, do I?'

'Unfortunately you do,' Samsa said.

Ryan Pritt looked round the room at the faces of the assembled cops. 'I get it. You guys don't believe me.'

'It's not that, Ryan. The thing is, sometimes people come in confessing to stuff they haven't done.'

'That's pretty damn stupid.'

'It happens. Which is why we have to ask questions. We need details.'

Ryan Pritt looked up at the ceiling. 'Okay. We went in the back seat of the car. She gives me this condom. I told her, I don't wear those things. No way.'

'So what happened next?'

'We argued,' he said. 'I wanted it straight. I wasn't shelling out sixty bucks for a condom fuck.'

'And the argument blew out of all proportion?' Samsa leaned a little closer to the man. *Why was he lying? What was in it for him?*

'I lost my temper,' Pritt said. 'I exploded, I guess.' He shut his eyes in the manner of a man replaying bad memories. 'She slapped me because I wouldn't let her out the car. She was beginning to scream.'

'Then?'

'I didn't mean it,' Pritt said. He hunched forward, laid his head on the table and began to sob silently.

'Take it easy, Ryan.' Samsa gestured to Duff. 'Get Ryan some water, Ed.'

Duff fetched a cup from the cooler and set it down on the table.

Pritt lifted his head, sipped and said, 'Thanks, thanks.'

Samsa said, 'She slapped you. She screamed. There was some kind of struggle.'

'Yeah, very brief,' Pritt said. He rubbed his eyes.

'You hit her?'

'One time. That was all.'

'Where did you hit her?'

'Here.' Pritt reached back, touched the base of his neck. 'In that area, roughly. First, I thought I'd just knocked her out. I grabbed her shoulders, shook her a few times, but she wasn't coming round.'

I shook her shoulders, Samsa thought. *I shook her shoulders. It wasn't you, Ryan Pritt.*

'So this one blow killed her,' he said.

'One blow, all it took,' Pritt said quietly. 'She was a frail little thing. Tiny . . .' He played with the corner of his mouth, touching it with a fingertip as if he were applying balm to a cold sore.

Samsa walked round the room. 'What was she wearing, Ryan?'

'Oh, real short skirt, a blouse you could see through. You know how hookers dress. Even in the rain.'

Samsa remembered the umbrella she'd been carrying.

How could he ask about that without opening a door he wanted to keep shut?

'Anything else, Ryan?'

'She had this bracelet.'

'Can you describe it for us?'

Pritt shook his head. 'Only that it was big.'

'Did you see the color of her panties?'

'I never got that far.'

'Okay. You hit her. Then what?'

'I found a place to dump her out in that field. I was desperate, I was freaked, you got to understand that.'

'You dumped her. Then what?'

'Then nothing. All I wanted was to get the hell away from there.'

Samsa asked, 'Why did you pick up this girl in the first place? You're married, two nice daughters. Why?'

'My wife's . . . between ourselves, I guess we don't get along in that one area,' Pritt said.

'You often use hookers?'

'Two times a month maybe. At most.'

'Had you picked up Cecily Suarez before?'

Pritt said he hadn't. He leaned back in his chair.

'Why have you confessed, Ryan?' Samsa asked.

'Because it's a burden, Lieutenant. It's like this big goddam cloud inside your head. It's this voice that won't stop talking in your ear. You don't sleep. You go around in a daze. You're scared. You feel like shit.'

Tell me about it, Ryan. 'So what do you want? To sign a confession?'

'Somebody take down my statement and I'll sign it.'

Brodsky said, 'It's customary to ask for a lawyer, Ryan.'

'Why shell out good money to those bandits?'

Brodsky looked at Samsa and said, 'A word.'

They went out of the interview room and stood together in the corridor. The chief asked, 'What's your impression?'

'I don't know.'

'He described the girl.'

'Up to a point, sure. He might be lying. He might have picked her up before.'

'Why would he be lying?'

'Why does anybody lie? Has he been checked out?'

'Cullinan did the background. Construction worker, two daughters. That's all on the level. No priors.'

'Everything he's told us he could have seen on TV, or read in the early edition of the *Gazette*. There's nothing new in his story, Al. There's no big surprise.'

'There's the bracelet,' Brodsky said. 'The way she was dressed. I don't remember these details going public.'

'Yeah, but I still say it's *possible* he picked her up before. She might have been wearing a bracelet then.'

'The gift horse, and you're looking it in the mouth.'

'I don't trust gift horses, Al.'

'Normally I don't trust them either. But this guy seems so . . .'

'Straight? Genuine?'

Brodsky said, 'Ordinary.'

'With a mighty conscience,' Samsa said.

'Some people have such things, Greg.'

'You want to book him?' Samsa said.

'I'd like to hold him until I hear from Zane that the blow on the kid's neck is consistent with what Pritt says he did to her. I also want a psychiatric report.'

'And if it gels, he's our man.'

'You got a better prospect?'

Samsa thought, *This is the easy way out. This is my escape route. But it isn't. It can't be. And you can't tunnel your way to freedom through Ryan Pritt.* 'No,' he said. 'I don't.'

'It's your case,' and Al Brodsky raised his hands, palms outward in a backing-off gesture. 'You play it any way you see fit.'

'I want to talk with his wife. See what his home back-ground is like. I want to know this guy before I reach any conclusion.'

Brodsky said, 'Always cautious.'

'Thorough,' Samsa remarked. 'I'll take Eve Lassiter with me. She's got a light touch with some people.'

They were about to step back into the interview room when a uniformed cop appeared at the end of the corridor and called out, 'Lieutenant? There's somebody waiting for you in your office.'

'Who?' Samsa asked.

The cop said, 'I'm only the messenger, Lieutenant.'

'See who it is, Greg,' Brodsky said. 'I'll keep chatting with Pritt in the meantime.'

Samsa, irritated by this interruption, walked to his office.

The man who stood beside the desk was fingering a photograph of Darcy. He looked at Samsa and said, 'I thought I'd drop in. See what the hive feels like. Maybe talk about this and that.'

Samsa stopped dead. *This is wrong.*

The man set down the photograph. 'Your daughter?'

Samsa nodded. 'What do you want to talk about, Boyle?'

Lee Boyle smiled, sniffed, ran the back of one hand across the tip of his nose. 'One or two things, I guess.'

'Be more specific,' Samsa said. *Boyle shouldn't be here*, he thought. He was uneasy, more than that. He fought back the feeling, the sense of menace Boyle had dragged inside his office. Boyle knows nothing. Absolutely nothing.

'I'm not sure you want to hear what I have to say in this particular environment, Samsa,' and Boyle gestured around the small office, encompassing more than this tiny space – the whole department, City Hall, the corridors of law and order and propriety.

Samsa said, 'Say what you're here to say, Boyle.' He couldn't keep a certain thickness out of his voice.

Boyle walked round the desk and settled in Samsa's chair. 'You know what I think?'

'Suppose you tell me.'

'I think you're going through assorted degrees of torment.'

'Why would I be suffering torment, Boyle?'

'Think about it,' Boyle said.

'Think about what exactly?'

'Almond.'

Almond, Samsa thought. *Where is Boyle going with this?* He said, 'First, get the fuck out of my chair.'

Boyle shrugged, rose. 'Like I say. Maybe we should continue this conversation someplace where you won't get so uptight.'

'What's wrong with talking right here?' Samsa listened to phones ringing. He heard Cullinan's voice in an outer office and a couple of traffic cops yack about an accident on the freeway. Phones, voices. These sounds came to him over a great distance, but they gathered intensity as they rolled in his direction. He saw a fly flit dangerously close to the whirring blades of the fan. He imagined the motor set in reverse mode and the fly sucked into the blades and butchered instantly.

'Nothing, I guess,' Boyle said. 'I don't give a shit basically. You want to talk about your accident here or some other place, it doesn't matter to me.'

Samsa suddenly had funny spots in front of his eyes, small dancing stars. Stress maybe. Blood pressure rising. *My accident.* He looked at Darcy's photograph. How bright and sharp she appeared. Her smile was open and innocent and imparted all the optimism of her age. He wanted to keep her this way, protect that innocence for as long as he could in a threatening world.

'Name a place,' he said, even as he knew immediately this was a mistake, a moment of weakness.

Boyle smiled and fingered the edge of Darcy's photograph. 'Now that's what I call good judgement, Lieutenant.'

30

LEE BOYLE ABANDONED THE STOLEN CAR – HIS THIRD IN THE last twelve hours – in a parking garage downtown, and began the search for new transportation. The trick to stealing cars was simple: don't get attached to them. He found a white Ford Taurus parked outside a health-food store in a side street, windows rolled down, keys *dangling* in the ignition. The owner must have stepped inside the store on a quick errand, mung beans or organic maple syrup, back in a flash, no sweat – *no car*.

Boyle drove through downtown, swung quickly past the Greyhound station – a seedy functional box surrounded by a stack of great smoking buses – and out to the freeway, thinking of young Ms Samsa, seeing her face in the photograph on Samsa's desk, the neatly written message she'd inscribed: 'Love to the Best Dad In the World, Darcy.' She had a mouth like a cherub waiting to be kissed. And her teeth, the *gleam* of perfection. It struck him that if you dyed the brown hair black, and the eyebrows, she'd look a lot like Almond, those deep dark eyes were similar, a reincarnation if you thought about it from a certain angle, a restoration of somebody you considered lost.

Maybe.

At her age she was delicately poised between obeying rules and flaunting them. The way Almond had been. Exactly.

Darcy Samsa. *Dar-cee*. Rolled off the tongue.

He was on the freeway a few miles before he took an exit ramp, checking his rear-view mirror. Now his mind went racing to the idea of Raseci, and he wondered if Bigshoes was tracking him. He'd seen no sign of him, which didn't mean he wasn't around somewhere. He'd also have minions who carried out tasks for him, such as surveillance. Boyle wouldn't know their faces or the cars they drove.

But they were there. This was indisputable. Gospel.

The dashboard clock registered 11:02. Time clung to him like a succubus. $10,000. He pondered Crassman briefly. A total write-off. Crassman probably had his guys – those hapless dickheads who looked like they were fresh from some Appalachian hollow where the barber had palsied hands – hanging out at the trailer park, armed and waiting for Lee Boyle to show and muttering about what they'd do to that goddammed *scumbucket* next time.

He wanted to arrive at the appointed place early, check it out. The last thing he needed was to be bushwhacked. He felt nervy, like a man committed to a roller-coaster trip, but midway through the heart-shaking ride wondering if he'd made the correct choice, except it was too late to disembark – unless you stepped out into space.

He parked the car, bought a ticket at the booth and passed through the turnstile. Stub in hand, he walked in the direction of the reptile house. The zoo wasn't upscale. The city didn't have the budget for natural habitats. The polar bear, slightly fortunate, had been given a tiny pit to himself, where murky water dribbled across a rocky formation. The creature looked mangy and sorrowful, like he was having dim memories of the carefree ice floes of his youth, before human assholes came and shot him with a trank gun and he woke up in hell.

Boyle kept moving, glancing around. A squall of red-assed baboons picked at each other's butts and chattered. There were very few customers: a bunch of schoolkids led by a guide, a couple of solitary browsers. The air was dead and heavy inside the reptile house, and there was that stale musk common to places where creatures are trapped.

Boyle, who found himself alone in the building, stared at a boa constrictor inside a glass case. Fat and motionless. In the next case rattlers lay coiled. All that pent-up venom.

At the sound of footsteps Boyle turned his face, saw the door open and Samsa appear with the sun behind him. Boyle tried to slough off his tension, tried to be cool, but the speed in his system jittered him.

The cop approached slowly. One of the rattlers struck the inside of the case, a whack of tail upon the glass. Boyle moved away slightly.

'Punctual,' he said to Samsa. 'I like that.'

Samsa said, 'Let's hear what you have to say, Boyle.'

Samsa had one of those thoughtfully still faces that might suddenly explode in animated expression. He looked, Boyle thought, a little on the haggard side. You needed to see under surfaces, though. The dark in Samsa's eye, presently calm, could smolder and turn to fury without warning.

'I agreed to meet with you, Boyle. I'm here and I'm waiting.'

'Don't rush me, Samsa. You can't afford an attitude problem.'

Samsa gestured round the reptile house. 'These some of your relatives?' He tapped one of the cases and a diamondback reared up an inch or so, roused from its torpor.

'You're a wag,' Boyle said. 'Except I'm not the snake here. I wasn't the one who picked up the girl. I wasn't the one who killed her.'

'*Killed* the girl? You out of your goddam mind?'

'Let's run through the facts, Lieutenant. You picked her up Monday night around ten.'

'You've got quite an imagination there, Boyle.'

'Then you drove her out to the Purchase place. You went off the fucking road in your Le Baron. Accident report number six-eight-two-zero, submitted by Frederick Trope, State trooper.'

'You must have accessed a computer to get that information. Initiative, Lee. So I had a car wreck. So what? It's a matter of record. The rest is bullshit.'

Boyle smiled. 'I admire you, Samsa. I'm in total awe of the way you handle two different worlds. One is all nice and respectable and wrapped in cellophane. The other's a black steamy hole. And you think you can keep them apart. You're the one with the bounteous imagination.'

'If this is all you've got to say, Boyle, you're wasting my time.' Samsa turned and took a step away.

Boyle said, 'You were *seen*, Samsa. The girl got into your car. You were spotted. I have an eyewitness.'

'This eyewitness has a name?'

Boyle nodded.

'But you're not saying who.'

'I look like a fool?'

Samsa stared at him hard. 'So all you've got is a wrecked car and an anonymous eyewitness. My guess is your erstwhile friend Cassandra, or whatever she calls herself. Her reputation isn't exactly unsullied, Boyle. You

241

think anybody's going to believe anything she has to say?' Samsa shook his head. 'Your story's a work of sheer desperation. You've got surmise and supposition, which amounts to thin fucking air. What you're doing is trying to divert focus away from yourself with this bullshit.'

'I don't think so, Samsa.'

'No? Let me show you the cards in my hand.'

'I'm all eyes,' Boyle said. So Samsa knew about Cassandra. He'd been digging.

'Your alibi frankly sucks, Boyle. Nobody can place you at Chang's at the time you stated. Your pals Plumm and Raseci don't have precise memories of when they saw you Monday night. They give vague a bad reputation. Rudolph Vass is another one that doesn't know the time of day. Your whole yarn's a sandcastle and the tide's coming in. This is a way of saying you have problems, Boyle. Real problems. In fact, you're up there on the suspect list. Way up. Certain parties downtown would like nothing better than for me to book you and lock you away without further ado.'

Boyle said, 'So book me. What's stopping you? Left your cuffs at the office? Here. Look. I'm holding my hands out. Take me downtown. Interrogate me. Lock me up. I'm a danger to society.'

'Unfortunately the law says I can't throw a guy in jail just because his alibi's like a fucking sieve. I need a little more than that, Boyle. I wish to Christ I didn't, but that's the way it's written. I'll tell you this much, though. It's only a matter of time before I nail you for the girl.'

Boyle thought, *This is your moment. Wipe the look off this fucker's face.* 'I happen to have something else, Samsa. Better than any eyewitness.'

Samsa didn't look interested. Or if he was he had ways of hiding it. Boyle placed a hand inside the hip pocket of his pants and left it there a moment. *I want to watch you sink, Samsa. I want to see the bubbles come up to the surface as you go down and down to where the bottom-suckers live.*

'What's in the pocket?' Samsa asked. 'Or are you trying to keep me in suspense, Boyle?'

'What an insightful guy you are,' Boyle said. He took out a sheet of paper, unfolded it and held it in his hand. 'This is a photocopy. The original is in a safe place. Here.' Boyle gave the paper to Samsa, who took it, gazed at it, then let it flop over in his fingers like something he wanted to drop.

Boyle reached out and retrieved the paper. He watched Samsa a second, then he glanced down at the Xerox.

In grainy light, face hidden slightly by the upraised collar of a sports coat, illuminated weakly by a street lamp, Samsa sits in his car, rolling the window up. The girl, slightly blurred by her own movement, is stepping in on the passenger side. She holds an umbrella at an angle away from her head, like she's about to fold it down. The expression on what you can see of Samsa's face is one of nervous fatigue maybe.

The car, you can tell from the badge visible on the hood, is a Chrysler.

And the girl, even though she's out of focus, is Almond. He knows the shape, the little skirt she's wearing, the chunky big bracelet you can just about see. He remembers her body when they made love on the bathroom floor. He imagines her on a slab in the morgue.

He raised his face to Samsa and said, 'So you see.'

Samsa gazed at a snake slithering across its cage. 'It's not a good image,' he said. 'It's blurred.'

Boyle had the impression that Samsa was talking to himself. His voice was strange and flat.

'It can be improved, Lieutenant. Technology's terrific these days.'

Samsa was still observing the serpent. 'I was running her off the streets, that's all. You see a kid like that cruising, you think of your own daughter . . .'

'I'm moved, Samsa. I'm deeply touched. I'm almost tearful. The lieutenant has compassion for hookers. It's something he doesn't want to discuss in his own office, so here we are in this fucking zoo having a secret meeting.'

'It's not a subject I wanted to talk about back there,' Samsa said.

'Why? Your colleagues might overhear, and they wouldn't understand the sheer fucking depth of your compassion? They'd think more salacious thoughts, huh?'

'Exactly.'

'Fine, fine. So if I show this picture to Fogue or Rebb, you wouldn't mind? If I took it to the Chief of Police, that wouldn't bother you? Is that what you're saying?'

Samsa didn't reply. He had the look of a guy who has just backstepped into a pile of dogshit up over the rim of his shoe.

Boyle laughed aloud. 'I didn't think so, Samsa. Here's another scenario for you to mull over: Almond's in your car, and you go skidding off the road and down into the field. And somewhere in that time frame your passenger, God rest her sad young soul, dies. Maybe she's giving you head as you're tooting along and you lose your concentration. Or maybe she's administering a hand job and your senses are otherwise engaged. Or maybe it's even more devious and deliberate than that. There's this dark side to you because you've been hanging around homicides for too long, and something's rubbed off and it's warped your thinking and you wonder, hey, what's it like to kill somebody, what's it like to snuff out a life, because you're sick—'

'No,' Samsa said.

'And after you kill her you fake the accident—'

'*No*,' Samsa said again.

'Whatever it is, *bang*, you go off the road. And the lieutenant, concerned about his reputation as a law-enforcement officer of some standing, has a big-time panic attack. He's got a dead hooker on his hands. But wait. The idea of the century comes to him. Why, he'll just *dump* the corpse and report the accident – minus any mention of the dead girl, of course. So he goes through with this chump scheme, and he thinks he's got his ass well and truly covered. Right? *Right?*'

Samsa pressed his forehead against the surface of a glass case. Sweat filmed his forehead. He had his hands clenched and white against his sides.

'*Right?*' Boyle asked again. 'You dumped the corpse. You falsified an accident report. Oh, you're in deep shit, Samsa.'

Samsa looked at Boyle and was silent for a very long time, as if a prolonged inner struggle were coming to some kind of resolution. 'You can't prove this. It's all guess-work.'

'Okay. I'll take the picture to your boss. You don't have any objections to that, I suppose.' Boyle folded the Xerox and turned away.

He hadn't walked more than a few steps before Samsa called him back. *I knew he would*, Boyle thought. *I see his fear. I can smell it.*

'You want money. It's usually money.'

'Money's always useful.'

'I'm not wealthy, Boyle.'

'And I'm not greedy. I call that serendipity.' Boyle thought a second. Ten thou to get Plumm off his back. Something for himself. 'Twenty-five K should keep your name out the papers.'

'That's a lot of cash.'

'But you're in a lot of trouble.'

'Look,' and Samsa stopped, his face devoid of color.

'I'm looking,' Boyle said.

There was a shiver in Samsa's voice. When he spoke, the words came out of some locked cellar deep inside. 'It was an accident, Boyle, a tragic fucking accident. I didn't kill that girl. I didn't mean for that to happen. Believe me, if I could go back and change things I'd do it. I'd give anything to be able to do that.'

'Nobody's going to give a shit if it was an accident or if you broke her goddam neck with your own hands,' Boyle said. 'It doesn't change the fact that this is an impossible situation for you. And just in case it sneaks across your mind to pull out your gun and shoot me dead in this big empty snake house, remember, you don't know where the original print is. You imagine I came here without taking some precautions?'

Samsa looked as if he was calculating in his head. 'I want the print, the negs, the photocopy or copies. Plural. I want all of that. Because I don't want you coming back at me again. You understand that. I give you the cash, I get the stuff, I never see you again. That's the end of it. You cross my path one more time, I can't be responsible for what I might do to you. You understand that, too?'

Boyle smiled. 'Gotcha.'

'Twenty-five thou. After that, I'm tapped out. I'm empty. Is that clear?'

'Transparent,' Boyle said.

'I can get it this afternoon. Tell me a place we can meet.'

'I'll think about that. I'll phone you at your office. Three o'clock say.'

Samsa said, 'You're scum, Boyle. A real piece of work.'

'You're not exactly a walking paragon of virtue yourself, are you?'

'I make one mistake, Boyle. One goddam mistake and—'

'What was it anyhow? A mid-life crisis? Or is it some-thing you do often – go downtown, slumming for a piece of young ass, a little stroll on the dark side to get your juices flowing? Whores excite you? Blow jobs in the front seat? A quick fuck with the seat inclined? Is it like that?'

Samsa made an angry sound that came deep out of his chest, and he shoved Boyle back against one of the reptile cases. He moved quickly, surprising Boyle with his agility and strength. His eyes were wild all at once, and Boyle, whose antennae were finely tuned to such things, felt the unmistakable buzz of serious danger.

He saw Samsa's hand come up and instinctively he ducked, feeling Samsa's fist skim his scalp and hearing the searing crack of glass in his ears. Samsa's knuckles were cut and blood was running down the glass, and one of the snakes, agitated, flicked a tongue against the splintered case. Samsa drew his hand to his side and held it with the other, and the look on his face was one of raw pain.

'Get the fuck out of my sight, Boyle.'

In the doorway Boyle stopped, looked back, saw Samsa, shoulders slumped, clutching his bloodied hand.

Lee Boyle thought, *You could almost feel sorry for Samsa.*

Almost. But he didn't.

31

RYAN PRITT'S HOUSE WAS LOCATED ON THE EDGE OF THE CITY in a new subdivision where building was still going on. The site had a barren unready feel to it, lawns not yet seeded, cement-mixers and construction trucks all over the place.

These half-made places depressed Eve, a feeling that wasn't alleviated by Samsa's brooding mood. She'd expected something different after last night: a smile, a touch, a reference to what had happened between them, which, in her mind at least, had been a wonderful thing. But he was slippery, hard to read. He looked vaguely *tortured*. She wanted badly to touch him, but she didn't. She wanted to ask about the bandage wrapped round his hand, but she hadn't.

She parked outside the Pritt house. A thin woman in a sleeveless floral dress was standing in the open doorway. Behind her two small girls concealed themselves shyly. Eve and Samsa walked up the unpaved driveway.

Eve introduced herself and Samsa, then asked, 'You're Jody Pritt?'

'Yeah. Come inside.'

The house was open-plan downstairs, with a kitchen situated at the back behind a service counter. The furniture was new, the sofa and matching armchairs wrapped in plastic.

'You want to sit?' Jody Pritt asked.

'Sure,' Eve said.

Samsa leaned against the counter and gazed at the two small girls, who were clutching their mother's dress.

Jody Pritt said, 'I don't understand what the hell's going on. Somebody phoned from the cops and said Ryan had confessed to some murder.'

Eve said, 'And we're checking his confession, Jody. You mind me calling you that?'

Jody Pritt, who had stringy mouse-colored hair of the unmanageable kind, made a small gesture of confusion with her bony hands. 'I just don't see it. I mean, Ryan's no killer. He might be a lot of things, but a killer?'

'When you say he might be a lot of things, what do you mean?' Eve asked. The woman, she noticed, was missing a tooth, lower left of her mouth. Her face was gaunt, almost bone. She had a translucent quality you sometimes saw on the terminally sick.

'He drinks in binges. He's in and out of AA. But a killer? If you saw him with these kids you'd see what a terrific father he is.'

A stale marriage, Eve thought. The roaming husband, the neglected wife. And when he was home Pritt gave all his attention to the daughters. It was a common story, but it didn't go any way to explaining why Pritt would kill. Or, alternatively, confess to a killing he hadn't done.

'He's been unemployed how long?' Eve asked.

'Four months. It's his choice. Look outside at the construction going on. If he'd wanted he could be working there. They offered him a job.'

'He turned it down?' Samsa asked.

'It's like he doesn't want to work,' Jody Pritt said. 'Like he couldn't see any future in it or something.'

'What about the mortgage on this house?' Eve asked. 'How does that get paid?'

'I had some money saved he didn't know about. But mostly that's gone now.' She blinked back tears. 'This dead girl was a hooker?'

Eve said yes, she was.

Jody Pritt picked up the smaller of the two girls and held her. 'I can accept the hooker, okay, because we're not what you'd call intimate much, frankly, and he's got needs I can't satisfy, but the rest . . .'

Samsa said, 'He's desperate to confess, Mrs Pritt.'

'That's what I don't get.'

Eve said, 'I have to ask you this, Jody. Has Ryan ever acted violently?'

The woman lowered the kid gently. The girl, blue-eyed and fragile, had a thumb stuck in her mouth. The other daughter was staring at the floor like a shy fawn.

'When you say violently, what do you mean?' Jody Pritt asked.

'Has he ever struck anyone? You, for instance?' Eve noticed from the corner of her eye Samsa glancing round the room. His impatience was almost palpable. He didn't want to be here. He had something else to do. What was wrong with him, for Christ's sake? He'd been off-key ever since that accident. He hadn't been himself. She had an urge to go to him and hold him and ask him what was wrong. *Open up your heart, Greg. You can tell me anything after last night, don't you realize that?* She pictured his car plunging off the road, plowing through the muddy grass of the Purchase property. The report she'd seen said the car had overturned, hit a tree. Something clicked inside her head, like the sound of a latch opening in a faraway room. She wasn't sure what it was, something to do with the Purchase property, Samsa's accident.

She caught herself drifting. Unprofessional. 'Has he ever struck you, Jody?' she asked again.

'Only when I deserved it. Like when I stepped out of line.'

'What exactly do you mean, stepped out of line?'

The woman ran the palm of her hand across the smaller child's hair. 'When he came home and I didn't have supper ready, for instance.'

'He hit you for that?'

'Or when I had a night out with friends and came back late, like after midnight.'

'Did you report any of these incidents to the police?'

'Report them? No way. They're private. They're part of a marriage.'

Eve thought of all the battered wives she'd known, and how many of them still kept buying into the idea that the occasional lash of violence was a component of marriage, something that happened between husband and wife, an unwritten conjugal law – I got what I deserved. I had it coming to me. He was within his rights. Why didn't they learn they could fight back?

'How often did this happen?'

'I don't know how often. Mainly when he was down about something.'

'How did he hit you? With his fist? His belt?'

'You really need these details?'

'It helps form a picture,' Eve said.

'Okay. He'd punch me. He kicked me a few times.'

Samsa asked, 'And you never thought about reporting him?'

'Like I said, it was between him and me.'

'It's still against the law,' Eve said.

'I didn't see it as being cop business,' the woman said. 'It's not like he's a savage. And he never hit the kids. He'd

251

never lay a finger on them. They're his little princesses.'

They were his princesses and you were his punchbag, Eve thought. She saw Samsa gaze at his bandage and a look of discomfort cross his face. She remembered the gentleness of his lovemaking, those hands upon her body. He was a good man, and a tender one, and whatever was bothering him now troubled her, too.

Jody Pritt said, 'I put some of the blame on the medication he takes.'

'What medication?' Eve asked.

'Those anti-depressant things.'

'You remember what they're called?'

'Ela-something. I don't remember.'

'Elavil?' Samsa asked.

'That's it. He started taking them about three years ago, last time he was out of work in fact. He was moping around, feeling pretty low. Then when he went back to work he just kept on taking them. I think they turned his head around.'

'In what way?' Eve asked.

'For one thing – and I know this is gonna sound damn strange – he suddenly decided one day he'd press his own clothes. He wouldn't let me iron anything. Said I couldn't do it properly. Remember, this is a man who never had any interest in these kinds of chores. He'd even press his shorts, his handkerchiefs, everything. He'd spend *hours* doing it. Then he got real weird about money. He started stashing coins and dollar bills all over the place. I'd find bills inside toilet rolls, coins hidden inside the kids' toys. He'd hide money in old wine bottles, beer cans, and he'd dig these little holes in the yard. I'm talking about pennies and quarters, not just bills. I asked him why he was doing it. He always came up with the same answer. "Because I don't trust the banks," he'd say. "They're in cahoots with the IRS."'

252

Samsa asked, 'Is he still taking the medication?'

'Yeah. But he added some others. So now it's like he takes three or four different kinds. Prozac. Librium. Something else.' She started to cry, raising her hands to her face and trying, Eve thought, to be brave. 'Sorry, I'm sorry,' and she drew the back of her wrist across her eyes.

'It's okay,' Eve said. 'Look, Jody. If Ryan's innocent, we don't want to see him serve time. That's why we need to discover if there's some reason he felt the need to confess to a murder he may not have committed.'

The woman said, 'They have the death sentence in this state.'

'You don't want to start thinking that way, Jody. Believe me. I'll need the name of his physician.'

'Dr Stanford,' she said. 'He has an office down on Rosemont.'

'We'll find him,' Eve said, and rose from the sofa.

'I have a favor to ask . . . I'd like to see my husband.'

'I can arrange that. I'll give you my card, and you phone me later this afternoon and we'll fix up a time. Okay?'

'Okay.' Jody Pritt took the card as if it were a lifeline to her future.

Samsa said, 'You might want to consider hiring a lawyer, Mrs Pritt. Your husband rejected the idea, but I think it would be in your best interests.'

Jody Pritt appeared not to have heard him. 'Ryan didn't kill this girl,' she said. 'No matter what he says.'

'I hope you're right.'

Eve stepped outside. Samsa followed. When they were back in the car she said, 'Violence and bad medicine. Did the medicine contribute to the violence? Or was he always going to be violent anyway?'

'Chicken and the egg,' Samsa remarked.

'And that manic behavior,' she said. She ran a hand through her hair, feeling strands made damp by humidity.

'Harriet used to take anti-depressants,' he said.

Was that the thing troubling him? More memories of Harriet? She wondered how she could rid him of a ghost. She put her hand on his knee somewhat tentatively, as if this action involved a great risk. He gave no indication that he welcomed the touch. She didn't move her hand away. She'd get through to him. She had great determination.

'What's the bandage for?' she asked.

'I cut my hand on some broken glass.'

She thought about saying something flippant – Let me kiss it better – but she didn't. 'You're out of tune today, Lieutenant.'

'Am I?'

'I imagined you'd be all smiles.'

'Maybe I'm smiling inside,' he said.

'I have a question for you. Is there going to be a repeat of last night? Or was it just a one-off thing for you?'

'What do you want it to be?'

'It didn't feel like a one-nighter from my angle. Or am I being too pushy?'

He placed his unbandaged hand on hers. 'No. It's just me being slow.'

'I enjoyed it. I enjoyed every second of it. I can't remember . . .' She let the sentence float off unfinished. She didn't want to talk about other lovers. 'Take your time, Greg. There's no hurry. No pressure.' He smiled at her and she said, 'You should do that more often. It brightens your face. You're a good-looking man, except when you frown.'

She started the car, drove away from the subdivision, headed through older suburbs toward downtown. She had to remove her hand from his knee to drive – a tiny wrench that took her by surprise: she didn't really want to let him go.

254

She braked at a red light. 'I think Pritt's a candidate. He's violent. He's clearly whacked-out on those drugs. He's got this manic streak.'

'Sometimes candidates don't get elected,' Samsa said.

She tapped her fingertips on the wheel. 'He loses his temper, breaks the girl's neck, dumps her in that field . . .'

The light changed to green. She edged the car forward, and she remembered that the time of Gregory's accident in the field coincided with the estimated time of the girl's death. And she recalled Joshua Gold's insistence – no, his *certainty* – that he'd seen Greg, more than once, cruising the streets.

But Joshua had been mistaken. Greg had told her so.

She cut this line of thinking dead. She disengaged the connection. It was a cop's habit, adding one fact to another, then to another, and sometimes the end result was all these little building blocks leaning in the wrong direction. *What was she thinking?*

Samsa said, 'I need to stop at my bank.'

'Sure,' she said, and she turned her face, pressed her lips against his knuckles and wondered about love, the way it could bomb you quite unexpectedly out of your senses like an incendiary device dropped from the sky.

32

SAMSA LEFT HIS OFFICE AND WALKED SEVERAL BLOCKS through the sapping heat. His hand ached and his shirt stuck to his skin. The envelope in the inside pocket of his sports coat felt bulky and alien.

Stan Rougier at the bank had asked, *You sure you want all this in cash, Greg?* Samsa wanted to say it's none of your goddam business, Stan. He'd withdrawn $15,000 from his savings account, which left a meager balance of $3,300. He'd also taken $10,000 from Darcy's college fund, thinking he'd replace it if he set aside a good sum from his monthly pay check – on the assumption he kept his job. Vicious circles. You pay extortion so you can keep on working to replace the money extorted from you in the first place. He was assailed by a deep loathing of Lee Boyle.

What could he have done anyway? Refused to pay? Listening to Eve interview Ryan Pritt's wife, a stupid parlor game without purpose – poor Eve going through her Q & A session and not knowing it was a fraud – he'd found himself seriously entertaining the idea of killing

Boyle, luring him to a deserted place and shooting him. But that wouldn't be the end of the whole thing. Boyle said he had a collaborator, and Samsa was inclined to accept this. The guy who'd taken the photograph, for starters. Maybe there was even more than one accomplice.

So Boyle dies, and somebody else steps into the frame and makes more demands. *You killed Lee Boyle, Lieutenant, and now the price has just gone up.*

This turmoil. This being nailed to a cross. He found himself imagining Xeroxes of that damning photograph all over the place, falling into God knows whose hands, and multiplying until everyone in the city had a copy.

Eve senses something isn't right, he thought. He could see the way she searched when she looked into his eyes. Lovely generous Eve – she was toting some of Samsa's burden without knowing what it was.

That's an awful lot of cash to carry around, Greg, Rougier had said.

But Boyle might have demanded more. Tell yourself you're getting off lucky. Of course, Boyle might be greedy, come back again. Confirmed dopers were notoriously twisted.

You'd have the print, the copy, the negatives. Even so, how could you predict *anything* in this strange inverted world? This deal with Boyle was flimsy, he knew that. But he'd bought his ticket and he was boarding the flight, even if he didn't know the final destination.

He turned a corner and walked a few more blocks until he came to a pedestrian precinct, cobblestones and Victorian lamps and expensive little shops. He stepped inside a vegetarian restaurant called the Bounteous Planet. The room, ferny and airy, skylights everywhere, was empty. He sat at a table and ordered coffee from a young waitress wearing heavy-framed glasses that added fifteen years to her face.

257

He sipped the coffee, his hand a little unsteady. He'd been sleeping badly, a few hours at most. Dreamless sleep, and yet he always woke with the feeling he'd just dreamed something dire. He looked at his bandaged hand, the cotton slightly pink. He remembered smashing his fist into the glass case and the snake rearing up, tongue flashing, eyes resolute.

Boyle entered the room carrying a manila envelope. He crossed the floor in that easy loping walk of his and pulled up a chair at Samsa's table. He had well-muscled arms, Samsa noticed. His body was in good shape, no suggestion of flab.

'How's the hand?' Boyle asked.

'Skip the pleasantries,' Samsa said.

'You might have severed an artery,' Boyle said.

Sometimes I wish I had, Samsa thought. *Sometimes I wish I'd died in that field.*

'Just give me the envelope, Boyle.'

'There's a way of doing these things. You get the envelope *after* I get the cash. It's not that I don't trust you, you understand.'

'But I'm supposed to trust *you*? Is that how it works?'

'That's the situation,' Boyle said. He opened a pack of cigarettes and lit one, despite the No Smoking signs. He flapped a hand to waft smoke away. 'This bothering you, Samsa? Say the word and I'll stub it out.'

'Smoke all you want. You might just get lung cancer one day and die in sheer fucking agony.'

'It's a chance I take,' Boyle said. 'We live in a diabolical age where all our sweet little pleasures contain a kernel of danger. Foods have toxic additives, tobacco's bad for you, booze fucks up your liver. And sex is taboo if you don't take care.'

Samsa looked into Boyle's blue eyes and thought they were just a little too bright, the pupils dilated. The way he spoke was a shade on the rapid side. Speed would ravage his good looks in a few years. He was already showing slight signs of mileage.

Samsa took the envelope from his pocket and slid it across the table.

Boyle picked it up, glanced inside. 'I'm not going to count it,' he said. 'See how I trust you, Lieutenant?' He shoved the envelope in a back pocket of his pants, and Samsa, with a sensation of sinking through tar, thought about Darcy, her college money, her future. His own savings also. Gone in a flash. Gone inside this creep's pocket.

Boyle placed his manila envelope on the table. Samsa didn't hesitate to open it. He saw the print, the creased Xerox, and a negative he held up to the light to make certain.

'You'll burn them, I guess,' Boyle said.

'What I do with them is my own fucking business, Boyle. I paid for them.'

'Tetchy.'

Samsa said, 'Don't cross my path again. You understand that.'

'We agreed that already,' Boyle said. He crushed out his cigarette in Samsa's saucer.

Samsa pushed his chair back from the table. 'One tiny thing intrigues me about you, Boyle. I understand you're from a wealthy family. Daddy's a hotshot capitalist.'

'I have that misfortune.'

'You started out with some terrific advantages, didn't you? So where did you foul up?'

'Who gives a shit. Here I am. As is.'

'A convincing argument for abortion, Boyle.' Samsa stood up. He had to get away. The idea of his cash lying in Boyle's pocket increasingly riled him.

Boyle reached out, clasped his wrist. 'Linger a moment, Lieutenant.'

'We're finished. Take your hand off me.'

The waitress came to the table with the coffee pot in her hand. 'Refill?' she asked.

Boyle switched into sunshine mode, which he could seemingly flick off and on at will. He smiled dazzlingly at the waitress and said, 'My good friend here is in bad need of one. Be a sweetheart and pour me a cup while you're at it, honey.'

The waitress fetched fresh cups and filled them, then wandered off.

Boyle said, 'I just happened to see on TV that you're in charge of the murder investigation. What a convenient situation. You're not about to collar yourself, are you?' He picked up the chunky metal salt shaker from the table, shoved it under Samsa's nose like a microphone and fired a few quick questions in the manner of an inquisitive broadcaster. 'Does some patsy get to take the fall, Lieutenant? Is that how it's going to pan out? Or does Almond get lost in a shuffle of paper? Tell me how you see the situation shaping up. Our viewers would dearly love to know.'

'Get that goddam shaker out of my face.'

'One last thing.'

Samsa waited. A pulse beat in his neck. His bandaged hand felt numb. He could see it in Boyle's expression, something else was coming, it didn't end with the 25,000 bucks, and he'd known that going in. But what were his choices? The only choice that mattered was one he'd already made in a rain-sodden field, and every move after that was forced.

'I need one small favor.'

'Fuck yourself, Boyle. *There's nothing left.*'

'This is a very small thing,' Boyle said.

'Boyle, listen good. I'm walking out of here. I'm going back to my office. We had a deal. I'll regret it to the day I die, but it's done.'

'Uh, it's not that simple, Gregory.'

'I *paid* you, for Christ's sake.'

'And I'm everlastingly grateful to you.'

'My heart is overwhelmed. Now I'm leaving.'

'A killer to catch, huh?' Boyle asked.

Samsa stepped away from the table.

'A killer to catch?' Boyle called out, laughing. 'Or some stupid fall guy?'

Samsa kept moving, seeking the doorway, the street beyond. He wanted the air out there, no matter how dense and polluted. He stopped when he heard Boyle say, 'Things got a bit mixed up, Gregory J. And I'm deeply sorry. But the woeful thing is – there's another print.'

33

JIMMY PLUMM LOOKED AT THE CASH PILED ON HIS DESK. HE slid a hundred-dollar bill from under a rubber band and held it to the light. Then he smelled it as one might sniff a cigar. 'I have to be careful these days, Lee. So many good counterfeiters around. So much sham money.'

'We're clear now,' Boyle said.

'Even steven.'

'Pleasure doing business with you,' Boyle said. 'Except for a little random violence and the daylight robbery of my Porsche.'

'Business is very cruel,' Plumm said. 'A moment, before you go rushing away, Lee. I'm curious. How did you raise this much money?'

Boyle tapped the side of his nose. 'No can say.'

'Daddy come good?'

'Daddy isn't involved.'

'Ah. You have other sources.' Plumm fingered a strand of long hair away from his shoulder.

Boyle was restless here. He didn't like Plumm, didn't like Plumm's office, the heavy brocade drapes drawn against the sunlight and the sense of being imprisoned in some eternal night. The desk lamp threw out a sickly light the color of a withered lime.

'Have a drop of port before you go, Lee.'

'Hate port, sport.'

'A little vino then? This is a red-letter day, after all. And to think I was worrying about you, imagining Raseci ruining that pleasant face of yours.'

Plumm was already pouring wine from a decanter into two glasses. He pushed one across his desk toward Boyle, who shrugged and picked it up.

Boyle sipped and said, 'Nice, very nice. I'd be happy to sit here all day, Plumm, but I have places to go. Do I get a receipt?'

'Very funny, Lee,' Plumm said. 'You won't let me in on the secret of this money?'

'I'll carry it to my grave.'

'Then we'll let it go like that, shall we?' Plumm extended his hand and Boyle took it. The handshake was too firm to be friendly. But you couldn't expect amiable gestures from Plumm. Even a handshake had to establish some kind of supremacy.

Fingers tingling, Boyle walked to the door.

Plumm said, 'Terrible thing about your girl, by the way.'

'Terrible is right,' Boyle said.

'You aren't in trouble with the police, are you?'

Boyle shook his head. 'No sweat.'

'Let's hope they catch the culprit.' Plumm had his glass raised in the air. 'And let's hope you're back in business before too long, shall we?'

'Let's hope.' And Boyle stepped out, took the stairs quickly. He was hyper. He had $15,000 in his pocket and he was free of Jimmy Plumm. *$15,000*. Great score. And so *easy*. Samsa had been backed up, manacled, stripped of options and going round in circles like a blind guy without his stick.

Boyle was *flush*. Money gave him a feeling of invincibility. What to do with all that bread. Out on the sunny street he remembered something Vass kept harping on – 'It's not too late to change your life, Lee.' With the bucks bulging in his pocket he could begin a reconstruction of himself, split from this city, do something with his future. Such as? Go back to college, get a degree? In what? Pharmacology, so you could design your own drugs?

The idea of buckling down and getting the brain refocused was a drag. Why work if you don't have to? When you can get other people to do it for you? Like sad little Almond. Nancy, that *cunt*, before her. And before Nancy, the French exchange student called Paulette, whose only true exchange had been one of body fluids.

Let's hope you're back in business before too long, shall we?

Yeah, let's.

Let's put our mind to work on that one.

He reached the Taurus, parked in the same alley where his Porsche had been vandalized. He got in, spread a little speed on the back of his hand, snorted – up up and away. His stash was practically gone. But he wasn't fazed. Nosiree.

He drove out of the alley, air-conditioner blasting. He headed for the freeway. He turned on the radio, found a Bach cello suite on a classical channel, sweet and deep and melancholic. This fondness for classical music was the solitary debt he owed Hugh, who had thousands of albums he played endlessly, and Boyle in his childhood had developed a liking for it. Which was about the only aspect of his youth Hugh had approved of, albeit grudgingly. Monique, of course, *she* went off to learn the violin at Hugh's insistence, despite having a tin ear and an aphid's brain.

His mind was fizzing. He came off the freeway, approached a stop sign, slowed. This was familiar territory. This was where he wanted to be.

He hung a right, parked under a tree, left the engine running. He was hot. He adjusted the flow of cooled air directly into his face.

There she is.

He saw her step out of a VW convertible a hundred yards away. He watched the guy behind the wheel skip lightly over to the passenger door and follow her up the drive. She turned to say something to him, and the guy reached for her hand and simultaneously thrust his head forward, obviously expecting a kiss, but it didn't come.

Instead she moved toward the porch. The kid, filled with youth's mighty persistence, went after her, caught her by the arm and swung her round to face him and she pulled away. She said something – he saw her lips move but couldn't read her words – and then she entered the house, running fingers through her brown hair as the door closed. Boyle thought he detected a certain weariness in her movements, the way her shoulders slumped.

A boyfriend? Or maybe this kid with the shiny black hair and model looks was just making a play for her, only he wasn't getting very far. The relationship, whatever it might be, had obviously hit some snags, and the young guy was applying pressure. The kid lingered on the shadowy porch a few seconds. Boyle could hear him call out quite distinctly, 'I love you, Darcy.'

She didn't open the door.

The kid charged down the steps and jumped back in his car. I love you Darcy. So that was the kid's pitch. I love you and my hidden agenda is I want inside your pants. And Darcy – was she holding out?

Well well. Young virgins might have visions of delight.

Boyle watched the VW swing in a loop and stream past

him. He slipped the Ford in behind the little convertible and followed it, seeing the cocky way the young guy drove, one hand loosely on the wheel, the other dangling over the side and tapping the panel. *Look at me, I'm young and horny and driving this neat little auto, and the breeze is doing these real nifty things to my hair.*

Boyle's mood was darkening swiftly. *I don't like you. Not even a little. I don't want you getting in Darcy's pants, buckaroo.*

He followed the VW several miles. The young guy turned the car into an alley behind a row of houses. He parked, ran a comb through his hair, checked his face in the mirror and then got out, hitching up his jeans with a swiveling little motion of his hips.

Mr Cool. God's gift. You think.

He pushed open an iron gate in a fence and entered a backyard.

Boyle parked the Taurus close to the mouth of the alley, exited the car, strolled to the gate. The yard led directly to the rear of a two-storey house. Boyle saw the kid stand outside a pair of sliding glass doors. He was waiting for something, tapping one foot, whistling, cheeks puffed. *He just exudes confidence*, Boyle thought. *He's young, the world at his feet. Fucking fool. Milk behind his ears.*

The glass doors opened, a girl appeared. She had yellow hair piled high on her head and wore a gray sleeveless T-shirt, cut-off Levis and red and blue starred boots that went halfway up her calves. She had big tits and her mouth was a slash of violet lipstick. Boyle, concealed by shrubbery, saw the girl draw the kid inside and slide the doors shut with a deft movement of her foot.

This is interesting.

First he drops off the lovely Nightingale, then he comes here to visit this chick who looks like she's just failed an audition for lead vocalist in a country band.

266

Boyle pushed the gate, entered the yard and made his way through the foliage to the back of the house. He edged along against the wall until he was within a few inches of the glass doors. A quick peek was all he wanted. A look inside.

So let's do it.

What's this?

The kid, his jeans rolled down to his ankles, ass bare, was ferociously humping the girl on the floor. She had her legs upraised on either side of him, and her cut-offs had been discarded and her sleeveless T-shirt pushed up around her neck. She was still wearing the tacky boots. They were going at each other like rutting skunks, the kid pumping away, the girl clutching him, her mouth wide open.

This young asswipe was playing goddam games with Darcy. He had his flash blonde cutey he was banging on the side. He dropped Darcy off after school and came straight here to get laid, which *could* mean he *wasn't* scoring with Darcy, who was the kind of girl you'd gladly introduce to your parents.

The bimbo was a dark secret stashed on the side, a girl you'd never take home to Mom and Dad in a hundred years.

Boyle didn't like this *at all*. It offended him deeply. He sometimes convinced himself into thinking he had a tiny pocket of decency left, and it was this fictive moral sense, exaggerated by chemicals, that was outraged by the kid's duplicity. *Fizz fizz.*

The greaseball cheapened Darcy. It was a goddam *insult*. And Boyle was filled with a hot flood tide of anger as he stood outside the doors and watched this savage coupling on the floor and listened to the first orgasmic sounds emerge.

He clenched and unclenched his hands time and again. Sweat poured down his face.

Darcy betrayed, he thought. *By this creep. This cretin.*

He'd open the glass doors and go inside and just do something about this whole goddam situation. But not now, he had an appointment to keep, one he didn't want to be late for.

With reluctance he had trouble overcoming, he turned and went back to his car, thinking of the treachery done to Darcy, and picturing her with her hair colored black and her mouth lipsticked and maybe some shadow under her eyes. *Yeah.*

34

SAMSA APPROACHED THE HATCH AND ASKED SERGEANT Docherty for the key. Docherty slid it across the surface of the counter and Samsa picked it up, closing his fingers around it. He looked along the corridor at the locked door. It was one thing to give Boyle your own money – an act that filled him with resentment so deep he couldn't begin to measure it – but this was something else.

There's another print—

Why had he imagined that Boyle would just take the money and cheerfully crawl away under a rock anyhow? Fear of exposure. Naïve optimism. At bottom, some huge blind primal need to trust, because he *hoped* with all his heart Boyle would keep his side of the deal.

And that, dear Christ, was a monumental stupidity, and he cursed himself for believing it could ever have been otherwise.

He moved along the corridor, thinking of Darcy and the great prairie spaces in their relationship. Quit the job, spend time with her, take early retirement, your pension –

but it wasn't enough to live on, let alone replace the college fund.

He slipped the key in the lock, turned it.

He'd never done anything like this in his life.

Sweat from his fingers adhered to the key. He entered the room, shut the door behind him, pulled the drawstring for the light. He was tense beyond reckoning. He stared around the windowless room, the shelves half in shadow, the piles of stuff stacked there. The air smelled of trapped heat and cardboard.

He'd do it quickly, he wouldn't even think about what he was doing, he'd be out of here in a few seconds, a minute at most. He walked to the shelves, moving past cartons and boxes filled with items wrapped in Ziploc bags – guns, money, clothing. You didn't know what you were going to find here: a bloodstained clawhammer, tufts of human hair, broken spectacles, false teeth.

The evidence room was a museum of horror.

There would be a box somewhere with the name SUAREZ, C, freshly inked on the side with a fat black marker.

The boxes were supposed to be alphabetized, but sometimes people didn't put things back where they belonged. He was searching for a carton marked WEEKS, BILLY LEE. Billy Lee Weeks, a known dope dealer, had been shot through the head in his suburban home six weeks ago by a cheap hood named Clarence Newborn.

Hurry hurry.

He found the carton stacked in the wrong place. He drew it forward, quickly looked inside, located what he wanted and stuffed it in the left pocket of his pants. He pushed the carton back in place—

'I was told I'd find you here.'

Startled, Samsa turned. Eve was standing in the doorway. He wondered how long she'd been there, if she'd

270

seen him rummage inside the box. He felt his tension grow as if it were pushing out barbed new shoots in the depths of himself.

'Eve,' he said. 'You surprised me.' He heard himself laugh.

'You look like a kid caught with a hand in the cookie jar.'

'Do I?'

'How is your hand, by the way?'

'It's fine.' But it still pulsed and he kept trying to ignore it.

She touched it gently and said, 'You need to change that bandage. I'll do it for you, if you like.'

'People are going to start talking if we hang around in here like this,' and he laughed again, thinking how shallow and insincere it sounded.

'People always talk. Haven't you heard I'm the scarlet woman of the department?'

'I don't listen to rumors,' Samsa said. He had an urge to hold her, to bury his face between her breasts. Just to be enclosed by her in a safe place beyond the reaches of the rancid waters rising around him.

'I've been looking all over for you,' she said.

'I was checking on something,' he said. 'It's not important. I can't breathe in this place. Let's get out of here.'

He opened the door, let Eve go out before him. Her scent hung delicately in the air. He locked the door and dropped off the key with Docherty. The narrow corridor, the green walls, the light strips overhead – these things combined to make him feel he was institutionalized, that this was not a police precinct but some hospital where he happened to be a patient whose illness no physician could diagnose.

Eve said, 'The shrink spent an hour with Ryan Pritt. That's what I wanted to tell you.'

271

'And?'

'According to the good Dr Mcalister, who likes to put things in layman's terms, Pritt is probably schizophrenic, a condition exacerbated by prolonged use of anti-depressants.'

'What does that mean in terms of his confession?'

'Mcalister wants more time. He did venture to say that Pritt's violent tendencies might just edge him in the direction of believing the confession. He emphasized *might*. Mcalister is never happy unless he's sitting on a fence. I also talked with Pritt's physician, who claims he only ever prescribed Librium. Which means Pritt's been getting drugs from other doctors.'

'So we wait for Mcalister to come back to us?'

Eve said, 'I guess we do.'

'And hold Pritt in the meantime.'

'Looks that way. He still rejects the idea of a lawyer.'

'How long will it take Mcalister?'

'He says a couple of days. Maybe more, maybe less.'

They were outside Samsa's office now. Phones were ringing non-stop in the maze of rooms, people hustling, shouting at each other, Billy Fogue blowing smoke, Cullinan complaining about something. For a strange moment all this sound was stilled and Samsa, as if struck by a sudden deafness, felt himself slide into a world of utter silence. It was a weird experience, like a blip on his mental screen. He was dizzy, too, and he had to lean against a filing cabinet. Then the strangeness passed and sounds came flooding in again.

Eve asked, 'Something wrong?'

'No, not really.' He wanted to shout, It's me you're looking for.

'You look white, Greg. Can I get you something? Water? Aspirin?'

'I'm *okay*, Eve.'

'Kind of snarly all of a sudden, aren't we?'

'Sorry, I didn't mean to be.'

She touched his arm and looked mildly distressed. Billy Fogue raised his face from his desk and said, 'Hey-hey, what's going on here? Touchy-feely time, huh?'

'Shut up, Fogue,' Samsa said.

'A *joke*, Lew Tenant. A joke, awright? Excuse me.'

'I'm laughing my goddam head off, Billy.'

'Somebody didn't *get* out of bed this morning, they *fell* out,' Fogue muttered.

Samsa entered his office and sat behind his desk. Eve leaned in the doorway. She looked good, red hair lustrous, those green eyes suggestive of limpid marine depths. She wore a black sports coat, a white T-shirt and gray jeans, all very plain and understated, but she transformed them. He wondered again if she'd seen him pull his stunt in the evidence room, but she hadn't said anything. Maybe she wouldn't mention it anyway. He had every right to be in that room.

But not the right to steal.

Al Brodsky materialized holding a plain brown envelope. 'Hey, Greg. I just got Zane's report here. You want to see it?' He tossed the envelope onto Samsa's desk. 'I don't think you'll find it entirely enlightening.'

Samsa opened the envelope, saw three typed sheets, the bottom corner of each initialed by Zane in purple ink. He always found coroner's reports masterpieces of cold prose. He scanned it quickly, '. . . petroleum-based prophylactic lubricant in vaginal orifice . . . evidence of intravenous use of cocaine hydrochloride . . .'

Brodsky said, 'The long and the short of it is she was killed by that notorious old culprit, a blunt instrument. A human hand would be consistent with the bruising, Zane says. Or a fall, if she hit the right object at the appropriate angle.'

273

Samsa stared at the sheets until all the letters ran as if they were moist. The dead girl distilled in three pages of forensic jargon. An epitaph in a chilly language.

Brodsky said, 'She's got some scratchmarks on her hands. Zane says they could be attributed to the fact that she might have come in post-mortem contact with some jagged "vegetable material". I like the word vegetable in there. Why couldn't Zane come out and say it was thorns, or something like that? If Pritt was carrying her around he could easily have brushed her against a bush.'

Stephen Rebb suddenly appeared behind Brodsky. His dyed hair must have been freshly tinted that afternoon because it was an almost cruel black, the kind you never saw naturally on any human. 'I was out all night,' he said.

'And?' Brodsky asked.

'The last recorded sighting I can find of our little hooker was on the night of her death.'

'Sighted by whom?' Samsa asked.

Rebb said, 'This stripper called Marilyn Cooley, aka Bonny Bodymachine, that works out of a place called the Zoom Boom Room over on Clitheroe, more commonly known as – no prizes for guessing, folks – Clitoris Street. Excuse my language, Detective Lassiter. Bonny says Cecily Suarez came in there around eight, looking to score coke. She was alone.'

Eight o'clock, Samsa thought. *She had roughly two hours to live.*

'Did she score?' Brodsky asked.

'Bonny is coy on that point,' Rebb said. 'She deals small-time, so naturally she isn't forthcoming. The kid hung around for a while, then split.'

'Back to work,' Brodsky said.

'An appointment to keep with her killer,' Rebb said. 'Nobody saw her after that. But those hookers tend to turn a blind eye. They see only what they want, and half of them are wasted anyhow. It's like a Masonic club, and if you don't know the right passwords you don't learn shit. I've been trying, believe me. And if I can't get anything out of them, it's damn sure nobody else can.'

Brodsky sighed. 'So what have we got? Not much of anything, so far as I can see. Unless you count the quote unquote confession. I'd love somebody to pop up out of nowhere and say, Guys, great news, I saw her get into Pritt's car.' He looked at Samsa, eyes suddenly wide. '*Speaking* of said car, has anybody gone through Pritt's? Searched for any trace the girl was ever in the goddam thing? Does anybody even know the *location* of the car?'

Samsa stood up. He'd overlooked this elementary procedure, something he'd normally have delegated without thinking. But it had been crowded out of his mind. 'Jesus,' he said, 'I must be slipping in my old age.' Trying to make light of his forgetfulness even as he wondered if he'd subconsciously ignored such a basic routine – because, God help him, he wanted to believe deep down in some dismal ravine of himself that Pritt was guilty, Pritt would take the fall.

'I'll get it done immediately, Chief.'

Brodsky said, 'Do that, Greg.' There was a stony little tone in the chief's voice, almost a reprimand. Brodsky the Blade. 'Then get back to me.'

Brodsky walked away.

'Oops,' Rebb said. '*Quelle* oversight, Lieutenant.'

Eve said, 'I'll see to it, Greg.'

'No, it's my fault, I'll attend to it myself.' He sat down again. He had a burning sensation in his ears. He looked at Eve. 'Why don't you find out the names of the other physicians who prescribed for Pritt, see if they can tell you anything about why they gave him these drugs.'

She seemed a little disappointed, as if she'd expected a more demanding task. 'Will do.'

Samsa listened to her footsteps in the outer office, and heard Fogue say something like, 'Is he a bear today, or is he a bear?'

Samsa said to Rebb, 'Keep checking.'

'I'll check what's left to check, but the cupboard's just about empty,' Rebb said. 'And that Jack Spratt lead, if you can call it a lead, fizzled out.'

There's a print, Samsa thought. And for a terrible second he thought he'd said it out loud without meaning to, but Rebb had already moved away.

For a time Samsa sat very still. He thought of Rebb snooping the dark streets and trying to reconstruct Almond's movements, of Al Brodsky's unexpectedly sharp little sound of disapproval. He thought about Eve coming across him in the evidence room, and the fact she knew he wasn't operating on all pistons – and he felt he was tangled inside a fabric that was about to unravel. Threads were popping audibly, and it was all he could do to keep them from coming asunder altogether.

He left his office and walked out of City Hall with the pilfered plastic bag in his pocket, his neck scorching his collar and his heart pounding, expecting at any moment to be stopped and interrogated and eventually disgraced.

35

BOYLE HEARD SAMSA'S VOICE THROUGH THE INTERCOM. HE
pressed the buzzer and listened to the cop climb the stairs.
He opened the door and Samsa entered the room and
said, 'I want in and out of here quickly, Boyle. Where's the
print?'

'First the stuff,' Boyle said.

Samsa took a plastic bag from his pocket, handed it to
Boyle, who dipped a fingertip inside and raised a small
quantity of the powder to his mouth. It had a rich bitter
taste.

'Now the print,' Samsa said.

'One crucial little test and the print's yours.' Boyle
removed another small amount of the powder and spread
it out on a mirror that lay on the coffee table. He chopped
it with his razor blade. This sacred ritual. He raised a
quantity on the tip of his finger and held it to his nose. It
roared into his bloodstream, no afterburn, no clogged
sinuses. 'I declare this is the goods, Gregory J.'

He went to the bookshelf, opened a copy of Coleridge's
Biographia Literaria, and slipped the print out from

between the pages. He gave it to Samsa, who folded it angrily in half, then folded it again and put it in his pocket.

'This is the end of it,' Samsa said.

'Totally.'

'You said that before.'

'I don't have another print. I just happened to kind of overlook the fact I had a copy. Confusion, probably.' This speed of Samsa's was brilliant. No bathtub crank. Boyle was riding a big smooth Cadillac through a sunny landscape.

Samsa walked to the window, looked down into the street. 'You had the second print all along, but I was dumb enough to think you'd keep your word. What the fuck does that make me?'

'That *rara avis*,' Boyle said. 'A trusting soul.'

'A fool,' Samsa said.

'But with honor, Gregory.'

Samsa turned from the window. He had a gun in his hand. He'd slipped it out of his holster and was pointing it at Boyle.

'You're not going to use that.'

Samsa held the gun level. 'I might, I swear to God, if I'm pushed another inch.'

'Nobody's going to push you again,' Boyle said. 'It's over.'

'This time I'm supposed to believe you.'

'There's no logic to gunplay. You're overlooking the fact I have at least one partner in this enterprise.'

'What if I suddenly decide there's only you and the rest is bluff?'

'I told you I don't work alone. When it comes to a camera I'm a buffoon.'

'And if I have a sudden brainstorm, say I lose control, the gun goes off. One dead small-time pimp. The world isn't going to attend your funeral, Boyle. Not many people are going to be crying into their hankies.'

'It's a big gamble,' Boyle said, wondering just how demented Samsa might be. 'You shoot me. An associate of mine shows up. You shoot him, too?'

'Maybe.'

'And then let's say, for the sake of argument, a third associate pops up. You do what? Just keep on killing?'

Samsa stepped across the room. He pointed the gun at Boyle's chest, and in that moment Boyle knew he wasn't going to pull the trigger. Something just yielded in the cop's expression: his purposeful look dissipated, his eyes lost their hard sheen. Boyle thought, *A scare tactic, a desperate little piece of improvisational theater.*

'Why kill me anyhow, Gregory? I'm the only guy you've shared your secret with, right? And if you think about it, that makes me your confessor. Stuff like that gets you all choked up – and stress is a killer, Lieutenant. I saved you money you'd have wasted on a fucking therapist. Look at it that way.'

Samsa let the gun hang at his side. 'My confessor,' he said. 'A pimp and a blackmailer and a speed-freak.'

'Life's like that, Gregory. Sometimes you just don't get to choose your confidantes.'

Samsa looked into Boyle's eyes, as if he were looking for something he needed to find. Boyle knew what he wanted: *reassurance.* No more demands. This was the final hook. The last print had been handed over and all the rest was silence. Welcome to hell.

Boyle felt the familiar mind-rush, the pulse-beats, words coming in a streak. 'Let me tell you how it's going to be, Gregory. You'll have some sleepless nights for a time, a few bad dreams, and you'll wake up sweating, and now and then you'll feel a little twinge of pain and guilt. But that's going to fade. Believe me.'

Samsa was concentrating, and even if his expression was one of distaste, you could see he wanted to buy into this picture of salvation. He wanted to believe Boyle was painting a true portrait of a guilt-free future.

Then Samsa shook his head in exasperation. 'What the fuck am I doing listening to *you*? Jesus Christ.'

'I'm only laying it out so you can look at it,' Boyle said. 'Anyway, from what I see on the TV you're off the hook. According to the intrepid reporters on the evening news, somebody's already confessed.'

'That confession's going to fall apart sooner or later.'

'Let's say it holds.'

'That's hypothetical, Boyle.'

'I'm fond of dickering around with the hypothetical. If it holds, do you go along with it?'

'Which is what you'd do in my position,' Samsa said.

'I wouldn't give it a second thought. I'd grab this sucker's confession with both hands, man. I'd fall on my knees and give thanks to the one upstairs, I'd stuff all my spare change in mission boxes for isolated priests baptizing savages in the jungles of Peru, then I'd go down the church and light a thousand candles. People in the wax business would be working night shifts. Wick-makers couldn't meet their quotas.'

Samsa said, 'You turn my stomach, Boyle.'

'I affect different people different ways, *amigo*.'

Samsa holstered his gun, then moved toward the door. Watching him, Boyle detected some slight resemblance to Darcy.

Samsa opened the door. His shoulders seemed to sag a little. 'I never want to see you again, Boyle. Under any circumstances. Not in the street, not in a bar, not in a restaurant. *Nowhere*.'

'Hey, I'm your genie, Lieutenant. Your wish is granted.'

'Enjoy the speed,' Samsa said. 'In fact, why don't you

do the whole three ounces in one swoop? Have yourself a hell of a trip, Boyle.'

Boyle smiled and said, 'One thing you might consider in future, Lieutenant.'

Samsa moved to the stairs. 'And what's that?'

'Save yourself further hassle and stay home with the little woman at nights.'

Samsa turned. He looked as if somebody had thrown a blazing firework into his eyes. He stepped away from the edge of the stairs, moved quickly and shoved Boyle against the door jamb, elbow pressed into Boyle's neck.

Boyle could see great heaving currents of hatred and hurt in Samsa's face. The pressure from Samsa's elbow was giving him trouble breathing. He flattened a hand against Samsa's chest and tried to push the cop away, but Samsa was like a stone wall leaning against him. What raw thing have I touched? he wondered. He smelled a faint medicinal odor rising from Samsa's discolored bandage, some kind of anti-bacterial cream maybe.

'Hey,' Boyle said, struggling a little for air. 'This is becoming a problem, Gregory.'

'*Never mention my family,*' Samsa said. He squeezed the words out angrily between clenched teeth. 'You understand that, Boyle? *Never, ever mention my goddam family.*'

'Jesus,' Boyle gasped.

Samsa relaxed his arm, drew it back to his side and moved toward the stairs.

Boyle shut the door, rubbed his throat and coughed. His telephone was ringing. He thought about ignoring it, but in the end he picked it up. It was The Kid. *Joshua* – the name came back to him now.

Silver? Or was it Gold? What did it matter?

'Anything nice happening?' Gold asked.

'It's too soon,' Boyle said, wishing he'd let the call go

281

unanswered. 'These things take a little time.'

'I guess. I was checking, that's all.'

'Listen, I have company. I'll call you back.'

'Can you give me, uh, an estimated time?'

'Later.' Boyle put the handset down. He didn't need to be hassled by The Kid. It could become a regular thing, The Kid calling to know what was going on. He might give him 500 bucks, keep him quiet. He might not.

He had to get out of here. Time was a force.

He rubbed his neck again and noticed the lit message digit on the answering machine. He pressed Playback and heard, *I don't know why I'm doing this, really I don't. I don't even know you . . . but you gave me your number and I figured, oh what the hell, I'd call . . .*

36

EVE LASSITER PARKED OUTSIDE THE APARTMENT BUILDING, and for a time didn't move. This was a tangent she really didn't need to explore. She remembered Greg in the evidence room, the way he'd spun round in astonishment when she'd spoken, the sense she'd had of just missing out on something – that tingly feeling of entering a space where some furtive activity has happened a split second before your arrival.

She opened the door of her car, got out and entered the building.

The carton she'd seen him shoving back in place was marked WEEKS, BILLY LEE. She was familiar with the case. A dealer shot in his home – banal, commonplace. Ed Duff was in charge of the homicide and Greg's involvement a supervisory one. What had he been looking for?

She felt locked out of an enormous secret he was keeping, and yet she wasn't sure she had any rights of access to his world. *You made love with him once, which didn't exactly give you a license to pry, but he was like a man trapped. An aura of despair hung about him. And I care,* she thought.

She knocked on the door of the apartment. She heard a voice calling out. 'Coming, *coming.*' The door opened.

She smiled. 'Can I come in?'

'Do you have a warrant, Detective?'

'A warrant?'

'Just my feeble little joke. Enter.'

Eve stepped past Joshua Gold, who'd recently showered and was wrapped in a blue terry robe, his hair wet and glistening. 'I hope you're not here to ask me to be a model citizen again.'

Eve shook her head. 'Not this time.'

'And you haven't come to arrest me, or have you?'

'Not yet,' she said.

'That's a relief.'

She sat. *Make an excuse, get up, leave. This isn't necessary.*

But it was. She couldn't leave it alone.

Gold began to fuss with his plants in the window, using an eye-dropper to apply a pale-green liquid to the soil and leaves. 'What can I do for you?'

'It's a little delicate,' she said.

'Ah, now I'm *intrigued.*'

She watched him a second, wondering at his nervous energy, the way he fidgeted with the plants. Despite his initial attempt at levity she had the strong feeling he wasn't happy to see her again, didn't want her here in his apartment.

'The last time we spoke you said you'd seen Lieutenant Samsa . . .' She paused. It wasn't too late to back off.

'Let me hazard a guess. You don't want to believe your nice lieutenant goes slumming for his pleasures?' Gold asked. 'You hold him in very high regard.'

'As a matter of fact, I do.'

284

'It shows on your face, Detective.' Gold ran fingers through his damp hair. 'But he's only human, after all. As my mother always says, even the Pope needs to take a dump *now and then.*'

'You're sure you saw him?' she said.

'You want me to say I didn't, don't you? The great man must be *positively* untarnished.'

'I don't want you to lie, Joshua.'

'Okay. I didn't see him. It was a fable, Detective, from start to finish. Really. What difference does it make in the long run?'

Maybe Gold was right. If Greg had had a need to go on nocturnal prowls, checking the scene, fantasizing, did it really matter? She could understand it up to a point. But it was more than this. She was chasing something else, and at the same time she didn't want to get close enough to bring it into focus. *Let it be.*

'Why would you make it up?' she asked.

'Oh, total mischief.' He moved across the room, sprinkled food in the fish tank.

'I asked the lieutenant. He says you're mistaken.'

Gold expelled air in a flustered way. 'What do you want me to say?'

Eve had no direct answer to this question. She'd need to dig too deep to come up with one, and she wasn't prepared for that archaeology of the self. She got up, looked at the pictures on the wall, Joshua's neat signature on each one. 'Nice work,' she said. 'I like it.'

'It's an old hobby, but way too expensive for me. I quit a while ago. Are you through with your questions, Detective?'

'You still say you made it up about the lieutenant cruising?'

'Ask my friends. They'll tell you what a prankster I am.'

He isn't telling the truth, she thought. *He's fudging.*

285

Only she wasn't sure why. She glanced again at the photographs – young muscular men with artfully brooding expressions, a whole lot of shadows.

'I don't mean to kick you out, Detective, but I have somewhere to go very soon,' Gold said.

'Why do I get this odd feeling you're protecting him for some reason?'

'Why would I want to protect the lieutenant? I don't have any good reason. It was a *story*, that was all. Accept that.' He looked impatient now.

'I'm having a hard time with it, Joshua.'

'Don't you ever make things up, Detective? Just for the sheer hell of it? Because you want to sort of spice things up. You want to pour a pinch of real *fiery* chili powder into everyday humdrum. Maybe you just don't have a malicious streak the way I do.'

'You're playing with me, Joshua. I don't like that.'

'I have to dress. I have to go out. I wish you'd believe me, I really do. I've given it my best shot, and if you won't accept that it's not *my* problem. I'll walk you to the door.'

She heard the sound of a buzzer going off in another room, and her first thought was of some household appliance – a microwave, a tumble-dryer – signaling the end of its operation. The noise agitated Gold, who looked suddenly anxious, as if the buzzer meant something urgent to him.

'What's that?' she asked.

He was ushering her toward the door. 'It's only my alarm clock,' he said.

'Funny time to go off,' she said.

He had his hand placed in the small of her back, edging her in the direction of the door, pressuring her. He wanted her out quickly, even feverishly, because the buzzer was ringing, because he wanted to turn it off, he *had* to turn it off, and she knew no simple alarm clock could have this

286

effect. *It was a timer*, she thought. *But not a clock. And whatever it was, he had to attend to it fast.*

'You're pushing me, Josh. I don't like being pushed.'

'Please. Just go.'

'Why don't you switch that thing off?'

'*Go*,' he said.

She swung round and faced him. The noise was coming from behind a door to the left. Gold, who looked stricken, flapped his hands in the manner of someone who doesn't know which way to turn.

'What's the big secret, Josh?' she asked, and she took a step toward the door.

'Wait,' and he tried to block her way.

'What the fuck are you hiding?' she asked.

'I'm not hiding *anything*.'

'You give a damn good impression of a guy who is,' she said, and she thrust a hand past him and grabbed the door handle. The buzzer kept going and going.

She twisted the handle, managed to reach beyond him and nudge the door with her foot, and it opened a crack.

'You lied to me, Josh.'

He shrugged and looked foolish, like an eavesdropper caught with his ear to a keyhole.

'Why don't you give me the guided tour,' she said.

37

BOYLE HIT THE FREEWAY AT NINETY MILES AN HOUR. HE HAD the windows *and* the air-conditioner blasting. The radio played a somber passage from Ravel's *Trio* for Piano, Violin and Cello, suggestive of a night funeral, slouched pallbearers shouldering a coffin under a full moon. It was Almond in the box, waxy and dead. *To cease upon the midnight with no pain.*

He wondered what she'd felt. If it was all over in a flash. Into the void immediately. He heard rats scamper in his skull. They were busy chewing things, building nests, breeding.

Who needs a boyfriend in the picture anyhow. He's bad news.

Braking only lightly, he left the freeway. The tires whined, rubber burning. He slowed when he reached the suburb, where it was all yield signs and intersections and kids on bikes half hidden under trees. He reached his destination, parked and got out the car in one fluid movement. He walked along the alley, came to the iron gate, opened it, wondered how much time had passed since he was last here. Sixty minutes max. He hoped he wasn't too late.

Sixty minutes was nothing when you were a kid with fire in your gonads. You could come and come again, maybe with a couple of cigarette interludes and some chit-chat between times.

Allow me to show you the downside of all this, asshole.

The rats were gnawing on timbers. *Chomp chomp*. The way to deal with them was to ignore them. They were figments anyhow, they were products of Samsa's dope. But that didn't go any way toward explaining why their small sharp teeth caused him flashes of pain in his head. Why he could smell their fur and their rancid breath and the small excited squeaks they made.

He looked through glass.

The pair on the floor were so caught up in their pursuit of the wild goose of gratification they didn't hear him. He stood and watched. He wondered how many times they'd fucked during the last hour.

He slid open a door and stood unnoticed.

What did he have to do to get some attention here? Introduce himself?

The girl opened her eyes and saw him, and with a look of surprise pushed the young man away from her. 'Who the hell are you?' she asked. 'Is this a robbery or something?'

Boyle said nothing. The rats had scurried away to some deeper level, and now there were steam valves opening in his head and hissing, a whole load of pressure. This was a real piece of chicanery going on here. This was dirty work.

The kid turned over and said, 'What the *fuck*?'

'What the fuck indeed,' Boyle said.

The kid snatched at his turquoise boxer shorts, which were lying at his feet. He got them straightened out and was drawing them up over his red erection when Boyle, stooping slightly, hearing the valves in his head release steam, punched him in the throat. Once, twice, a third time in quick succession. 'She's way.' *Punch*. 'Outta.' *Punch*. 'Your.' *Punch*. 'League.'

The kid moaned and the girl, covering her tits, yelled. 'What the fuck do you think you're *doing*?'

Boyle sideswiped her abruptly, a knuckle job. He felt her teeth against his bone. She flopped over, dazed, drooling blood. The kid was feeling his larynx with anxious fingers. 'Oh, man,' and his voice was just above a croak.

'I hate fucking turquoise,' Boyle said. 'If there's one color that goddam pisses me off it's turquoise.'

'Who are you?' the kid asked, froggy-voiced.

'I'm the fucking avenging angel,' Boyle said. 'I punish guys for their sordid deeds. I'm the one who tells you you're shit, you piece of scum.'

'You're insane, crazy fuck.'

Boyle pressed himself down on the guy, throttling him one-handed, driving his head into the floor. The sheer energy he felt. The unfettered strength to destroy. 'What's your name, asshole?'

'Nick.'

Boyle hammered him across the face with a solid fist. The kid's eye began to darken and swell almost immediately. 'Nick who?'

'Mancu . . . so. *Shit*. What's this all about?'

Boyle relaxed his grip a moment. 'This is about the company you keep, fuckhead.'

'What company?'

Boyle got up, walked a few paces away, seething, boiling, his heart like a yo-yo, then he turned round and kicked the kid in the mouth. He felt the lips yield to slackness, and the slackness give way to an open hollow. 'I've taken a fucking serious dislike to you.'

Wiping blood from his lip, Nick Mancuso said, 'What the fuck have I ever done to you? I've never even—'

'You don't have to do any one particular thing for me not to like you,' Boyle said. 'I flare up at stuff other people wouldn't even notice, hotshot.'

'Look, hey, please, leave us alone, go away. I don't know what you want. Here, take my watch. It's a Rolex.'

'Fuck your watch,' Boyle said. 'Did Daddy buy it for you, huh? Daddy lay out the bread for your goddam Rolex?'

'Yeah,' Mancuso said.

'Good old Daddy. May his name be blessed.' Boyle reached down, gripped one of the kid's nipples and twisted it viciously, then slapped his face back and forth.

'Hey – hey – *hey*,' Mancuso kept saying, blinking, trying to twist his head out of the way.

'And the car? Daddy buy the fucking car?'

'He helped.'

'I bet he did. Good for picking up babes, huh? A genuine pussy-wagon, huh? Chicks just want to jump in that car, right? It's a piece of shit, that's what it is. A piece of goddam flash German shit.' He was in freefall, hyper-sthenic, charged with the need to keep havoc going. He walked to the mantelpiece, where various sports trophies were lined up. He swiped his hand across them, and they tumbled to the floor and rolled away.

'*Why?*' Mancuso asked.

'You stay the fuck away from her,' Boyle said.

'Who?'

'Don't fuck with me, lover boy.'

Mancuso was looking at the prone girl, who was breathing badly. 'She's hurt.'

'That's the whole idea,' Boyle said. What else could he smash? What else could he just fucking destroy? He saw the fireside implements, horse-headed brass doodahs.

291

Monique had taken riding lessons – dressage, of course – every Saturday morning. One time, when she was eleven, she brought home a ribbon she'd won and Hugh hung it on the wall of his office. It was probably still hanging there, that goddam green ribbon, a souvenir of Monique's achievement. She had a horse called Mambo, a monster skewbald that had died in mysterious circumstances.

I poisoned its fucking food, Boyle thought. *You never even knew that, did you, Monique? You wept in the stable over the horse's big dead body. I can still hear your tears, you spoiled bitch. I can still see the truck from the abattoir coming to dispose of Mambo, the horse stiff, mouth gaping. I can remember feeling absolutely great. I remember the foul stench of the truck.*

He gripped the poker and hauled it out of the stand. He whacked it through the air, listening to the swish it made. Mancuso was starting to rise, hands held out in front of him, shaking his head as he watched the poker lash space.

'No,' he said.

Boyle stared at this spoiled-brat kid with his swollen eye and his mouth running blood. He heard the sirens of chaos, the whole choir of destruction singing in his head. 'You ever fuck her, Nick?'

'Who?'

'Darcy, you asshole.'

'Darcy?'

'You ever FUCK her, I asked.'

'No, I never did.'

'But you try.'

'Sure I try.'

'She doesn't let you.'

'Listen, why don't you put that poker down?'

'You tell her you love her?'

'Yeah, I tell her that. It's true.'

'Lying fuck.' Boyle whipped the poker just under Nick

292

Mancuso's nose. The kid stepped back fast. 'You tell her you love her because you figure that's the *numero uno* route to screwing her. But the thing is she's too smart for you. You're unworthy. You're some links down the great chain of life, Nick. She's floating on the pond like a lily, and you're down there in the dark-green slime with the fucking mosquito larvae. This blonde heap of shit is your level, just about.'

'What's Darcy got to do with you?'

'That's none of your goddam business. You just stay the hell out of her life,' Boyle said. He sliced the air with the brass poker. Mancuso stepped further back. The blonde, Mandy, raised her face and made a small choking sound of pain. She gazed at Mancuso, then at Boyle, as if she were trying to piece the events of her world together.

Don't bother, sweetheart, Boyle thought, and hit her across the skull with the poker. He hit her a second time smack on the forehead, and she fell back silent.

Mancuso, lowering his head like a young bullock, charged suddenly, roaring aloud as he came across the floor, and his skull struck Boyle in the chest. Boyle was thrown against the wall and lost his balance, sliding on one of the silver trophies on the floor, going down on his ass and striking out furiously with the poker, catching Nick Mancuso on the kneebone and feeling it snap under the force of brass. The kid crumpled and fell, hugging the knee to his chest and gasping with pain.

Boyle rose and stood over him. 'You stupid fucker,' he said.

He hit him time and again with the poker, working up a frenzy, a crescendo of rage, and then it wasn't just this kid he was beating to pulp, it was everybody who'd ever crossed him, everybody who'd interfered with his life, everybody and anybody who'd acted against him to his detriment: judges, lawyers, cops, social workers, professors, psychiatrists, counselors, Hugh – especially Hugh – and the world, the fucking world. Up and down and up and down, brass rising and falling, the kid's face mashed potato, welts rising on his body, and the choir singing full-throated in Boyle's ears, *He will awake no more, oh, never more*, and up and down, and on and on, the brass stick whacking cartilage and bone and ligament. *No refuge! No appeal!* Just metal hot in his hand and speed roaring through his system and *the abysses of the sky and the wild earth* and the kid bleeding and bleeding on the floor.

Breathless, elated, Boyle dropped the poker, which fell without any sound that he could hear.

38

SAMSA ENCOUNTERED THE REPORTERS AS SOON AS HE
entered City Hall. Linda Kisminski from Channel 5, Vic
Sebley from Channel 7, some print journalists, camera-
men – jackals snapping around him.

'Is there any more info on this confession?'

'Can you name the guy?'

'Any chance of an arrest soon?'

Flustered, Samsa said he had no comment to make, it
was too soon. Standard guff and the reporters wanted
more. A flash popped, a video camera was pushed toward
his face, Kisminski shoved a microphone in front of him,
and Vic Sebley – sleek and bow-tied – was trying to get
close. Samsa shoved his way past, but they came after
him, hunting in a pack.

'Just tell us the name of the guy.'

'Is he guilty or is he not guilty? What's the feeling in the
department?'

Samsa, crowded and hassled, repeated what he'd
already told them.

Vic Sebley said, 'Come on, Greg, give us something we

can get our teeth into. Throw us a hunk of meat.'

'If you'll be good enough to excuse me.'

Linda Kisminski, persistent and fizzy as ever, followed him. 'Greg, be a sweetheart, give me *something* I can use? What's the skinny?'

'Jesus, Linda,' Samsa said. 'Later, later. Don't you guys ever listen?'

He made it to the top of the stairs that led down to the department offices. He descended without looking back, although he could hear the usual complaints the frustrated pack always made when they had to pull in their claws: 'It's like the Kremlin used to be around here at times. You can't squeeze a cent's worth of info out of anyone.'

He wondered how news of the confession had leaked anyhow, but it was fruitless to speculate. News always seeped out of the department. It had always been that way. The only surprise was that Ryan Pritt's name hadn't yet been revealed.

He went toward his office, pausing to tell Billy Fogue to have Pritt escorted to the interview room. He stood in front of the fan a few moments, opened the top button of his shirt, loosened his necktie, and thought about the journalists and how they snooped, digging away at the topsoil, scratching until they'd reached the place where the skeleton was interred. And then they exhumed it, they picked at the bones. They were all investigative reporters these days. They never left anything alone.

A scary prospect.

He was thinking about Darcy, wondering if he should call her and tell her there was no chance he'd be back before very late. But she'd have guessed that by now. He looked at his desk clock. Seven twenty-two. In the course of one long ruined day he'd depleted his bank account and stolen drugs from the evidence room, and in his hip pocket he carried a photograph that could destroy him. The other material from Boyle he'd already ditched, tearing it into tiny strips and flushing it down the toilet and watching it swirl away like the pieces of a jigsaw that had never been designed for assembly. And this last print, tightly folded in his pocket – he'd do the same thing with that.

The last print. If there was another one, if Boyle even so much as *tried* to put the bite on him again, he'd kill him. Regardless of consequence. You couldn't go on living with this palpitating menace. It was like existing in a freezing fog, waiting for an avalanche. But what would the death of Boyle accomplish? It wouldn't dissipate the fog. The avalanche, threatening and amorphous, would still be hanging in a precarious icy mass above him.

Still, the idea of emptying his gun into Lee Boyle's skull was tempting. He imagined the weapon bucking in his fist. But he wouldn't feel it, he'd be in that place where violence consumed everything.

Fogue put his head round the door. 'Pritt's ready.'

Samsa left his office and walked down the corridor to the interview room, where Ryan Pritt, smoking a cigarette, was seated at the table. A uniformed cop called Levine was also present, a young guy new to the department.

'Lieutenant,' Pritt said.

'Hello, Ryan,' Samsa said. He pulled up a chair and sat down.

'Checked out my story?' Pritt asked. He looked and sounded cheerful. He might have been asking an innocuous question: *Seen any good movies lately?*

'We're working on that, Ryan,' Samsa said. 'We'd like to look at your car. We have to check everything. You understand that.'

'Sure,' Pritt said.

'Where can we find the vehicle?'

'My car's in the garage at home, Lieutenant. The obvious place for it.' Pritt crushed out his cigarette.

'We need to run a few tests on it. Fingerprints and stuff.'

'You'd be wasting your time,' Pritt said.

Samsa glanced at Levine, who had an impassive face. *Of course we're wasting time*, Samsa thought. *We're going through this routine because it's necessary, not because it's useful, not because it has anything to do with truth. We're doing it for the benefit of Levine here. For Al Brodsky. For the department. Checking 'facts' that exist only inside your head, Ryan.*

Pritt said, 'See, I didn't use my own car to pick up the girl. I hear these stories about vice cops taking down license-plate numbers of cruisers for possible prosecution. I don't know if they're true, but it's crazy to run risks when you don't need to . . . I stole a car.'

Risks, Samsa thought. This from the guy who refused to wear a condom with a hooker. 'You *stole* a car?'

'Yeah. Well, borrowed is how I think of it. I do it every time I go down to that neighborhood.'

'You remember the make?'

'No, I don't. American, but I don't recall the brand.'

'Where did you steal it?'

'A street downtown. Primrose, I think . . .'

Samsa asked, 'Where did you leave it after?'

'Back where I found it.'

'You returned it to the same spot?'

'Why not? I couldn't just abandon it. It was bad enough stealing the thing in the first place.'

'Even in your panicky state of mind, you pulled your-self together enough to return the car to the same place?'

'I was thinking more clearly then. I was over the initial shock of what I'd done.'

Yeah, Samsa thought. *Naturally*. 'You remember *anything* about this car, Ryan? Color? How the interior looked? Anything like that?'

'Black leather seats, I think. Not genuine leather. Naugahyde. I think the car was dark brown.'

'A brown American car with a black interior.'

'Is that a problem?'

A brown car, black interior. A car with no unusual identifying features, no singularities. A car that couldn't be tracked down. A car that existed in Pritt's dream world, the same place where he'd killed a hooker and was overwhelmed by guilt.

'The thing is, Ryan, if we can't locate this auto, how can we be sure you picked up this girl? You see what I'm saying, don't you? The car, in all likelihood, would provide corroborative evidence. Without it . . . I don't know.' Samsa heard an echo of Boyle's deep voice. *I'd grab this sucker's confession with both hands, man.*

'Try to remember anything you can about the car,' he said. This mockery. He had to *believe* in it. In his heart, in the fiber of himself.

'The fact I can't remember the goddam car doesn't affect my confession,' Pritt said, looking stubborn, jaw thrust out a little way. 'Look, I came in here of my own free will, I want to make a statement none of you guys seem prepared to take. I killed the goddam girl, Lieutenant. It's plain and simple. What more do you want?'

Samsa strolled around the room. This was being handed to him on a plate, for God's sake. Pritt knew enough basic details about the death of the girl to be convincing, and the car was way out there in the wild blue yonder. And the confession was a document that would bestow a kind of normality on his life. Just thinking this made him feel cowardly, shrinking inside himself, a husk of a person.

You could be pragmatic about it. You could tell yourself

that it made no sense for an experienced law-enforcement officer to trash his career and his usefulness on account of one misjudgement. It was a waste. You could go on and on, until you were inextricably lost in elaborate justifications.

But there was a bottom line. And it was silence. A big silence. You'd get your broken tooth fixed, the bruise would fade, you'd go on seeing Eve, maybe you'd even fall in love with her, who could say? But there would always be the big silence. There would always be that sense of balancing on the head of a pin, that fear of ultimate discovery. Even if he wrote down Pritt's confession himself he'd feel the dead girl's presence for the rest of his life.

He walked back to the table and stared at Pritt. 'Why the fuck are you doing this, Ryan?'

'If you don't want my confession, get me somebody that does. Get me that guy Brodsky.'

'You want to see your name in the papers, Pritt? Is that it? A little notoriety? A splash on the evening news? Or are you so fucked-up in your head you don't know what the hell you're doing? Tell me about all the little pills you pop. Have they seriously disrupted your reality?' He was aware of Levine just then, and wondered how the young cop felt to see his lieutenant lose his cool so easily.

'I don't need this,' Pritt said calmly. 'Maybe it's you should be taking the pills. What is it with you anyhow? You don't *want* me to be guilty?'

Samsa leaned across the table. *This is the place where you're all tangled up. Accept the confession. Don't accept it. Let Pritt walk out a free man. And then what reasons do you give to Brodsky and the department? What do you say? He was unconvincing, Al. I couldn't hold him.*

Why was that, Greg? Why was he unconvincing?

Because. I decided so. Call it instinct. A hunch, Al.

300

Pritt was standing now. 'Get me Brodsky,' he said.

'Let's just relax, Ryan, what do you say?'

'You're the one who's uptight, not me.'

'I shouted, okay, I didn't mean it,' Samsa said.

'I guess this is a high-pressure kind of job,' Pritt said. 'Things get you down. I know about pressures, believe me.'

Samsa's eyelids felt heavy. He was beginning to fade in and out. He said, 'What I want you to do is think really hard about all this, Ryan. Concentrate. See if you can remember any details about the car. Even the smallest thing could be useful. Meantime, I'll discuss the situation with Chief Brodsky. Then we'll see.'

See what? he wondered. It was just something to say, words you tossed out. He smiled at Pritt and walked to the door. 'Levine will take you back to your cell, Ryan. We'll talk again later.'

Samsa went out into the corridor. He walked a few yards, paused a moment to drink from a water fountain. Bending to the spout, he closed his eyes and imagined himself drinking from a mountain stream, the air around him chill and clear and his heart filled with the joy of being, and if he opened his eyes he'd see mountains, deep green valleys, a hawk circling freely and full-winged in the sky. But the water tasted of the chemicals the city treatment-plant pumped into it.

He splashed his face, let water spill down his shirt, then went back to his office. He'd phone Darcy now, check in on her. The good father. He reached for the phone and was halfway through punching the numbers when Al Brodsky appeared in the doorway.

Samsa put the handset back. Brodsky tossed a sheet of paper on the desk. Samsa picked up the sheet, which was pale-blue and flimsy, the kind used in the department for telephone messages. He stared at the handwriting and somehow couldn't get beyond it to the message it contained, as if the meaning of the words were imprisoned within the letters.

'Life's a fucking bitch sometimes,' Brodsky said.

39

DARCY RODE THE BUS INTO THE CITY. SHE GOT OFF NEAR THE Greyhound station, a grubby neighborhood, full of drifters and panhandlers. She was wolf-whistled a couple of times, a few 'hey, babes'. Her black linen skirt was short and her white off-the-shoulder blouse revealed maybe a little too much. She thought her make-up made her look nineteen or twenty.

She crossed the street and walked a few blocks to a bar called Chang's. The sun was beginning to set, the sky hazy.

She knew absolutely nothing about him – what he did for a living, his background – yet here she was strolling toward a bar where she'd arranged to meet him. *You're out of your head*. It had seemed such a damn good idea at the time because Nick had been argumentative after school, getting on her nerves, nagging at her about the next step in their relationship, like it was a goddam ladder you climbed. Wasn't she ever going to 'come across', 'put out' – phrases she thought sexist and cheap, especially when they were delivered in a wheedling tone of voice designed to make her feel guilty for not fucking him.

'I'm a guy, I have needs, you don't seem to understand that, what are you, like this professional virgin?'

'Yeah, well I have needs too, Nick,' she'd said. 'And you're not exactly meeting them either. You think with your dick.'

'I love you, Darcy' – like that smoothed over all the cracks.

Then Nick had driven away in his small rasping car and the house had begun to feel like a tomb. There was no sign of her father, *as usual*, and she was bored, boxed in. And then she'd played piano for a time in a listless manner before she'd decided, *Oh, just do it, go ahead, pick up the telephone. Get out of this rut, this funk, this big empty house.*

Face it. There was something interesting about him. She couldn't say what exactly. He was an *adult*, and Nick – Nick was a big horny kid. This flattered her to some extent, sure. But it wasn't just flattery, because that alone wasn't enough to have brought her downtown to meet a stranger.

Sit with the clones. Conform. Be like everyone else.

Now *that* was the real turning point. He couldn't have known he'd thrown down a completely irresistible challenge when he'd said that. Until that moment she'd been quite prepared to step on the bus and ignore him, but he'd really stung her with those comments. And when he'd shoved his phone number into her hand she'd known there and then she'd call him.

Conform, she thought. Y*ou just don't know me, whoever-you-are.*

She'd never been in a bar before, didn't have ID, wouldn't be served. The whole thing would be mortifying. She hesitated on the sidewalk.

Then he appeared in the doorway. 'Coming in or not?' he asked.

'I wasn't sure this was the right place,' she said.

'There's only one Chang's,' he said. He put a hand on her elbow, steered her inside the crowded bar, edged her through the throng to a table at the back of the big room. She was conscious of pink plaster flamingoes all over the place and the smell of his aftershave and the way his silk shirt shone.

'What would you like to drink?'

'Oh . . . rum and Coke?'

'*Uno momento.*' He went to the bar. She watched him force his way through. She barely had time to scan the room – which was filled with some business types, a few overdressed girls, groups of young men – before he came back carrying two drinks.

'Bacardi okay?'

'Sure. What's that you're drinking?' His glass contained a red-yellow liquid.

'A Suffering Bastard. Which translates into, you drink too many of these and you wake feeling embalmed. You look lovely by the way.'

The compliment embarrassed her. She wasn't going to say anything in response, though. Hadn't she read somewhere that it was a mark of maturity when you knew how to accept praise with graceful silence? She'd go with graceful silence.

'*A full-born beauty, new and exquisite,* quote unquote.'

'Shelley,' she said.

'I'm impressed.'

He pushed a pack of Camel Lights across the table. She took one, and he lit it for her with a Zippo. She wondered what would happen if somebody she knew walked in, a friend of her father's, say, or even her father himself. Oh Christ. She tasted her drink, made a face.

'Don't like it?' he asked.

'It's strong.' An unsophisticated response. She shouldn't

have said anything. 'It's good though.'

'Tell me about your family,' he said.

'There's only my father. My mother died a year ago.'

'That's too bad. How did she die?'

'She killed herself. You won't mind if I don't really want to talk about it?'

He looked genuinely sympathetic. 'What does your father do?'

She said, 'He's a cop.'

'A *cop*? Oh-oh. You mean I'm drinking with a policeman's daughter, who's obviously – whisper it – under the age limit for alcohol consumption? I'll be clapped in irons. Sent to the brig.'

'Only if he finds out, and I won't tell him.'

'I like secrets,' he said.

'What about you? What's your story?'

He drummed the top of the table with the palms of his hands. 'I'm a failed neurologist. So I took up spodomancy by way of compensation. You want to know what spodomancy is, don't you? Flick some cigarette ash in the ashtray.'

She did so, puzzled. He studied the ashes. 'You're going to have a long life and I see many babies. I also see a number of ocean voyages.'

'Really,' she said. 'What is it you do?'

'You don't buy the neurologist bit and you don't believe I can divine the future from the pattern of ashes?'

'Not a word.'

'You don't believe in myth and magic? Spells and incantations and casting the runes?'

'Do you?'

He shrugged and appeared to drift a moment. 'I believe everything in the world happens for a purpose,' and he leaned toward her in an earnest way she found a little unsettling, unexpected. Was he putting her on again? Or

306

was there some nugget of sincerity in what he was saying?

'Running into you, for example,' he said. 'I don't believe that was random.'

'You see that as part of what – like a design?'

'Everything's part of a design.'

'What kind?'

'That's the big question,' he said. 'I think everything fits together in some way. The trick is to fathom the pattern without a blueprint. Think of life as walking a high wire blindfolded.' He looked at her darkly and then laughed all of a sudden, and the veil of seriousness lifted. 'Okay. You prefer mundane truth? I taught college for a couple of years, gave up and went to Tibet in search of deep truths – which is what you do when you don't know what you're supposed to be doing. And then I came back here last year, and now I'm looking round for some business opportunities.'

It sounded plausible, but there was a light in his eyes that suggested a certain amount of bull, as if he wanted to project an image of himself that was part truth, part fabrication. 'What kind of business?' she asked.

'The only criterion is I make money. I like money. I make no excuses for liking it either.'

'You don't care how you get it.'

'So long as I stay on the good side of the law, he said to the cop's daughter.'

'Oh, forget I'm a cop's daughter,' she said. 'Were you born here?'

'San Francisco. I came east for a three-year gig at Rutgers teaching freshmen comp. Making freshman bozos construct simple sentences. Brain-dead kids with rich daddies. Who needs them?' He sounded bitter. She wondered why, if maybe he'd had a bad experience teaching. He said the word 'freshmen' as if it was an insect he'd found in his drink.

He pushed his glass toward her. 'See what you make of this cocktail.'

She tasted. It wasn't subtle. It burned in her chest like a blowtorch. 'What is *in* that stuff?'

'You don't want to know,' he said.

'Do your parents live out west?'

'Why don't you ask me my sign?'

'Your sign?'

'I'm only pointing out the drift in our conversation,' he said. 'All that background text and hubbub – who cares about it? Somewhere along the way of such chat your star sign inevitably comes up.'

She'd been making small talk, that was what he was saying. She felt annoyed with herself. This is the big world, Darcy, and you're not sure how to behave in it. He placed his hand over hers. The touch shocked her a little. She looked at his face and saw an expression of deep interest there, a probing, as if he wanted to get beyond superficialities as soon as he could. She slid her hand out from under his and helped herself to a second cigarette, which he lit for her. She never smoked except at parties. But she felt like smoking up a storm now.

'I don't even know your *name*,' she said. 'I can't believe I'm sitting in a bar drinking with a guy I don't know.'

'Vass. Lee Vass. Originally Russian. Vassinsky. Shortened somewhere along the way. Probably at Ellis Island. Maybe now you'll tell me your name.'

'Darcy,' she said.

'Darcy. I like it. It suggests stately homes, ivy on walls, butlers carrying trays, menials grooming horses. Oldie worldie.'

The alcohol was going to her head. She felt sober still, but a touch lopsided. And suddenly liberated. No Nick to bother her, no empty house to press down against her.

308

'You called me a clone,' she said. 'Which I regarded as an insult, Lee Vass.'

'That was a ploy. I knew all along you were a free spirit.'

She liked the sound of that. 'And I'm still puzzled why you phoned at three in the morning. And please don't deny it was you.'

'I didn't phone. I swear.'

'I *know* it was you.'

'Ah happy Lycius – for she was a maid more beautiful than ever twisted braid.'

'I don't know why you're hiding the fact,' she said. 'What's the mystery? You asked to talk with my father. Why?'

He crossed his heart. 'There's a mistake here. It wasn't me. What possible reason would I have for calling at – what time did you say? Three in the *morning*? Just drink up. We've got places to go.'

'Like where?'

'Here and there. Lee's tour of the city.'

She finished her drink and followed him out to the street, thinking maybe, just maybe, she was mistaken about that phone call. The last of the evening's sunlight came back off the rooftops with a soft glow, as if the world were filled suddenly with thousands of haloes. She saw pigeons in scattered leaden flight. He took her by the hand and began to run along the sidewalk, and she laughed as she tried to keep up with his pace.

'Where are we going, Lee?'

'You'll see.' He kept running faster, turning a corner into an alley.

'Are you always in such a hurry?'

'Always.'

He stopped alongside a white Ford and took the keys from his pocket.

'Where's the big blue thing with the fins you were driving before?'

'Gone and forgotten. Jump in.' He held the passenger door open for her, and just for a second she hesitated. She wasn't sure why, some tiny flicker of uneasiness, a sense of irresponsibility. Then she thought, *Screw it, I'm getting into this car. I'm doing what I like.* She stepped in and snapped her seat-belt buckle in place.

'Unbuckle it,' he said.

'Why?'

'It's just one more goddam restriction. Life's all petty rules and stupid little laws. Wear your seat belts. Don't smoke in public buildings. Fuck all that. You get tired of people telling you what to do.' He reached out and unclasped the buckle of her belt, and she felt the light pressure of his hand against her hip a moment, an intimacy that both disturbed and pleased her. She slumped back in her seat, stretched her legs, felt comfortable now.

He started the car and roared out of the alley. He drove with a furious recklessness, just making the lights before they changed to red, swerving once to avoid a bus disgorging passengers.

'You drive like a lunatic,' she said.

'Maybe because I am one,' and he glanced at her.

She said, 'I have nothing against lunatics.'

'Good. I'm a crazy bastard. You'll love me.'

No, she thought. *But I like you.*

He parked the car in a side street in a neighborhood she didn't know. Old crumbling tenements, a kind of broken-down cool about the place. He got out, walked round and opened her door. Tugging on her skirt, which had risen up her thighs, she slid out. She hoped she didn't appear clumsy. She noticed the way he looked at her legs. Not in a sneaky manner, but with open appreciation. He grasped

310

her hand, helped her onto the sidewalk. Nick was never this courteous.

She didn't know where she was and she didn't know where she was going either, but it didn't matter, she had her hand in Lee's and he was leading her, and she didn't mind being led, being directed. It was his script she was following anyhow.

They walked a few yards before he drew her down a flight of steps to the basement of a building. She heard the lazy sound of a blues guitar being played somewhere, and then he was escorting her through a doorway into a badly lit room. It took her a few moments to get used to the gloom – candles on tables, a dull purple lamp on a small stage, where an old guy sat hunched over a guitar, black skin dyed blue by a trick of the light. The air was dense with smoke, and when you breathed it felt raw against the back of your throat. And it wasn't just tobacco. She detected reefer, rich and bittersweet.

Lee pulled out a chair from a table and she sat. He asked her if she wanted rum and Coke again, and she nodded, watching him disappear into the murk. She looked round, conscious now of other people at tables, faces glowing in the light from the candles that burned in red glass jars. It was the kind of place that might get raided at any moment: clandestine, somehow *exciting*. She listened to the guy on stage sing, *Black gal, black gal, don't lie to me. Tell me where did you sleep last night?* He had a voice like pebbles rattling inside a drum.

She saw Lee coming back through the haze. He sat, gave her the rum and Coke. He was drinking Heineken from a bottle. He placed his hand over hers and rubbed her skin with the tip of his thumb for a time. Then he leaned across the table and blew in her ear, and his breath tickled her. She laughed, pulled her head to one side, listened to the singer: *I slept in the pines where the sun*

311

never shines, And I shivered with cold, deadly cold.

She drank and felt the surge of alcohol to her brain. 'Are you trying to get me drunk?' she asked.

'Why would I do that?'

'Because. You might have devious motives.'

'Do you want me to have?'

She looked at him over the small red flame of the candle, and saw how the flickering light played in his eyes and created shifting shadows on his face and made the thin gold chain around his neck glitter. *Lee Vass, who is he really? Do you really want him to have devious motives? How are you supposed to act?* She drank more, felt loose, relaxed. She'd discarded the idea that her regular little world might intrude here – nobody she knew was going to see her in this place. She could be somebody other than the lieutenant's daughter for once. She could reinvent herself, drift into a pretend identity.

'I don't have a secret agenda,' he said. 'What you see is what you get.' He held the cellophane from his cigarette pack directly in the flame of a candle and it burned yellow with purple disturbances.

'And what is it I see?'

'People see different things in me,' he said. 'What you see is up to you.' He inclined his head and turned her hand over and kissed the palm. She'd never been kissed there before. It was a strange sensation, like a gentle electric current had been applied to a sensitive point. She closed her eyes. What was she getting into? She edged away from him, looked at him, saw how his face seemed to float on candlelight and his blue eyes reflected flame. *It's all going too fast*, she thought. *Slow down. Apply the brakes.*

'Your skin tastes nice,' he said.

'Nice. How?'

'Imagine if a starry sky had a flavor. It's like that.'

312

A starry sky. She laughed. He massaged her fingers slowly one by one.

She said, 'Lee, you're too old for me.'

'It's you that's too old for me,' he said. 'I'm very young inside.'

She felt his other hand on her knee beneath the table. '*Lee . . .*'

'I love your skin,' he said. 'I could develop an obsession about it. They'd have to whisk me off to some psychiatric clinic and experts would discuss my condition, which they'd call Vass's Syndrome. Men from Vienna would be hired on a consultancy basis. They'd make me lie down on couches and plumb the cesspool of my childhood.'

'Cesspool? That's a funny word to describe your child-hood.'

He didn't appear to hear her. 'You know what they'd find? This crusted surface they'd have to shatter with jack-hammers. Then, if they got through that, they'd reach murky water where they wouldn't be able to see a goddam thing. Just this rancid dank place with no rapid whirlpools spinning, and no mermaids, and no plant life.'

She didn't know quite what he was talking about, but somehow it didn't matter. She understood she was approaching a boundary she shouldn't cross, but she didn't want to quit. She was enjoying the way her percep-tions were suddenly spilling one into another, as if her brain were undergoing some weirdo renovation. 'You know what I'd like?'

'I'm here only to serve,' he said.

'Grass. I'd like to smoke grass.'

'No problem,' he said. He got up from the table and disappeared somewhere. She finished her drink. She clapped when the singer ended his song and started another. *I ought to go home*, she thought.

Lee returned and handed her a thick joint, which he'd

313

already lit. He also had another rum and Coke for her.

'You think it's okay to smoke it here?' she asked.

'Consider this club a free-enterprise zone. Anything goes.'

She put the joint to her lips. It took only moments for her to feel the effect, and suddenly the music was rich with hidden revelations. Strong grass, mind-blowing in a dreamy way.

Lee leaned across the table and touched her hair. 'You okay?'

She passed the joint back. 'Oh, I'm fine, just fine.' *Scrambled Darcy.*

'Don't smoke too much of this,' he said. 'It's Thai, and I don't want you turning into a jellyfish because the night is still young. And miles to go et cetera.'

She raised a hand to look at her watch, then changed her mind. Time wasn't real. You couldn't touch it, you couldn't taste it. 'Tell me if I'm red-eyed,' she said. 'I don't want to go home all bloodshot.'

'Your eyes are beautiful and clear,' he said. 'You're not going home yet anyway. Hang loose.'

'I don't think I can get any looser,' and she laughed in the way dope makes you laugh. The whole world was a cheerful shambles.

'Drink up,' he said.

She finished her first drink and started on the second. Actually her third, if you counted the one she'd had at Chang's – but who's counting? The music was pounding inside her. Lee was still stroking her hair, but there was no urgency in the gesture, only a slow soft caressing. She felt joined to him in an easy way, his hand and her hair fused together.

'I am *stoned*,' she said. '*Really* stoned. I'm not going to freak, am I?'

'Would I let such a thing happen to you?' He had a

strand of her hair twisted around a finger. 'Finish your drink. Let's get out of here.'

'You don't ever sit still, do you?'

'I like to keep moving. Move move move. Mr Motion. That's me. Everything's a rush, everything's a blur.'

She drained her glass. She started to rise. Uh-oh, wobbly, legs like paper. She heard herself laugh at her own imbalance. Lee put an arm around her waist and led her toward the door.

'I like this place,' she said.

'You'll also like the next one.'

They were back on the street. It was dark and the street lamps had come on. They walked to his car and he opened the passenger door for her and helped her into the seat. She was dizzy a moment, but the feeling passed and she felt relaxed again, as if the air around her was warm water frothing in a jacuzzi. She reached for her seat belt – automatic pilot kicking in – and then she remembered she didn't need the goddam thing. Suddenly the whole idea of seat belts was *amazingly* silly.

She listened to the hum of the engine. She was aware of how light from the street lamps seemed to be threaded together in some way, as if the night was filled with electric linkages. Shiny beads.

Lee stopped the car in a backstreet where there were no lamps, and he flipped on the interior light.

'Pit stop, Darcy.' He had a plastic bag of white powder in his hand.

'Cocaine?'

He smiled. 'What else?'

'I've tried it before.'

'You want to try it again?'

'Sure.'

'You'll need this,' he said. He handed her a rolled-up twenty-dollar bill. He laid some of the powder on the

315

console between them. She noticed how it twinkled here and there, like it contained fragments of crushed gems.

She angled her head downward, held the bill to her left nostril, sniffed up some of the powder, then repeated the action with the right. She felt it hit the back of her throat. She raised her head up quickly. Her nose stung inside. 'Woooee,' she said.

'Let's go,' and he drove out of the street, heading this time for the freeway entrance, and she wanted to ask where he was taking her, but she felt dislocated suddenly, as if her head was going in several directions at the same time, and all the lights of the freeway were unnaturally bright and her heartbeat was a little skippy. She wasn't sure she enjoyed this effect. It wasn't anything like the short-lived euphoria she'd had with cocaine before – this was different and harsh, almost menacing, like it was about to create dark unpredictable cracks in herself. This was flying with no sense of anyone in the cockpit.

She rolled down her window and the night air made her feel a little better. *Speeeeding* along and wondering if her emergency brake worked. She said, 'The coke I had last time was nothing like this. My pulses are *thumping*.'

'You probably had crap,' he said. 'This is *primo*.'

She felt the breeze in her hair. She dangled an arm from the window. She'd done too much too soon, that was it – booze, reefer *and* coke – and they were bombarding her senses like tracer-bullets, and now the suburbs alongside the freeway were fuzzy and so faraway they might have been constructs on a strange moon seen through a beveled telescope. Lee had one hand lying casually against her hip, his fingertips making small circular motions. And then he lowered his hand to where the hem of her skirt lay high on her leg, and he raised the skirt a little.

He rammed the car up a freeway ramp and she was swung to the side by the sudden swerving motion. He laughed as he screeched into a parking lot and brought the car to a dead stop. She looked through the windshield at a neon sign a hundred yards away that quivered in her vision.

'Uh,' she said. 'Is this what I think it is, Lee?'

'What do you think it is?' he asked.

The sign was red and discolored the sky above it. The Wayside Motor Lodge.

'One drink, Darcy.'

Before she could say anything, he was out of the car and holding open the passenger door for her, and she slid from her seat, feeling giddy. She was sweating and her hair was damp and yucky against her scalp.

'Lean on me if you need to,' he said. 'That's what I'm here for.'

40

SAMSA LOOKED THROUGH THE GLASS DOORS INTO THE BACK-
yard. In the alley behind the house an ambulance spiked
the dark with sharp turning lights, and a patrol car
flashed red, white and blue. Cops in the yard searched the
shrubbery under brilliant lamps that had been rigged up.
He thought of the Purchase field. How could he not?

He had a hard time drawing his face away from the
glass. He didn't want to look back at what lay in the
room. He turned anyhow and saw Charlie Bird, a tall man
whose head was a little too tiny. Bird reminded him,
fittingly, of a stork, even in the manner he walked,
delicately picking up his feet and avoiding anything that
lay on the floor – in this case, trophies and silver cups that
bore the name Mandy Robbins, and prizes for athletic
achievements, swimming, track and field. The girl who'd
won these trophies lay half naked near the fireplace. Her
eyes were closed and the lids were like blood-red coins.

'This is savage,' Charlie Bird said. 'I never seen anything
this bad before.'

Al Brodsky said, 'It's goddam brutal.'

Beyond a closed door directly behind the chief, bewildered grief-struck people filled a corridor – relatives, neighbors, a priest who'd hurried to the scene and was out there whispering the only thing he could: platitudes. The shock of homicide. You never think it's coming to your house, touching your family.

Samsa shifted his eyes. He had an acid pain in his stomach.

Nick Mancuso lay close to the girl. His face was demolished, hair thick with drying blood, bare upper body covered in deep incisions. He'd been beaten to death.

Charlie Bird said, 'We're looking for a guy hauling around some serious rage here. *Psychopathic* rage.'

Samsa turned his face from the two dead kids. His mind wandered to Darcy, and he wondered how he'd tell her about this. Murder was vile, but there was an added element here: betrayal. Nick had strayed.

Charlie Bird crouched near the fireplace. 'The poker's missing,' he said. 'These fireside sets always have a poker.'

'Could be your weapon,' Brodsky said.

Bird stood up and looked across the room at Samsa with a muted form of sullen hostility: *What the fuck are you doing here, this one is all mine, Pharaoh*. This was Bird's zone and Samsa, who felt like an interloper, gazed around, anywhere to take his eyes away from the sight on the floor. He saw the posters on the wall, mainly jock heroes, basketball superstars. He noticed a single bed in the corner and thought of the passion that must have flared up between Nick and Mandy, something so strong they couldn't even wait to make it as far as the bed.

'The girl's parents were gone all day,' Bird was saying. 'This is what they come home to.'

Brodsky said, 'Maybe there's a jealous boyfriend.'

'Who knows. Who knows anything these days,' Bird said. He looked inside the fireplace, reached up into the

319

chimney and rummaged. He straightened his back. His hands were sooty. He was the kind of guy who didn't mind getting his hands dirty.

Samsa said, 'I don't know how I'm going to break this to Darcy.'

Charlie Bird looked puzzled. 'Who's Darcy?'

'My daughter,' Samsa said. 'She'd been seeing Nick Mancuso.'

'High-school romance?' Bird asked.

'Something like that.'

'I'll have to talk with her. Maybe she'd know if Mandy Robbins had a boyfriend somewhere. Maybe the guy walked in and found them screwing, lost control, went berserk big-time.'

'I'll talk to her for you,' Samsa said.

'She's your daughter.' Bird half kneeled alongside the dead boy, and stared at him as if he were about to give him a lecture on morality. 'So Nick was seeing Darcy and fooling around on the side. What kind of kid was he? Or do I have to ask?'

Samsa said, 'I only met him a couple of times. Seemed nice enough. Maybe trying too hard to please. Over-polite.'

Bird said, 'You wonder what's happening to the world.'

Samsa walked out into the hard sharp lights in the yard and watched men search the bushes silently. He took his cellular phone from his pocket and punched in his home number, but Darcy didn't answer. He let it ring a long time before he shut his unit off. If she wasn't at home, where was she? He tried to remember the names of her close friends. Ginny somebody. Maybe that's where she was.

Ginny who? Last name beginning with F?

Or maybe she was asleep and failed to hear the ringing.

Jesus Christ. How do you convey such horror to your own daughter? His bandaged hand pulsated.

Al Brodsky came and stood at his side. 'You talked to Pritt about that car?' he asked.

'He used a stolen vehicle. He can't remember the make. It's all very vague.'

'A stolen car. That's really helpful. What do you plan to do with him, Greg?'

'I'm waiting, see what Mcalister says.'

'You know, I'm beginning to feel like a juggler with too many hoops in the air,' Brodsky said. 'We've got thirty-seven unsolved homicides still active on the books. No, make that thirty-nine now. If Pritt's confession hangs together, it's one we can chalk off the list.'

Samsa thought how the numbers could pile up and defeat you. You could get crushed by the dead weight of statistics. All that grief out there in the city. All that badness. Sometimes the city seemed to hang over him like a big black nuclear cloud.

'You don't need me around here,' he said. 'Bird has it under control. I ought to see what Darcy has to say.'

'Good idea,' Brodsky said. He stepped a little nearer. 'You took your eye off the ball, Greg.'

'About Pritt's car, you mean?'

'Yeah. Maybe there's too much on your plate. Do you think that's it?'

'I'm tired. That's what I think.'

'You can't let yourself get tired on this job.'

'Is this a dressing-down, Al?'

'If it is, I'm soft-pedaling, believe me. Go home. Sleep. You look wasted.'

Samsa walked out into the alley where he'd parked his car. He drove in the direction of his house. He traveled a couple of blocks before he tried to call home again. Still no answer. *Where is she?* He couldn't remember the last name of her friend yet. Flynn? He chastized himself for knowing so little about Darcy's life.

I took my eye off more than one ball.

It was going to be okay. He'd see lights in the house, she'd be upstairs safe in her bed. He reached 1900 Devine and slid the car into the driveway. The house was in darkness. He got out and moved to the porch, fumbling for his door key. Okay, she didn't leave any lights on. Usually she did. This time she just forgot. That was the simple explanation. He unlocked the door, stepped inside, flipped on a light switch and breathed the still warm air of the hallway.

'Darcy,' he called out.

He climbed the stairs. He pushed open the door of her bedroom and turned on the light – no Darcy. He went through the house uselessly calling her name. There was clearly some very simple answer. There had to be. *What the hell was her friend's name?* He entered the living room, switched on a lamp, had the very strange feeling that the piano had been played recently and the vibration of a note still lingered at a sub-audible level. But that was nonsense, something shaped in the crucible of his growing panic.

He went to the table, where the address book lay, flicked the pages, F, F for Flagg, there it was. Ginny Flagg. He dialed the number and a sleepy-voiced woman answered.

He said, 'This is Gregory Samsa. Darcy's father? I hate to call at this hour. Is my daughter there?'

'I haven't seen her.'

'I'm trying to locate her.'

'Kids. They just don't think,' the woman said. 'They go AWOL without telling you. You have my sympathy.'

I don't want your sympathy. I want my daughter. 'You mind asking Ginny if she knows where Darcy is?'

'I'll try. She's probably sleeping.' The woman was gone a long time, and when she returned she said, 'No, Ginny doesn't know where she could be. I'm sorry.'

'What about other friends?' Samsa asked.

'You tried Lindy Prosecki's number?'

He couldn't remember ever having heard of Lindy Prosecki. 'I don't have it,' he said.

'Four zero nine, seven nine eight eight.'

Samsa scribbled this down, apologized again, then called the number he'd been given. He got an answering machine. 'We are not here to take your call . . .'

He hung up, walked into the kitchen, filled a glass with water and drank quickly. He saw his face reflected in the window, and for a moment was startled. He ripped off his bandage, looked at the dark cuts, and remembered Nick Mancuso. His own wounds were pitiful by comparison. He went to the bathroom, found some fresh bandage and wrapped it clumsily over the hand.

Darcy, where are you?

He went back into the living room. The trick was to relax. She'd have a good reason for not being here. He sat by the telephone, wondering who he could call next. He heard a sound on the porch, a footstep, and he thought, *Okay, here she is.*

Relieved, he went out into the hallway and opened the front door.

Eve was standing in the shadows. 'Is this a bad time to call?'

41

LEE BOYLE DREW THE CURTAINS. HE HEARD THE GIRL IN THE bathroom. He saw her bent over the washbasin, running cold water across her head and saying how very hot she felt. The inferno of crystal. She was in that clammy stage, sweating, too hyped after her last blast. He stepped into the bathroom and hung a towel around her neck.

'You'll be okay, just go with it,' he said.

She said nothing, kept her head under the faucet. He placed a hand flat against her spine, thinking what a delicate creature she was, how perfect the spinal column and unblemished the skin. Youth in all its intricate wonder.

She said, 'I shouldn't be here.'

He dried her face and hair with the towel, gently, gently. 'You're doing fine.'

'I shouldn't *be* here,' she said again. She gazed at her face in the mirror above the basin. 'I don't feel good.'

'Relax.' He led her out of the bathroom and made her lie down on the bed.

She shut her eyes. Her hair created a wet stain on the pillow.

He opened the little leather shaving-kit bag he'd brought up from the car. It contained his rig, cotton balls, a spoon, a nylon stocking, a tube of Preparation H for concealing tell-tale marks on the arm – and his gun, because he was carrying 15,000 bucks in his pocket, and maybe 3,000 dollars worth of crank, bounty worth protecting.

He placed the rig on the coffee table. The needle was brilliant steel. Shakily, he put a portion of finely chopped crystal in the spoon, added water from a glass, then tore a small chunk of cotton from one of the balls and dropped it in the spoon with the mixture. He tied the nylon stocking around his left arm – an intricacy he had down to an art – and flexed the arm. The big boost was coming. The fast shuttle to Ampsburg.

Darcy turned on her side and gazed at him. He pierced the cotton swab with the needle and filled the syringe, feeling the vein rigid in his arm, the tick-tick of glorious expectation, and always that annoying little voice somewhere at the back of his head – *Lee, lay off.*

She propped herself up on an elbow. Her face was white. 'I feel sick again. I think I want to throw up.' He watched her rise unsteadily from the bed. She slid against the door jamb, stumbled into the bathroom.

He pushed the needle into his vein, the galvanizing contact of steel and skin, a rapturous puncture, crank shooting through him like rocket fuel. He made up a second batch in the spoon and filled the syringe again.

Bless you, Samsa. For the money. The dope.

And your little girl.

You are my benefactor and I your confessor. The world is finely balanced.

He walked into the bathroom.

325

She was leaning over the basin. He stood behind her, massaged the back of her neck, then slid his hand down her spine to her waist. He pushed his body against hers. She lifted her head up from the basin. Her eyes were filled with water. She reached for a towel and buried her face in it. He shoved himself more forcefully against her. Her stomach was flat against the rim of the basin. In the mirror he saw his face loom behind hers.

She slipped the towel from her face and said, 'Lee, please . . .'

'We make an attractive couple,' he said.

'You're hurting me.'

She pushed against him, trying to turn and face him, but he kept her locked in place. She didn't say anything. She lowered her head and gazed bleakly into the porcelain.

He reached down, raised her skirt up, felt her shiver. 'You're not afraid of me, surely?' He rubbed her buttocks softly through the silky material of her panties. Oh yeah, firm young flesh. Nothing was more tasty than young meat. Old men everywhere should have daily access to this diet. She wasn't resisting and she wasn't encouraging either, she was just standing there with her back to him and her eyes directed into the basin, and this lack of participation bothered him. He tugged the panties down a little way, creating his own slow striptease gig, and thinking, *Move it, baby, move it. Respond.*

Samsa's child. Consider this, Lee, you've set loose the hounds of fucking *havoc* on this family: plundered Samsa's bank account, forced him to break the law he's sworn to uphold, degraded him – the man was on his *knees* goddamit – and now you have the daughter in a motel room, and she's so fucked-up she doesn't truly know where she is or what she's doing here, and that's the way you want it. Poor Samsa with a dead wife, and this sweet little girl with no mother.

You are a mean sonofabitch. What are you?

He slid her panties down past her thighs, lowered himself on one knee and kissed her ass lightly and saw how goosebumps appeared on her skin. He pulled the underwear to her ankles, parted her legs, then he stood up and felt her tremble against him. He was trembling also, trying not to. He saw her face in the mirror again, her eyes shut and her angelic mouth halfway open, as if she meant to sing but couldn't remember the melody. I'll make you sing, little one. Lee H. Boyle will bring a song to the nightingale's throat.

And he plunged the needle in his left hand into her left arm, scoring a vein. She cried out, jerked her arm away, knocked the syringe out of his hand and it clattered into the sink. She said, 'Oh, Christ, no,' and she stared at her arm. The vein issued a drop of blood.

'That wouldn't have happened if you hadn't moved,' he said. 'You didn't get all of it. Goddamit.' He looked at the syringe in the sink. Saw milky liquid leak from the tip of the needle.

She tore a sheet of toilet paper from the roll on the wall and placed it over the blood. 'I didn't *ask*,' she said.

'It's good speed.'

'*Speed*,' she said.

'You've already been doing it up your nose. This way it just kicks in that little bit quicker.'

'Coke. You said it was coke.'

'Coke's for weenies who want a short lift. This is more long term, way more intense.'

She dabbed frantically at her arm with the tissue even though the vein had quit bleeding. He said, 'It's no big deal, for Christ's sake. It's not going to kill you.'

'What's going to happen to me?'

327

'The amount you've had? You'll feel energetic. As for sleep, forget it.'

He pulled her toward him, held her head against his chest, smelled her wet hair. She was fragile. She was lost in this world. *I'll show her the way. I'll take her places she's never been.*

She slumped a little in his arms. His head ached suddenly, a deep booming in his skull, suggestive of cannon fire. He picked her up, carried her into the bedroom and laid her on the bed. She was so light it felt like he was carrying nothing at all. She was Almond's weight.

He reached down and disentangled her panties from her ankles, let them fall to the floor. He slid her skirt up and she made an effort to force his hand away. Coy. He hated coy.

He didn't want this situation to turn sour. He had plans, cap P.

'Why did you come up here in the first place if you're going to be this unco-operative?' he asked. 'I said I'd get a room and you said that was fine with you. What was it? The booze talking? The dope? Or did you just like the idea of walking a precarious line, huh? Thought you were a big girl?'

Her eyes were wide and a little crazed. She didn't know speed, didn't know what to expect when it rushed through you. She turned her face to one side. 'I'm feeling sick. I want to leave, Lee.'

'Back to Daddy,' he said.

She started to rise, slid in a cumbersome way from the bed to the floor. He drew her up to her feet and shook her a couple of times with a vigor he couldn't keep in check. 'Back to fucking Daddy,' he said.

'I just want to go home, Lee. *Please.*'

'I just want to go home, Lee, please.' He pulled her face

toward him, cupped her chin in his hand and squeezed. 'Your daddy. The good lieutenant. You want to hear a nasty little truth about your daddy? He's *bad*. Your precious daddy killed a hooker. Picked her up, I don't doubt he fucked her, then killed her in a field.'

She tried to step back, but he held her face firmly, squashing her mouth. He had a strange experience, a little mind-shift, as if a crawlspace in his head had collapsed, and just for a moment he thought she looked more like Monique than Almond. Resemblances everywhere. Hadn't he sometimes thought that, from a certain angle and in a certain kind of muted light, Almond had faintly resembled his sister? Hadn't he found in that vague similarity some little nut of pleasure and glee? It was Monique he was sending to strange motel rooms. It was Monique walking the streets for him. Monique spreading her thighs for strangers in beds with gray sheets, or participating in seedy hurried couplings, or quick BJs in the back seats of cars. Then this thought dissipated, and he couldn't remember how accurate the memory was. Faces rushed at him – this one, that one, he couldn't keep them apart.

He shut his eyes and opened them again. This girl was Darcy Samsa, definitely. Chemical overspill. Warnings from Brain Central. Truant synapses rushing from classrooms screaming.

'You're saying . . . What are you saying? My father killed somebody?'

'Yeah, and he's trying to keep it to himself, but *I* know. I know the whole fucking *story*. Oh, he's up shit creek, little Darcy. He's well and truly up shit creek.'

'My father would *never* kill anybody. You're out of your mind.'

'Ask him yourself. Hey, Daddy, you kill a girl called Cecily Suarez?'

'*Cecily Suarez?*'

'Go to the horse's mouth, babe.'

'I'll call him, I'll do it now.' She stretched an arm toward the phone.

'I don't think this is such a good time,' he said. He knocked the receiver out of her reach and it fell to the floor.

'You're a lying bastard,' she said.

He slapped her once, hard. She had to learn who was in control here. Her head snapped back. Blood leaked from her nostrils, and he was strangely moved by this sight. He grabbed a tissue from a box on the bedside table and applied it to her nose. She kept her eyes shut tight.

'Let's get one thing clear, babe. You're going nowhere unless I say so.'

She yanked herself free and made a movement toward the door, and he caught her before she'd gone three feet and tossed her down on the bed. He lay on top of her and she turned her face this way and that. *I have the power*, he thought. He kissed her, found her unyielding, forced the kiss on her, felt the wet warmth of her mouth. This is the way it's done, Darcy. I explore the contours of your body, all the secret cavities. I go where I like.

He gripped her arms, turned her over and tugged the skirt down her legs. He was hard, *hard*. She was speaking into the pillow – 'No no no' – and she was kicking her legs, thrashing around underneath him. She swiveled somehow, turning on her side, and he tried whispering in her ear, 'We'll go away. Your father won't find us in another city, you'll change your name. Life is going to be nice, I promise you. Just the two of us. We'll go to a place where music and moonlight and feeling are one.'

She clawed at his cheek, raked it. He could feel she'd drawn blood. Okay, he'd do this the hard way. He reached over to the coffee table, grabbed his bag and took out the gun. 'You see this?' He was feeling quirky hot flashes go through him like fireballs roaring down a tunnel.

She pressed herself against the headboard. How young she looked. How scared.

'Now. You are a microsecond away from oblivion. Try to get it through your head what we're here for. Okay?'

She smoothed hair from her face and looked up into his eyes, and he had it again, that flash of Monique. Get the fuck out my brain, Monique, go play with that lumbering bespectacled husband of yours, Austin I-am-a-big-time-money-maker Arganbright.

He was limp all of a sudden. Fucking Monique was still in his head, and he could see her wedding cake decorated with rainbow frosting. She liked goddam rainbows, considered them symbolic of something, he couldn't remember what. Some New Age guff.

This is the speed at work, buddy. This is years of self-destruction screeching back at you, and you are not silencing it.

The girl was sniffling.

He hated that sound. It reminded him of Monique weeping over her horse – *Oh, Daddy, bring him back to life, please*. Stamp your feet all you like, sister, the nag is plain fucking *dead*. Daddy can't do a Lazarus act for you. Hugh isn't Christ, despite what he might think.

He got up from the bed and walked up and down the room. A crack of pain shot across his scalp, and he was suddenly plunged back into that nocturnal world where people waited for him outside closed curtains. There were shadows in parking lots, men sitting in motionless cars, phones were tapped. Okay, you could blame the dope, but this *felt* real. He couldn't deflate this panicky feeling, this need to move.

He imagined Jimmy Plumm saying to Tom Bigshoes, *It*

331

might be interesting to know how Lee came into money. What scam does he have going? I want a cut of it. Break a few bones if you need to. He also imagined Samsa coming after him with a posse of his cop buddies and finding him with his daughter in a motel room. He could imagine even Rudy Vass turning against him in some foggy serpentine way.

And cops, there were always cops, black patrols of them, and he pictured them finding the poker he'd hidden in a place he considered altogether appropriate, *ironic even.* And though he'd wiped it clean, they probably had some kind of hypersensitive equipment that could pick up a fingerprint on Mars, for Chrissakes. All this was a marquee collapsing on him, tons of canvas, a hundred poles, miles of rope, the whole fucking business.

'We need to get out of here,' he said. 'We need to get the fuck out of this city and begin all over again.'

She stared at him. Wet eyes. 'I don't understand what you're saying,' she said.

'You don't have to understand. Nobody's asking you to understand. We move, that's all. Too many people know me around here. You see what I'm saying? People know me, I have all kinds of pressures coming down on me.'

He stuffed the gun in his bag and tossed the rig inside and all the rest of his stuff. *Lee Boyle is freaking*, he thought.

He grabbed her by the hand and stepped into the corridor, dragging her behind him. Halfway toward the elevators he experienced a razor-sharp pain at the back of his eyes, so fierce it sucked all the air out of him and dimmed the lights around him.

Is this it? Is this the legendary Seizureland, that theme park for dying speed-freaks? His heart was charged with explosives.

When the elevator arrived he hustled Darcy inside the mirrored cab, seeing multiplied reflections of his own pale image, sweat bright on his face, eyes feverish. As the elevator descended he had the thought that there were at least six Lee Boyles and Darcy Samsas riding down this shaft to God knows where.

42

SAMSA STARED OUT AT DARKNESS, HOPING HE'D SEE DARCY appear. But the street was silent and dreadful.

'When did you last see her?' Eve asked.

'This morning. No, yesterday morning. God, I'm losing track of time.'

He looked at Eve. She hadn't said why she'd turned up at the house. She seemed unusually reticent, as if she had some preoccupation beyond Darcy's troubling absence.

'You've tried her friends?' she asked.

'I called a couple of them. Nothing. The only thing I know for sure is that she isn't with Nick Mancuso.'

'I heard about that.'

'You also heard the circumstances.'

Eve nodded. 'Nick and this girl, yeah. If Darcy's already learned about that she can't possibly be handling it very well.'

He thought of Darcy out there on her own, perhaps wandering in a private blue haze. 'I phoned downtown,' he said. 'I gave the guys a description of her, but I don't know what she was wearing. I looked through her closet, but I can't tell what's missing.'

She sat on the stool at the piano, leaning forward a little and looking at the floor. She seemed downhearted. He walked across the room and touched her shoulder, and she edged almost imperceptibly away from him.

'Something bothering you?' he asked.

'Just Darcy.' She looked at her watch. 'Does she ever stay out this late?'

'Not without telling me she's spending the night with a friend or going to a party,' he said. He bent down, put his hand under her chin and lifted her face so he could see her eyes. 'There's something else on your mind.'

She got up from the stool and moved away from him. 'No,' she said. 'How's your hand?'

Changing the subject, he thought. Fine. Whatever was on her mind couldn't be forced out. She'd tell him when she was ready. 'It's okay. I bandaged it up again,' he said.

'You didn't do such a great job, did you? It's like something on a mummy.'

He made some passing reference to the logistical problems of bandaging your own hand, then he returned to the window, the silent street, the lamps that attracted a blizzard of moths.

'I can't stand this goddam waiting,' he said. 'Maybe I'll drive around, see if I run into her.'

'What if she comes back when you're gone?'

'I'll take my phone. I'll call the house every ten minutes or so.'

Eve said, 'You want company?'

He told her he'd welcome that. They went outside.

She said, 'Let's take my car.' Her mood was off-center, she'd retreated to a place he couldn't locate. He thought of Harriet suddenly, but Harriet's silences were profoundly different, deep and mysterious. With Eve you knew something was simmering just below the surface.

She drove a couple of blocks and Samsa, thinking how uniform the neighborhood was, gazed out at trees and houses. Three a.m. and quiet, nothing moving on the streets. His mind was skipping like a flat stone thrown across water. Where to look? Where to begin? Down through the suburbs and into the city centre. And if she *had* gone there, why?

Here and there porch lights burned, some yellow, others orange. So many houses, windows, rooms. And all so goddam ordinary to look at. It was in one such ordinary house that Nick Mancuso and Mandy Robbins had been bludgeoned to death. Surfaces told you nothing.

'Is there any special direction you want me to take?' Eve asked.

'Just drive around,' he said. The pointlessness of this, scanning the night, hoping she'd materialize. He remembered stories of people who'd just vanished off the face of the earth. The department had scores of unsolved cases. Missing persons, people who'd fallen into mysterious cracks and were never seen again. And then he remembered how he and Darcy had mentioned the subject of runaways.

You'd never do that, would you?

Run away from home? Come on. I can't imagine the circumstances.

He beat the palm of his hand against his thigh. Why wasn't he receiving signals from that source people called paternal instinct? Why wasn't there some gut feeling to inform him he was worrying fruitlessly? Instead his mind was filled with shadows and his instincts were persistent little beeps of apprehension.

Eve said, 'She's a kid, and sometimes kids forget

about time. I used to worry my mother to death.'

'Darcy's usually good about these things,' he said.

'So this one time she forgot.'

He wondered why he wasn't convinced by that. 'Even when she cuts classes she doesn't hide it,' he said.

'She's open and honest,' Eve said.

'Yeah, she is.'

'But you don't *really* know that, do you? I mean, there's a sense in which we never know other people, isn't there? We go along thinking we do, then something happens right out of the blue, and all of a sudden your ideas of somebody else get changed around.'

'Why don't you just *say* what's bugging you, Eve?'

'Let's look for Darcy, okay? Let's concentrate on that.'

'But there's something.'

She stared ahead. 'Let's try and find your daughter, Greg.'

He fell silent. Okay, her barricades were up and this wasn't the time to storm the fortress. He looked out, saw a twenty-four-hour convenience market, bright and white. In the darkness of the vicinity it was like a big fluorescent spaceship, just landed.

They traveled in silence for a time through an assortment of neighborhoods that became progressively more mean, more shabby, the closer they got to the edge of downtown. He was trying to bring Darcy's face into sharp focus, wondering if there was any truth to the idea that if you could visualize a lost thing you could find it – but he supposed that only worked if you were the one who had misplaced it originally. Stupid thoughts, stoked by panic. His feelings were turning bad, his head was spinning. She's out there somewhere and I'm never going to find her again. I'll spend the rest of my life looking for a girl whose photograph is inside a missing persons folder that grows more and more musty with every year that passes. But you'd never forget. You'd look for ever. You'd imagine you caught a glimpse of her in a mall, a department store, a passing bus. Your life would be one of checking out reported sightings. You'd live on hope.

He took out his cellular phone and punched in his home number. No answer.

Eve asked, 'Where now?'

He had no directions to give. 'Anywhere,' he said.

'We might as well go downtown,' she said.

Somehow it didn't matter where she drove, the idea was to keep moving and looking. Downtown was a drab mausoleum at this hour. The streets were lifeless, save for a few cars and a couple of drunk pedestrians shuffling along unsteadily.

Eve turned off the main drag a few blocks before City Hall. She drove past the old Rialto Hotel, and Samsa glanced at the awning, the lights in the lobby.

Then she hung a left and they were moving into a neighborhood where he didn't want to go. He had the urge to tell her, No, not this way, but he didn't say so, he couldn't explain that this area was the last place on earth for him. But Eve was driving there anyhow, and suddenly there were ghostly girls and boys lingering on sidewalks, watching the car approach and probably thinking, *This might be a customer, some late-night score*. There were twenty or so, and they moved toward the curb, desperate to do business, gesticulating, calling out. Eve slowed the car a little, and he wondered why.

Hands reached out from the sidewalk, signs were made. A girl in short tight spangled pants swiveled her pelvis and laughed, another flashed a breast, cupping it in her hand and thrusting it forward as if she had a thirsty infant to feed. A slinky boy in a leather jacket and tight jeans clutched his crotch. Samsa noticed he had platinum-dyed hair.

338

'We're not going to find Darcy in this place,' he said.

'Oh, you never know what you're going to find down here,' Eve said.

He didn't like that cutting little note in her voice. He remembered what Joshua Gold had told her: *He saw you cruising, Greg.* Did she believe Gold? Had something happened to make her imagine Gold was telling the truth? He dismissed the questions. He didn't have space in his mind for anything but Darcy, finding Darcy, turning this goddam city upside down if he had to.

Eve was moving the car slowly along the edge of the sidewalk. Somebody on the curb reached out and touched the window on Eve's right, leaving a smear of what looked to Samsa like Vaseline – he couldn't tell – a greasy streak of something or other. He wished she'd give the goddam car some gas and get out of here. What was she playing at, idling along like this?

He said, 'Let's blow this place.'

'You want a change of scene? Okay, you got it. I'll give you a change of scene.' She accelerated away from the sidewalk. She drove without saying anything, taking corners fast, making her tires screech and leave echoes between buildings. She drove like this for several blocks, manic, like she didn't give a damn.

'For God's sake, slow down,' he said.

'You want slow? I can do slow.' She had the car crawling now, fifteen miles an hour.

'What the hell is your *problem*, Eve?'

'I don't have a problem, Greg.'

'Pardon me for thinking otherwise,' he said. 'Ever since you showed up on my doorstep you've been wound like a goddam clock.'

She pulled the car over and laid her face for a moment against the wheel. He touched the back of her neck, even though he understood it involved a risk because he had

339

the feeling she didn't want to be touched. She stared through the windshield at the dead street ahead. She didn't look at him.

'I'm fine, Greg. I'm perfectly okay.'

'No, you're not.' He wanted a cigarette suddenly. He hadn't smoked in years and now he wanted to light a cigarette he didn't have. Craving nicotine. He didn't know what to do with his hands. He punched his home number into his phone and, as before, received no answer.

He tapped in a second number and heard Duff's voice. 'Anything happening? Anybody seen my daughter?'

'Not so far,' Duff said.

'Call me at once if you hear anything.' Samsa cut the connection. He turned to Eve. 'Look, if you don't feel like driving, I'll do it.'

'I don't mind,' she said.

They passed the Greyhound station where a bus from a faraway city was disgorging weary passengers. The light from the terminal building was muted, dreary. A few taxi-cabs idled outside the station. Two uniformed cops were standing close to the doorway, nervy and vigilant. This area was a hang-out for small-time drug dealers, and sometimes there were occasional disputes that turned violent. It was also a place where runaways disembarked. He found himself imagining Cecily Suarez stepping off a bus right here, in a city that was strange to her, a place chosen at random because she didn't have enough money to get any further away from home. He wished to God she'd had a few more dollars to spare.

'Say something, Eve. Explain this ... this mood. Please.'

'I have my highs and lows, Greg. I have my expectations and my disappointments, like everyone else.'

'So you're disappointed with something. That's a start.'

340

'Sometimes I just hear things crashing in my head. Does that make sense to you?'

'Explain some more,' he said.

'You were the most honest man I knew.'

'But something's happened to make you think otherwise,' he said, and he could feel it coming, rumbling in the distance as it rolled toward him, a runaway train unstoppable and gathering speed. He looked down at his hands flattened against his legs. The bandage was coming undone. He hadn't bound it properly, he'd left loose ends. He'd left loose ends all over the place. *Eve knows. Somehow she knows.*

She said, 'I don't have a clue what I believe any more.'

He heard his phone buzzing. He snatched it out of his pocket and held it to his ear. *It has to be Duff*, he thought. Darcy's been picked up by a patrol car and she's safe.

'Hey, Lieutenant, *sir.*'

No, he thought.

'*She seemed at once some penanced lady elf, Some demon's mistress, or the demon's self.*'

'Why the fuck are you calling me?'

'*I took compassion on her, bade her steep her hair in weird syrups*, Lieutenant, *sir.*'

'Talk sense, for Christ's sake.'

'I'm talking good sense, and you're too moronic to know. *Tell me only where my nymph has fled.*'

Samsa said, 'Darcy. You're talking about Darcy.'

'Oh, you're one bright sonofabitch, Gregory J. You want to know where your nymph has fled, don't you? Huh?'

'If you touch her, if you fucking harm her—'

'*She began to sing, happy in beauty, life and love and everything.*'

'Where the fuck are you?'

341

'I don't know for sure. But I see a sign that says, *All hope abandon ye who enter here*. Now where do you suppose that might be?'

The line was dead and the phone sticky in his unsteady hand.

43

SHE SAT IN THE CAR AND WATCHED HIM STEP INSIDE A PAY-
phone adjacent to a darkened gas station. She thought,
Take a chance and run, but he was only ten yards away
with the gun in his hand, and even though he held it
loosely at his side, he could easily aim and fire if she made
a wrong move. She curled up in the passenger seat. He
came back and got in behind the wheel. He slid the key
into the ignition. His movements were weird, spazzy, like
he had no control over his muscles. His face was sweaty,
as if he'd come from a steam bath.

'I just spoke to your daddy,' he said.

'What did you say to him?'

'I had this overwhelming urge to toss a little *gasolina* on
his bonfire. Now Daddy's worried sick. He's gnawing on
his fingertips. He's all chewed up.'

She stared at the road ahead. She imagined her father's
state of mind. 'You told him I was with you?'

'I pointed him in that general direction,' he said.

'He'll come after you. You know that.'

He laughed. '"A man, to be greatly good, must imagine

intensely and comprehensively. He must put himself in the place of another. The pains and pleasures of his species must become his own."'

What was he talking about? The dope in her system wasn't helping her think clearly. She was alert, but she had druggy distortions in her head, and thoughts slipped like fish through nets. Only one emotion kept coming back to her with leaden consistency: dread. Where was he taking her? What did he plan to do with her? He'd rambled on about driving her to another city and starting some kind of new life – *together*, for Christ's sake.

Like how? Lovers? Did he imagine that?

He pulled the car over. She recognized the neighborhood. The dark swath of greenery on her left was Ludlow Park, about five miles from her home. She watched him shove more speed up his nose, spilling a bunch of it in the process. His nostrils and his upper lip were white and sparkling, and dope had fallen into his lap, but he didn't notice. He was totaled.

'I could have been greatly good,' he said. 'You know what held me back? Because people are all so fucking *unworthy*. So totally immoral. Like your daddy. You know how much money he paid me?'

'I don't believe he gave you any money,' she said.

'Check it out. Fifteen K give or take.' He tugged bills from his pockets and tossed them flamboyantly in the air, a downpour of fifties and hundreds floating and falling inside the car.

'And where do you think all the dope came from, huh? He stole it for me. Because I know his big secret, nightingale.' He drew a hand across his brow.

'You're dreaming,' she said. 'All this stuff about him killing that girl. You made it up. I know my father. I know what he's capable of and what he's not.'

344

He didn't seem to hear her. 'I'm always dreaming. Around the next corner, somewhere over the big fucking rainbow, is the place where my dreams will come true. Who needs reality? Reality's a pisser, a downer. You, now. You're out of a dream. *I arise from dreams of thee*, you know what I'm saying? Never knock dreams, babe. They are the *stuff* of life.'

He slid his hand up her leg, touched her thigh. She thought, *I can distance myself from his damp hot touch, squeeze it out of my mind*, but then she was jolted back into the motel bedroom and the fear she'd felt when he'd produced the gun and she knew he could do anything to her he pleased. She could still feel the sting of his slap like a thorn embedded in her cheek.

What am I going to say if I get through this nightmare? I went out with this guy willingly to a motel room? I halfway imagined I wanted him to make love to me, then it all spun out of control? Was it like that? She couldn't remember with certainty. All she could bring back to mind was the memory of wanting to do something *risky*. Something different. Picking up a challenge. *Darcy comes of age, daringly.*

Stupidly.

A couple of hundred-dollar bills lay in her lap, caught in the creases of her skirt. She felt Lee's hand motionless and moist as a basking crab on her skin. Sometimes he emitted a tiny gasp, which might have been a sound of pain, she wasn't sure. He was forever dabbing his shirt-sleeve against his face, so that sometimes the wheel was unattended and the car veered to the edge of the sidewalk, and she wanted to reach out to take control, but she was afraid of his reactions. He was erratic, careless, volatile.

She was unaware of the cop car behind until it flashed its rooflights and its siren whined once. Lee looked in the

345

rear-view mirror and said, 'Say absolutely nothing. I'll do the talking. You got that?'

She twisted her head. She was blinded by the way the spinning lights fragmented the dark. She saw somebody get out of the cruiser and come towards the car in brisk strides. *Rescue me.*

The cop inclined his face and Lee rolled down the window.

'Problem, officer?' he asked.

'Please step out of the car,' the cop said.

Darcy looked at the cop's face. She'd met a few cops through her father, but this one was new to her. *Scream,* she thought – but Lee had the gun stuck in the pocket of the door and he could reach it in a second. And he'd use it. She had no doubt about that. She wondered how she might get a message to this cop. What pantomime move she might make. What sign.

'Give me one good reason why I should step out of the car.'

'Because I'm telling you.'

'Because *you're* telling me? I have every goddam right to know *why* you want me to get out of the fucking car. Or did we vote some Fascist government into power when my back was turned? Huh?'

'Get out. Just do as I say.'

Lee drew his hand across his mouth. 'What is your problem, man?'

'Don't make this any harder than it is,' the cop said. He was very young. He'd cultivated a tiny mustache to give himself a dimension of authority. But there was stress in his eyes, maybe the fear of confrontation.

'I'm asking what rights you have,' Lee said. 'Isn't that simple enough for you?'

'A car that fits the description of this one was reported stolen,' the cop said, and he laid a hand on the door

346

handle, drew the door slightly open. 'Get your ass out. *Now.* Where I can see you.'

Darcy heard herself say, 'Wait—'

The cop seemed to notice her for the first time, and, alerted by an instinct of danger, probably baffled by the sight of so much cash lying around, reached for the gun on his hip and dragged it out, but he was cumbersome and inexperienced, and he hadn't made the right moves. Lee shoved the door open violently, and it rammed the young policeman in the gut, and then Lee had the gun in his hand and was firing it – once, twice, Darcy's head reverberated – and the cop staggered back like a man whose legs had turned to flawed glass under him. He fell down in the grassy verge of the street and lay still, and Darcy couldn't get the scream out of her throat.

She was aware of motion, the stolen car traveling at speed, Lee saying, *Oh lift me from the grass, I die, I faint, I fail,* and laughing vigorously.

'You shot him,' she said.

'Yeah I shot him. So?'

'You *killed* him.' She had a wild teeter-totter feeling in her stomach. She could see the cop falling even now, and the dread she'd been feeling deepened. She'd never seen a man shot before. She didn't know what to do with the image of the cop, where to put it, how to stick it into a compartment where she wouldn't keep seeing it.

Lee said, 'Maybe he's dead, maybe he's not. The thing is, it doesn't matter, it doesn't belong inside my equation. Do you know what I'm saying? He was in the wrong god-dam place at the wrong goddam time. Some people have a knack for that. Some people just don't see the fucking boundaries. They want to get inside your life and eat away at your plans like maggots. They want to keep you squashed and down.'

He might have been speaking in a language of lost

347

tongues. She didn't understand what he was talking about. He was driving through neighborhoods she didn't recognize, heading for a destination only he knew. Then he stopped the car, and sat back with his eyes shut and a pained frown on his face and he groaned. 'Oh *shit,* this is bad, this is really downright kick-ass *baaad.*' He put a hand flat to the side of his skull. 'It's like some fucking monstrous kid who's been given a set of drums for Christmas, and the little cocksucker won't stop beating on them.' He was sweating so profusely he might have been ice melting. His eyelids fluttered. 'Somebody take his fucking drums away.'

She thought, *I could run now while he's like this.* But, as if he'd read her mind, he pressed the electronic door lock in the key. She heard all the doors of the car click shut.

He said, 'You stay with me. Don't fuck with me like that cop back there.'

'I'll stay,' she said.

'Yeah, you'll stay. Damn right.' He groaned, inclined his face, pressed his fingertips firmly into his scalp. 'Because I need you.' And he began rambling about sea blooms and the sapless foliage of the ocean, losing it completely. Sometimes he punctuated his words with a small laugh, which wasn't exactly a joyful sound, but sad in some way.

Then he appeared to gain control of himself. She couldn't decide which was more dangerous: these times of composure or the flights he took into lunacy. He turned his face and smiled at her in a woozy way. 'We'll look back at all this one day from a long distance, and we'll laugh,' he said.

'Laugh at what, Lee? You're not even going to get me out of this city. My father will have cops everywhere looking for me.'

'Your father the whore-killer,' he said. 'Your father,

big-time guardian of morality. This is right, this is wrong. Don't do this, don't do that. Who the fuck does he think he is? Your father couldn't handle traffic duty, for Christ's sake. Your father couldn't even write a goddam parking ticket. He's through. He's all washed up. Maybe he'll find a job as a security guard working the night shift at some piss-ant factory. If he's lucky.'

'Stop,' she said. 'Just *stop*.'

'Your daddy's so much shit. He's like something came down a sewage pipe. He's waste. He's human crap that happens to carry a badge. The truth upset you, huh? Is that it? Hey, face it, people don't ever come up to expectations. You think the sun shines out their ass, but that's only because you're wearing gold-tinted lenses. You see what you want to see. You blind yourself.'

She wasn't going to listen. She didn't have to hear this. The man Lee was talking about wasn't anybody she knew, certainly not her father.

He turned the key in the ignition.

'Where are we going?' she asked.

'Sightseeing,' was all he said.

44

SAMSA HEARD HIS FOOTSTEPS CLATTER ON THE MARBLE floor, and the strange hush of the vast interior of City Hall, unlit except for a few pale lamps in the lobby. High black spaces hung above him, and the central stairway terminated in midair as if it were unfinished. Eve, hurrying after him, might have been nothing more substantial than an elongated shadow he cast. He rushed in the direction of the department offices, taking the stairs rapidly. He needed help if he was going to find Darcy.

Duff was leaning against the corner of his desk with a phone in his hand. There was motion in the rooms behind Duff: the night cops doing paperwork at their desks, a handcuffed guy with a sky-blue bandanna knotted on his head being booked. The air smelled of stewed coffee and the afterburn of the absent Fogue's cheroots. Stephen Rebb, yawning, wandered into view.

This is the high noon of my panic, Samsa thought.

Duff put his phone down as soon as he saw Samsa. 'I was just trying to call you, Lieutenant. I don't know if this relates to your daughter, but we have an officer down—'

'Who?'

'Kid called Ron Askew.'

Samsa didn't know the name. 'How bad?'

'He took two slugs, one in the stomach, the other in the shoulder. He's on his way to County. He's conscious, but kind of in and out.'

'Come to the point, Duff.' Samsa tried to check his impatience, but he was beyond etiquette.

'Askew stopped a car reportedly stolen. A white Ford Taurus. The driver shot him. Askew says there was a girl in the car. Short hair, brown, brown-to-black. Askew says she resembled the description we issued of Darcy. The driver was a blond guy of about thirty, who acted like he was stoned out of his skull.'

'Boyle,' Samsa said.

'Boyle? *Lee* Boyle?' Rebb asked. 'Your kid might be riding around with *Lee* Boyle?'

'I don't think there's any *might* involved, Rebb. Don't ask me how it happened, but it did. That's all I know.'

'Like a kidnap thing?' Rebb asked.

'I don't know if it's a kidnap thing. I don't know what it is.'

Samsa looked at Eve's concerned face, then at Duff and Rebb, and beyond them to the cops in the other rooms, some of whom had become aware of the lieutenant's presence and were listening.

'Where did this happen?' he asked.

'Stafford, where it intersects Dolores Drive,' Duff said.

Dolores Drive. He knew where it was located. He knew where it led.

He headed at once for the stairs. Eve followed him up. He crossed the lobby, stepped out into the street. It was empty, but it was an emptiness that assaulted him, coming at him in brutal waves of silence. He had the feeling the city was one he'd never visited in this lifetime, and yet it was familiar in the unsettling way of dreamscapes.

He got inside Eve's car, closed the door. She sat behind the wheel.

'Boyle didn't actually *say* she was with him, did he?' Eve asked.

You want to know where your nymph has fled, don't you? Huh? It didn't take a whole lot of literary analysis to understand he was talking about Darcy. 'She's with him all right. I don't have any doubts about that, Eve. What really worries the hell out of me right now is his record of violence.'

Samsa stopped dead on the last word of his sentence, remembering what Rebb had said about a girl called Nancy, how Boyle had beaten her so badly she'd ended up in hospital. And he imagined Boyle threatening Darcy, hurting her. He tried to excise that thought.

'What do you imagine happened?' Eve asked. 'He went to your house, lured Darcy away on some pretext?'

'He's smooth when he wants to be,' Samsa said. 'I can see where he might be impressive, if you're a fifteen-year-old girl. Maybe Darcy went along with him willingly. I don't know.' He recalled something from Boyle's rap-sheet. *Sex with a minor.* He had an image of Boyle and Darcy locked together, Boyle fucking her. It took some effort to eject this picture from his mind, but somewhere at the back of his head it continued to unwind, like a video cassette playing in the next room.

Eve said, 'He could have used force.'

'He could have.' Samsa tried to picture Boyle calling at the house, grabbing Darcy, hustling her off inside a car. But she'd have yelled, drawn attention to the situation, and the Petersons next door, neighborhood eagles who missed nothing, would have heard her and called the cops.

'We'll look in the general neighborhood of Dolores Drive to start with,' she said.

'Fine,' he said. Where else? It was all they had to go on. He pictured Dolores Drive, darkness on either side of it. Why that direction? Why there into the quicksands of his own life?

Eve drove quickly. Samsa, dry-mouthed and tense beyond his experience, pondered the destruction Boyle had wreaked on his life. It was like surveying driftwood on a lonesome stretch of beach. He stared ahead, tried to concentrate only on his daughter. But there was an unfinished conversation with Eve, and even if he would have preferred to avoid it, he drew a deep breath and said, 'You were saying something before about my honesty, I remember. You were talking about your disappointment. I guess you want to pick up the threads of that?'

'It can wait.'

'I don't want it to wait,' he said.

'This isn't the time, Greg.'

'Make it the time,' he said. 'I can't take your moods any more, Eve.'

'Okay. That's what you want.' She removed something from her pocket and flashed it in front of him.

He didn't want to see whatever she was holding.

She shoved it toward him, and he squinted at it, then closed his eyes, searching his mind for some tiny corner where he might be safe. But all he could see was his daughter's face, and all he could hear was Lee Boyle's voice: *All hope abandon ye who enter here.*

45

DARCY SHUT HER EYES AND PRESSED HER KNUCKLES INTO HER lids, seeing bright visual flashes, and thinking they had a name, *phosphenes*, something like that, and if she just concentrated on unusual words she'd be fine, she wouldn't need to listen to what Lee was saying.

But his words filtered through anyhow. 'The way I see it, they'll love you. They'll wait in long lines for you, babe. I imagine you in a wine-colored velvet skirt, not too short, and maybe a pricey lace blouse. No see-through crap. Something with class. And we'll stay away from the streets, because it's a snake-pit down there. It's going to be hotels, good hotels. I don't want you out there with the goddam riff-raff. You're better than that.'

She peered at him through slatted fingers. His face was white and glistening. The gun lay in his lap. The leather bag with the dope sat on the console. Much of the dope was spilled. Money was strewn inside the car. Everything was chaos and displacement.

'This is a fresh beginning. Gleaming spires in the distance. Lee is moving up in the world. Lee will have a kidskin Filofax and a state-of-the-fucking-art cellular phone and a car that has taste written all over it.'

She saw this future he was talking about. He couldn't possibly be serious. But he was. He was animated and purposeful and his voice was resolute, and he was chopping the air in karate fashion with one hand to emphasize everything he was saying.

'You think—? You're *crazy*,' she said.

'I have been told that on more than one occasion, nightingale. Always by wrong-headed people lacking perception. People who cut me down, took pot-shots at me. The trees are thick with snipers. My head's always in somebody's cross-sights. Not this time, because Lee has had *enough*. You understand what I'm saying? Lee takes no more shit.'

She was traveling through another person's nightmare, the strands of somebody else's reality – or in Lee's case no reality at all, but some kind of deformed relationship he had with the world.

Phosphorite.

Just keep the words coming, Darcy. Just fill your head with words.

He said, 'I'm not saying it's going to be easy at first. I realize that. You'll probably hate yourself, you'll definitely hate *me*, but we'll get round that. The trick is, you don't think about what you're doing, you just numb yourself. After a while it comes naturally to you. It's just a job you do.'

It comes naturally. Going to hotel rooms to fuck strangers. She pictured herself taking her clothes off, fat men pawing her, slobbering over her, screwing her, she thought of dirt under fingernails and sweat and bad breath.

'And if any of the customers step out of line – hey, I'm there to see you're protected. I'll look after you all the way. And we won't work it too hard, we'll do it nice and easy.'

Yes, Lee. Whatever you say, Lee. She looked from the window and wondered about her father, where he was, why he wasn't looking for her, why she didn't hear the wail of sirens. She saw houses float past, and then abruptly there was darkness and the lit streets were left somewhere behind and the car was traveling through a black wormhole in the texture of space.

Phosphate.

But the words weren't working. She couldn't play this game any longer. She couldn't hide from her predicament. She looked at the oil-black landscape on either side of the road, which was narrow and unmarked, and she realized where she was, and that the city was slipping away behind her, her father receding, the notion of safety diminishing.

'You're a natural,' he was saying. 'The way you walk. From the hips, you know what I mean? With a little pelvic thrust that says, Hey, guys, consider it a privilege just to *breathe* the same air as me. And that mouth of yours – people will think you stole it from an angel. We'll need to color the hair, I figure. Red? No, I don't think red. One of those offbeat colors – purple? A streak of gold? Not too much, though, because we don't want you looking tacky. When you strut inside a room I want men going fucking wild with desire. I want them drooling because a goddess has condescended to visit.'

He was expelling his words like tiny torpedoes of air. She was looking into the darkness, thinking, thinking, fearful, seeing the headlights gleam on the blacktop. Humor him. Go along with him. Crossing him now was dangerous. *Think.* Nobody's going to help you out of this. You're on your own.

She said, 'It all sounds terrific, Lee.'

'It *is* terrific, no two ways about it,' he said. 'First time

I saw you, I thought, She's the one, she's my girl,' and he reached out to touch the back of her hand. 'Or maybe it was when I heard your voice. What the hell. It doesn't matter, does it?'

She couldn't stand the feel of his skin. She was aware of blackness zooming past. Do something. But what? The only thing that came to mind was risky and dangerous, but she was beyond thinking of any consequences, all she wanted was to disrupt a sequence of events that in Boyle's mind was inevitable. Becoming a whore. His.

Just do it.

She hesitated a moment and then thought, *Go for it, now or never*, and made a grab for the wheel, thinking she could make the car swerve, maybe crash it, derail everything somehow. But it was a hapless effort, doomed from the start because Boyle anticipated her. He was too quick, he struck her wrist with the hard edge of his hand, and she pulled her arm back to her side.

He braked, turned to her with a fierce look. 'What the *fuck* do you think you're trying to do? You could have killed us both, for Christ's sake. Did you imagine you could somehow get away? Huh? Some crazy notion of freedom entered that little head of yours?' He smiled suddenly. 'Oh, you are precious, nightingale. Totally precious. Devious and sly. You've got the instincts of a whore. See, you're halfway there already. Just don't *ever* think about fucking with me again. Any time a similar stunt pops into your head, take my advice and strangle it at birth.'

He laughed in a discordant fashion, and turned off the blacktop at a place where the incline into the field was gradual and easy, and then he was driving through long stalks of grass that slowed the progress of the car, and straight ahead was a big tree made white by the glossy glare of the headlights.

'Now the sightseeing,' he said. 'And after that we move move move, *all hastening onward*, and no more fucking *games*. One more off-the-wall prank and you're a dead little girl and Daddy's going to have to arrange a funeral. Think about that, nightingale.'

46

SAMSA LET THE PRINT SLIP OUT OF HIS HAND. IT FELL DOWN the side of his seat and he didn't reach to retrieve it, didn't want to touch it.

'They've been blackmailing you,' Eve said. 'Gold and Lee Boyle.'

'*Gold?* I didn't know Gold was involved.' Gold and Boyle conspiring in the fissures of the city: Gold taking the furtive picture, Boyle exploiting it.

'I can just *about* understand you picking up that girl. Just about. And I can see how your reputation would be compromised seriously after the accident. And maybe I'm being naïve and idealistic, but what really blows me out the water is the fact you didn't tell the truth from the beginning, because in the long run it's easier—'

'*Easier?* When you're faced with the dead body of a young girl you don't always make the right choices, Eve. All that training you get to stay composed in the face of pressure, it's nothing, it goes haywire. You create a lie and suddenly everything's built around it, and you can't see a way out because you can't go back and undo it—'

'By covering it up, you *compounded* it, for Christ's sake. You got yourself tangled up in this whole diabolic mess, going through the motions of an investigation you knew was a total fiction. And now Darcy's out there . . .'

He laid his cheek against the window of the car. What did he feel anyway? A release? Or a darker guilt? It didn't matter now.

She said, 'I thought seriously about never mentioning this to you and just choking it down and going on as if I'd never learned about it in the first place. But I can't live like that, Greg. I'd see you every day. There would be this effort at pretense, and I wouldn't know how to carry that off.'

'You'll go to Brodsky,' he said.

'That's not up to me,' she replied.

She had an expression he'd never seen before on her face – pinched and sorrowful, and her green eyes were a shade darker. There were right ways to do things, and wrong ways, and she knew the difference. *And you, Samsa, in the most terrible overheated moment of your life, you forgot.*

Eve said, 'I'll ask for a transfer if it comes down to that. I'll make up some excuse: I need a change of scenery, I'm tired of homicide, whatever. But I won't tell him what I know, Greg. It's up to you to straighten it out.'

He looked at the street ahead. The city was dead space in which his daughter was lost. He half imagined she'd suddenly materialize in the darkness unharmed, she'd come strolling along the sidewalk, that Boyle's phone call was just a cruel hoax.

'I had you up on a pedestal,' Eve said.

'Where I didn't belong.'

'More naïvety, I guess. That was my mistake.'

'We all make them,' he said.

360

'I thought . . . well, maybe we had the germ of some-thing. Stupid me. *Naïve* me.'

'And now it's changed. What happened between us is just something hit by a fucking truck and bleeding at the side of the road. Is that how you see it?'

'I should have left it alone,' she said. 'I shouldn't have gone back to see Gold, I shouldn't have looked inside his goddam darkroom. The timer on his developer was buzzing and I keep hearing it—'

'You did what you had to,' he said.

'And what good has that done?'

'You can sleep nights,' he said.

'I'm not so sure. How much has this cost you so far?'

He told her.

She said, 'You gave him twenty-five thousand dollars. You stole State's evidence and *handed* it over to him. And now he's got your daughter. This guy has it in for you in a big way.'

I killed his girl, Samsa thought. *He thinks I still owe him. And the last installment of the debt is Darcy.*

'You forgot one simple truth,' she said. 'Blackmailers always come back, Greg. Always.'

'I didn't forget it,' he said.

'You hoped he'd just *evaporate*?'

'I don't know what I hoped. Maybe he'd just see the well was dry and take a hike. I don't *know*.'

She drove for a few moments in silence. 'Gold is terrified. He'll testify against Boyle in the matter of ex-tortion. He wants very badly to be law-abiding. Basically he doesn't want to be a piece of gay white ass in a prison.'

Samsa wasn't interested in what Gold would or wouldn't do. 'There's only one thing on my mind right now. Everything else can keep.' He looked at her, searched her face for some tiny glimmer of sympathy, but found none.

She said, 'I keep wondering what you would have done if I hadn't gone back to see Gold. Would you have kept up this masquerade? God, I want to believe you'd have come to your senses, because basically I always considered you a decent man, Greg. I'll never *really* know now, will I?'

'Then we're in the same boat,' he said. He touched her hand and she permitted the contact a moment before she drew away.

The car was beginning to rise up through narrow streets in the direction of Dolores Drive. He glanced back and saw the city spread out below in spidery interstices of light the color of jaundiced flesh.

Dolores Drive. It was a narrow blacktop that sliced through the badlands where everything in his life had gone wrong. He thought of the great dark unkempt mass of the Purchase property that lay on either side of Dolores.

And he wondered why Lee Boyle had taken Darcy into that vicinity.

Dear God.

If Boyle had taken Darcy anywhere close to the Purchase property, he could have only one reason for doing so.

Samsa could think of no other.

Boyle was redressing the balance of things as he perceived them. Squaring the accounts. The debt paid in full.

We're even now, Samsa.

He leaned forward in his seat, staring ahead, seeing nothing, listening to his own roaring pulses. The field filled his head. Damp grass, a branch cracking and falling, wheels spinning, metal crunching against wood.

'Pull over,' he said.

'Pull over? Why?'

'Just do it, Eve.'

'I don't see the reason for—'

'Pull over, I said. Here.'

'Okay, *Lieutenant*,' she said. 'Whatever you say.'

She braked, looked at him in a puzzled way.

'I'll drive,' he said. 'Change places with me.'

She shrugged, stepped out of the car reluctantly and slammed the door.

He slid his body behind the wheel, saw Eve walk round the hood to the passenger side. He waited until she was reaching for the handle of the door and then slammed his foot on the gas and drove forward. In the rear-view mirror he saw her standing in the middle of the street, a diminishing figure with one arm raised in a gesture – of what? Anger? Bewilderment?

It didn't matter what she felt. He was the one who'd constructed this nightmare. He was the one who'd have to go into the depths of his own creation. Nobody else. It was beyond police business now, outside the law, it lay in that uncertain territory where no book of procedure dictated the rules.

He was alone.

47

THE FORD STAMMERED TO A HALT ABOUT FIFTY YARDS FROM the tree. Boyle cursed, turned the key, heard the engine hack. He twisted the key again, then again, nothing. Out of gas, okay, that wasn't going to be a problem. He wouldn't allow it to become one. It was a minor inconvenience. Don't blow it up into something enormous.

'What are you going to do now, Lee?' she asked. She looked into his blue eyes by what scant moonlight there was, and they were cold, like icicles hammered all the way into his skull.

'I'll steal another goddam car,' he said. 'There's a whole suburb over there filled with them,' and he pointed into the distance, where dim streetlamps were visible way beyond the foliage. Then he swung round and kicked a front tire of the Ford in a petulant way and said, 'The fucking fuel gauge is probably faulty.'

He stopped himself. Waste of energy kicking rubber. He'd forgotten why he'd driven down here in the first place, then it came back to him, and he gripped Darcy by the wrist and walked to the tree. 'The guided tour,' he said. 'This is the spot where your daddy crashed his car. You can see the gouge.'

She found herself staring at the tree. She didn't want to look. Didn't want to listen to him.

'Touch it. Try to picture Daddy smacking into this. Imagine a little girl dead.'

'No—'

'Just do what I fucking *say*, for Christ's sake.' He seized her hand and forced it against the trunk, and she didn't have the strength to resist.

She encountered a jagged indentation with her finger-tips. Something moved in the crevice – an ant, a spider. She drew back, alarmed. She watched Lee stick his fingers into the gash. Ants, scores of them, criss-crossed his hand. He imagined them working their way into his flesh, tunneling into his veins. He thought of himself as a building occupied by busy black tenants always making demands. He brushed them off.

He walked around the tree. A large branch lay some feet away. 'This probably came off when he whacked into the trunk.' He stared into the distance and had the strange feeling that just beyond the range of his vision a hooded figure lingered in the bushes, one crooked finger beckoning from the fold of a long sleeve, a voice saying, *Step right this way, Lee. I'll take you to a place nobody ever comes back from.*

'Your daddy dumped her like a piece of trash. Just walked off the scene. Free as a bird. You think I'm making this up?'

She shook her head. *I don't know what you're making up and what you're not*, she thought. *All I know is you scare me to death. All I know is I want to be a million miles away from you, a galaxy away.*

He grabbed her arm again and pushed her forcefully back in the direction of the car. He began to rummage inside the car, gathering money together and stuffing it in his pockets, rescuing his dope, some of which lay spilled on the floor and the console. Working quickly. Gotta move. Get out of here. Time is an eagle.

She watched him move around in a frantic way. He raised to his nose a little pile of speed balanced on the back of one hand and sniffed deeply. How could he keep doing that stuff on and on?

He finished collecting his money and then –

– wowee, here it comes, the rush, the familiar big jolt. He had the feeling that his skeletal structure was changing, as if pins had been implanted to hold his bones together, knobs of steel, little screws. As if he'd undergone surgery, his skin peeled back, men in surgical masks screwing bolts into his exposed skeleton. His skull had been reassembled too, the cracks fused together with thin metallic stitches, but they weren't holding, they were beginning to come undone, and with each pop there was a tiny hand-grenade burst. When he stood upright from his bending position, he heard the pins creaking inside him and his skull splitting open.

He shivered and rubbed his hands together briskly, thinking how even the bones of his fingers felt odd, like they were steel inserts under his skin. He licked his dry lips. Numb, tasted of stone. 'Now it's time for some grand theft auto. Then we're history, kid. We are truly *history*.'

And he bent down, groped around in the dark below the exposed roots of the tree, then rose with something in his fist. He looked at the girl and said, 'Can I trust you?'

She nodded her head slowly. She couldn't see what he had in his hand. He concealed it, tucking it in his waistband, his shirt hanging over it.

'Can I? *Can I?*' He grabbed a sleeve of her blouse, pulled her close to his body and listened to the heavy way she breathed and felt how her heart thudded. *This is the power.*

'Yes,' she whispered.

'Yes what?'

'Yes. You can trust me.'

He gripped her hand, twisted her fingers back until she made a low moaning sound. 'Again,' he said.

'You can trust me, Lee. I *swear . . .*'

He released her and thought, *Not for a moment, nightingale.*

48

HE DROVE AT HIGH SPEED THROUGH STOP AND YIELD SIGNS, saw the dull moon rush behind clouds. He parked at the edge of the blacktop and scanned the expanse of the field. The property was a motionless sea that had sucked all light out of the sky.

He scrambled down the slope.

He wanted moon. He wanted light.

I want Darcy back.

At the bottom of the slope he found himself ankle-deep in the puddle where the girl had died.

He'd hoped never to return to this place. Yet here he was.

His shoes squelched. He walked through the grass, saw the Ford when he was about thirty yards from it. The door on the driver's side hung open and the interior light burned a muted yellow-brown. He approached quietly, carefully.

No Boyle. No evidence of Darcy.

He saw some dazzling little swirls of white dust on the console: spilled speed. A key dangled from the ignition.

He looked at the instrument panel, saw the red glow of the battery and oil-pressure lights, and the fuel gauge, which registered a bright red E.

Boyle had run out of gas.

Samsa backed away from the car. He touched the gun holstered at the base of his spine. Reassurance. He circled the big black tree slowly, approached the fallen branch, half imagining he'd stumble across his daughter's body. His breath was like a dense gas in his throat, and he had the shivery feeling of trespassing on somebody's grave. Boyle wants to close the circle, wants a reckoning, and so he brings Darcy to this specific place in this wilderness because he has a demented notion about the poetry of justice, and it has to be as neat and exact as a fucking couplet, two girls dead in the same godforsaken field.

Samsa stepped quietly round the fallen branch. The silence was huge and overwhelming. The sullen secretive hour before dawn. Everything sleeps.

Please don't let anything happen to her.

If it's not too late already.

Head inclined, he listened for a sigh, a twig breaking, the whisper of clothing against stalks of grass. Anything. But the dark was still and mute and unforgiving. He stared at the lights of Chackstone. They were fuzzy and faraway.

There was a brief shifting of cloud and a sparse milky light spilled across the landscape, but it lasted only long enough to glaze the tree where the Chrysler had come to a battered halt, then was drawn back behind cloud cover.

Samsa moved away from the tree. The dark was crowded with apprehensions, flutters of awful anxiety. In some places the grass grew knee-high and parted grudgingly when he forced his way through. He had the odd feeling he was somehow seeking another version of himself in this wild meadow, a spectral Samsa who'd taken a wrong turning. He wanted to catch this phantom and warn him. Do it differently, make another decision.

He paused, tried to empty his mind of extraneous stuff. *Nothing else matters here except Darcy.* Concentrate on her. But suddenly he couldn't picture her face clearly, couldn't bring her to mind. He experienced a thrum of alarm. She was fading away, disappearing. He quickened his pace now, pressured by the sudden fear that Boyle may have killed Darcy and concealed her in an obscure corner of this field, and then entered the subdivision in search of a car to steal. Maybe he was already long gone. Maybe he'd never be found. Maybe he'd vanish into a remote part of the continent, another name, an assumed identity . . .

Or just maybe Darcy was still alive, and Boyle had other plans for her that Samsa couldn't begin to guess. Consider that. Yes. Why not. This slender thread of hope propelled him, and he started to run. The lights of the subdivision burned a little brighter beyond the trees and the cedar fence. The grass impeded him and he had to force himself, *push* himself. The bandage around his hand had unraveled almost entirely and flapped as he moved. The trees at the edge of the property were a hundred yards away, and he could see orange street lamps beyond, the tops of red-shingled rooftops, chimney pots. He was going as fast as he could now, conscious of the wet sound his shoes made and the creaking of blades.

'You make way too much noise, *amigo*.'

Samsa stopped dead. He hadn't seen Boyle emerge from the trees. He'd been too focused on the lamps, the fence, finding Darcy. Boyle's shirt hung outside his pants and he had a gun held firmly in his hand.

'Where is she?' Samsa asked.

'Paternal instincts,' Boyle said. 'I wonder what they feel like.'

'Where is she, Boyle?'

'Marriage and babies don't come into my general equation. Maybe when I'm old and wasted and drooling in front of a fire on some fucking freezing wintry day, and my pants are damp with piss, I'll wish I had a daughter that came to visit. You think that's likely, Samsa?'

'Where the fuck is Darcy?'

'Darcy, Darcy,' Boyle said. 'You should have taken better care of her, Samsa. You don't seem to do too well when it comes to little girls in general, do you?'

Samsa's urge was to rush Boyle, shatter his face, blow after blow after blow. Destruction. But Boyle had that gun in his hand.

'That dope has done a fearful number on me, Samsa. What was in it? My heart has been doing loops. It's like there's this dangerous little stunt pilot in my goddam chest. And *he's* on speed as well—'

'One more time, Boyle. *Where's my daughter?*'

Boyle came nearer. He placed a hand on Samsa's shoulder. '*Whither fled Lamia?*'

Samsa said, 'Spare me the goddam quotes,' and moved slightly, but Boyle's hand remained on his shoulder.

'You know they're looking for me,' Boyle said. 'Everybody's looking for me: you, your cop buddies, Jimmy Plumm, two goons despatched by a guy called Crassman. Fuck only knows who else. I am being *hounded.*'

Samsa thought, *He's gone, scattered.* Tiny white flecks of spit adhered to the corners of Boyle's lips. He was moving his jawbone from side to side as if it were locked too tight. He looked unhealthy, affected by a general air of extreme edginess, and there was a touch of desperation in his dry voice. The hand on Samsa's shoulder fluttered and trembled. He considered the gun in his holster, weighed his options, which were seriously limited by the pistol in

371

Boyle's fist. And Boyle, primed like a detonating device, had to be handled with enormous care.

'You could always give up,' Samsa said.

'As in surrender?'

'You could give me the gun.'

Boyle tightened his fingers on Samsa's shoulder. 'It's not like I don't appreciate the offer, sport. The thing is, it doesn't fit my future plans.'

'You don't have a future.'

'Oh you're wrong, you are so *very* wrong. Me and Darcy have all kinds of plans. She's such a willing girl, Greg.'

Samsa struggled to keep the tone of his voice calm. 'What does that mean exactly?'

Boyle brought his face very close to Samsa's and winked. Samsa saw the lid lower over an eye that was slightly bloodshot, and then open again. The gesture was furtive and obscene, insinuating that a sexual transaction had taken place between Darcy and Lee Boyle. Bad pictures rushed into Samsa's head, and he tried to shove them aside, but they created a disturbing kaleidoscope of images, flesh superimposed on flesh. His daughter in this creep's bed. That intimate locking of parts. He labored to hang on to whatever control he had of himself, because it would be fruitless to enrage the man, and kamikaze to strike out at him.

Boyle said, 'The circular nature of things is downright fucking astonishing at times. You took my girl away from me. Now I've taken yours. There's a power in nature, a balance. I feel it at this very moment. I'm standing here and I can feel the whole field hum under my feet, and I'm overawed by this dynamo, Gregory. I am flooded with notions of a lovely symmetry. You feel it, too?'

He's tuned to other dimensions, Samsa thought. Mad

rooms where he can't be reached. 'I'm not blessed with your insights,' he said.

Boyle dropped his hand finally from Samsa's shoulder and stared out across the meadow as if he'd heard something move in the black grass. His eyes probed the dark and he frowned. 'They're out there. They're coming toward me. You hear them? Listen. Listen real hard. Tell me you don't hear people out there in the grass.'

'Sure. I hear them.'

'Don't patronize me, Greg.'

'I said I *hear* them. People moving. Voices whispering. Yeah. I hear them.' Samsa had the odd feeling of standing on the threshold of Boyle's speed-afflicted fucked-up world, a place of derangements and bizarre anomalies, where silences were translated into sounds, light into dark, life into death. He watched Boyle wipe the back of his hand with his arm, and just for a moment what he felt wasn't loathing but some mutant form of pity, a sensation that came up out of nowhere and surprised him. *He isn't worth it. This is a weakness in yourself, a chamber of misplaced charity in your heart. Boyle shot a young cop, blackmailed you, ruined you, stole your daughter. He isn't worth pity.*

Boyle said, 'This fucking stunt pilot insists on flying his little plane again,' and he laid a hand upon his chest, and worked his jaw from side to side again, like a man who has just had gum-stiffening oral surgery. He inclined his head toward the center of the field, his expression that of somebody listening very hard to hear through reams of static and interference.

'Your best bet is to give me the gun,' Samsa said, 'and tell me where Darcy is.'

'Assuming she's anywhere,' Boyle said. 'You bandy the present tense around too freely, Lieutenant.'

'What the hell are you trying to say?'

Boyle smiled a little thinly. 'Am I getting past and present all mixed up, huh? What do you think?'

Assuming she's anywhere, Samsa thought. Boyle was fueling his dread. His worst fear was one he didn't want to confront – that Boyle's realities had collided, and in one of them Darcy was dead, in another she was still alive, and he didn't know which to believe. He was unsteady on his feet for a moment. He felt heat rush to his head and heard himself say, 'They're getting closer, Boyle. I'm catching all kinds of sounds now. You haven't got a chance in hell.' And he thought how easy it was to believe that the grass concealed figures fanning out in all directions, how easy to enter into Boyle's whacked perceptions.

Boyle said, 'Shut up, let me think. I can't think with you droning on. Jesus Christ.'

'Listen,' Samsa said. 'Somebody just said your name. Did you catch that? "There's Lee Boyle."'

'Shut the fuck up.' Boyle raised a hand and, open-palmed, smacked Samsa across the side of the face.

A whining went through Samsa's ears like a chill wind. He wouldn't listen to it, he'd ignore it. He'd keep jerking Boyle's chain, pushing him, niggling him. Screw the risk. 'Didn't you hear it, Lee? They'll shoot you. They don't give a damn about you. But I can promise you safety. I won't let them kill you, Lee. You have my word.'

'I don't need the word of some fucking hypocrite cop. I'm still in charge of my destiny. I am *this* close to pulling the trigger, sport.'

'Before you reach a decision about shooting me, just tell me where Darcy is.'

'And put your mind at rest?'

'You're running out of time,' and Samsa glanced back, seeing a half-assed moon pock the grass. 'Did you hear that, Lee? The distinct sound of somebody chambering cartridges. *Click click click.* One cartridge, two, three.'

374

Boyle stared into the reaches of darkness. 'Yeah, I heard.'

'They're not far away, Lee.'

Boyle said, 'I hear them, I fucking *hear* them. Don't keep reminding me.'

'Thirty, forty yards tops—'

'I said don't keep *reminding* me.' Boyle raised a hand and swung it against the side of Samsa's neck, a chopping blow Samsa had no time to avoid. He felt the thud of Boyle's fist, and for a second he was dizzy and listed to one side. But he wasn't going down. He was determined to keep his balance, pain be damned.

Lee Boyle pointed his gun toward the field – the big dark silence he'd populated with figments. Then he directed the weapon at Samsa, but there was a look of uncertainty on his face. His attention, already fractured by chemicals, was divided between what he believed lay out there in darkness, and Samsa.

Samsa said, 'Shoot me, *sport*, and you're a dead man. Because my colleagues hidden out there are wired for instant response. Besides, they've taken a very serious dislike to you.'

Boyle, the sweat on his white face silvered by the moon, turned his head this way and that like an animal perplexed by an array of dangerous scents.

'Hand me the gun, Lee. Do yourself a favor.'

Boyle pointed the pistol at Samsa, then swiveled it once again toward the wilderness, then back at Samsa.

'This is something of a *bind* for you, Lee,' Samsa said, and thought, *Where is Darcy?* The question lodged in his head like a conundrum he couldn't solve, didn't even want to entertain.

Boyle pressed his hand flat upon his chest, and his face contorted as if he'd swallowed something sour, and his mouth opened slackly. 'Shit, this is *hurting* again. And I'm

375

oozing pints of sweat. Did you spike that dope, Samsa? Did you say to yourself, I'll poison this ice before I give it to him? Just a few drops of something toxic, not enough so he'd notice immediately? More a cumulative effect, huh?'

'You need treatment, Lee. You need your stomach pumped—'

'You poisoned me, didn't you? You put bad shit into the speed.'

Samsa said, 'Maybe it was bad to begin with. And you're OD'ing.'

Boyle grimaced, pushed the gun into the side of Samsa's neck. 'You motherfucker. You stepped on the dope with *poison*.'

Samsa felt the discomfort of steel pressed against the muscles in his neck. Stress. Cold fear.

'What is it, Samsa? Arsenic? Is that what you used? Weedkiller? Something like that?'

'You've lost it, Lee,' Samsa said. 'You've really lost it.'

Boyle prodded the gun harder into Samsa's neck. 'So have you, *amigo*. Welcome to the chump's club.' And he laughed for no reason Samsa could tell, a dry back-of-the-throat laugh that sounded like sand being shifted around.

Boyle took a few steps back and lowered the gun from Samsa's neck. He doubled over, clutching his chest. 'This goddam pain is *crucifying* me. I can't breathe.'

'Let me get you to a hospital.'

'Stay away, don't come near me.'

'Give me the gun—'

Boyle fired the weapon wildly. A flash, a roar. The shot split the air and the dark was suddenly filled with movement: crows cawing as they flapped across the field. Boyle went down on one knee, head inclined forward. He was breathing in a labored manner, and his shirt was soaked black with perspiration. Samsa again thought of reaching

376

for his own holstered weapon, but Boyle was still holding the gun aimed generally in his direction.

'I won't miss next time,' Boyle said.

Samsa, deafened by the gunfire, said, 'They'll move in now, Lee. You know that, don't you? I can hear them coming. Listen.'

Lee Boyle raised his face toward the field. His eyes had the glazed look of a man in serious pain. 'Yeah, I hear them, Samsa.'

It was a moment of inattention on Boyle's part, a tiny window of chance, and Samsa understood he had to take it, because it might never open again. He moved quickly, crossing the space between himself and Boyle. Boyle turned his head, saw Samsa rush him, brought up his gun. Samsa launched a foot, clipped the pistol, watched it fly from Boyle's hand, then reached back to draw his own gun. But Boyle reacted with unexpected haste. He lunged at Samsa's legs, caught them, caused Samsa to lose his balance and fall into the grass. And then Boyle was on top of him even as he pulled something out of his waistband, something that had been concealed by his overhanging shirt, and he whacked it down toward Samsa, who twisted his face away at the last possible second, hearing a *whish* of air, seeing the pale orange-tinted implement in Boyle's hand. Boyle raised it again, and Samsa, trapped by Boyle's surprising strength, kicked and shoved to get out from under the man. But he was locked in place and couldn't reach his weapon, and the implement, a hard metal rod, was coming down again, and this time it struck his scalp and he felt a searing sensation and his field of vision was dark around the edges. Boyle struck him again. Samsa felt the metal split the skin of his cheek and thought, *He's killing me.*

He caught Boyle's arm, struggled to keep it from coming down another time, pushed with all the force he could collect, muscles straining. He looked into Boyle's eyes, listened to the strange angry whimpering Boyle made, and he felt a rage equivalent to Boyle's, and realized he was imprisoned with Boyle in the same raw airless space, beyond any considerations except survival.

'Your little girl fucks like a well-oiled machine, Samsa.'

Boyle's broken whisper was accompanied by a small stressed smile. Samsa shifted his hand from Boyle's arm, caught the man's lower lip and yanked it downward with his fingers. Then he tried to raise his bandaged hand and force it into Boyle's eyes, but the hand was as useful as a damaged paw, and Boyle pulled his face back beyond reach.

'Your little girl's a whore. She blew me, had me doing fucking cartwheels of joy. Almond suck *your* cock, Lieutenant?'

A whore. Samsa felt a choking sensation. Weakening, strength seeping out of him, the lights between the trees dimming. He needed to make one great effort to get out from under Boyle. Where was Boyle finding his energy? Speed, what else, the same speed that devastated him also galvanized him.

Boyle raised the tool yet again, and suddenly Samsa realized what it was, saw the horse-head glimmer faintly.

He felt the poker smack against his forehead and felt a pain too severe to quantify. He imagined this same implement raining down from Boyle's hand and Nick Mancuso trying to crawl out of range, begging for mercy where there was none to be had, plodding on hands and knees as Boyle lashed him time and again in a rage that was beyond rage, a murderous fury. *And this is going to happen to me. I am going to die in this place, never knowing what has happened to Darcy*.

He couldn't feel his face. He knew it had to be shattered. He caught Boyle's hand, twisted it, hoped if he

378

could bend the hand back the poker would be released and fall away, and all the time Boyle was whispering, 'A well-oiled machine, a slut, she gives head like there's no tomorrow,' and Samsa said, 'You lying bastard,' and then quit listening. Boyle's words were so much empty air, and Boyle's weight was squeezing the life out of him. He had the feeling he was being forced into the ground and sooner or later the earth would just open up and he'd be gone, and all at once he was drifting toward a realm of incongruously placid thoughts, such as a man drowning was said to experience, a sweet torpor, a dreamy descent.

Boyle said, '*Au revoir,* sport.'

No, not yet, not like *this*. Samsa concentrated with intense purpose, fighting not only Boyle, but also the strange soporific sense that possessed him, and he forced the heel of his hand under Boyle's chin and *thrust* with all the strength he could muster. Push, push, the situation finely balanced, his diminishing strength pitted against Boyle. He felt Boyle's head go back an inch or so, and he kept shoving, because if he didn't he knew he'd slip back down inside that enticing lethargy and that would be the end. His lungs were constricted and blood ran into his eyes, but he couldn't quit now, wouldn't quit. He had to keep forcing Boyle back.

'Dear sweet Christ,' Boyle said.

And Samsa felt Boyle yield and slump a little, and he gazed into the man's face and saw something abruptly shift and change there, saw eyelids flutter. The architecture of his face appeared to implode. The mouth was wrenched to one side, and Boyle was rolling away from him, turning over in the grass and gasping. Samsa, barely able to rise, got to his knees. A voice in his head told him, *Go for your gun*, but his movements were slow motion, and even when he had the weapon in his hand he was halfway certain he was dreaming. He crawled toward Boyle, who lay flat on his back with his arms at his sides and the poker held limply in one hand.

'This what I'd call . . . acute gridlock on Cardiac Boulevard.' Boyle's voice was choked and distant, like a man speaking through a tightly bound gag.

Samsa, drenched in blood, bent over Boyle.

'Last rites?' Boyle asked.

'Go fuck yourself,' Samsa said. 'Where's Darcy?'

Lee Boyle clutched his chest. His skin was the color of wet paper. 'It's a little too late for Darcy.'

'What the fuck does too late mean?'

'She got lippy, *amigo*. I had to . . .'

'You had to *what*?'

'Kind of quiet her down.'

'Quiet her down? What have you done with her, you fucker? What are you saying?' And Samsa thought, *What small strand remains of your better instincts tells you to do something. This man is dying, call an ambulance, something.* But he didn't give a damn, he was beyond all the niceties of civilized response. Way beyond. Further than ever in his life. 'You killed her? Is that what you're telling me? You killed Darcy?'

Boyle blinked, gazed at Samsa. '*Our Adonais has drunk poison.*'

'You're a piece of shit, Boyle. Unspeakable shit.' Samsa heard the sound of a tide in his brain. He imagined Darcy was crying out to him. She was being swept away on these waters, drawn out into darkness, and he couldn't reach her, and her voice was fading.

Boyle had a small sunken half-smile. '*I am borne darkly, fearfully, afar*. Samsa.'

Samsa drew himself up on his knees, looked down at Lee Boyle and raised his gun. Boyle lifted a hand, tugged Samsa's sleeve, held it. The gesture was beyond Samsa's interpretation – a plea for mercy? A request to hurry the inevitable?

Samsa felt an immense despondency that deepened when he fired the first shot into Boyle's stomach and watched the body kick. He fired the second shot into Boyle's neck, the third into his skull. And then he emptied the gun blindly into Boyle before he dropped it in the grass, rose and stumbled away into the trees, swaying from side to side as he went, thinking of going through the cedar fence, some vague notion of making a phone call, although he wasn't sure to whom. He was conscious of the moon flying free in the sky and a rash of stars shining weakly beyond. He walked between the trees, concentrating on the lights that appeared to recede the closer he came, as if everything in the world was being sucked away from him, until eventually there would be nothing. And Darcy was lost to him, the way Harriet had been lost, and any chance with Eve, too. His whole life was an accretion of losses.

He kept moving. Overhanging branches caught his face, but he didn't feel them. The world was all illusion. He wondered if this was what dying felt like, if the pressure inside his skull was more than the brain could withstand, if there was cerebral damage, and too much blood lost. He slipped, inclined his body against a tree for support, and drew air into his mouth. He was going back inside the dream again.

Dreaming of his daughter now.

He imagined he saw her sitting with her back to a tree, her face tilted to one side, her mouth bound with strips of a white ectoplasmic material, her hands tethered behind her by more of the same binding. He dreamed he went toward her, slid down onto his knees, placed his hands on either side of her face and looked into her eyes. Her upper body was naked. He heard her utter a strange little sound.

381

And then he was no longer sure of anything. He was adrift at that strange juncture where reality and illusion conflicted.

The same place where Lee Boyle had lived much of his life.

'Darcy,' he said.

Then it was dark, very dark. And Samsa, faintly conscious of the whirring spinning lights of police cars beyond the fence, was disintegrating.

49

PALE GREEN GHOSTS CAME AND WENT. A PERIOD OF DRIFT.
Samsa was X-rayed and brain-scanned and shot with
painkillers. He had no true sense of time and the dope
made him feel disembodied during his waking moments.
And yet something kept sneaking into his mind with a
certain urgent clarity, something he knew he was
supposed to do, *obliged* to do.

He had a room to himself, a narrow hospital bed, a
window shaded by a yellow blind. The walls were light
blue. He felt connected to his environment only in a tan-
gential way. Through his pain, which the morphine could
only dim, he had recurring images, some of them involving Lee Boyle, but there was an unreality to most of them,
as if Boyle were a person he'd invented on the worst day
of his life.

Once he dreamed of Harriet in a bathtub of rose-
colored water, and saw wet curls of her razor-chopped
hair float on the surface like dark wasted flowers. He saw
Boyle standing over the bathtub, saying, 'She's never
coming back, sport,' and dipping his hand into the

discolored water, parting Harriet's pink-tinted legs, smiling.

Samsa woke, remembering a fact he'd forgotten: Harriet had shaved her pubic hair too. Then sliced her veins.

Nightmares. Pictures shimmered.

He was thirsty. On the bedside table somebody had left a glass of water, which he managed to sip through an angled straw, but the effort drained him and the water tasted stale.

A physician came to check on him, a young man – too young, surely, to have graduated medical school – with a thick mass of dark hair and Coke-bottle glasses. He spoke of a hairline fracture in the forehead, serious lacerations to the cheek and scalp, like somebody reciting a threnody. Samsa listened to this list of his injuries, but couldn't relate them to himself. The physician talked about treatment, painkillers, bedrest. He said he believed time was the best healer, finally. Stitches in the scalp and cheek would dissolve eventually, obviously leaving scars, but they'd fade. The bone in the forehead would knit back.

'All in all, the prognosis is good, Mr Samsa. It might have been much worse. Your daughter's waiting to see you. Keep it down to a few minutes, okay?' The physician left.

Darcy came into the room. She was dressed in blue jeans and black T-shirt and sneakers. She drew a chair up to the bed and held his hand. She was uncomfortable, her movements awkward.

'You look . . .' she said.

'I look what?'

She didn't answer.

Samsa thought, *It's been a bad time, I'm not supposed to look great*. Darcy's hand was cold. He remembered the obscenities Boyle had whispered, and he wondered.

She began to cry quietly, reached for a tissue on the table and held it to her face. 'I swore this wouldn't happen,' she said.

He squeezed her hand. She crumpled the tissue and looked at the window and appeared annoyed with herself. 'I keep thinking about Nick . . .'

'We'll get beyond that. Somehow we'll get through all that.' Samsa reached for his water, spilled some slicks down his chest. His hand, he noticed, had been newly bandaged.

'Will we?' she said. She gazed at him. Her brown eyes seemed wary. He thought, *They're not the eyes of a fifteen-year-old girl any longer. The child is gone.*

'It seems to me there's a whole lot to get through,' she said. 'Maybe too much.'

Samsa floated just a moment, a little morphine shift. 'Whatever it is, whatever it takes, we'll do it.'

'How?' She bent forward, laid her head on the bed. Samsa stroked her hair and felt an awesome sadness. He had no answer to her question. He might have uttered words like fortitude or courage, or platitudes about how life goes on and you pick up the pieces. But these would have been porous noises lacking substance. His own actions had allowed Boyle to vandalize their lives, and the destruction had to be mended. He didn't know what it would take. What adhesive. How long.

Darcy raised her face. Tears crossed her cheeks and gathered at the edges of her lips. He'd never been able to bear the sight of his daughter crying, and it was even worse now. This sad girl with the pretty face broke his heart. He thought about the accumulation of neglect. The way time dwindled and every day was one day less left to you. And you never really noticed because you imagined an unlimited future, some form of immortality. Wrong.

'How?' she asked again.

'When I get out of here we'll go away somewhere,' he said. 'Let's do that.'

She reached for another tissue and blew her nose. 'I *encouraged* him, for Christ's sake. He *attracted* me.'

For a moment Samsa didn't know if she was referring to Nick or to Boyle, then he realized. 'How were you supposed to know what he was really like,' he said. He heard his voice catch at the back of his throat. There was a fade taking place inside him, the yellow blind shedding sunlight, Darcy's face going in and out.

She flicked hair from her forehead. She walked to the window and pulled back the blind. He wished he could go to her, soothe the hurt and bewilderment she carried. As a kid she'd come to him, never to Harriet – bruises, cuts, scrapes – and he'd always magicked them away.

But this was something else. This would take more than pretend.

She walked back to the bed. 'He said,' and she paused. 'He said something about this young girl. Something about you killing her.'

'And you want to know if it's true?'

'Is it?'

Samsa was aware of an intersection here. One way carried him in the direction he'd been traveling lately, back into lies. The other was different and unexplored.

'He was blackmailing me. But I didn't kill anyone.'

'Tell me about it. I want to know.'

'When I'm more alert I'll explain.'

'So he lied, that's what you're saying?'

'He had his own brand of truth,' Samsa said.

'But he lied, didn't he?'

Samsa remembered: *Your little girl's a whore. She blew me, had me doing fucking cartwheels of joy.* Boyle's delusions. 'Yes. He lied.'

She lifted his hand and held it to her lips. 'They'll throw me out of here if I don't go now.'

'Will you manage at home?'

'Haven't I always,' she said.

'If there's anything, I'm sure you can phone Eve,' he said.

'She hasn't called, you know. I can't figure it. I thought she'd be asking for health bulletins every half-hour.' Darcy stepped away from the bed and opened the door. 'Al Brodsky wants to talk to me about what happened. I'll come back tonight.'

He watched the door close and wondered about Eve, why she hadn't telephoned, why she hadn't paid a visit. She'd changed towards him. But he wanted to see her regardless. He wanted her presence, even if there was nothing left to build on between them.

He lay for a time with his eyes turned to the blind. Then, through his exhaustion and pain, he remembered what it was he needed to do. He raised himself on one elbow, picked up the phone, punched in the department's number and asked to be connected to Ed Duff.

Darcy goes down the corridor, passing orderlies, nurses. Thinking of her father's broken face. Stitches, swelling. Thinking how he must hurt. Thinking of Nick beaten to death with the poker. Thinking of her father being lifted onto a stretcher. Brodsky, who'd appeared out of nowhere, had supervised the bearers. 'Easy now. Don't rush him. Easy easy. He's precious cargo.'

Thinks of Lee. She doesn't want to.

He rips off her blouse and tears it into shreds.

He ties her hands behind her back with the strips.

This comes back to her, the way it has kept coming back since it happened. Before dawn. Twelve hours ago, more.

He's forgotten all about stealing a car. It's slipped his mind, what's left of his mind. He doesn't care any more. He's reached an extreme of himself.

He says, 'Let's see what you're made of.'

He holds it in the palm of his hand. 'Let's see if you can get me going.'

And then he pauses and listens to somebody trampling through grass.

'Not a sound out of you, understand?'

He stuffs her mouth with ragged strips of her ruined blouse.

'I'll be back,' he says.

And later, a long time later it seems, there's gunfire. And then her father is coming toward her.

Not Lee. He's never coming back again.

Except in her dreams.

Al Brodsky arrived at five minutes past seven. He pulled a chair up to the side of the bed. 'How's the patient doing, Greg?'

'I've had better days,' Samsa said. He'd been dozing fitfully, dreaming of Darcy, though he couldn't remember anything specific.

Brodsky placed a brown-paper bag on the bedside table. 'Grapes. Seedless, so you don't have to keep spitting.'

'Thanks,' Samsa said. He was hoarse.

Brodsky said, 'Nice room.'

Samsa waited for the question he knew Al had come to ask. But Brodsky appeared hesitant, as if he were unsure of Samsa's state of mind and how morphine might have affected it.

'I had a chat with Darcy,' he said. 'I get the strong feeling she's not telling me everything. The situation she was in, the stuff Boyle put her through, the boyfriend killed . . . it's only natural she'd keep some of it to herself, because she hasn't had time to put the pieces together in any coherent way. I'll talk with her some more tomorrow. But you know what I think? She's gonna need counseling down the line, Greg.'

Samsa's face was stiff and ached. 'You may be right, Al.'

Brodsky drummed his fingertips on his knees. 'According to Zane's report, you fired six shots into Boyle.'

'I don't remember how many exactly,' Samsa said.

Brodsky reached out, plucked one of the grapes and popped it in his mouth. He chewed a moment, then spat out a seed into the palm of his hand. '*Goddam*. They were marked seedless in the supermarket. I can't believe that.'

He looked back at Samsa. 'The thing is, some hotshot investigator in Internal Affairs is going to ask why you had to shoot him six times. It's the kind of thing I'd understand myself. The guy's trying to kill you, you defend yourself. And you're not thinking right, you don't know what he's done with your daughter, you're desperate, out of control.'

Samsa said, 'Is this important, Al?'

'Not to me, but some of those guys don't like cops firing guns needlessly. They're gonna ask you if it was necessary to use that much ammunition. *I* know it's bullshit. *You* know it's bullshit. But it's the kind of bone they love to chew on. The worst expression in their whole vocabulary is *excessive*, applied to a cop who's used a gun.'

Samsa was light-headed, drifting again, when what he really needed was focus and clarity for a few more minutes.

Brodsky said, 'All I'm saying is, expect to be questioned. Be prepared.'

'You're beating around the bush, Al. You didn't come here to talk about how many times I fired my gun.'

389

Brodsky paused. 'No, you're right.'

Samsa shifted his head on the pillows. His forehead throbbed, but he didn't want to ring the nurse for a painkiller just yet.

Brodsky said, 'You phoned Ed Duff earlier. You ordered Pritt's release.'

'Yeah, I did.'

'So naturally I'm very curious. We have a guy panting to confess, and you want him sent home? We haven't even had the psychiatric report yet.'

Samsa experienced a moment of tension, and then he thought, *There's only one way to go. There are no options. There had never been any, not really.* 'Pritt didn't kill the girl, Al.'

'How can you be so sure of that?' Brodsky asked.

Samsa told him.

He told him without halting. He heard his own voice echo in his head. It was easy, so damn easy, he'd expected it to be wrenching and difficult. He felt the lifting of an iron burden. An amazing calm settled inside him. Brodsky looked down at the floor as he listened. Halfway through Samsa's narrative, the chief got up and walked round the room in an agitated way, then returned to the bed.

Samsa finished. He was conscious of his systems beginning to shut down.

Al Brodsky stared at him. 'Why the fuck didn't you come to me in the beginning,' he said.

'What would you have done if I had?'

Brodsky said, 'That's not the question any more, Greg. The question is, what am I going to do now?'

'There's nothing you can do,' Samsa said.

Brodsky looked pensive. 'Let me run something past you. We free Pritt, okay. We make some cursory inquiries into the girl's death, under my direction. They don't lead anywhere, of course, then it begins to fade away, the newspapers and the TV lose interest because it's stale, it's yesterday's news, then we quietly shut the book and Cecily Suarez goes into the unsolved bin. Who's ever going to ask, Greg? Who's ever going to start poking round?'

'We bury it,' Samsa said.

'Exactly that.' Brodsky sat on the edge of the bed. 'Look, you've got a lot of time under your belt in the department. Why waste it all on account of one mishap?'

Mishap, Samsa thought. A mishap was when you stubbed your toe in the shower. Slipped on a wax floor. 'You'd do that for me.'

'You're a good cop, Greg. A good friend.'

'You understand what you're suggesting?'

'Fully.'

Samsa leaned back and shut his eyes. Back behind his desk in two or three weeks, however long it took him to mend. Working cases. Living among the city's dead. The brutality. The savagery.

'We never talk about this again,' Brodsky said. 'Subject closed. This conversation never happened.'

It was tempting. Samsa opened his eyes. 'I don't think so,' he said.

'Say again?'

'It's over, Al. I've got a bad taste in my mouth, and I don't think it's associated with the drugs they've been shooting into me. It's all over.'

'Look, maybe you're too doped out to get this, Greg. I'm offering you an escape route. I'm going out on a fuck-ing limb for you —'

'And I've said I'm grateful. But this is the end of the line.'

Al Brodsky got up from the bed and frowned. 'You're talking like a crazy man.'

'I don't think so,' Samsa said.

'Tell you what. You sleep on it. See how you feel in the morning. A new day, a clear head. Things'll look different.' He patted his pockets as if he were checking on something, then stepped toward the door. 'I'll see you tomorrow, Greg.'

Samsa didn't answer. Alone, he rang the bell for the nurse. He thought of twenty-one years dissolving all around him. A dead past. He still had Darcy to deal with, his story to tell all over again. He wondered how she'd react.

He was asleep before the nurse arrived.

And he didn't wake when Darcy came and sat alongside him for fifteen minutes and gazed at his face. Before she left she placed three oranges and a Snickers bar on the table.

Samsa woke in bright daylight. He was aware of somebody standing in silhouette at the window.

'I brought you flowers.'

He raised his face from his pillows. From the corner of his eye he noticed carnations in a vase on the table. And oranges and a candy bar from somewhere.

'Don't look at me unless you want to be frightened,' he said.

'I already looked. You don't scare me.'

She turned and approached the bed.

He said, 'I didn't think you'd come.'

'Darcy phoned me. Did she tell you? She needs somebody to talk to.'

'She can talk to me,' Samsa said.

'I guess it's another woman she wants right now, Greg. She's hurting.'

'I know she is.'

'I mean *hurting*. And she's lonely.'

'With any luck I'll be out of here in a few days—'

'She doesn't want to be on her own, Greg. So I took the liberty of asking her to stay at my place. At least until you're home again. She's lost and confused at the moment, and if I can help her I will.'

Samsa wanted to hold her hand. He wanted her to come close enough so he could reach out and touch her. He smelled her scent. He was reminded of her bedroom, the robe sliding from her body, that sweet giddy time.

'You don't mind having her as a room-mate?' he asked.

'I get lonely sometimes too.'

'What about . . .' The leaden density of unfinished questions. He wasn't sure he wanted an answer.

She said, 'You and me? Is that what you want to know? I haven't thought about it.'

'Will you?'

'Where do you pick up the threads? Where do you start again? I don't know.'

'You go back to the beginning,' he said.

'What did we have anyway? One night, Greg. That's all.'

'Does it have to stop at one night?'

She sat on the chair by the bed and looked at him. 'You're not a pretty sight, are you?'

'Was I ever?' He gazed at her. 'Has Pritt been released?'

'I hear Brodsky wants to hold him.'

'I ordered his release,' Samsa said.

'Did you? When?'

'Last night. I think it was last night. I'm not keeping up with time all that well.'

She sat very still. 'Did you say why you wanted him freed?'

'I explained it all to Brodsky.'

'All?'

Samsa nodded.

'How did he react?' she asked.

393

Samsa was remembering Al Brodsky's visit. The past can be disregarded. The job is still yours. This conversation never took place. There was another level of reality, Samsa thought, where Brodsky operated, a place where deals were struck and never recorded, and exchanges that took place never actually happened. A world of convenience. Lies of omission.

I've been in that world, he thought. *Where the currency is concealment.*

I know exactly what I'm going to do.

He reached for the telephone and pressed the numbers that would connect him directly to Al Brodsky. He was aware of Eve watching him. The sun caught and fired her red hair. She looked wary, defensive, as if she didn't want to give any of her trust until she was certain. And perhaps not even then.

Brodsky came on the line. 'Greg,' he said.

'I've slept on it, Al.'

'And?'

'That conversation we never had,' Samsa said.

'What conversation?' Brodsky laughed.

'Send Pritt home, Al.'

'Let me ask you one question, Greg.'

'Go ahead.'

'You know the consequences for you?'

'Just send him home.'

'You're on your own now,' Brodsky said. 'You know that, don't you?'

'Yeah. I know that.'

Brodsky said, 'Questions will be asked about Cecily Suarez, and I'm obliged to answer them. Because if you don't want the deal I offered, consider it withdrawn as of now. It saves me the hassle of playing around with the truth. And if they crucify you in public, don't expect to hear a squeak out of me on your behalf. If your name's bruited about and vilified in newspapers, I'll be taking my annual vacation. Nothing personal, you understand.'

'Florida?'

'Where else do I ever go?' Brodsky hung up.

Samsa put the phone back and looked at Eve.

She was quiet for a long time before she said, 'It's some kind of start.'

He agreed. It was some kind of start. He didn't know how much of one.